The Flower Reader

Elizabeth Loupas lives near the Elm Fork of the Trinity River, halfway between Dallas and Fort Worth, Texas. She hates housework, cold weather and wearing shoes. She loves gardening, animals and popcorn. Not surprisingly she lives in a state of happy, barefoot chaos with her delightful and slightly bemused husband, her herb garden, her popcorn popper and two beagles. *The Flower Reader* is her second novel.

The Flower Reader

Elizabeth Loupas

arrow books

Published by Arrow 2013

10 9 8 7 6 5 4 3 2

First published in Great Britain in 2012 by Preface Publishing

20 Vauxhall Bridge Road
London, SW1V 2SA

An imprint of The Random House Group Limited

www.randomhouse.co.uk

Addresses for companies within The Random House Group Limited
can be found at www.randomhouse.co.uk

The Random House Group Limited Reg. No. 954009

A CIP catalogue record for this book is available from the British Library

ISBN 978 0 09957 152 0

The Random House Group Limited supports The Forest Stewardship Council® (FSC®), the
leading international forest-certification organisation. Our books carrying the FSC label are
printed on FSC®-certified paper. FSC is the only forest-certification scheme supported by the
leading environmental organisations, including Greenpeace. Our paper procurement policy can
be found at www.randomhouse.co.uk/environment

Typeset in Fournier MT by Palimpsest Book Production Limited,
Falkirk, Stirlingshire

Printed and bound in Great Britain by
CPI Group (UK) Ltd, Croydon, CR0 4YY

In loving memory of my mother
Descendant of a long line of Scots

Margaret Fleming Gross
1913–2010

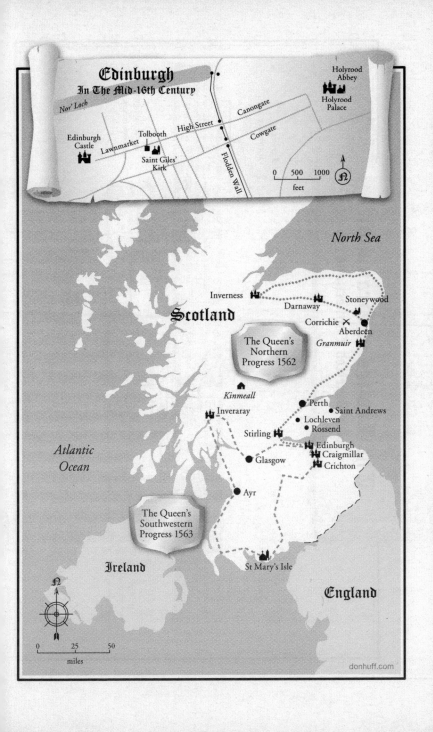

Edinburgh
In The Mid-16th Century

Nor' Loch

Holyrood Abbey

Holyrood Palace

Canongate

High Street

Cowgate

Edinburgh Castle

Lawnmarket

Tolbooth

Saint Giles' Kirk

Flodden Wall

0   500   1000
feet

North Sea

Inverness

Stoneywood

Darnaway

Scotland

Corrichie

Aberdeen

Granmuir

The Queen's Northern Progress 1562

Kinmeall

Perth

Saint Andrews

Inveraray

Lochleven

Rossend

Stirling

Atlantic Ocean

Glasgow

Edinburgh

Craigmillar

Crichton

Ayr

The Queen's Southwestern Progress 1563

St Mary's Isle

Ireland

England

0   25   50
miles

donhuff.com

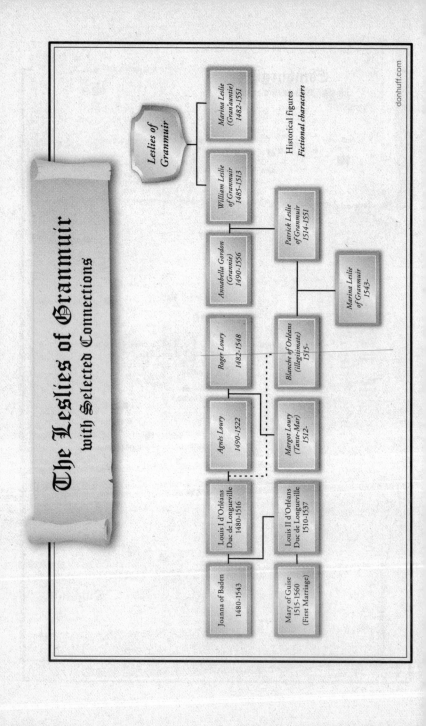

The Leslies of Granmuir
with Selected Connections

Leslies of Granmuir

Historical figures
Fictional characters

Marina Leslie (*Gran'auntie*) 1482-1551

William Leslie of Granmuir 1485-1513

Patrick Leslie of Granmuir 1514-1551

Annabella Gordon (*Grannie*) 1490-1556

Marina Leslie of Granmuir 1543-

Roger Loury 1482-1548

Blanche of Orleans (illegitimate) 1515-

Agnès Loury 1490-1522

Margot Loury (*Tante-Mar*) 1512-

Louis I d'Orléans Duc de Longueville 1480-1516

Louis II d'Orléans Duc de Longueville 1510-1537

Joanna of Baden 1480-1543

Mary of Guise 1515-1560 (First Marriage)

donhuff.com

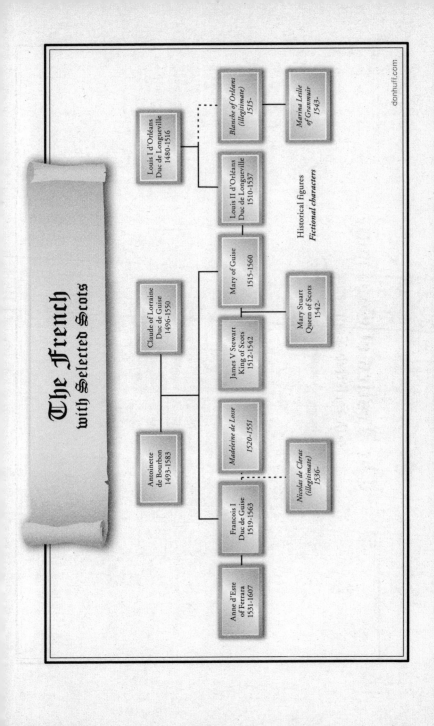

The French
with Selected Scots

Louis I d'Orléans
Duc de Longueville
1480-1516

Blanche of Orléans
(illegitimate)
1515-

Marina Leslie
of Granmuir
1543-

Louis II d'Orléans
Duc de Longueville
1510-1537

Claude of Lorraine
Duc de Guise
1496-1550

Mary of Guise
1515-1560

Mary Stuart
Queen of Scots
1542-

James V Stewart
King of Scots
1512-1542

Antoinette
de Bourbon
1493-1583

Madeleine de Losse
1520-1551

Nicolas de Clerac
(illegitimate)
1536-

François I
Duc de Guise
1519-1563

Anne d'Este
of Ferrara
1531-1607

Historical figures
Fictional characters

donhuff.com

2

10 June 1560
Edinburgh Castle

I hated the queen, hated her down to the deepest marrow of my bones.

I was a fierce and graceless fourteen-year-old when my grannie died and the queen took me away from Granmuir, kicking and crying, to shut me up at court. She gave me three years of luxury and learning, I will give her that, music and poetry and polish, but no fresh salt-scented air, no wheeling guillemots, no Aberdeenshire flowers and no huge silver sky stretching down to meet the sea. She took me away from my home. She took me away from Alexander Gordon, my soul and my heart. She ruined my life. By the Green Lady of Granmuir, I hated her.

How could I hate her so, and love her too, with all my heart?

Now she was dying, Mary of Guise, Queen Regent of Scotland, my *belle-tante*, my foster mother, my liege lady, my adversary, dying in the night under a waning moon. And everyone in Edinburgh, everyone in the castle, everyone in the queen's own bedchamber, was waiting for the queen to die.

My knees hurt. The stone floor was hard; older and more important folk had claimed all the places on the carpet. In unison with the ladies in front of me I prayed, half-drowned in a haze of beeswax and perfume, sweat and sickness, my Latin phrases perfect but meaningless. In my heart I was praying hard for Alexander Gordon, my own darling dear, my golden love, to come for me. We would go home, the two of us, be married at last and be happy forever.

The queen's French-born ladies knelt close around her; the truly brave ones told their rosaries, bead by defiant bead, under the narrow eyes of the Protestant Lords of the Congregation. Lord Erskine and young Lord Seton kept close, as did the half-outlaw Earl of Bothwell and the queen's inscrutable French secretary, Monsieur Nicolas de Clerac. Lord James Stewart was in and out of the room, the bastard son of the queen's dead husband – when I looked at him I saw narcissus for self-interest and snapdragon for deceit.

Why flowers? I always saw flowers in people's faces and eyes, and the flowers told me what was inside the person, what they had done, what they would do. When I touched a flower or breathed its scent, I saw things. It was an old, old trait in the Leslies of Granmuir, and my great-aunt, whose name had been Marina Leslie just like mine, had taught me to use it when I was a wee bairnie. People said I looked like her – my dark brown hair that caught tortoiseshell gold streaks from the sun, my sea-coloured Leslie eyes. People also said she was mad. She never married, Gran'auntie, and lived alone in Granmuir's north-east tower which we called the Mermaid Tower. She fought a running war with my grannie, my father's mother, who was practical as iron nails, managed Granmuir single-handed, and did not believe in flower reading.

'Rinette.'

Surprise rippled through the people packed into the chamber.

How could it be the queen's voice, when she had not spoken for days?

'She is asking for her daughter,' said Lady Bryant. She was one of the dearest of the queen's friends, a lady who had come with her from France and married two Scots lords in succession. 'The little queen, *la Reinette*.'

'Rinette,' the queen said, a second time. '*La jeune floromancière*. To me.'

I did not move. If I am very still, I thought, they will not see me here.

'No, it is the Leslie girl she wants, I think.' Lady Bryant put her ear down close to the queen's lips. 'That *farouche* child who sees fortunes in flowers.'

'Yes,' the queen said. Her voice was faint and laboured. 'Rinette Leslie. I would speak with her. *Vite*.'

Lady Bryant looked straight at me. So much for invisibility. 'Come here, my girl,' she said. 'The queen is asking for you.'

I stood up, my knees stiff and aching. Could I run? Would they stop me?

Of course they would.

I walked across the chamber, feeling the blood rush up hotly in my cheeks as people stood aside to make way for me. Their faces were like moonflowers in the dark, turning towards me, round and white with the black anthers and stamens of their features in the centre. Moonflowers . . . harbingers of dreams and prophecies and madness. What madness was coming, what prophecies, what dreams?

'Madame,' said Lady Bryant. '*Voici la petite* Leslie.'

The queen opened her eyes. Guise eyes, designing and subtle. They saw into my soul: *I know you want me gone*.

You have held me captive for three years, for the sake of your statecraft. I want to be free.

3

You will be free soon enough. Until then, I am still your queen.

I curtseyed and said aloud, 'What is your wish, Madame?'

'I wish you to read the future.'

Holy Saint Ninian, did she not realise everyone in the room could hear? The room was packed with Protestants who saw witches in every corner, and even the Catholics were quick to see heresies.

'The flowers are only an amusement, Madame.'

'Even so, I wish you to prophesy.'

It was impossible to disobey. 'I will need flowers, Madame.'

'Fetch them.'

'Yes, Madame.' I curtseyed again but could not find the will to move. Lady Bryant gave me a push and I stumbled back; that broke the spell of royalty and death. I made my way to the door through close-packed bodies, dressed in fur despite the heat, silk and gold and jewels, with avid eyes and mouths whispering behind their hands. I could hear words, random, sibilant. *Superstition. Sorcery. Heresy.* Once I was out of the bedchamber I gathered up my grey camlet skirts and ran like a wild thing, down the staircase, out of the palace and into the clean silver moonlight, through the quadrangle and across the upper ward to the hedgerow beside Saint Margaret's ancient chapel. There I threw myself to my knees – I felt no pain this time – and gulped in fresh air, the scents of woodbine and hawthorn and sweet briar rose. Far far off, down the firth, the sea.

I breathed. The moon climbed higher. I broke off a branch of hawthorn and brushed the velvety blossoms back and forth over my face. It calmed me, as the touch of flower petals always did. I would not go back inside. I could not go back inside. The queen regent was the last link with my childhood; Grannie was dead, Gran'auntie Marina was dead, my father was dead. My mother might as well have been dead, immured as she was in her convent in Paris.

But I did not want to think about that.

'Mademoiselle Leslie.'

I started round, clutching the branch of hawthorn. One of the thorns pricked my finger. It stung.

The queen's French secretary Nicolas de Clerac stood there in the moonlight. He was all in black and white, attenuated, long-legged and graceful as a heron; the only colours about him were the sapphire in his ear and his shock of russet hair.

'The queen wishes to know why you are taking so long,' he said.

'Can you not guess?'

'I can.' He stepped closer and held out his hand, as if to help me to my feet. Rings glinted, more colours – blue and green and deep purple. How Alexander would laugh at the rings, at the courtier's refinement, the French-style *maquillage* of kohl and silver around his eyes. 'It is hard to see her dying. But there is not much time. Gather your flowers and come back inside.'

I did not take his hand. After a moment he withdrew it.

'I must choose the ones that speak to me,' I said. I held out my finger over the hawthorn; a drop of blood fell, black in the moonlight. Hawthorn meant death, but there was no blood in the queen's dying; was someone else to die as well? 'Why do you think she asked for this? She has never asked me to read the flowers for her before, not once in three years.'

'I do not know,' he said. 'But she has a reason. Even dying, she is more subtle than all the Lords of the Congregation at once.'

Subtle knows subtle, I thought. I did not like him. No, it was not that, not exactly; I did not trust him. If I were to choose a flower for him, it would be trailing nightshade with its bell-shaped

flowers of Tyrian purple, its sweet showy berries – and the contradictory deadly danger within.

I gathered up a fold of my skirt and filled it with honey-scented
woodbine and the cup-shaped pink-and-gold roses of sweet briar.
I tried to leave the hawthorn behind but it called to me so insist-
ently I felt thorns pricking me all over. Reluctantly I took a branch,
then another, then more, until my skirt was filled with masses of
the foamy white blossoms. The pricking sensation stopped. I said,
'I am coming.'

He did not offer his hand again. We went back to the queen's
chamber. It was not so crowded now; both Protestants and
Catholics had withdrawn, offended by the queen's request and
unwilling to be in the same room as a foreseeing.

'A moment of solitude, if you please,' Mary of Guise whispered. 'Rinette, you will stay.'

I felt like a fawn in a snare, afraid to breathe. Monsieur de
Clerac and the ladies withdrew, murmuring the queen's request
to those who remained. There were coughs and more disapproving
whispers. Silks and velvets rustled. The door creaked on its hinges.
Finally it creaked again as it closed. I knelt beside the queen's
chair, the flowers heaped in my lap.

'Madame,' I said. 'I am here.'

'This happened – so quickly,' the queen said. Her face and
hands and legs were grotesquely swollen. 'I did not have a chance
to prepare.'

'I am sorry, Madame,' I said. What else was there to say? 'I will
tell you what the flowers say to me, if that will give you peace.'

'No. That was only a ruse, to frighten people out of the room.
I want you to help me, and it must be a secret.'

My breath stopped again. Fear squeezed my throat and melted
my heart and made my legs tremble. 'But Lady Bryant, Lady

6

Drummond – Lord Erskine, Lord Bothwell, Monsieur de Clerac – they are your friends, they have been your friends through the years, surely they would be better to confide in than I. I am no good with secrets.'

'That is why I chose you. The others, they would be questioned. No one will think of you, *ma fille précieuse*. Come closer.'

I crept closer and put my forehead down against her hands. The doctors had ordered her rings cut off, the beautiful rings she cherished – her wedding ring with its royal Scots lions engraved on either side of a fine diamond; mourning rings in silver for each of her four dead sons, the two Longueville boys resting at Châteaudun and the two Stewart princes in Holyrood Abbey; a magnificent table-cut ruby on a band enamelled in the Guise colours of red and yellow; her signet ring with its crown and rock cut deeply into the gold. Now her only jewels were onyx and ivory rosary beads, looped and sunk deep in translucent dropsical flesh.

'There is a casket,' she whispered. 'I have had no chance to put it away. Swear on your life you will take it out of the palace and put it in its proper place.'

'I want to go home.' I knew I sounded stupid and childish but I could not stop myself. 'Madame, I do not want your casket. I do not want your secrets. I only want to go home to Granmuir.'

'You still hate me so, *ma petite*, for bringing you to court?' The queen lifted one hand, groaning softly with the effort, and gently stroked my hair. 'You were like a bone between two dogs, Rothes and Huntly, Leslies and Gordons. They both have claims – you are a Leslie, of course, but your grandmother was a Gordon, and your Alexander was Huntly's ward, before he came of age.'

'You yourself granted Granmuir to me as a royal fief.' We had argued this over and over; I hated to be arguing again as she lay dying, but I could not help myself. 'As the king your husband granted it to my father, and James IV to his father, and back a thousand years.'

The queen's mouth twitched. 'Not quite that long,' she said. 'And with your grandmother dead, you were safer here.'

'Alexander would have protected me. I would have protected myself. I know you meant well, Madame, but I have hated it, being here at court.'

'I will keep you no longer. I ask you for this one thing, then you may go and fight your own battles – although I warn you, you will fall into Rothes' power the moment I am dead, and he will never allow you to marry the Gordon boy.'

'I will escape him. I will refuse any other marriage.'

'May God give you strength. Rinette, *écoute* – time is short. I am your queen. By my first marriage I am your aunt, and you know I loved your mother as my true sister. You must do as I ask you. Swear it on the cross.'

I bowed my head and looked at the flowers I had gathered under the moonlight. Hawthorn for death, dappled with blood, with woodbine twining around it. Woodbine . . . a twining, a net, a snare. Woodbine whispering, *You are meant to be here in these bonds and you must do as she says.* The briar rose, so sweet, lying beside the others. Not entangled. There was freedom and sweetness to come, if I did as the flowers instructed me: endure the death – *do not think about the blood, there is no blood here so what death is the hawthorn foreseeing?* – accept the bonds and embrace the sweetness to come.

I kissed the queen's crucifix. In a shaky voice I said, 'I swear it, Madame.'

'In my oratory.' The queen turned her head slightly. 'The prie-dieu. There is a cupboard, and the casket is in it.'

8

I lifted my head and looked. The prie-dieu did indeed have a cupboard under its shelf, two doors carved with the double-barred crosses of the House of Lorraine. Dread prickled over my skin, but the promise was made. I rose to my feet, stepped over and knelt down before the prie-dieu, reached under the shelf. The cupboard was closed with gilded latches. I opened them.

Inside I felt an oblong box of polished metal, its top slightly domed, textured with repoussé metalwork in rows like ornately embroidered ribbons. By touch I determined it was perhaps a foot in length, perhaps a little less, with two small handles on either long side, hinges on one short side and a lock on the other. When I drew it out I could see it was fashioned of silver with the edges and decorations picked out in gilt. Engraved on all four sides was the letter F in the Roman style, under a crown.

'I have it, Madame.' I carried the casket to the queen's chair, knelt down again, and put it into her hands. 'Is it a holy relic to comfort you?'

'It is not a relic, *ma petite*, but it comforts me to have it safely in my hands while I am still alive to protect it, and to know you will take it afterwards to its proper place.'

I ran my fingertips over the pounced silver designs of hunting scenes on the side of the casket. In the flickering candlelight the figures almost seemed to move. 'Do you have a key, Madame? Do you wish me to open it for you?'

The queen's voice was weaker. 'I have a key, yes, but I do not want you to open it. What is inside is for my daughter alone. They have all tried to steal it away – James Stewart and the Lords of the Congregation, Huntly and his Catholics, the English, French agents of the Medici woman, so many. You must hide it, *ma petite*, as I will instruct you, because they will try to steal it again. And if the day ever comes that my daughter returns to

Scotland, you must give it to her the very day she sets foot on Scottish soil.'

'You are frightening me, Madame.'

The queen grasped my wrist. Weak as she was, her grip was hard; the rosary beads felt as if they were cutting into my skin. 'You are clever, I know that. You can outwit them. No one will suspect you, and in the eyes of the world the casket will simply disappear. The key . . . it is on a chain at my belt, in a jewelled box like a reliquary. Take it. Put it with the casket.'

The passion in her voice seemed to use up all her strength and breath, and she fell back, gasping. I fumbled among the scissors and needle-cases and pomanders at her waist and found the golden box, as long as my forefinger and studded with jewels. I detached it from its chain and pried its halves apart; inside there was a silver key, wedged tightly so it would not rattle.

'I have the key, Madame.'

'*Bon*. The casket's proper place – Saint Margaret's Chapel – where blessed Margaret herself prayed. There is a hidden vault – underneath – no one knows – the Abbot of Dunfermline, where Saint Margaret is buried, always kept the secret.'

She gasped for breath again and stopped.

'A hidden vault?' I said. I did not want to feel curious but could not help myself. 'How can I enter it?'

'A passageway,' the queen said, very faintly. 'From the vaults under the Great Hall, here in the Castle. The fireplace there – the panelling on the left – count up from the floor twelve, and from the side four, and look for the cross – go down – follow the crosses. Never tell anyone, Rinette. Never tell anyone—'

Her voice failed. She struggled for breath and found none. Her hands fell away from the casket. In a panic I thought – what can I do? I have to call them, and they will all come rushing in. How can I take the casket out of the chamber when they all want it and will be looking for it? It is too big to hide in my sleeves or skirt.

The queen did not breathe again. She remained sitting upright, her eyes half-closed. Her lips were parted, as if to say one more word. But no more words for Mary of Guise, queen and queen mother, Regent of Scotland. No more words ever.

I had not thought I would cry but I could feel tears filling my eyes and streaking down over my cheeks. Think, think. There had to be a way.

They would be looking for a casket closed and locked and hidden away – but open and filled with flowers – overflowing with the flowers of sorcery and carried before their eyes—

I do not want you to open it. What is inside is for my daughter alone.

You are clever, I know that. You can outwit them.

I unlocked the casket. Even with my hands shaking, it was easy to turn the key, so easy – the queen herself must have unlocked it often. The lid swung back. I gathered up all the flowers, the hawthorn and sweet briar, and stuffed them in on top of – I caught only a glimpse – a book of pages sewn together with black thread, a packet of folded papers bound with a net of scarlet cords, sealed with scarlet wax, with writing in rusty-looking ink. The flowers covered it all. I filled the hollow of the lid as well, and pushed the jewelled box and the key in among the blossoms. Then I wrapped the woodbine recklessly around it all and let the ends trail down.

I pushed myself to my feet. 'The queen is dying!' I cried.

The women and the lords and the Protestant minister Mr Willock flocked in like gannets, sharp-eyed and gluttonous for news. I stood fast, holding the casket filled with flowers as if it were a shield. Surely it was only the stir in the air from all the people running into the room that made the flowers move, made the woodbine vines float and curl. Surely it was nothing but the heat in the room that made the pink buds of the hawthorn seem to open themselves before my eyes into starry white flowers.

Mr Willock passed close and one of the trails of woodbine caught on his sleeve. He slapped it away as if it were a serpent.

'Get away, girl,' he said. 'You have no business here with your mummery.'

I kept my head down and curtseyed humbly. Lady Bryant and Lady Drummond had begun to cry. Lord James Stewart came in with the Earls of Argyll and Rothes close behind him. They made no pretence of grieving for the queen, but went straight to the oratory and began to rifle through the prie-dieu. So for the moment at least the Earl of Rothes had more important things to think of than one unmarried Leslie girl and her castle by the sea.

I began to edge toward the door. People pressed away from me so as not to touch the flowers. I caught a glimpse of Lord Bothwell and Nicolas de Clerac speaking to Lord James and the earls, over by the poor queen's prie-dieu. Voices were raised. Bothwell was swearing at Lord James in both Scots and French. It made a good distraction.

'The queen is dead,' Mr Willock said. 'Idolatry is dead in Scotland.'

I pressed the silver casket close to my body. God speed you, Madame, I thought. I will see your casket safe under Saint Margaret's and then I will be away from the court forever. No one paid any more attention to me. I walked out of the room with the silver casket and the masses of flowers in my arms.

2

I did not keep my promise to hide the queen's silver casket in the secret vault under Saint Margaret's. Not that night, at least.

I had a little household of my own within the court – my aunt Margot Loury, my mother Blanche of Orléans' legitimate half-sister whom I called Tante-Mar, and my maidservant Jennet More, my own age, the daughter of the castellan of Granmuir. They could not have been more different. Jennet was tall, stout, freckled and outspoken; Tante-Mar was tiny, frail and ferociously devoted to proper manners, always contending, I think, for some sort of equality with my mother's grand birth as the bastard daughter of the Duke of Longueville. I had never known my French *grandmère* Agnès Loury, the farmer's wife who caught the duke's eye so briefly, but I suspected my mother was like her – dazzlingly beautiful, passionate, devoted to one thing and one thing alone. For my mother it had been my father, Patrick Leslie of Granmuir. After his death at the end of that terrible year in France I might never have existed for her at all. She disappeared into the Abbey of Montmartre in Paris to spend the rest of her life in prayer for him, and I was left to the queen regent to foster, and to Tante-Mar, who loved me as my mother never did and came home to Granmuir with me for the sake of it.

I had barely reached my tiny chamber and begun to tell them of the queen's death when a blow on the door behind me swung it open, hard enough to crash against the wall.

Tante-Mar screamed. Jennet knocked over the one candle; it rolled across the stone floor, casting grotesque streaks and flashes of light on the face of the man in the doorway. For a moment he looked like a hobgoblin from hell; then the candle went out and in the light of the small fireplace he was an ordinary man-at-arms again, snub-nosed and ruddy, wearing the Earl of Rothes' livery.

Tante-Mar clutched her rosary. Jennet stared, open-mouthed. I put the casket and the trailing flowers down on the table. There was a three-legged stool pushed up beside it.

'The Earl of Rothes wants Lady Marina Leslie brought back upstairs right away,' the man said. He put one hand on his sword-hilt. 'To protect her, like. That's you, am it not, my lady?'

I caught up the stool, swung it hard by one of its legs, and knocked him stone cold unconscious.

'*Sainte Mère de Dieu*, Rinette!' Tante-Mar cried. 'Have you gone mad?'

'I have not,' I said. 'Get your things, whatever you want to keep. Hurry. We are off to Granmuir and we do not have long until the earl sends more men. Where is Wat?'

Jennet, pragmatic as the day is long, knelt beside the uncon-scious soldier and began tying his wrists and ankles together with his own bootlaces. 'Stables,' she said. She bounced up and began collecting a bundle of clothes for herself and one for me. 'You want that frippery casket in here?'

I handed it over — no time for hidden crosses and secret vaults, but would not the casket be just as safe at Granmuir? — and wrapped poor trembling Tante-Mar in her heaviest mantle. I took her bundle and muffled myself up in my own cloak. 'Ready, Jennet?'

'Ready.'

We ran for the stables, the three of us. They were across the upper ward and past the gate, and poor Tante-Mar was half-fainting by the time Jennet and I dragged her to the door of the wattle-and-daub stablemen's hut and pounded on it vigorously.

'Wat!' I cried. 'Wat Cairnie!'

He opened the door at once – he too had been awake, then, waiting for Mary of Guise to die. He was stout and sunburned summer and winter; I had grown up with him and he was the closest thing I had to a brother.

'The queen?' he said.

'Dead. *Requiescat in Pace.*' I crossed myself. Wat and Jennet did the same. Poor Tante-Mar just gasped and wheezed and clung to her rosary. 'Rothes wants to take me now – we have to run for Granmuir.'

'She's already cracked one of the earl's men over the pate with a stool,' Jennet said. 'More'll be coming.'

'I'll saddle the horses.' Wat, thank God, was as pragmatic as Jennet. Both their families had served the Leslies of Granmuir for generations and not much surprised them.

'Jennet, you take Lilidh,' I said. Lilidh, sweet-tempered namesake of white valley lilies, was my own mare, half-Andalusian and the fastest horse in Aberdeenshire. 'Ride for Glenlithie and tell Alexander what has happened – beg him to ride back with you to Granmuir as fast as ever he can.'

'Aye.'

'Wat, take Tante-Mar pillion – she cannot manage on her own, and we have only two more horses. Bad enough the Earl of Rothes is after us, without having the Sheriff of Edinburgh chasing us down for horse-reiving as well.'

Jennet was already in the saddle. Lilidh tossed her head and whickered. 'We can't hold Granmuir against the earl,' she said. 'Young Master Alexander's got no soldiers to bring, and you've got only Wat and Master Norman and Robinet and the boys.'

'I do not need soldiers,' I said. I swung up astride the hammer-headed chestnut, tucking my skirts around my legs. Thank God the grey camlet was thick and serviceable. 'Just Père Guillaume.'

'The auld priest? You think you can pray away the earl's army?'

Wat was mounted as well, with Tante-Mar behind him clinging fast. He wheeled his gelding and the three of us clattered out towards the Constable's Tower. It was a dangerous ride down from the castle rock, and none of us spoke as the horses picked their way.

'I do not have to pray them away,' I said, when we'd reached the bottom. I kicked the chestnut to a canter and we swept down the West Bow and through the Grassmarket three abreast in the moonlight. At the West Port a watchman stepped out in front of us; I threw him a coin and he opened the gate. 'All I have to do is marry Alexander. Then neither Rothes nor Huntly will have power over me, or Granmuir, ever again.'

We reached Granmuir in three days. Jennet and Alexander were a day behind us; the sun was setting behind the forest when they arrived at last, bursting free of the trees and galloping hard along the clifftop causeway connecting Granmuir to the mainland. I knew him instantly, Alexander, my Alexander, by the sun striking gold from his hair like the gold of a yellow iris, a fleur-de-lis, the flower of princes, of beauty and light. He rode wholly at one with his long-legged Spanish stallion. No one rode like Alexander Gordon.

No other riders. No pursuit. For the moment, at least.

I ran towards the gatehouse. Young Davy More waved the blue-and-gold colours of Granmuir and shouted in Gaelic as the riders thundered through. A flash of mud-spattered white – Lilidh, pacing the stallion, with Jennet More dragging back on the reins. For a few moments there were trampling hooves everywhere, iron shoes sparking against stone, heads tossing and foam flying. Alexander kicked his feet free from the stirrups and slid out of the saddle like an acrobat. I threw myself into his arms.

'Alexander,' I cried. 'Alexander, Alexander, my darling—'

He cut me off with a kiss, then another and another, hard and exuberant. He smelled of sweat and male and excitement. I wrapped my arms around him, dazzled.

'They are close behind us,' he said. 'Rothes' men. Is the priest ready?'

'In the church. Hurry.'

Hand-in-hand like children we ran for the church, with Jennet behind us shouting orders for the care of the horses. Tante-Mar and Wat Cairnie were waiting to witness our vows. Just as we reached the ancient chapel, Davy More shouted again.

'Men a-coming, flying the Earl of Rothes' colours! Good ten or twelve, closing fast.'

We crowded into the church. Wat Cairnie shut the doors – the wood was strong enough but worn, light showed through the planking, would it hold? – and pushed a heavy bench up against them. Père Guillaume had lit two candles on the altar and laid out his stole and missal; the scent of beeswax and primordial holiness inside the little stone structure was stronger than any incense. My exhilaration turned to solemnity.

'This is not the wedding I would wish for you, *ma douce*,' Tante-Mar said. There were tears in her eyes. 'You have no proper dress or veil, no procession, no maids to attend you. But look, I have brought a bit of lace – it was your mother's. And her turquoises. They will protect you from evil, and at the new moon—'

'I want nothing of hers,' I said. 'Just as she wanted nothing of me.' To soften the ruthless truth of it I hugged Tante-Mar's shoulders. Her bones were thin and pointed as birds' bones.

'Step forward, *mes enfants*.' Père Guillaume was a tiny, fragile-looking man, his cassock and surplice made of undyed wool from Granmuir's own sheep. What little hair he had was the same colour, thin and curling. 'I am prepared. Monsieur Alexander, have you a ring?'

'I have this.' Alexander took his own signet ring from his forefinger – heavy gold incised with the three boars' heads of Gordon and the tree trunk cut into five pieces that represented Glenlithie. 'A bit large for my lady's finger, but it will have to—'

There was a hammering on the door – fists. Booted feet, milling about and kicking. A voice cried out, 'Ho there! Open the door!'

Wat Cairnie stacked a second bench atop the first. 'I'll hold the door as long as I can, Rinette,' he said. 'Get on with your marrying, but best be quick about it.'

'Oh, Alexander.' I clasped his hands in mine and kissed the ring with passionate intensity. 'Oh, my dear. I do not care how big it is, I want no other ring. Thank you. I love you.'

'I will have a true marriage-ring made for you later, gold with sapphires and pearls from the River Tay by Glenlithie. I love you, Rinette.'

Sword-hilts and clubs began crashing against the door. Someone cried, 'They've got it blocked! Get a ram!'

Père Guillaume kissed his stole and put it around his neck, then took up his missal. His hands shook. 'Alexander Gordon and Marina Leslie,' he said, raising his voice against the clamour outside the church. 'Have you come here freely and without reservation to give yourselves to each other in marriage? You must each answer separately.'

'I have,' I said. I felt as if I were filled up with love to the top of my head, as if it were shining forth from my whole face like light. I held tightly to Alexander's hands.

'I have,' Alexander said.

'Will you love and honour each other as man and wife for the rest of your lives?'

'I will.' We both said it at the same time.

A great crash against the door, and splintering wood. Tante-Mar screamed and ducked back against the wall. I jumped. Alexander dropped the ring; I caught it only at the last moment.

'Join your right hands,' Père Guillaume said, 'and declare your consent before God and his Church. Be quick, *mes enfants*.'

'I take you to be my husband,' I said. I had the ring tight in my left hand. There was more – better and worse, sickness and health, in bed and at board – but no time for it. Who needed it? It was all there in the word *husband*.

Alexander was breathing hard. He began, 'I take you—'

Another crash, and the doors burst in. Wat Cairnie was thrown off his feet and fell, stunned by a flying piece of the splintered wood. Alexander and I turned in one movement – half-married, oh, Saint Ninian protect us, give us just a few moments more – to face the soldiers.

'This is a house of God,' Père Guillame said. He could barely make himself heard. 'Take yourselves off at once, lest I pronounce the anathema upon you.'

'I hold with no such papistical notions.' One man stepped through the ruins of the door ahead of the others, dark and rough-hewn, with a brutal look about him. He was dirty and unshaven. So is Alexander, I thought, and yet he looks like an angel – and there was a deep crease between his brows, a perpetual scowl. 'We are here in the name of the Earl of Rothes, clan chief of the Leslies, to take his vassal Lady Marina Leslie under our protection. Do not oppose us in this and no one will come to harm.'

'Protection!' Alexander stepped forward, drawing his jewelled filigree dagger with a flourish. He was so tall and light-footed and shiningly golden, so much the opposite of the thick-muscled gracelessness of the soldier, that my heart broke with the sheer beauty of him. 'Abduction would be a better word. I am Alexander Gordon of Glenlithie, near kin to the Earl of Huntly, and this lady is my affianced wife. Touch her if you dare.'

The dark man looked at Alexander for a moment. There was silence in the little church. Then with one well-practised and ringing arc of movement he swept his sword from its scabbard – plain workmanlike steel with no jewels or fancywork. He levelled it at Alexander's heart. The dying light of the sun through the broken door edged the glittering blade with blood-red.

'I am Rannoch Hamilton of Kinmeall, and albeit I'm wife's kin to the Earl of Rothes I wouldn't call it near,' he said. The mockery was heavy in his voice. 'I dare. And I have ten men at my back to dare with me. Put by your blade, laddie.'

I felt Alexander's arm tremble. Eleven men, I thought. Eleven men with swords against Alexander, with only a dagger. Wat down and unconscious. Tante-Mar and poor Père Guillaume frail and terrified. Alexander, my love, stand strong, stand strong. I closed my fist around the ring as if I could give him strength and nerve by means of it.

The dagger dropped and clattered on the floor. One cabochon ruby broke loose and skittered over the worn stone like a shining ladybird.

'Good.' The dark man sheathed his blade with the same careless, economical skill he had used to draw it. 'Now, my lady, we'll trouble you for food and ale and a night's rest, and you'll be accompanying us back to Edinburgh in the morning.'

'That I will not,' I said.

My blood was pounding in my ears and my hands were cold as ice. I could still feel the ring in my left fist, the gold suddenly cold too. I thought, It is not Alexander's fault. He is alone against them all. I love him. It is not his fault.

I lifted my head and stepped forward. I meant to smile, but I felt my lips draw back to bare my teeth like an animal's. Straight into the eyes of this Rannoch Hamilton of Kinmeall I stared; what I saw was blackness. Surface glints of cruelty, sensuality and animal self-interest. Crude amusement at first. Then the beginning of wariness.

I said in a voice that did not sound like my own, 'I am the Lady of Granmuir by blood descent, and I hold Granmuir as a royal fief – the Earl of Rothes has no authority here.'

'The queen is dead,' Rannoch Hamilton said. 'Your royal fiefdom means nothing now.'

I had known he was going to say that, and I had my answer prepared. 'Then I claim sanctuary here in this holy place, in the name of God and Our Lord Jesus Christ, and Saint Ninian who built this church with his own blessed hands.'

The men behind Rannoch Hamilton began to murmur and shift their feet. The Lords of the Congregation might be telling themselves they had outlawed the old religion, but men's hearts and souls did not change so quickly. The followers would never break the law of sanctuary – they would withdraw. It was only their commander who mattered.

'Saint Ninian is nothing to me,' Rannoch Hamilton said. His voice was hard. 'And I have my orders. Back to Edinburgh you go, my lady, will you or nill you.'

He stepped forward, deliberately kicking aside Alexander's dagger. Alexander and Père Guillaume stepped back. Tante-Mar had made her way across to where Wat Cairnie lay and was tending to him. He was moving, lifting his head – he was not dead, thank God. I stood my ground, feeling faint and sick with the effort of it.

'And will you strike me down?' I said. 'Will you bind and gag me like a criminal? Because you will have to, Rannoch Hamilton of Kinmeall. I will never set foot out of this church willingly. I have claimed sanctuary at God's own altar, and sanctuary I will have.'

'I care not for your papist God. I've bound and gagged women before, and will do it again with pleasure.'

He stepped forward again. I did not move.

'You do not care for God?' I said. 'Care, then, for the old gods of the Picts, who were worshipped in this very spot before the Christians came. There is a sea god who will drown you if you touch me, and creatures with claws and teeth who will eat your eyes. There is a god of this rock who will call the cliffs themselves to shred your flesh from your bones.'

'*Ma fille, ma fille.*' It was poor old Père Guillaume, behind me, tugging at my sleeve. He sounded as if he were crying. 'Do not say such terrible things.'

'I care for no gods at all,' Rannoch Hamilton said. He sounded less sure than he had before. Behind him, the soldiers were slipping away, one by one.

'Then take care for the goddesses.' I was just as terrified as the others but I would have died before I let him see it. The only goddesses I knew were the gentle spirits of the flowers, but even gentle spirits could be dangerous when threatened. 'You take pleasure in binding? There is a Green Lady of Granmuir, who will come in your sleep and wrap her woodbine around your cock and balls and pull it tighter and tighter until *they turn black and fall off*.'

Involuntarily Rannoch Hamilton crossed himself.

'There!' I could have screamed with exultation. 'You dare sign yourself with the Christian cross in full Catholic fashion, and deny me sanctuary when I have claimed it?'

The man's face reddened. Like most of the others who supported the Lords of the Congregation, he would have been born and brought up a Catholic and his Protestantism was a thin polish on instinctive old ways. He looked around to see if his men had caught the forbidden gesture, and saw they were gone. The jingling of bits and clattering of hooves in the distance made it clear they were making for the mainland, away from churches and gods and women who dared claim sanctuary in their own names.

'Have your sanctuary, then, and be welcome to it,' he said. There was a dangerous glitter in his dark eyes, and the line between his brows might have been cut with a knife. 'This will not be the last of it. The Earl of Rothes will have your damned sea-rock in the end, my lady, and when you go to the stake for your heresy, I'll be there to cheer you to hell.'

He turned and walked away. I could hear him shouting for his horse. All the anger and power drained out of me. I turned and threw myself into Alexander's arms.

'Finish it.' I started to cry. 'Finish it now, oh, my love, and never, never leave me.'

He put his arms around me but I could feel distance in him. I looked up. His face was white. Behind him Père Guillaume was doubled over, gasping for breath, as if he had been struck hard in the chest.

'I am sorry,' Alexander said. 'I should have—I should have—' He did not seem to know what he should have done.

'No! Oh, no, Alexander, my love. He had ten men. They would have killed you. I could talk to them, trick them – I am a woman, I am the one they wanted, they did not dare do harm to me.'

A little colour came back into Alexander's face. 'You are a woman,' he said slowly. 'Yes, of course they did not dare touch you. I drew my steel on them. It is not my fault I had only the dagger and he had a sword and ten men.'

Suddenly I realised I still had Alexander's ring clenched in my fist. I took his hand and pressed it back into his palm. 'Take it,' I said. 'Père Guillaume?'

'*Ma fille*,' the old priest said in a shaky voice. 'The soldiers are gone. There is no need for hurry now. I would hear your confession first, and give you penance – you are in a state of mortal sin, to say such things as you said to that man.'

'But I saved us!' I was surprised and hurt. I wanted only to be Alexander's wife, now and forever. 'I saved us all.'

'Even so, you cannot be married until you do penance.'

'He is right, Rinette.' Alexander was himself again, tall and golden and full of lordly confidence. 'Confess and do penance, my love, and we will forget all this. You cannot be a proper wife with such – thoughts – in your head.'

I stared at them, one after the other, speechless. How could they be wrong, the holy old priest who had christened and confirmed me, and the beautiful man I loved with all my heart? What would they do, what would they think of me, if I refused?

'I will do it,' I said, 'because I love you, and because the only thing I want in the world, the only thing I have wanted since I was twelve years old, is to be your wife.'

Alexander kissed my forehead and slipped his ring back on his own finger. 'Tomorrow, then,' he said. 'Père Guillaume?'

'Yes, tomorrow. Come, *ma fille*.'

I clasped my hands together and followed the priest with every appearance of meekness. I love you, Alexander, I thought. I will do anything for you. But still – it was I who saved us all.

3

That night I did my penance kneeling on the cold stone of Saint Ninian's, my arms outstretched, trembling with strain and fatigue as I recited the *Pater* one hundred times. Old Père Guillaume would have remitted the penance if I had wept and begged, but I would not beg because I was not sorry. In fact, I was proud of what I had done. I had driven the enemy from Granmuir and I was willing to pay the price.

And my reward, oh, my reward – my reward came the next day when Alexander and I were married at last, with the sound of the sea sighing gently through the broken door of the church and with all Granmuir's people gathered round to bear witness: Tante-Mar, of course; her cousin Robinet Loury, who had come from France with her and acted as Granmuir's master-at-arms; my dear Jennet with her father Norman More, the castellan, his wife Bessie and Jennet's younger brother Davy; Wat Cairnie with a bandage wrapped pirate-style around his forehead. I imagined Grannie in the shadows, upright as a poker, and my beloved Gran'auntie with her arms full of windflowers. I imagined my father, handsome, dark-haired, laughing, his eyes the colour of the sea. Leslie eyes, like mine.

My fine court gowns of silk and lace had been left behind in Edinburgh; I wore a plain high-necked dress of sea-green

Florentine serge with only one petticoat. For Tante-Mar's sake – and only for Tante-Mar's sake, not because I missed my mother, no, not at all – I wore my mother's lace veil, with her chain of turquoises braided in my hair and looped over my forehead. I wondered if she would sense, in her convent far away in Paris, that my father's presence had come home to be with me.

Afterwards we feasted. Everyone from Granmuir village on the mainland was invited into the castle's Great Hall for roasted mutton and pork pies, stewed chickens and braised pike in spicy-sweet cinnamon sauce. We danced, to the harp and pipes – not the mannered dances of the court but the boisterous jigs and reels of the countryside.

Then as the moon rose my husband – my husband! – and I walked up the ancient circular staircase to the chamber at the top of the Mermaid Tower, the north-east tower of Granmuir castle. It was all so unlike the court weddings I had seen – no processions, no ribaldries, no chattering ladies and gentlemen. Just the two of us. We undressed each other, slowly, so slowly. The shutters were open to the sea and the stars and the sweet June darkness.

'Alexander,' I whispered. 'Oh, my love.'

He was beautiful. Can a man be beautiful? Alexander Gordon was. He was like an archangel, his golden hair silver in the starlight, his shoulders broad and elegant, fine muscles perfectly intertwined under the smooth skin of his arms and chest. But no archangel was ever so naked. No archangel was ever so male.

'Do you like looking at me?' he said.

I reached out and touched his left forearm. There was still a slight irregularity in the line of the bones; I would not have noticed it if I had not known it was there. 'Yes,' I said. 'Do you remember the first time we saw each other? Grannie had just finished splinting your arm. You were naked then, too, or at least partly naked. She told me not to come in, but I did anyway. I loved you then, the moment I saw you.'

He laughed. 'You were only a little girl.'

'I was not. I was twelve. Some girls are married when they are twelve.'

'Only princesses.'

'I have royal blood – somewhere, I think. Perhaps on the French side. I loved you, but you did not even notice me. You were only afraid your horse had been hurt when you fell.'

He threaded his hands through my hair and drew my face close to his so he could kiss my mouth. 'It was a Glenlithie grey,' he said. 'I loved it like you love your flowers. Do you remember the first time I kissed you?'

'Do you think I would ever forget? We were hiding in the garden. Grannie had made me swear I would not let you touch me or kiss me—'

'—and so of course you came straight to me and begged me to touch you and kiss you,' he said. I slapped at him in mock indignation and he laughed. 'We planned to run away together, that afternoon. I had come of age by then, and we could have gone to Glenlithie. You showed me some yellow flowers you'd planted, and told me you could dig them up and carry them with you.'

'Irises. Golden flags. Your flower, Alexander.'

He caught me up in his arms. 'You are my flower,' he said. 'My beautiful wife.'

I kissed him. He tasted like wine and cinnamon. I wanted him so much I was afraid I would faint with it. I was afraid – suddenly I was terrified and I did not know why.

'Where would we be tonight,' I said, 'if the Earl of Huntly's party had not stopped to hunt at Granmuir that day, and if your Glenlithie grey had not fallen with you? Oh, Alexander, it frightens me. Such a small thing, and our whole lives were changed. What other small things—'

'Shhh.' He put his finger against my mouth. 'It did happen, and we are here.' Slowly he drew his finger down over my chin, along the line of my throat, to the hollow between my breasts. 'We can touch and kiss each other now, all we want.'

I gave myself up to him, and we did everything we had ever wanted to do.

We lived in that tower room, Alexander and I, for the next few days. We learned each other's bodies down to the last scent and texture and curve and fold. We sat cross-legged on the bed, giggling like children, and ate honey-soaked cakes until the counterpane was covered with crumbs and we never wanted to see honey again. We drank wine until we were dizzy. We watched the sea, the sunrises, the stars, the change in the moon from a gibbous half-circle to a waning crescent. And on the last day, I showed him the queen's silver casket.

'What is in it?' he asked.

'I do not know. She told me not to open it – whatever is in it, is for her daughter, the French queen, if she ever comes back to Scotland.'

'Do you have a key?'

I opened my hand to show him. 'Yes. But the key is for the French queen as well. I must not open it. I promised, sweetheart.'

He leaned forward and kissed my mouth, slowly and deliciously. 'The old queen is dead and the French queen will never know,' he said. 'Open it. I want to see.'

'I promised.'

He licked the corner of my mouth, then kissed his way along my jawline. My whole body quivered and tightened. 'Open it,' he whispered, close against my ear.

'We will just look. Nothing more.'

He laughed and sat back. 'Nothing more.'

I fitted the key into the keyhole. The scents of hawthorn and woodbine and briar rose suddenly seemed to fill the room. I shook my head. Not real. Just memories. Mary of Guise was dead and that was what the hawthorn had foretold – *but the blood, what about the blood?* – and the woodbine meant entanglement, binding, my promise. Yes, I had promised. But what harm could it do to look, just look, nothing more?

I turned the key and put back the casket's lid. Alexander leaned forward, his breath sweet and warm against my cheek.

There were still a few dried petals inside. I brushed them aside – they clung to my fingers and I shook them off – and took out a stack of papers, sewn together with black thread into a sort of small book. There was a dark spattered drop beside the stitches – a blot of ink? Or blood, a needle thrust unwisely through the paper, a finger pricked?

'Do you recognise the handwriting?' Alexander took the packet and turned over the pages. The paper was beginning to discolour. 'It is all in some sort of cipher. But look at the headings on each page.'

'It is the queen's hand.' Was the drop of blood the queen's also? I read off the single words at the tops of the pages as Alexander turned them over. 'Hamilton. Stewart. Gordon. Hepburn. Douglas. She is writing things about all the great lords, secret things.'

'Secrets they would rather keep hidden, I suspect.' He turned over the pages with more and more excitement. 'Look, a woman's name – Margaret Erskine. Her husband's favourite mistress, Lord James' mother. That is one I would like to read. Do you think we can decipher them?'

'No,' I said. 'They are for the young queen, not for us. Please, Alexander, put them back.'

He laughed and put the book of papers back in the casket. 'There's another one,' he said. 'No, not a book, a packet, papers folded up tight – God's belly-bone, sweetheart, I have never seen anything quite like this before. Red cords, tied together in a net, all around it, and at least a dozen red wax seals. Unbroken, so even the old queen never opened it. Do you recognise the device?'

Imprinted deeply into the wax, a sun and five stars.

Over two fixed stars, three superior planets conjuncted in opposition to the sun.

'I recognise it,' I said.

'Well? Whose is it?'

Reluctantly I said, 'A French doctor and seer with whom the queen had correspondence from time to time. Monsieur de Nostredame.'

'Nostredame – do you mean Nostradamus? The man who writes the almanacs and the books of prophecies everyone is mad to read?'

'Yes.'

'I wonder why he was sending sealed packets to the queen. I thought the Medici woman in France was his patron.'

'She is, but he wrote to the queen regent as well. Perhaps others. Alexander, put it back. I should not have opened the casket.'

'Someone has written on the outside,' he said. 'It is in the same hand as the ciphers, so it must have been the queen. *Pour Marie seule – les quatre maris.* For Mary alone – the four husbands.

He must have prophesied the young queen will marry four times. Well, everyone says the little King of France is a sickly stripling.'

'Alexander, it is for the young queen alone. Please put it back.'

He grinned at me. 'Not even a tiny peek? Queens' husbands are great matters.'

'Not even a tiny peek.' A chill had run through me. 'Put it back, quickly. These secrets are not for us, Alexander. I do not want to meddle in anything to do with Monsieur de Nostredame.'

He put the packet back in the casket. I could tell he was reluctant. Then he kissed me and sat back. 'Put your casket away then, sweetheart. Let us have some more wine. It is almost time for supper, I think, and we had best put on some clothes.'

I closed the casket and locked it, then jumped up from the bed and carried it over to my particular hiding place, a loose stone in the wall under the window. I had been hiding things there for as long as I could remember: dolls, bracelets, dried flowers, bits of poetry. Gran'auntie's herbals were there, crammed with crumbling pressed leaves and flowers, scribbled with bits of folklore, commentary and poetry in her tiny bird-track handwriting. I loved looking at the herbals.

I never looked at the one other thing left of my childhood treasures: my mother's storybook. Perhaps inspired by Gran'auntie, she had written it herself and drawn the pictures, coloured and gilded them; the tales, she had said, were country folk tales her own mother had told her and *contes-de-fées* she had learned from other books. How I had loved it when she read to me, when she came home from the court with my father. Even though their visits were rare, I memorised the stories and knew when she left out so much as one word.

No one knew about my secret hiding place, not even Jennet

or Tante-Mar. But Alexander was my heart, my husband, my own flesh. I had no secrets from him.

I put the casket and the key on top of the books, and fitted the stone back into place. Then I hurried to wrap myself in my night-gown, so I would be presentable when Jennet arrived with our supper.

4

From that day to this, here is what happened.

The poor little French king died in December, to the surprise of no one. This left the young Queen of Scots a widow at eighteen. The Lords of the Congregation were firmly in the saddle here in Scotland, and no one dreamed that Mary of Guise's Catholic daughter would do anything but find another Catholic husband with another European crown.

At Granmuir, we were far from crowns and politics. We brought in the harvest on the mainland and sheared the sheep; I laughed at Alexander, who was happy to spend our estates' revenues on fine clothing, horses and hawks and dogs, but looked at me with blank horror when I suggested he shear a sheep or two himself. We celebrated our first Christmastide, and around Epiphany, I began to suspect I was with child. By the beginning of Lent I was certain. When I told Alexander, we cried together for the joy of it.

By Easter Day, however, he had grown restless and cross-grained. He was not used to such isolation, he said. He was not born to be a countryman. He rode to Aberdeen twice, on some matters of business – to do with his estate at Glenlithie, he said. He began to talk of the pleasures and prestige of court life. I reminded him that with the queen in France and the Lords of the

Congregation ruling the country, there was no court. We had sharp, childish quarrels and reconciled blissfully in the Mermaid Tower, with the sea roaring around us.

In June the news broke that the Queen of Scots was coming back to Scotland after all. Her marriage negotiations were being thwarted at every turn by Catherine de' Medici; perhaps the Queen of Scots thought that in Scotland she would have more freedom to find a new husband. Perhaps she simply wanted to be queen of her own court again. In any case, the Lords of the Congregation turned their Protestant coats and invited her back, Catholic or no, because her pretensions to the English crown gave them a bargaining chip to use with the Queen of England.

At Granmuir I began to make plans to go to Edinburgh to meet her.

Tante-Mar and Jennet did everything they could to dissuade me. Alexander forbade me, with frightful oaths. The journey down to the capital, he said, would be exhausting, agonising, and dangerous to me and to the baby. He would not allow me to go. He would lock me in the Mermaid Tower before he allowed me to go. It puzzled me that he was so determined to remain at Granmuir when all through the spring and summer he'd been pining to get away.

For the first time, we quarrelled in earnest. I swore I would go to Edinburgh. I would go if I had no one but my mare Lilidh to accompany me. I am not sure why I was so determined. Yes, I had promised the old queen, but I had already broken my promise to her twice – once when I fled Edinburgh with the casket instead of hiding it under Saint Margaret's, and once when I showed it to Alexander. Perhaps it was because my poor promise was so broken and tattered that I was determined to fulfil what remained of it.

I was only sure that I would go, and give Mary Stuart the silver casket. Alexander gave in eventually, and we went together.

It took ten days, because we rode slowly and rested along the way; when we finally arrived in Edinburgh I was exhausted and sore. We settled ourselves at the Earl of Huntly's town house with the rest of the Gordons to await the queen. She arrived on a Tuesday, the nineteenth day of August in the year of Our Lord 1561, a day or two before she was expected. The royal apartments at Holyrood Palace were not even prepared, but only a palace would do for her; so after descending upon an assemblyman's house at Leith for her midday dinner – can you imagine the panic of the assemblyman's wife? – to Holyrood she went.

Edinburgh went mad with excitement.

Alexander and I went to Holyrood that very afternoon. I told her ladies I had a gift to present to her, a relic of her own mother who had charged me to keep it safely against the young queen's return. I did not tell them what it was – that, I thought, could wait until I was in the queen's own presence. Oh, but the queen was *très fatiguée*, her ladies replied. She would see me next week or the week after. She was sure that since I had kept her dear mother's treasure safe for a year and more, I could keep it safe for a little while longer.

I was furious. I had come all the way from Granmuir; I had quarrelled with my darling Alexander and risked my precious baby to come. I was tired and aching and humiliated. Since I had been with child, my emotions seemed wilder, closer to the surface.

I decided to fulfil my original promise and no more: I would put the casket in Mary of Guise's secret hiding place under Saint Margaret's. Then I would write the Queen of Scots a letter telling her the whole story, and go home.

*   *   *

Even Edinburgh Castle, high on its ancient rock over the unsettled city, was crammed with people who had come to the capital to welcome the new queen. Fortunately most of them, including the men-at-arms and the palace servants, were taking advantage of the excitement to carouse and play the pipes in the palace yard. Alexander and I were able to slip into the Great Hall of the Royal Palace without anyone paying a blink of attention.

A passageway, Mary of Guise had whispered with her last breath. *From the vaults under the Great Hall. Never tell anyone—*

Alexander carried the casket in a saddlebag of plain leather slung over his shoulder; in his hands he carried two lanterns. I had a few flowers tucked in my pouch, picked from the sadly neglected knot garden in Saint Anne's Yard outside the south wall of Holyrood: roses and clove pinks, rosemary from the old queen's overgrown topiary, and wildflowers, marguerites and yarrow and ragged-robin, which had crept in as wildflowers will do. The rosemary was for the memory of the old queen, the cultivated roses for the young one. The colour was right, pale pink, but the flowers themselves were wrong – did that mean the young queen did not belong at Holyrood? The wildflowers, chance-blown, chance-found, would tell the fate of the casket itself.

'Look here,' I said. 'By the fireplace.' I crouched down, clumsy with the babe in my belly, and ran my fingers over the panelling. Up from the floor twelve what? There were no lines, no seams in the polished panelwork. No crosses evident in the rich grain of the wood. When I tapped and pressed at random, nothing happened.

'I do not see why you think you must follow the old queen's directions now, sweetheart,' Alexander said. He sounded sulky and restless; he had wanted to stay at Holyrood with the courtiers who were flocking about the young queen like sheep to a bell-wether ewe. 'And I do not want to return to Granmuir without at least being presented to the queen.'

'I want to go home,' I said. I could see the irony – two weeks ago I had been quarrelling with him because I wanted to come to Edinburgh – but I was still angry over the queen's snub and did not care that I was inconsistent. I began measuring up from the floor and over from the side by finger widths. Nothing. 'Are you not even a little curious about a secret vault under Saint Margaret's? The chapel is hundreds of years old and they say there were other holy places there before it, on that very spot, from the times before the Christians came. A vault underneath – it could be thousands of years old.'

'Thousands of years of rats and spiders. And anyway, Edinburgh Castle and Saint Margaret's are built on solid rock. Not likely the savages could have chipped a vault underneath with bones and stones.'

I measured up with hand widths. Fingers together. Nothing. Fingers spread wide – and there it was. Worked so intricately into the grain of the wood one would never see it unless one knew exactly where to look – a tiny cross, not a double-barred *croisette de Lorraine* but a cross saltire, Saint Andrew's cross, the mark of Scotland from the time of the Picts. The wooden panelling was comparatively new but whoever had carved the little cross had been marking something ancient and singular.

'I found it,' I said. Alexander leaned down to look. I pressed the spot firmly and felt the panel shift. With an eerie shrieking sound it turned and revealed a narrow opening.

'You will never fit through, sweetheart, not with the baby.'

'I can fit.' I began to wriggle through the opening. Hold still, I thought, my littlin, my bairnie-ba. Press close. We're going on a great adventure. One last deep breath and I was through.

'Light,' I said.

Alexander passed me the lanterns and the bag with the casket, then turned and stepped sideways through the opening so easily he might have been performing a *ripresa* as part of a court dance. I could have smacked him. We both looked down: stone steps, rough-cut and thick with dust, spiralled away into what seemed the depths of the earth. There was no handrail.

'Take care,' Alexander said. 'I will go first, and manage the lanterns and the casket.'

I kept one hand against the wall and the other stretched out in front of me, to catch Alexander's shirt if I should slip. The shape of his shoulders was so familiar and so beloved, yet at the same time with his face turned away he might have been a stranger. It seemed as if we went around and down and around and down forever. At last we reached the bottom.

'Follow the crosses,' I said.

The lanterns cast ghostly shapes and shadows on the rough-hewn stone. There had been vaults under the palace and the upper ward for a hundred years and more, since James Stewart the second of the name, but this was different – this was a narrow passageway chipped out of the living rock, much older than the vaults. Every hundred steps or so I saw another cross. Seeping water and the passage of time had worn away the sharp edges of the carvings.

'I wonder if there is treasure hidden away in the secret chamber.' At last Alexander seemed to be falling under the spell of the old queen's secret. 'Why would they do all the work of making these tunnels, if not to hide something valuable?'

We went on. The walls of the passageway began to look different; the stone seemed moulded or melted, and no longer bore any mark of tools. The rock both underfoot and overhead was curved, and there were narrow ledges like steps at the sides. Three more crosses and we came out into a chamber. The light from the lanterns flickered over rounded walls and an arched vault overhead with bubbles and drips in the stone like an upside-down pot of porridge. Under our feet the rock was smooth as polished marble, with deep cracks running at random angles. The air had been getting harder and harder to breathe and here in the eerie empty chamber it was thick and stale and smelled of stone and rainwater and eons of time.

Alexander put the lanterns down and crossed himself. I wrapped my arms around the round weight of the baby. It was very still, as if it could feel awe even in my womb.

'How did it come to be?' Alexander whispered. 'It is like a bubble in a bog, only all in solid rock. The floor's like melted sugar that's been cooled too fast and crackled.'

'I do not know. I wonder who made the crosses, and how they knew Saint Margaret's was overhead. Look, there is a niche in the wall.'

We crossed the chamber. The niche was clearly man-made; there were tool-marks. I took the branch of blue rosemary flowers and the pink rose blossoms out of my pouch and put them inside the niche. The rosemary had remained fresh, its scent sharp and astringent, but the roses had wilted. The young queen, then, would not have the strength and purpose of her mother.

'Put the casket in,' I said.

Alexander took the casket out of the leather saddlebag. The light from the two lanterns played over the silver – freshly polished, just before we left Granmuir – and the repoussé ribbons worked into the casket's domed lid appeared to twist and flicker. He put it in the niche, cushioned by the rosemary and the roses.

'Now let us get back above ground, sweetheart,' he said. 'I am feeling faint and the lanterns will not burn much longer. The air is dead.'

'A moment.' I took the rest of the flowers out of my pouch. Clove pinks, yarrow and ragged-robin. Half the meaning of the flowers was in which ones chose to present themselves. The other half lay in myth and legend, shaped and deepened by Gran'auntie's teaching and by what the flowers themselves whispered to me.

The clove pinks were variegated, almost black at their hearts but with white edging on their jagged red-violet petals. They had remained fresh and their distinctive spicy scent strong. *Misfortune*, they breathed. *Bad luck*. Jagged streaks of white – old age, an old woman with white in her hair, white she covered with jewelled coifs. Mary of Guise, perhaps? The young queen, many years from now? I myself, at a great age? Whoever the old woman was, she and the casket and bad luck would be folded together like the clove pinks' petals.

And then the ragged-robin, sunrise pink, its narrow, deeply lobed petals as shaggy as a moor pony. Wit and ardour – whose? *The next person who touches the casket will have a fierce heart and a clever tongue. Me?* I thought in return. *Not you*, the ragged-robin whispered. *Not you*.

Alexander, then. Surely he has a fierce heart and a clever tongue.

The ragged-robin was silent.

I turned my attention to the last blossom, the yarrow. Tight clusters of small white flowers smelling of cabbage leaves. Some called it the devil's nettle, but the flower itself whispered of witches – *witchcraft, spells, incantations and fear*. And at the same time, confusingly – *a dream of one's own true love*.

My hands shook as I packed the flowers around the casket. Misfortune, witchcraft, fear, and even possibly some unknown person taking the casket from the niche. Some other person who knew the secret of the passageway and the crosses. Perhaps not all of it was true. Sometimes the flowers were wrong. Sometimes I myself was wrong in what I heard, or how I interpreted it.

'Now we can go, my love,' I said. 'I am fainting for fresh air as well.'

We made our way back through the passageways. As I climbed the stairs my legs were shaking and the baby was heavy inside me. Back through the narrow secret door into the Great Hall of the Royal Palace. In the fresh air the lanterns burned brightly again. I pushed the panel shut and the hidden lock clicked.

'Listen to the pipes,' Alexander said. He had thrown his head back like a restive colt, ready to run. Clearly he was longing to be part of the excitement, to dance and eat and drink with the rest of the city. 'Let us go down into the street and find a tavern with good wine and a meat pie or two. You have not eaten all day, sweetheart.'

It was true. Perhaps that was why I felt so faint and dizzy. Perhaps that was why my belly was cramping.

'Only for a little while.' I could hear the edge of a whine in my own voice and it made me angry with myself. 'Some food, yes. Then I must sleep. Please, Alexander.'

'You felt well enough to wander through miles of vaults and tunnels under the Castle,' he said. 'I went with you. I helped you. Now you are too tired for a bit of enjoyment for me?'

I said nothing. In silent animosity we made our way out into the upper ward. There is Saint Margaret's, I thought, there is the hedgerow where I picked hawthorn and woodbine and sweet briar the night the old queen died. Hawthorn for death, woodbine for binding, sweet briar for joy to come. What joy? Coming when?

We passed through the castle yards and down the long steps. By the time we reached the High Street at the bottom I was sweating. The August night was warm and humid and the street was packed with people; torches streamed fire and soot. The screeching of the pipes and rebecs and the chanting of psalms was jarring. The individual familiar smells of sweat and smoke, spilled wine and hot meat from the cookshops, combined into an overpowering and stomach-turning stench.

'Alexander,' I said. I had to scream, or try to scream, to make him understand. 'I am going to be sick.'

'A fine time to be sick,' he shouted back petulantly. 'All right. We will go back to Huntly's house. There will be people there to look after you.' He didn't say, *And then I can come back out and do some proper celebrating*, but he might as well have. 'We should have stayed there in the first place, and your wretched casket be damned. Come on, it is just a little further.'

He put one arm around me and used his other hand to push passers-by aside. I squeezed my eyes shut and willed myself to walk. The ache in my back was fierce. Just a few more steps. A few more steps.

'Make way!' Alexander said. 'This lady is unwell. Make way—'

He broke off with a strange sound, half-shriek, half-exhalation. His arm fell away from my waist and he lurched to one side. I staggered and opened my eyes and saw the flash of a dagger's hilt and a flood of glistening black in the torchlight, bursting from his throat. His eyes were open, shocked more than anything, not angry or frightened. Blessed Saint Ninian, it was blood, Alexander's blood – *blood on the hawthorn, blood and death* – it was hot and sticky and smelled like salt and rust and raw meat and it was all over my breasts and arms. The spurting slowed. He tried to speak – his lips moved but there was nothing but a grunt of air and a bubbling from the nightmare slash across his throat. The shock in his eyes hardened into blankness and he collapsed.

I caught him as he fell. His weight dragged me to the stones of the high street and pinned me there. I tried to scream but I had no breath. I heard someone laugh and say, 'He's drunk.' A filthy boot struck my cheek as another man pushed past. I sobbed and tried to curl up to protect the baby. More boots, stepping on my hair, crushing my headdress, tearing my skirt. The smell of the blood was overwhelming, and I retched in the street. My belly rippled and contracted. *Alexander, Alexander. God help me, my bairnie, I am sorry, sorry, sorry . . .*

The boots stopped. Shouts, and the unmistakable sound of a blade being drawn, the whistle of steel against leather. A torch falling. Kicked away, but a shoe, not a boot, a shoe of fine soft and polished leather, a long leg with a silk stocking gartered in silver, standing over me and stretching up as if it would never end. Painfully I turned my head. The torch rolled and struck flashes of light off the guard and pommel of a sword, slicing through the air in a circle and creating a magic space of safety around me. Gilding, scrollwork, silver inlay. A hand in a black leather glove. Hair like fire. Angel or demon?

Somewhere a bell rang.

The pain in my belly was tearing me apart.

Nothing more.

5

*A*lexander, Alexander . . .

I felt hot and sick and too light to keep my body connected to the earth. I smelled blood. Was it Alexander's blood, glistening in the torchlight? No – a man with a French-accented voice was saying, *We must stop the blood or she will die,* and so it must be my own.

I looked down. Time was wrong. It was a year ago, a lifetime ago, and there I was in the upper ward of Edinburgh Castle the night the old queen died, holding my finger over a mass of hawthorn. *A drop of blood fell, black in the moonlight. Hawthorn meant death, but there was no blood in the queen's dying; was someone else to die as well?*

Oh, Alexander. Oh, my dear love. Oh no, oh no—

I opened my eyes.

I had been dreaming something terrible, but it had slipped away and I felt only the lingering fear and horror. Dream, dream, only a dream. Thank God it was only a dream.

Why did I hurt so much? I felt as if I had been cleft in two with an axe. And why did I feel – different, too small, too light? Where was I? Where was Alexander? And why was there a baby crying?

'She is awake.' A woman's voice, soft and deliberate and at the same time chillingly cold. 'Bring the babe.'

I turned my head. There was a woman standing next to the unfamiliar bed I lay on. I knew her. At least, I knew I had seen her before. I knew I did not like her, did not trust her – but I could not remember who she was.

She placed a swaddled infant on my chest. At least that explained where the crying was coming from. The poor wee bairnie screamed. I turned my face aside and pushed it away.

'Take her,' the woman said. 'She is your daughter.'

'That she is not,' I said. My throat was sore and my voice sounded wrong, hoarse and scratchy. 'Where is Alexander?'

'Your Alexander is dead.'

Your. Alexander. Is. Dead.

Words. They did not come together to mean anything to me.

I looked at the woman, at the way her lips hardly moved at all when she spoke, at the ruined traces of sensuous beauty in her cheekbones and eyes, and I knew her. It was Lady Margaret Erskine, one-time mistress of old King James, mother of Lord James Stewart who was the secular leader of the Protestant Lords of the Congregation and said to be the king's favourite bastard. What was she doing here now? Where was I?

The baby was still crying.

Your Alexander. Is dead.

'No,' I said. I felt quite calm, because clearly Lady Margaret did not know who I was. She was talking about some other Alexander. Or else she was stark daft. First she thought the crying baby was mine, then she thought Alexander—

—a flood of glistening black in the torchlight, spurting, bursting from his throat—

No. I would not remember.

'No,' I said again. 'Not my Alexander. My Alexander is—is—'

My voice shook so badly I could not go on. My whole body

46

began to tremble. I squeezed my eyes shut as tightly as I could. The dream was coming back and I did not want to see it.

'Alexander Gordon of Glenlithie,' Lady Margaret Erskine said, 'is lying before the altar in the nave of Holyrood Abbey, his throat cut to the bone.' She bent closer, her eyes burning. Her breath smelled of wild arum lilies, sulphurous and overripe. 'Your Alexander is dead.'

Your Alexander is dead.

I knew it was true.

The baby was still crying in the background and my body hurt and I knew she was right. It was my baby. A daughter. I did not care. I did not want her. I did not want to live in a world without Alexander Gordon.

So this was what my mother had felt. This was why, when my father died, she had abandoned me to pray her life away in a French convent. I had cried for her and missed her and hated her for so long, my beautiful, evanescent mother who had lived at court with my father and descended on Granmuir two or three times a year like a dayflower suddenly blossoming, to read me stories. Now – now I understood. The dayflower was sometimes called widow's tears. Her widow's tears had blotted her out. I felt a wave of love for her, love I had not felt since before we went to France, before the year that cut my childhood in half.

There were no convents left in Scotland. I would die. It would be easier.

I turned my face away but cold fingers forced me to turn back. Nails pointed as claws sank into my cheeks and the wild-arum scent was hot in my face. Wild arums, cuckoo-plants, devils-and-angels – whatever they were called they meant concealment, sexuality and the boundary between life and death. If you stirred a cup of rainwater sunwise and dropped in a wild-arum seed it would tell you how long a sick person would take to recover by the number of times it circled. If you stirred the water widdershins and dropped in the seed—

'Where is the casket?' Lady Margaret Erskine whispered. 'I will not let you die, Rinette Leslie, until you tell me where you have hidden the old queen's silver casket.'

—*where you have hidden the old queen's silver casket.*

But she had not seen me take the casket.

How did she know?

I did not care. It did not matter. No one would ever find the casket, safe underneath Saint Margaret's Chapel, wreathed in flowers in that mysterious bubble in the ancient rock. I could slip away into soft black unremembering and no one would find the silver casket until the last trump sounded.

Shocks of pain, sharper than the rest. I opened my eyes again. She was slapping me, the old witch. I saw her hand come down again and heard the cracking sound and felt the sting and the jolt of my head on the pillow.

'You have a daughter,' she hissed. 'Alexander Gordon's daughter. She has been baptised, with the queen herself as godmother – Mary Gordon she is, now and forever. Are you coward enough to leave her an orphan?'

Mary Gordon. It made her real and I did not want to think of her as real. Mary Gordon of Glenlithie and Granmuir.

'She will have Granmuir,' I said. 'And Glenlithie.'

'She will not. The Earl of Rothes will have it, and Huntly will have Glenlithie, and she will be a beggar with no place in either household.'

For the first time I felt a thread of feeling, pulling me back to life. Granmuir, my Granmuir, my garden by the sea. Rothes wanted it and I had thwarted him when I ran away and married – oh,

Alexander, Alexander. My beloved, my husband. So much blood. And we had been quarrelling. Stupid senseless meaningless anger the last thing we both felt, and then the knife flashing—

'Rothes will have Granmuir,' Lady Margaret said again. She had found a weapon and clearly she meant to use it. 'He will marry your daughter to one of his retainers. Or who knows? She might die – babies die so easily. She is a Gordon and that gives Huntly claim. He and Rothes hate each other. How easy to put a pillow over her face in the night. Then Glenlithie will be Huntly's forever.'

I opened my eyes. She had shaken her headdress crooked, slapping me, and I could see streaks of white in her hair. Streaks of white in an old woman's hair – I had seen it before but I could not remember where.

'Granmuir is mine,' I said.

'If you die it will be yours no longer.'

I hated her and I did not want to live but she was right. The thread of feeling twisted itself with another, and another, and became a living cord drawing me back to the world.

'Tell me where you have hidden the casket.'

Another thread, braiding itself with the rest. How did she know? No one knew, no one but Alexander and me. Tante-Mar and Jennet might have guessed, but they would never betray me. How did Lady Margaret Erskine, the old king's mistress, the bastard pretender's mother, creature of courts and plots and power, know what I had hidden at Granmuir for a year, what I had brought to Edinburgh to give to the young queen?

'I do not know what you mean,' I said.

She put her hand on my forehead, suddenly gentle. Had she realised, perhaps, that threats and slaps would never persuade me? 'You will understand,' she said, 'when your daughter is older. A

49

mother will do anything for her child. We are not so different, you and I.'

I turned my face away, but she bent closer. 'My son was born to be king,' she whispered. 'His father wanted to legitimise him, did you know that? He petitioned the pope to dissolve my marriage to Robert Douglas, so we could marry and I could be his queen and James could be his true heir.'

'He married Mary of Guise instead,' I said. 'Leave me alone.'

'Mary of Guise is dead and her daughter will bring nothing but conflict and sorrow to Scotland. We will send her home to France – she will be happier, in the end. Give me the casket – my James will use the contents wisely.'

'I do not have it.'

'Your Alexander died because of that silver casket. You will be next. Tell me where it is and save yourself. Save Scotland. Tell me, and James will arrange everything – you will be safe to take your daughter and live on your sea-rock in peace.'

Your Alexander died because of that silver casket.

Because of that silver casket.

It stunned me. It was like a knife to my own heart.

Was she right – was it about the casket, then? Not some random footpad in the crowd intent on Alexander's purse, but a deliberate assassination, a murder, ordered by—

By whom?

Why Alexander? Why not me?

A final thread, stronger than all the rest, hot as flame and red as blood.

I would live, then, and I would find out who killed Alexander Gordon. I would find out, and before I went home to Granmuir with his daughter in my arms, I would have revenge.

6

Alexander Gordon of Glenlithie, Lady Margaret had said in her fetid wild-arum whisper, *is lying before the altar in the nave of Holyrood Abbey, his throat cut to the bone.*

Then to the nave of Holyrood Abbey I would go, as soon as I could stand on my own two feet.

Lady Margaret thought I had chosen to live because of Granmuir and my daughter. She was partly right and I would let her continue to think that. I even allowed her to put the poor screaming babe to my breast, although it hurt when she sucked and there seemed to be precious little there for her. At least afterwards she stopped crying and slept.

I allowed the serving-women to give me meat broth and a few sops of bread in wine. I continued to swear I knew nothing of any casket. Lady Margaret knew I was lying, of course, but what could she do? At least I was making an effort to live. The knowledge of the casket's hiding-place would not die with me, not yet.

After an hour or two she went away. She would come and speak with me again when I was stronger, she said. I did not answer her, and off she went. Three women remained. One was richly dressed in black with pearls in her ears, and gave orders in Scots with a distinct French accent; the other two were stout Edinburgh girls who did as they were directed and said nothing.

'I am Mary Livingston,' the Frenchwoman said. 'I am in the queen's personal household, and she herself has charged me with your care. I grew up in France with her and it is so strange to be back in Scotland again – I hardly remember it and can barely speak Scots any more.'

'My name is Marina,' I said. I could not bring myself to say either Gordon or Leslie. 'For the sea, because my home is by the sea. I'm called Rinette.'

Mary Livingston smiled; her round freckled face was much better suited for smiling than for looking serious and sad. Then she remembered I was new-widowed and made herself look sad again. 'You must rest and get better,' she said. 'This is Alisoun and this is Elspeth. If there is anything you want, you must tell us.'

'I would like more broth and bread, please. Help me to sit up.'

I did not really want the food but I knew I had to eat. They piled pillows behind me. I was dizzy for a moment, but I ate more bread soaked in rich meat broth and my head cleared.

'What day is it?' I asked.

'It is Friday,' Mary Livingston said. 'Your babe was born very early Wednesday morning, and this is Friday night. It will be time for vespers soon.'

The queen had arrived on Tuesday morning. It had been Tuesday night when—

I could not think it.

'Where are we?' I asked instead. 'How did I come here?'

'In Holyrood Palace. The queen has settled here for the moment – her apartments are in the north-west tower, just at the end of the gallery.' She gestured to the door of the tiny room. 'Her own physician has been charged to attend you, and of course I myself, and Alisoun and Elspeth here. Monsieur Nicolas de

Clerac brought you here – he was passing by in the High Street when you fell, and rescued you from the crowds.'

'Nicolas de Clerac,' I repeated. 'He was the old queen's French secretary.'

'He returned with us from France. He is a great *ami* of the young queen, who loves him for her mother's sake.'

'And the baby.' I still could not quite call her by name, or say the word *daughter*. 'She was baptised?'

'Oh, yes, after such a birth, the queen felt it was best to baptise her at once. She held your beautiful little girl in her own arms and spoke the responses as godmother, while Père René performed the ceremony.'

'Lady Margaret said—' I stopped. I closed my eyes. It was easier to say it in the dark. 'She said my husband had been – Had been taken to the Abbey.'

Mary Livingston took my hands in hers. She had warm, strong hands. I felt a sense of white violets about her, simple and joyous, although with the deep purple of mourning in the centre hinting at darkness to come. 'He lies in the Abbey,' she said gently. 'With all honour. The queen has seen to everything.'

So I knew where I was, and what day it was, and what time it was. I knew where they had taken him. I had the twisted cords binding me to life – Granmuir and Mary Gordon, guilt and vengeance. All I wanted now was to get up and walk to the Abbey and see for myself that the terrible thing I remembered was in fact the truth.

I opened my eyes. I took a deep breath and shifted myself in the bed, stretched out my legs and put my feet on the floor. It was plain stone, and cold. I straightened my knees and stood up. My legs trembled and I could feel the blood seeping out of me.

'Please help me get dressed,' I said. 'My own people, from Granmuir — have they been sent for?'

'They have,' Mary Livingston said. 'The queen sent a messenger the very night the babe was born. They should be here in a few days. Rinette, *ma chère*, please lie down again. It is too soon for you to be out of your bed.'

'I want to be dressed. I want to go to the Abbey.'

'Oh, Rinette.' She put one arm around me. 'You will never be able to walk so far. You have had fever, you have lost so much blood. Stay here with your babe and rest. He will understand.'

'I want to go to the Abbey. Please help me wash and dress.'

I saw her look at the other two women. They all thought I was mad with grief. Well, let them think so. I had to see him.

Reluctantly they fetched warm water and fresh linens and a clean dress I had never seen before. It was black silk with a stiffened collar in the French style, the sleeves faced and lined in white linen embroidered with blackwork. Which one of the queen's ladies had been judged close enough to my own height and size and so been ordered to give up one of her dresses? Not Mary Livingston — she was considerably shorter and broader than I.

At last I was ready. Elspeth was chosen to remain with the baby. I leaned on Mary Livingston's arm with Alisoun on my other side, and with both of them protesting at every step we made our way along the gallery and through the palace's private entrance to the ancient nave of Holyrood Abbey.

It was long and narrow, with rows of columns like clustered flower stems on either side of the nave, creating two aisles. The tall pointed windows beyond the aisles were ghostly dark; the sun had long since gone down. At the crossing between the transepts a bier had been set, with two candles burning, one at either end.

Yes, there was a body on the bier, I could see that much. But I could not recognise it as Alexander unless I went closer.

'I will go in alone,' I said. 'Please wait here.'

'You cannot walk that far.'

'I can. I must be alone. Please.'

'May the Holy Virgin walk with you,' Mary Livingston whispered, and she let go of my arm.

I took one step, and then another. The stone floor of the church was scarred and I could see marks of fire on the pillars. I knew the tale, of course: the English Protector Somerset's men, twenty years ago, burning and looting the church, stealing the great font of solid brass, stripping the lead from the roof. But the nave remained, silent and holy, filled with the tombs of kings, smelling of ancient stone and centuries of incense. Each step took me closer to the bier. At the crossing, the ruined remains of the transepts stretched away darkly on either side. I stopped.

Alexander, Alexander . . .

He lay with mourning candles at his head and his feet, his hands crossed over his breast. He wore strange black clothes, borrowed clothes, just as I did; his own shirt and doublet and hose – his shirt which I had stitched with my own fingers! – would have been too bloodied. His face was uncovered, his profile serene as it gazed up to the vaulted roof of the church. God, how white he was. Only his hair was the same, shining in the candlelight. Its curls made me think of the petals of his golden iris. I reached out and touched it. It felt the same, silky but at the same time strong and springing away from his scalp.

His eyes were closed.

I touched his cheek.

Cold. Slack and softening, where in life it had always been warm and firm.

Alexander . . .

I may have cried it aloud. I know I threw myself down over his chest and clung to him even in his borrowed clothes and with his flesh beginning to dissolve away into corruption, and screamed and screamed. I knew I was screaming because it hurt my throat. How could this have come to be? Why were we not at Granmuir, safe and happy beside the sea with our daughter all our own and not a queen's godchild?

Because you insisted on going to Edinburgh.

Alexander's voice.

Because you would not rest until you had taken the silver casket to the queen.

I scrabbled for his face, his mouth – he could not be speaking, he could not. His head fell to one side away from me. The wound across his throat had been roughly stitched together with black thread. There was still blood, dried black. Whoever had washed him had done it carelessly. Some flakes of the dried blood had cracked and come away when his head moved.

I would be alive if it were not for you and your silver casket.

'No,' I said. I felt sick with horror and guilt. 'Oh, no. Forgive me, forgive me.'

I put my hands on either side of his face, as I had done so often in life. He felt like an image in soft, cold clay, but I had disturbed him and I had to put him right. I turned his head and as I did the candlelight struck a spark of crimson fire from the spot under his ear where the dried blood had flaked away.

I touched it. A jewel. A ruby. My thoughts lurched to Alexander's own dagger, jewelled and filigreed, falling to the floor of Saint Ninian's Church at Granmuir. This jewel was different, not a cabochon but cut with facets and polished to catch the light; it had nothing to do with Alexander and if it was lodged in his terrible wound there was only one place it could have come from.

The assassin's dagger. Something in the violence of the cut, the agony of Alexander's convulsion, must have broken the ruby free—

'Madame.'

I started around and almost lost my balance. A man stood behind me, tall and angular, all arms and legs but for the breadth of his shoulders. I thought at first he was a ghost but then I realised he was dressed in black and silver in a thoroughly modern style, and with red-gold hair like banked embers in the darkness. His eyes were edged with kohl and a diamond glittered in his left ear. Where had he come from? Where had Mary Livingston and Alisoun gone, that they did not come to my aid?

'Your ladies are still in the back of the church,' the man said. His voice was familiar. 'I mean you no harm, I swear it. We have met before, although you may not remember me – I am Nicolas de Clerac, and I was in Mary of Guise's household as one of her French secretaries. I have come back to Scotland with her daughter to serve in a similar capacity.'

'I remember you,' I said. I remembered also that I had associated him with nightshade, beautiful to the eye but deadly. 'I did not like you or trust you then. What do you want with me now?'

He smiled, just a little. 'I see one does not have to guess to know your true feelings,' he said. 'I want nothing from you, Madame, other than to know you are safe, and to offer you my *condoléances*. I went to the room where you had been lying-in, and found it empty.'

I remembered him from the night of the old queen's death, yes, but there was something more. Not just his voice and his hair and his face with its hard bones and austere features – yes,

austere, for all the Frenchified cosmetics. Something more immediate. His clothes – black, like all the queen's household, but
particularly elegant, shoes of fine soft and polished leather, his
long legs in silk stockings gartered with silver—

*Monsieur Nicolas de Clerac brought you here – he was passing by
in the High Street when you fell, and rescued you from the crowds.*

'It was you,' I said. 'In the street. When— ' I choked on the
words.

He inclined his head. 'It was my good fortune to be in the
street for the celebrations at just that moment. I wish I could have
been there soon enough to save your husband's life.'

'Did you see?' I reached out and grasped his doublet. I would
wrinkle the pristine black figured silk. I did not care. *'Did you
see who killed him?'*

He took my hand. I think he meant to hold me up if I fainted.
Or perhaps he was just concerned for the line of his fine clothing.

'No,' he said gently. 'He was dressed in dark clothes and a
hooded cloak, but so were a hundred others. It happened very
quickly. He may have meant to kill you too, Madame. He made
no attempt to steal your husband's purse or dagger, so I do not
believe his motive was simple thievery.'

Lady Margaret Erskine had said the same thing. *Your Alexander
died because of that silver casket.*

'What, then?' I said.

He looked away for a moment, into the half-ruined choir behind
the crossing. Did he see the ghosts of long-dead Augustinian
canons there? I thought I heard a rustling sound, soft footfalls,
as if the monks were pacing in procession. For all his elegant and
elaborate clothing and cosmetics there was a contradictory sense
of asceticism about Nicolas de Clerac; I could just as easily see
him in a habit and cowl.

He said, 'I do not know. But if you will allow me, I will make an effort to find out.'

I was beginning to feel dizzy and I was not quite sure I had heard him correctly. I pulled my hand away from his. 'Why would you do that?'

'Perhaps because I was so close by when it happened,' he said. 'Perhaps because I believe it is in the queen's interest to discover the truth.'

'I will learn the truth for myself.'

'Madame, you may still be in danger. Come, let me escort you back to your chamber. Your husband is safe here, and your place is with your child.'

That made me angry. It was not for Monsieur Nicolas de Clerac to tell me where my place was. Nor did he have any legitimate reason to offer to help me. My legs were shaking and I was beginning to feel that too-light feeling again, but I had enough of my wits about me to pretend to accept his offer. Better to keep the devil at the door, as Jennet would say, than to turn him out of the house. I would keep Monsieur de Clerac at my door until I could find out what his motives were.

'If you wish to help me, look at this,' I said. 'Whoever washed and dressed him and laid him here did not pay close attention to – to his wound.'

Nicolas de Clerac frowned. 'What do you mean?'

I stepped close to the bier again. With one fingertip I touched the ruby, still stuck in my husband's dried blood. 'This is not his. He never drew his own dagger and he was no courtier to be wearing earrings or jewels.'

'Where do you think it came from?' Nicolas de Clerac bent his head to look more closely; his own earring winked in the candlelight. 'It is too small to have been set in a ring.'

'It could have been set in the murderer's dagger.'

'If so, it would be a valuable piece, not an ordinary assassin's weapon. Stones of that size are not usually cut with facets. May I remove it?'

'No.' I pushed his hand aside, more violently than I intended. He stepped back instantly. 'I will take it.'

'Of course, Madame.' His voice was soft and formal.

I put one hand on Alexander's forehead and smoothed back his golden hair. One last time, one last touch. Then I took the ruby. It came away easily. A few flakes of long-dried blood clung to my fingertips.

I will see justice done for you, I thought. I cannot say it aloud for it is not something I wish anyone else to hear. But I will see justice done. I swear it.

'Perhaps one day you will allow me to examine it,' Nicolas de Clerac said.

'Perhaps.'

My voice was beginning to sound as if it was coming from far away. I could hear the footfalls of the canons again, pacing, pacing. They sounded so real I jerked around, looking over my shoulder. I saw no one.

'Madame, please allow me to call your women to you.'

'I can walk. Thank you for your assistance, Monsieur de Clerac, you may go.'

With my head high, I turned to walk down the nave again. After one step I fell face-forward into his arms.

I heard him calling for Mary Livingston. I heard her speaking to him in French, and Alisoun's stout Edinburgh Scots in the background. I felt fury and humiliation that he would see me so weak and helpless. Worst of all, in the end he picked me up like a child and carried me – carried me! – out of the Abbey church.

He smelled of bitter orange and myrrh. I knew he could not truly smell of the narcotic gold-and-purple nightshade flower, but for me he did. Through it all I clung to the ruby.

I thought: Why did he come to the Abbey church, Monsieur Nicolas de Clerac, courtier and so-called secretary and very plate of fashion that he was? Was it truly for nothing more than to offer his condolences to a grieving widow? Or did he, too, think to find some trace of evidence connected to Alexander's death?

Find it, or suppress it?

Was it nothing but chance that he had been so fortuitously close at hand to fight off the assassin, once the deed was already done?

And why did he offer to help me find out the truth?

I should not have let him see the ruby. If he was part of a conspiracy, he could warn the true assassin to hide the jewelled dagger, or throw it into the sea. Yet Mary of Guise had loved and trusted him, and he was clever behind all the flamboyance. That was clear enough.

I floated higher and higher, until I was far away from them all.

7

I refused to call my daughter Mary. The queen had chosen that name, not I, and I resented her interference. But the christening was done, and Mary Gordon she was in the eyes of God and man. In my own mind I made it into Màiri, which meant 'bitterness'. Her birth, after all, had been a bitter, bitter thing.

She had Alexander's hair, golden and soft as the finest silk. It curled. I had no sense of the princely golden iris for her, though, with its intimations of sun and wind and blood. She was a wild rose, pink-and-gold, sweet like the rose's scent – but also bitter like the tea made from the hips in the fall. Bitter, but bracing and healthful in the end.

I had thought I could never love her. How wrong I had been. I loved her fiercely and completely, with every last shred and tatter of love I had left in my heart.

I was not allowed to take her with me to the requiem mass, of course. I was almost not allowed to be present myself, after my collapse in the Abbey. But a week had passed and I was stronger and clearer of mind. Tante-Mar and Jennet and Wat had arrived from Granmuir and closed ranks around me. Mary Livingston went back to the queen with many protestations of lasting friendship. I put the ruby in a silver locket Jennet bought for me in the

High Street, and I wore it day and night. I was wearing it as Tante-Mar helped me to dress, on the morning of Alexander's funeral mass.

'I want to go to the mass, Tante-Mar,' I said. 'It has been a week, and I am much better and stronger.'

'A proper lady's prayers are said in private,' Tante-Mar said. 'And in any case, my Lord Huntly's making a bear-garden of the arrangements after the queen's priest got knocked about last Sunday. You had best keep out of his way right now.'

'I am not afraid of the Earl of Huntly.'

'Nor I,' Jennet said. She was sitting with Màiri in her arms, rocking her as she slept. 'I'll go with Rinette, Mistress Margot, and you can tend to Màiri.'

'I cannot stop you.' Tante-Mar had seen me through too many escapades as a child at Granmuir to have any illusions as to my obedience. 'But I warn you – you will be sorry if you go. Catholic masses are not safe places to be these days, under the best of circumstances. And Huntly is using the young master's requiem for his own purposes.'

'All the more reason for me to be there.' I had made a place inside myself, a smooth stone-hard bubble like the chamber under Saint Margaret's, and to that I had banished my grief and guilt and terror. No one, not even my dear Tante-Mar, would know they were there. 'Someone must mourn him properly.'

'Oh, my dear.' Tante-Mar put her arms around me. Perhaps she saw more than I gave her credit for seeing. 'Very well, go and bury your dead. But take care, and mark me – if you want to go home to Granmuir, the less Huntly sees of you, the better.'

'I do not want to go home to Granmuir,' I said. I surprised myself, saying it out loud for the first time. 'Not yet. I am going to make a place for myself here at court, and I am going to find out who killed Alexander and why. Then we can all go home together.'

The long nave of Holyrood Abbey, so dark and empty the last time I had seen it, was filled with light streaming in through the rows of pointed windows. People crowded the church, far more than would have come for Alexander Gordon's sake alone. They were divided into two groups – plainly dressed townspeople at the back, and courtiers at the front, around the bier. Alexander's body had been placed in a coffin, and the coffin covered with a pall bearing the arms of Gordon and Glenlithie, hastily and crookedly embroidered in azure and gold.

Wearing my own borrowed black dress and a white mourning veil, with Jennet at my side to steady me, I walked down the south aisle. No one paid any attention to me.

'We will suffer no idolatry in this church. It is now the parish church of the Canongate, and it has been cleansed of popish beads and prayers, once and forever.'

I recognised the speaker by his long and luxuriant beard: it was Master John Knox, the leading evangelist of the Protestants. At his right stood the Earl of Rothes, head of the Leslies, with a cadre of his own supporters.

'This is a private obsequy.' That was Huntly, head of the Gordons and the greatest of the Catholic lords, thick-muscled and running heavily to fat, his reddish mane and beard grizzled with white. The Cock of the North, his Highlanders called him, and his face was red as a cock's wattle. In the High Street Jennet had heard whispers he was disappointed by the queen's lack of Catholic zeal; he was disappointed as well by her appointment of her Protestant half-brother Lord James Stewart as her chief councillor. The word *rebellion* had not actually been spoken, not yet, but Huntly was a grandson of James IV by the king's natural daughter Margaret Stewart, and if he could take the Highlands with him, he might even lay hands on the crown itself.

"Tis bad enough the queen bows down to the idol in private,' Knox said. He had an orator's voice and it carried throughout the nave. 'This church has been purified and is now used for proper services. We will not see it defiled again, queen's household or no.'

'The queen has proclaimed,' Huntly said, 'that no one should molest her private household in their practise of the true religion, on pain of death.'

Blessed Saint Ninian! Tante-Mar had been right – Huntly was using the occasion to challenge Master Knox over religion. Grief and outrage overcame my good sense and I stepped forward, straight between the two men.

'It is my husband who lies murdered in his coffin there,' I said. I could speak clearly and strongly because my feelings were safe in their stone-hard bubble. 'Would you defame his memory by coming to blows over his very body?'

They were shocked into silence for just a moment, all of them. I walked on past them and knelt at the bier. Jennet knelt beside me.

Of course they began to shout at each other again the moment I had passed by. I did not turn around to look, but from the noise I could tell fights had broken out. The mass was never said. I never saw the queen's poor priest, but afterwards was told he fled for his life. I concentrated my thoughts, like the light of the sun through a curved piece of glass, and focused them on my husband.

Alexander, I thought. I do not know how you betrayed the secret of the silver casket or why, but betrayal or no, you did not deserve to die for it. I will find the man who murdered you and I will see him hang for it. You will rest peacefully, my love, I promise you.

A hand came down on my shoulder, heavy and possessive.

'Get up,' said the Earl of Huntly. His voice was deep and gruff, nothing like a cock's raucous crow. 'They are gone. You are a brave lassie, and a credit to the boy.'

I rose. My knees hurt, and Jennet steadied me. When I turned to face the nave I saw that although Knox and his townspeople had gone, a considerable crowd remained. Huntly, of course, with half-a-dozen stout Gordons. Rothes and his Leslies. Lord James Stewart, the queen's half-brother. I wondered if it had been his presence that had quelled the fighting. Behind him stood Nicolas de Clerac. One might say he was effacing himself, but for the fact that with his height, his russet hair and his outrageously rich clothing, such a thing was impossible.

'I will go now,' I said.

'I will take you home to Aberdeenshire,' the Earl of Huntly said. He sounded inordinately pleased with himself. 'You and the babe Mary Gordon. Your husband was my ward, you know, and he held Glenlithie in fief to me. You can rest at Strathbogie Castle until a new – arrangement – can be made for you and your estates.'

'She is a Leslie of Granmuir.' It was the Earl of Rothes, the opposite of Huntly in every way, younger, leaner, his eyes set close together and his light brown hair cut short and neat around his ears. Unlike the others he was clean-shaven but for a narrow moustache. To my horror I saw Rannoch Hamilton of Kinmeall, with his permanent scowl, among the cadre of men behind him. 'Gordon child or no. I will take her to Leslie Castle, and if any

arrangements are to be made for her and for her daughter's inher-
itance, I will make them.'

*But take care, and mark me – if you want to go home to Granmuir,
the less Huntly sees of you, the better.*

Wise Tante-Mar.

'I will go nowhere,' I said. My own cool-headedness amazed
and rather frightened me. 'I will consent to no new arrangement.'

Arrangement, of course, meant marriage. How dare they speak
so casually of a new marriage for me, over my Alexander's very
coffin? Outrage stiffened my spine, and gave me the will to set
my own wishes against those of great noblemen.

'I want to stay here, at court,' I went on. 'I will remain at
Holyrood for now, and petition the queen for a permanent place.'

'That you will not,' Huntly said.

'You will do as you are told,' Rothes said, at the same time.

'You are fighting over her like two dogs over a bone,' said
Lord James Stewart. 'It is unseemly in the house of God.'

His voice was crisp and autocratic, and silenced them both. I
remembered I had once seen snapdragons and narcissus as his
flowers, for deceit and self-interest. He had changed, in the year
I had been away at Granmuir. He had been king in all but name,
after all, being both a Stewart by blood and the secular head of
the Lords of the Congregation. Snapdragons and narcissus still,
but intermingled with them cinquefoil for worldly power.

'If I may make a suggestion, my lords?' It was Nicolas de
Clerac. He sounded like every diplomat in the world ever
sounded, graceful and diffident. I wondered why he always
seemed to be at hand to engage himself in my affairs. 'The queen
has taken an interest in the matter of Madame Gordon and her
child,' he went on. 'Although of course she could not be present
here today, I am certain she will have something to say about

Madame Gordon's future. It might be wise to wait upon her judgement.'

I did not particularly want to be a chattel of Queen Mary, any more than I wanted to be a chattel of Huntly or Rothes, but for the moment that seemed to be my best chance of staying in Edinburgh and gaining access to the court. I said, 'Monsieur de Clerac is right. The queen is my daughter's godmother, and has preserved my life with her kindness. I cannot leave Edinburgh unless it is by her order.'

'The more fool you,' the Earl of Huntly said. 'I will have a few Gordons about, regardless, just to be certain there is no connivance to abduct you or your babe.'

'I will match every Gordon with a Leslie,' said the Earl of Rothes between his teeth. 'Granmuir has been a Leslie demesne for two hundred years and I will not see it fall to the Gordons because of one foolish girl. They were married without my permission – I will have the marriage set aside and the brat made a bastard. Then you can whistle to the wind for your claim.'

'Enough, my lords.' Lord James stepped between them. Bastard though he was, he had royal presence; I could almost understand his mother's obsession with making him King of Scots. 'Monsieur de Clerac is correct – it is for the queen to decide. You, Mistress Rinette—' He gestured imperiously to me, and I could not help but admire how neatly he had avoided identifying me as either Gordon or Leslie. 'Return to your apartments in Holyrood. Remain there, if you please, until the queen summons you.'

I curtseyed with every appearance of obedient docility. 'Yes, my lord,' I said. 'By your leave, my lord Earls.'

I leaned heavily on Jennet's arm – only partly for effect, as I was beginning to feel light and shaky again – and started down the nave. I had not taken three steps when a dark figure overtook me and stepped into my path. With the light streaming in from the west door of the church and outlining the thick-muscled, threatening figure of the scowling man, I was transported briefly back to Saint Ninian's, when he had broken down the doors of the ancient chapel and stormed in to stop my wedding.

'This woman is a witch,' said Rannoch Hamilton of Kinmeall.

There was nothing but emptiness in him, where I would have ordinarily sensed a flower essence. I had never met any other person who did not have some correspondence to a flower or plant, however faint it might be. He looked me in the eyes and smiled and said, 'Better to burn her, and her brat with her, and take her godforsaken castle by right of arms.'

All of them stepped forward, Huntly and Rothes, Lord James and Nicolas de Clerac. None of them wore arms in the church, and if it had not been for that there would have been steel drawn. Even Jennet put one arm around me and clenched her other fist as if to fight. I myself felt as if I would fall over on the paving stones.

'Hold, Kinmeall,' said Rothes. He sounded as if he were calling off his man for form's sake only, and one day might actually find his vicious threat a suitable alternative. 'The queen must have her say, but afterwards we will have ours as well.'

'You will have no say—' Huntly began.

'While all you fine gentlemen brawl and brangle,' Jennet More said in her broad Scots, 'my lady is a-fainting. Make way, if you please.'

It was the one thing that could break the impasse, barring me actually falling down and cracking my head on the stones. None of the men would give way to the other, but they all stood back in the face of a determined, sharp-tongued Aberdeenshire maid-servant who cared nothing for courts or lords.

8

They left me alone for the rest of the week, and past another Sabbath; Jennet told me Mr Knox had preached a thundering sermon vilifying the mass, and the queen had summoned him to court to account for himself. I knew a similar summons would eventually come for me, but I put it out of my mind. I held my Màiri, my bitterness, and told her every story I could think of about her father. The Earl of Huntly made arrangements for Alexander's body to be sent to Glenlithie and entombed there with his father and mother; I had wanted him at Granmuir but my wishes were not consulted. I ate, and slept, and walked in the gallery morning and evening. By the time the queen's summons came, I had recovered much of my strength and clarity.

I would say I was my old self again, but I was not. That hard place like a bubble of stone inside me had been growing. I felt as if the stone was taking me over, bit by bit.

The queen received me in an antechamber at the base of Holyrood's north-west tower; it had been furnished with carpets and hangings figured with the arms of Scotland and of France. Another room opened to the left, and in the right corner there was an opening to a stone spiral staircase, half-hidden by a millefleur tapestry showing the three Fates spinning, drawing out, and cutting the thread of life. Lord James Stewart was present, and Monsieur Nicolas de Clerac; the queen's other close advisor, Sir William Maitland, had already been sent hotfoot to London to sweeten the temper of Queen Elizabeth there. Mary Livingston fluttered her fingers to me surreptitiously from beside the queen's chair, where she stood with another lady I did not know.

And, of course, the queen herself. I curtseyed deeply. I had been practising, because curtsies are not easy when one's legs are still weak and shaky, and I did not want to make a fool of myself by falling over. I straightened up – and for the first time since we were children I looked straight into Mary Stuart's eyes.

How to describe her, this girl my own age who was twice a queen, who was called the most beautiful woman in Europe, who was educated and polished to an exquisite sheen by the sophistication of the French court? She was tall – that was perfectly clear even though she was seated – and willow-slender. She had bright golden-russet hair, sleeked back in a French hood of black velvet heavily embroidered with pearls, diamonds, jet and silver thread. Her almond-shaped eyes were virtually the same colour as her hair, amber-gold, with heavy half-lowered eyelids and long glinting golden lashes. Of her face, though, I was struck mostly by the height of her forehead, a smooth rounded curve of white, white skin. It gave her a look of archaic dignity, like the queens in old portraits and illuminations.

Sensuality shimmered around her, so intense it was almost visible. Her perfume – was it perfume, or was it her natural scent? – was a heady distillation of lilies and roses, musk and honey and seaweed. I had smelled it before, and after a moment I placed it: peonies. She was a peony, glorious but fragile, its petals scattered by the least wind or rain. A white and pale pink peony with its black seeds symbolising melancholy and nightmares. I would have expected something grander, a crimson rose or a lily the colour of fire.

You are out of your place with crowns and thrones, Madame, I thought. You would have been happier with a simpler life – a pretty château in Touraine, a fine young husband to adore you, babes of your own to ride their ponies round and round in the garden. But simplicity you have never had, nor will you ever, until later, much later. And I do not think you know or understand the effect you have on men who breathe your scent.

'My Marianette,' she said.

It was her childhood nickname for me. That year in France – the year I was eight years old, the year that that changed everything for me – she had stubbornly refused to call me 'Rinette'. It was too like *la Reinette*, the little queen, which she herself was sometimes called. So she ran the two versions of my name together – Marina and Rinette – and had come up with 'Marianette'. I did not like it because it sounded like *marionetta*, which was what Queen Catherine de' Medici called her grotesque Italian puppets. *La Reinette*, the little queen, just laughed and used it all the more.

'Circumstances have delayed our reunion until now,' she went on. Her Scots was perfectly serviceable despite the throaty softness of a French accent. 'I condole with you upon the death of your husband – I too am a recent widow.'

'Thank you, Madame,' I said. 'I condole with you also.'

'I have known Marianette since the year my mother came to visit me in France, the year 1550 when I was eight,' the queen said, to the others in the room. 'Sir Patrick Leslie of Granmuir was in my mother's household, with his wife Blanche, called Blanche d'Orléans because she was an illegitimate daughter of the old Duke of Longueville. She was a half-sister to my mother's first husband, and my mother was kind enough to call her sister.'

I stood like a stone. I did not want to hear her tell the story of my mother.

'Just as my own mother was preparing to go back to Scotland the following year, a terrible thing happened – a fever struck the court, and Sir Patrick Leslie died. That in itself was bad enough, but Lady Blanche proceeded to go mad with grief. She was attached to her husband to an excessive degree.'

'Madame,' said Mary Livingston. 'Perhaps this is not the best—'

'She was taken in by the Benedictine Sisters of Montmartre outside Paris, and to everyone's astonishment refused to leave. She is there to this day, to the best of my knowledge. Does she write to you, Marianette?'

'No,' I said.

'Then perhaps she has died, as my own mother died. I am told you have a gift for me, a token from my mother?'

She smiled. She knew the tales would be all over the court by suppertime – my mother, a French duke's bastard, had gone mad and abandoned me. That, her expression said, would put me in my place. Lord James and Nicolas de Clerac, on the other hand, standing behind her where she could not see their faces, had the expressions of men who knew there was a prize to be had and were straining every nerve and sinew to snatch it up first, out of the other's very hands.

They knew about the casket. Lady Margaret Erskine had known. It was impossible, but here it was. And of course if Lady Margaret and Lord James and Monsieur de Clerac knew I had the casket, and knew there was something valuable inside it, who else knew?

How had they found out?

The only person who did not know, it seemed, was the queen herself.

'I do not have it with me, Madame,' I said. 'Please, may we speak privately?'

'I have no secrets from my brother and my most special advisor.' She gestured to the two men. 'Beaton, you and Livingston may go.'

The two ladies curtseyed and went out.

'Now,' the queen said. 'Tell me of this so-mysterious object.'

I hesitated. I had promised Mary of Guise I would not unlock the silver casket; should I tell the queen what I had seen inside? Or was it better to pretend I had kept my promise and knew nothing of the contents?

The old queen is dead and the French queen will never know. Alexander's voice, sweet with honey and kisses. *Open it. I want to see.*

Alexander had known. He had seen the contents of the casket, and he had seen me hide it in the niche under the window of the Mermaid Tower.

I wanted to run away and find a quiet garden where I could be alone with the flowers and the sky and sort out what all this meant. But of course I could not do that. The best thing I could think of to do was to pretend I knew as little as possible.

'It is a locked silver casket,' I said slowly. 'What is inside I do not know, but your mother, may God keep her—' I crossed myself, and the queen and Monsieur de Clerac did the same. I think I was as much asking absolution for my lie as wishing rest to Mary of Guise. Lord James, being a Protestant, did not make the gesture. 'Your mother wished you to have it, from the first moment you touched your foot to Scottish soil. She required me to promise. That is why I asked for an audience on the day you arrived.'

'C'est fascinant, hein?' the queen said. For the first time she opened her eyes completely. They shone like topazes. 'I wish to see it at once. Is it in your chamber? Have you a key?'

'It is put away safely,' I said. 'And, yes, I have a key. I—'

'I will send men-at-arms to take possession of it immediately.' It was Lord James, with his king-in-all-but-name voice. 'This is business of state, Mistress Rinette, and not something for a girl like you to be meddling in.'

'Perhaps we should send royal men-at-arms,' Nicolas de Clerac said in a mild voice. 'We would not want the contents of the casket to end up anywhere but in the queen's own hands.'

Lord James, not surprisingly, bristled at that. 'Do you imply, Monsieur, that I myself would take anything from this casket before presenting it to my sister?'

'James, James!' the queen laughed. Her eyes glinted with pleasure – she was enjoying it all, this conflict between the two men and her own power to stop or encourage it as she pleased. ''Sieur Nico, you are terribly improper to make such an imputation. Apologise at once.'

Nicolas de Clerac bowed, his face expressionless. 'As you wish, Madame,' he said. 'My lord, I beg your pardon for my – impropriety.'

The queen rose. She was tall – strikingly tall – even taller than I had guessed. She overtopped me by a hand's width at least, and her brother by two or three fingers. Monsieur de Clerac kept his head bowed, disguising the fact that he was the only one who could have looked her straight in the eyes. I wondered if he was doing it deliberately.

'Let us go and find this casket at once,' she said. 'Perhaps my mother left jewels in it. Perhaps she wrote me letters to assure me of her love. We will find it and open it together, and it will be an amusement for the day.'

'No,' I said.

They all looked at me. The queen's expression was quizzical

– she was thinking, plain as day, that she must have misunderstood me, as no one ever refused her what she desired. Lord James looked angry and offended. Monsieur de Clerac – 'Sieur Nico, the queen called him, with such charming intimacy – looked curious and at the same time apprehensive. He was the only one, then, who really believed I would refuse to give up the casket to the queen.

If I gave it up, I would be no one again – just Rinette Leslie, eighteen years old, so unfortunately widowed and with a baby girl, prey to either the Earl of Huntly or the Earl of Rothes, whichever could fight off the other. My royal charter had died with Mary of Guise; I would be pressed hard to marry some stranger, so as to give one of the earls the overlordship of Granmuir. Oh, Granmuir, my home, my gardens by the sea. They would take it, and fortify it, and with it they would control the shipping lanes to the low countries, the ancient drovers' roads down through the Mounths. I might be allowed to live there and I might not. All because I would be no one, with no power to stop them.

But I had the casket.

If I kept the casket, I could bargain with them.

I could say, *No marriage, not now, not ever.*

I could say, *Granmuir is mine and mine alone, a royal fief as it has always been.*

I could say, *When the murderer of Alexander Gordon hangs in the Tolbooth of Edinburgh, I will put the silver casket into your hands.*

I had broken my promise to Mary of Guise already. If I did this I would shatter it to splinters. I would be doing a wrong I had never thought I, Rinette Leslie, could do. A deliberate mortal wrong.

Very well. I would do penance. I had done it before, after I'd faced down Rannoch Hamilton and his men at Saint Ninian's. I would do it again, whatever it was, for Granmuir and for justice.

'No,' I said again. My voice did not sound like my own, but of course I was not myself. It felt strange – terrifying and at the same time exhilarating. 'I will give you the casket, Madame, only when you give me what I ask in exchange.'

'But it is mine,' the queen said. 'My mother wished me to have it, you have said so yourself.'

'You are playing a dangerous game, Mistress Rinette,' said Lord James. His voice was sharp and harsh as a cheese-grater, and I could see he was expending considerable effort to keep himself from grasping me by the neck and shaking my secret out of me. He knew what was in the casket. He had to know.

'It is not a game. It is a simple exchange.'

'What is it then,' said the queen's 'Sieur Nico, soft as silk and practical as iron nails, 'that you wish the queen to give you in exchange for the casket?'

'Two things,' I said. 'First, protection from the Earl of Huntly and the Earl of Rothes. I do not wish to marry again, and only the queen has the power to hold the earls off and confirm Granmuir to me and to my daughter as a royal fief. I would have my estates for my own and the queen's promise that I will not be compelled to marry.'

'That is not so unreasonable,' Nico said. 'What do you think, Madame?'

'I think Marianette should give me my mother's casket first, and ask her favours afterwards.' The amusement had gone from the queen's eyes, and her lower lip was thrust out. It was astonishing – for a moment she looked exactly as I remembered her in France so long ago, when we were both eight years old and had hated each other for no particular reason, as children will do. 'I do not understand why you think this a matter fit for bargaining over, as if we are all fishwives in the marketplace.'

Nico and Lord James looked at each other sideways. The queen did not see. I did. There was a whole conversation in that single look.

'The casket is more than a simple heirloom, Madame,' Nico said. 'There are reasons why your mother told this girl to give it to you the moment you touched your foot to the soil of Scotland. Reasons why she went to such lengths to preserve it from the Lords of the Congregation.'

'The regent was a fool,' Lord James said. 'And Mistress Rinette would be better off to give us the casket now, then keep her tongue in her teeth and marry as her betters command her.'

'If my dearest mother wished me to have this casket and what it contains, then have it I will.' The queen's voice shook. 'You will not prevent me, brother James.'

Lord James made an exasperated sound, like a man at cards who has overplayed his hand too early in the game. 'I do not wish to prevent you, sister.'

Nico turned back to me and said, in his silk-and-nails voice again, 'Your first wish is not unreasonable, Mistress Rinette. What is your second?'

They were both calling me *Mistress Rinette* now, as if I had no surname at all.

'I wish to see the person who murdered Alexander Gordon brought to justice,' I said. 'Both the assassin himself, and if he was paid, the person who ordered it done. I wish to have a place here at court where I can see for myself that inquiries are being made, and even take part in the inquiries if I wish to do so. When these persons, whoever they are, have been tried and hanged and are in their graves, Madame, then I will give you your casket and go home to Granmuir.'

Silence.

I looked at the three of them and wondered if the person who had ordered Alexander's death was here in this luxuriously appointed chamber, looking back at me.

'I will have nothing to do with any such bargain,' Lord James said. 'Sister, my advice to you is that you shut Mistress Rinette up in some suitable place—'

'How unfortunate that all the convents have been suppressed,' Nico de Clerac murmured.

Lord James narrowed his eyes. 'In some suitable place,' he said again. 'Put her child out for fostering, send her household away, and feed her bread and water until she decides to see reason.'

'I disagree,' Nico said. 'Madame, I believe if you treat Mistress Rinette with harshness, it will only further harden her resolve. Am I not correct, Mistress?'

He was. I said nothing.

'So we are back where we were, so many years ago in France,' the queen said. She looked directly at me with those heavy-lidded golden eyes – she had such power and she did not even seem to be aware of it. '*Reinette* and Rinette, at odds. You will find I am no longer a little queen, Marianette, a toy queen as I was then. I am here to rule, and rule I will.'

I lowered my eyes. I would not speak, but I would show her deference – that always pleased her.

'This, then, is my decision,' she went on. 'I will put you in a place among my ladies, but you will be close to me and watched. You will not be compelled to marry and your estate will be protected while you are at court. However, I will not confirm you in full possession of your estate and its revenues until you have given me this casket.'

She was cleverer than they gave her credit for. I said, 'And my husband's murderer?'

'I can make no promises. Surely you understand that. But I will order a royal inquiry to be commenced.'

I bowed my head to her and curtseyed deeply, to make it appear that it was I who was submitting to her will and not the other way round. 'I agree with your decision, Madame.'

'Now,' she said. How quickly she could change from one attitude to another. 'Tomorrow I leave Edinburgh for a short progress to the north. All the court is to accompany me, but in your delicate state of health, Marianette, you must stay behind.'

'I will remain here, Madame, and await your return.'

'See that you do. I will appoint men to accompany you if you go out.'

'I understand, Madame.'

'I will not have you giving my mother's silver casket to anyone else.'

'I will give it to you or to no one, Madame,' I said. I meant it. It could moulder under Saint Margaret's forever, but for the power it gave me to get what I wanted. 'I look forward to the day when I will place it in your hands.'

9

'There's a gentleman asking to see you, Rinette,' Jennet said. 'Don't know who he is, but he's a sleekit-looking fellow with fine clothes and an English manner of speaking.'

I was sitting in the middle of the bed playing catch-my-finger with Màiri. Her tiny perfect fingers were astonishingly strong, and she curled them around my own forefinger with a will. I could actually lift her a little, with just her fingers clinging to mine. She was a month old today.

'Did he not give his name? Almost all the court is away on progress with the queen, and I know no one else in Edinburgh.'

'Wetheral, he said his name was. No title, just plain Master Wetheral.' She made it sound as if he was lying about it. Truth or lie, it was not a name I had ever heard before.

The last fortnight had been quiet. There were two equerries with royal badges on their sleeves who stood outside my door every day like thistles, stout and prickly, and I had seen no one else but Tante-Mar and Jennet and Wat Cairnie and my precious Màiri. I had not set foot out of Holyrood Palace other than to walk for an hour each day in the gardens. Lilidh had been brought to Edinburgh and I longed to ride, even a sedate well-cushioned walk down the High Street and back with Wat at Lilidh's bridle. Tante-Mar forbade it; no riding for me till the new year, she said, after such a difficult birth.

I was numb and listless with the unchanging round of my days. I longed to ask questions. I longed to look at every dagger at every man's belt from one end of the city to the other, to see if there was a ruby missing from it.

'The royal guards,' I said. 'They did not stop this Master Wetheral?'

'Gave him a bit of a look-over, but no, they didn't stop him.'

'Very well. I shall see him. Where is Tante-Mar?'

'In the chapel, same as always.'

'Will you stay here with Màiri, then?' I climbed down off the bed and shook out my skirt. The plain russet-coloured Cambrai linen was creased and crumpled, but it hardly mattered if I was only to speak a few words with a stranger. An English stranger.

'Cry out if you need me,' Jennet said. 'But he's a soft-looking fellow, for all his breadth. One good whack with a stool, and he'll be cold senseless on the floor.'

She was trying to coax me to smile, I knew. I tried, I truly did. Perhaps I succeeded, just a little.

In the outer room a gentleman of ordinary height and a blocky, thickset mien awaited me. Jennet had been right – he was sleekit, his thick silver hair pomaded and combed straight back from his low forehead, his clothing well tailored and pressed, his boots polished, his hands clean and soft. His head seemed to be set directly upon his shoulders, with no neck to speak of. He bowed with a courtier's polish.

'Mistress Leslie? Please allow me to make myself known to you – I am Richard Wetheral, and I am a member of Master Thomas Randolph's household. Master Thomas, as you may know, is with the queen on her progress, but he asked me to call upon you while he was away.'

Even his voice was smooth. He spoke Scots as if it was his native tongue. Perhaps it was; enough Scotsmen had turned their coats and joined the English over the years. Thomas Randolph was the Queen of England's agent – supposedly her confidential agent but everyone knew – and he'd pursued English interests in Scotland even in the days of Mary of Guise. He was an open Protestant and deep in the pockets of the Lords of the Congregation. Master Wetheral, then, would be a Protestant as well.

'Good day to you,' I said. I made my voice cool; I did not particularly want to talk to him but at least it made a change. 'I have little hospitality to offer, but please sit.' There were two chairs and a small table in the antechamber. No other furniture. No stools. I wondered if I could lift the table. He waited until I was seated – sleekit manners as well – and then settled himself into the other chair.

'First, allow me to offer Sir Thomas' condolences and my own, upon the death of your husband,' he said. 'A terrible thing, and in the course of such joyous celebrations.'

Neither you nor your Sir Thomas knew Alexander at all, I thought. You certainly do not know me. What reason do you have to come here offering condolences?

I said nothing.

'You may be thinking Sir Thomas and I did not know your husband,' he said, as if he could see inside my thoughts. 'But in a way, we did. Sir Thomas had been corresponding with him over the past few months. I carried the letters, and met your husband twice in Aberdeen.'

'You met him?' I remembered those days when Alexander rode from Granmuir to Aberdeen. He had said he was dealing with matters related to his estate at Glenlithie. It was after that he began to talk of courts and pleasures and prestige. 'In Aberdeen?'

'Indeed I did. A very fine young gentleman, if I may be so bold as to say so.'

'Why? What did Alexander have to do with an ambassador of the English queen?'

Master Wetheral looked down at his soft white hands. He wore three rings, two on one hand, one on the other. One of them was a ruby, cut with facets. I wondered if he owned a dagger.

'It is a matter of some delicacy,' he said. 'Did you know, Mistress Leslie, that your husband was in possession of a – relic – of the late queen regent, Mary of Guise? He was a close and trusted friend to her, I am sure you know that much.'

'He was *what*?'

'He was one of her Scots equerries, and like a son to her. Her own sons had died, as of course you know. Your husband was exactly the age of Prince James, her eldest Stewart boy, born on the very same day – it was a bond between them.'

'That is not true, Master Wetheral.' I was so taken aback by the fanciful untruth of Alexander being born on the same day as poor ill-fated little Prince James that I could not quite absorb the greater lie, that Alexander had been an equerry to Mary of Guise. 'Alexander would never have said such a thing, so I cannot believe you ever actually met and spoke with him as you claim to have done.'

He looked at me thoughtfully. Most men would be angry to be called a liar so baldly. I wondered if Master Wetheral even remembered how to be angry, or if he had been a diplomat – and probably a spy – for so long that ordinary feelings were lost to him.

'I assure you, Mistress Leslie, I did meet your husband twice in Aberdeen,' he said. 'But whether or not these meetings took place, and the truth or untruth of what he told me, are of secondary importance. What is most important is this relic he had, from the hands of the queen regent. He promised it to Sir Thomas, and through him of course to the Queen of England herself, in exchange for a suitable recompense. My purpose here – aside from condoling with you as young Sir Alexander's widow – is to find a way for that promised exchange to take place.'

I had never in my life heard so many elaborate and meaningless words in one speech. 'Let me be plain, Master Wetheral,' I said. 'Whether or not Alexander met you in Aberdeen, I cannot say – he did ride into the city from time to time to deal with matters of business. But he was certainly not born on the same day as either of the little princes. He had nothing to do with Mary of Guise. He did not possess any relic, and if he did, he would not have sold it to the English. You have been misled.'

Master Wetheral ran one hand over his mane of grey hair, as if to smooth down strands that had risen with horror. 'You claim, then,' he said, in his diplomat's voice, 'that your husband did not possess a silver letter-casket which once belonged to Mary of Guise? A casket filled with the queen regent's own most private papers?'

. . . *a silver letter-casket which once belonged to Mary of Guise* . . .

Oh, Alexander. How does he know this? How many times did you betray me?

'Yes,' I said, with perfect truth. 'I claim exactly that. My husband never possessed such a casket.'

'Is it possible he had it hidden away, and did not tell you?'

'No. It is not possible.'

I thought back to exactly who had been present at my own audience with Queen Mary, when I admitted to having the casket and made my own bargain to exchange it for – what had Master Wetheral said? A suitable recompense. Queen Mary herself, of course. Lord James and Monsieur Nicolas de Clerac. The two women, Mary Livingston and Mary Beaton – they had been sent away but could have been listening at the door. Had someone whispered a word to someone else that I was in possession of Mary of Guise's silver casket? Was all this blather of Master Wetheral's a fiction, because his master had learned I had the casket and wanted a way to make me feel obligated to sell it to him?

'It appears we are at an impasse,' Master Wetheral was saying. 'Perhaps I should approach the matter somewhat differently, and tell you what we believe to be in this casket, and what Sir Thomas is willing to pay in exchange for it.'

'Perhaps you should not.' I rose, and of course Master No-Neck Sleekit-Manners was required to rise as well. 'Please tell Sir Thomas this – if such a silver casket exists, and if there are private papers inside it, Mary of Guise would have intended it for her own daughter and no one else.'

'It exists,' Richard Wetheral said. His mask of perfect polish slipped a bit and I saw a glint of the ruthlessness beneath. 'And Mary of Guise is dead and gone. Your husband accepted an offer of one thousand gold sovereigns, an English barony and a place at Queen Elizabeth's court, in exchange for the casket and its contents. A similar arrangement can be made for you, Mistress Leslie. Surely it would be better than to be kept here as you are, no better than a prisoner.'

'I am not a prisoner.' I was furious and sick with betrayal and a little frightened to think such a price had been offered for the casket. 'I am Queen Mary's lady, here at Holyrood instead of on progress with her only because I am recovering from the birth of my daughter.'

'Ah, yes, your daughter,' Richard Wetheral said. 'I have children of my own, in London of course, and I miss them. Will you permit me to meet your little girl?'

'I will not,' I said. Children in London! I did not believe it for a moment, and I was certainly not going to allow him anywhere near Màiri. 'Master Wetheral, you are a fool and so is your master if you think I would ever leave Scotland. I am a Leslie of Granmuir, and a Leslie of Granmuir I shall remain until the day I die. I have no need for English gold or English titles.'

'So you do have it,' he said.

'I do not.' Not entirely a lie, because I did not actually have the casket in my possession. Not that I cared whether or not I lied to him. 'Good day to you, Master Wetheral.'

He bowed and went out. I stood looking after him, too stunned even to call for Jennet.

Did you know, Mistress Leslie, that your husband was in possession of a – relic – of the late queen regent, Mary of Guise?

It could not be true. Alexander would never have said such a thing, never have claimed the casket as his own, much less offered it for sale. One of the queen's ladies had listened at the door during my audience with the queen, and whispered a tale of a silver casket to the English agent Randolph. He had put his head together with the silvery head of his lackey Wetheral and they had concocted a tale of correspondences and meetings with a murdered man who could not give them the lie. They had hoped their tale would shock and unnerve me so much I would simply hand the casket over, take their damned English gold and disappear over the border to some dreary English manor.

The more fools they.

I told the queen's men, my two upright thistles, that I wished to receive no more visitors until the queen returned. Perhaps a changeless round of days was not such a bad thing after all.

* * *

'You look white as new cheese,' Jennet said, when I went back into the bedchamber. 'What did he say to you?'

'He told me – things.' I wanted to call them lies but I could not quite force myself to do it. I sat on the bed and Jennet put Màiri into my arms.

'What kind of things?' she asked.

'Jennet.' I bent my head and touched my lips to Màiri's forehead. It was warm and soft, so soft. She smelled of soap scented with wild roses. She looked so much like him, with her golden hair and fair skin. 'What did you think of Alexander?'

There was a long silence. Màiri gurgled and made bubbles with her lips.

'Jennet?'

'He was beautiful as the day was long,' she said. 'I'll give him that, and gladly. He meant well, I think – he loved you, as much as he could love anyone other than his own self.'

I swallowed. I could not look at her.

'I know how much you loved him, Rinette. But you were a twelve-year-old girl when you met him first, and he was a sixteen-year-old boy – you thought he was a hero, the sun and moon and stars. You nursed him with his broken arm – what girl wouldn't have loved him, helpless and handsome as he was? I was half in love with him myself.'

'But you did not stay in love with him?'

'There was no one telling me I couldn't love him, as your grannie and Madame Loury were doing with you. Nothing makes a girl love a boy more than telling her she can't have him.'

I thought about that for a while. It was true. First Grannie and Tante-Mar, then the old queen – they had separated me from Alexander and it had only made me want him all the more.

'He came to Granmuir when I needed him,' I said.

'That he did. But in Saint Ninian's Church – Madame Loury told me – he didn't fight for you.'

Tears burned in my eyes.

'No,' I said. 'He did not fight for me.'

'There's something you're not saying.' Jennet wrapped a curl of Màiri's golden hair around her fingers. 'It's been a-poisoning you, Rinette, and it's something to do with your Alexander.'

I took a deep breath. If I said it, I would have to believe it. I still had time to stop. I still had time to tell Jennet it was nothing, nothing to do with Alexander.

'Rinette,' she said. 'Tell me, hinnie.'

'He betrayed me,' I said. After those first words the rest of it came pouring out. 'Jennet, do you remember the silver casket the old queen gave me, the night she died?'

'I do.'

'Alexander took it from my secret hiding place and opened it and made notes about the contents and he wrote *letters*, Jennet . . . letters to Lord James . . . the Queen of England's ambassador . . . I do not even know who else, great people. He asked them for money and favours. He tried to *sell* the old queen's silver casket, and he put himself in danger and he may have put us all in danger, and if I cannot ward them off the queen can force me to marry where she wills – and *I could lose Granmuir*.'

I realised I was screaming at the last, shaking with anger. Màiri started to cry; Jennet took her from my arms and tucked her into her cradle. Then she came back and put her arms around me, as gently as if I too were a tiny child.

'Mary Mother, Rinette, I'm sorry – you know we'll all help you however we can. But in truth, I'm not surprised. He would never have been happy at Granmuir, your Alexander. And he would have worked it around in his own head to believe he was doing it for you. He would have convinced himself, in the end.'

'It has to be why he was killed,' I said. 'Perhaps he betrayed someone else. Perhaps someone betrayed him. Perhaps someone just wanted to stop him. Oh, Jennet, I loved him so much! I see him every time I look at Màiri.'

'And so you should. Still it's a good thing to face the truth, Rinette, because then you can decide what to do and it'll be a clean choice.'

'I will never stop loving him, no matter what he did.'

'First love is first love. No woman ever forgets.'

I looked up at her. 'Who was your first love, Jennet?'

She smiled. 'I haven't met him yet. I've dreamed him, though. Do you think I've never gone into the fields at midnight on Saint Agnes' Eve, and thrown my grains of wheat, and said my prayer? *Bonny Agnes, let me see, the lad who is to marry me.*'

I smiled through my tears. 'I hope you meet him soon.'

'So do I.'

'I will still have justice for Alexander. Whatever he did, he did not deserve to die like that, with his throat cut in the High Street.'

'Justice is a fine thing,' Jennet said. 'But take care how you go after it. It's not worth dying for.'

10

The queen's party returned to Edinburgh at the end of September, and she settled herself into her tower again. Holyrood Palace sprang to life from one day to the next, with courtiers and ambassadors, workmen with tapestries and carpets and paintings, laughing ladies and gentlemen who stood in twos and threes and sometimes exchanged forbidden kisses when they thought no one was looking. Mary Livingston came to see me, and helped me embellish my wardrobe so I would not look like an Aberdeenshire country lass when I took up my promised position among Queen Mary's ladies. She brought lengths of silk and velvet that were gifts from the queen, laces and ribbons and even a cloth-of-silver forepart and a pair of black velvet sleeves sewn with tiny pearls. As she laid it all out on the bed she told me the gossip of the progress – the queen's bedcurtains set afire in Stirling Castle, and later the queen collapsing in a fainting fit in the streets of Perth.

'You should have seen Lady Huntly at Stirling,' Mary said. 'Once we'd put the fire out, she told a story of an old prophecy that a queen would be burned alive at Stirling. Lady Huntly keeps familiars, you know. It is she who will be burned alive if she does not take care!'

'Was the queen actually burned?'

'Only a little – not even enough to leave a mark. Jean Argyll tipped over a candlestand and the bedcurtains caught. The queen was more excited than frightened – she said the fire and the prophecy proved she was the rightful Queen of Scotland.'

'Of course she is the rightful queen.'

'Not to everyone. Not to the Protestants. People meet her in the streets with dead cats dressed up as priests, and their poor little heads shaved.'

'Is that what happened at Perth?'

'I am not sure – I was far enough behind her that I did not see. It was 'Sieur Nico de Clerac who was close beside her, and carried her into a house when she fainted away. He was in great favour just then – the queen was angry with Lord James for interrupting her mass at Stirling.'

I put my left arm through one of the sleeves. It was worked with couching in silver thread, and the pearls were sewn at each point where the lines of the pattern intersected. It was too long for me but it could be altered. 'Is the court all still in black?' I asked.

'Yes, until the anniversary of the French king's death in December. Although one sees a great deal of silver and pearls and white as well, and all shades of grey from willow to dove-colour to Isabelline. There is to be a great banquet and masque this Sunday, to wish farewell to the queen's uncle the Grand Prior, the Seigneur de Damville, and some of the others who are going back to France. The queen wishes you to be present – your forty days, your first *deuil*, have been accomplished and it is perfectly seemly for you to return to the world as long as you remain in blacks and whites.'

'Who else will be there?' I laid the sleeve against the length of black velvet. The blacks did not quite match, but of course black was irksome.

'Oh, everyone.' She laughed. 'Master Buchanan has written the masque all in Latin, about Apollo and the muses, with ten speaking parts. The queen herself will play Apollo, and the Grand Prior will play Clio – he says the Knights of Malta go back so many hundreds of years he is perfect for the muse of history. Monsieur de Damville is Erato, for he is always writing love poetry to the queen. They rehearse every day, and we all laugh so much to see them tripping over their silken draperies.'

'The queen is playing Apollo? A man's part?'

'Oh, yes. That is the joke, you see – the queen plays Apollo, and all the muses are played by gentlemen. The Marquis of Elbeuf is to play Thalia – he is the youngest and most charming of the queen's uncles. Sir John Gordon, Huntly's son, has a part as well, as does the queen's half-brother Lord John Stewart of Coldingham. Then there is 'Sieur Nico, and of course the two poets, Brantôme and Chastelard. The queen coaxed and coaxed to get Lord James to take part, but he's far too much of a Calvinist to wear a dress, even in a masque.'

I felt a pang of heartache. How Alexander would have loved such merriments. How perfectly he would have played the part of Thalia or Erato.

'There will be more thundering sermons from Master Knox, I think.'

Mary Livingston laughed. 'That is what Bothwell said. You would know Bothwell, I think? He was a great supporter of the old queen, and his sister Janet is to marry Lord John Stewart around Epiphany. It will make him part of the queen's kin, which of course annoys Lord James no end.'

I remembered Bothwell. He made me think of comfrey – hairy and just poisonous enough to make one's skin itch, with tuberous flowers in clusters like the fingers of grasping hands, so astringent there was an old tale they could restore a woman's virginity. Bothwell could have made good use of that, with all the virgins he was said to have despoiled. He had rough manners and an even rougher way of speaking – he knew obscenities in at least four languages, and he was liberal with them – but Mary of Guise had liked and trusted him. I tried to imagine Bothwell in female draperies and found myself laughing aloud. It was the first time I had laughed since Alexander's death.

'Surely Bothwell is not wearing a woman's costume?'

'*Mon Dieu*, no. Although he laughed at the prospect, just as you did.'

'So if all the gentlemen are wearing women's draperies, what is the queen wearing?'

'She has directed the construction of the most beautiful costume – a short draped boy's tunic in pure white, with taffeta hose in pale tawny-colour so that at first you think her legs are bare.'

'Surely not!'

'Oh, yes, surely so. She looks exactly like a beautiful Greek boy on the side of a vase. She will be masked as a swan – the swan is Apollo's bird, you know – and the swan's great wings sweep out from her shoulders and trail behind her, all made of white silk and feathers and spangles. Wait until you see. It is *magnifique*.'

I knew I was gaping at her, but I could not quite swallow my amazement. I tried to imagine such a costume at the court of Mary of Guise, and of course I failed. At last I said, 'Do you have a part?'

'No. No other ladies. Only the queen and her gentlemen-muses.' She hugged me, one arm around the shoulders in a friendly, careless way. 'Do not look so shocked, Rinette, such masques are all the style in France, and the whole evening is arranged to honour the queen's French uncles. The rest of us will wear our own clothes, and perform the important rôle of the amazed and entertained and oh-so-pleasantly shocked audience. Do you have black slippers to wear with all this?'

'No. Only these russet ones.'

'I will lend you a pair of my own. You must look *à la mode* for your first appearance as one of the queen's ladies.'

And so I wore the queen's gifts of black velvet and cloth-of-silver and Mary Livingston's black satin slippers on the Sunday night when the masque was performed. The queen was the cynosure of the piece, tall and slim and straight, her long legs perfect in their boy's hose of tawny taffeta, her eyes glittering with pleasure through the slanting eye-holes of her swan's mask. The wings were dazzling – great sweeps of snow-white feathers, jewelled and sparkling with crystals, framing her face and drifting out behind her, trailing languidly as she moved along the blood-red Turkey carpet which had been laid out in the gallery. She spoke Apollo's part in perfect Latin – well, it sounded perfect to me, although of course all the Latin I knew would fit into a tillie-pan, and a small one at that – and danced with unearthly grace and dignity. She could not have been more French at that moment, and I saw Lord James watching her with a disdainful look on his dark Scots face. Of course, he was her brother. Every other man in the room, Catholic and Protestant alike, watched her with simmering desire.

The Frenchmen acquitted themselves with style, clearly accustomed to taking female parts. The Scots gentlemen were more self-conscious, and tended to laugh when they should have been declaiming serious Latin epigrams. Just as young John Sempill of Beltrees made his entrance as Terpsichore, muse of the dance, wafting his draperies from side to side in a way that made all the ladies in the audience giggle, a short, compact gentleman in sober black silk stepped up beside me.

'Madame Rinette,' he said quietly, in a strongly French-accented voice. 'A word, if I may.'

I did not remember seeing him before, and his appearance was oddly soldierly amid the rich clothes of the courtiers and the whimsies of the masque. His hair was cut short; his eyes were greenish-grey, so pale they looked as if they had been bleached by seeing too much for too long.

'Forgive me, Monsieur,' I said, 'but if I have been introduced to you, I do not remember.'

'Blaise Laurentin, *à votre service*,' he said. 'You might say that I am in the French ambassador's household, although I am not exactly in the employ of Monsieur Castelnau himself.'

'Very mysterious,' I said. I did not want to talk to him. I wanted to watch the masque.

'I would like to call upon you privately,' he said. 'I understand you have already spoken to Master Wetheral, and before you pursue your – acquaintance – with him, I have a matter of some urgency to discuss with you as well.'

'I cannot imagine what urgent matter we might have to discuss.' The queen was declaiming in Latin again, her voice clear and pure as an angel's. She looked like an angel too with the fantastic trailing wings and white silk tunic, all but for the endless legs in their flesh-coloured taffeta. 'I do not know you, Monsieur, and I do not care for the implication that you are watching my visitors.'

'Anyone can watch men go in and out of Holyrood. I wish to speak to you about your husband, Madame – I have met him, you know.'

I felt a hot flush mount in my cheeks and forehead. No, I thought. Not another one.

A little unsteadily I said, 'I do not know how that can be so, Monsieur. My husband never went to France. Perhaps you have confused him with another—'

'He was Alexander Gordon of Glenlithie, Lord of Granmuir in the right of his young wife. You, Madame, are Marina Leslie of Granmuir. There is no confusion.'

'Whatever it is you have to say, I do not wish to hear it.' My heart was thudding and my inwards had turned to liquid, and I felt a desperate desire to run away. 'Please excuse me, Monsieur, I do not feel well.'

He closed his hand around my wrist. His fingers were cold; they felt boneless and unnatural, like vines. An image of wild white bryony flashed into my mind, twining and curling, the flowers shrivelling before my eyes to leave fetid berries the color of diluted blood. *Navet du diable*, they called it in France, the devil's turnip, for its fleshy white root.

'Let go of me,' I said.

'I will speak with you, whether you will it or not.'

His words were startlingly loud, because the chamber had suddenly fallen silent. The queen had broken off in the midst of her declamation to Terpsichore. Terpsichore herself, in the person of John Sempill, had stopped waving her – his – her spangled pasteboard lyre and was staring openly. The musicians had lowered their instruments.

'You are interrupting the masque,' the queen said in a cold voice. She did not even call me by my name. 'Is it not rather soon for you to be quarrelling with a lover, you who wish so passionately to take vengeance for the murder of your so-beloved husband?'

Everyone turned to look at me. I felt a scalding flush of humiliation, from my borrowed slippers to my hairline – I might have been on fire and I knew they all would see it and read it wrongly. Even if I could have thought of anything to say, I do not think I could have controlled my throat and tongue and lips well enough to say it. The Frenchman, damn him to the deepest pit of hell, was still holding my wrist, apparently as frozen as I was by the queen's sudden and open displeasure.

'It is Monsieur Laurentin who interrupts, Madame.'

From behind me, a man's quiet voice with the razor-edge of ruthlessness. At the same time, a hand in a silver glove closed itself around Blaise Laurentin's forearm just so, and with a little grunt of pain the Frenchman let go of my wrist. I turned my head, and there I saw the queen's advisor and secretary Nicolas de Clerac, costumed as Urania, the muse of astronomy, his white silk tunic and gathered mantle embroidered with scattered silver globes and compasses. There were blue and silver streaks of paint around his eyes. All the same, he did not look foolish or mischievous as the other gentlemen did; woman's costume or no, if I had met him alone in a dark place I would have been afraid of him.

'It does not matter which one of them it was.' The queen sounded petulant, but at the same time her golden eyes feasted upon Nicolas de Clerac. 'The masque is spoiled regardless.'

'With you as its centrepiece, Madame, it cannot be spoiled no matter what happens,' Nico said. 'I am sure Monsieur Laurentin will make no more difficulties, and Mistress Rinette is entirely innocent in the matter. Is that not so, Monsieur Laurentin?'

His fingers tightened around the Frenchman's arm again.

'Yes, of course,' Laurentin said in a tight voice. 'I mistook her for someone else.'

'Sieur Nico smiled and let go of his wrist. 'And Mistress Rinette herself wants only to see the rest of the masque. Is that not true, Mistress?'

'Yes,' I said. I did not look at him. I looked at the queen in her magnificent costume. 'You are as beautiful as a dream, Madame, and I have never seen such a masque before.'

Which was all perfectly true. Even so, I was saying it deliberately to flatter her, and I hated myself for falling into the same game as the rest of them.

'We shall continue, then,' the queen said. 'Monsieur Laurentin—'

She meant to dismiss him, that was clear. But he was already gone.

'You broke off at the fourth couplet of the epigram to Terpsichore,' Nico de Clerac said. He stepped back into place, paying no more attention to me. The queen smiled straight into his eyes and began to speak again. Terpsichore danced – quite gracefully for a man, although John Sempill was an agile fellow who was called 'the dancer' for his nimble footwork, and had probably been chosen to play the part because of it – and the masque proceeded. I might have disappeared like a wisp of smoke, and I was glad of it.

I could not help but wonder, though, why Nicolas de Clerac had intervened when he did. Once – when he'd defended me from the unruly crowd on the High Street, with Alexander lying dead in my arms – might have been simple chance. Twice – when he materialised out of the darkness in Holyrood Abbey with his offer of help in finding Alexander's murderer – was far less likely to have been chance. Three times—

Three times was not chance at all.

4 January 1562
Crichton Castle, Midlothian

'It is so cold,' the queen said. 'It is just so *cold.*'

She had been shivering and huddling on a stool in front of the fire since yesterday, when we had all arrived at Crichton Castle. I was at my wits' end. Her half-brother Lord John Stewart of Coldingham was to marry the Earl of Bothwell's sister Janet Hepburn in just a few hours and the whole point of the court coming to Crichton was for the queen to grace the wedding with her presence. Her presence in front of a fire in her bedchamber, wrapped in two fur-lined cloaks and an old wool plaid, was hardly what either Bothwell or her brother had in mind.

'This cold is *la morte*, Madame, for anyone so fragile and beautiful as you.' Pierre de Chastelard was kneeling at the queen's side. He had one of her hands pressed to his cheek, outrageous presumption in a raggle-taggle French poet whose verse was nothing but an over-embellished imitation of Ronsard's. 'Let us run away, back to the sweet Loire Valley where Christmas is kept properly by proper Catholics.'

I wanted to crack him over the head with the queen's gilded silver necessary-pot, which I had just carried into the chamber after rinsing and polishing it at the stable-trough. Since the débâcle of my first appearance at court, at the masque of Apollo and the muses, I had been relegated to the most menial, least public tasks in the queen's household. She was certainly not going to allow me to steal attention away from her at any more public events.

'Madame,' I said, keeping my voice soft and deferential, 'your brother's wedding is to be at four of the clock, in just two hours, and then there is a great banquet and celebration afterwards. You must put on your gown and have your hair properly arranged. Allow me to call Fleming and Seton, at least, to attend you.'

'Madame,' whispered Monsieur de Chastelard, in his feather-soft French-accented Scots, 'allow me to throw the clock out of the window into the snow.'

The queen lifted her head. Her cheeks were pinkened from the heat of the fire, and her eyes sparked with sudden annoyance. Her whole expression came alive for the first time since we had arrived at Crichton. 'Do not be ridiculous, Pierre,' she said. 'The King of France, my father-in-law, gave me that clock, and it is far too beautiful and valuable to be cast out of the window.'

She stood up. The plaid fell away from her shoulders into a multicoloured pile of rough wool behind her; her height and ethereal slenderness made her seem not quite human. Her hair was loose and shining, the very colour of the fire, falling away from the rosy-white height of her forehead. I had learned not to be surprised by her sudden changes of mood but I would never understand how she managed it, changed herself from light to dark, dark to light, in the space of a breath.

'You may go, Pierre,' she said with hauteur. 'I must be dressed.'

'I will serve as your *valet-de-chambre*,' the poet said. 'I will kiss your feet and roll your stockings oh-so-deliciously up the glorious length of your legs.'

'I will call my brother and have him stab you *à l'Ecossais*,' the queen said coldly. 'Through and through, Scots-style, a thousand times. Do not presume too far, Monsieur de Chastelard.'

The poor poet looked confused and hurt; he seemed even less able than I was to follow her quicksilver changes in temper. But people said he was mad with love for her, which I was not.

'I beg your pardon, Madame,' he said, with exaggerated formality. 'I beg your permission to withdraw from your royal presence.'

'Go.' She had already lost interest in him. She walked over to the table before the window – the iciest spot in the room, and yet suddenly she did not seem to feel the cold at all – and put one hand upon the clock. 'I remember the day King Henri gave this clock to me, the day of my betrothal in the grand new *Salle des Caryatides* in the Louvre. We danced afterward – oh, how we danced.'

The poet crept away unnoticed.

'There will be dancing tonight as well, Madame,' I said. 'The Earl of Bothwell has spared no expense in lighting or firewood, so it will be warm and bright. There will be music and every kind of wonderful delicacy to eat and drink – after all, it is not every day that an earl's sister marries a king's son.'

'Just look,' the queen said, as if I had not spoken at all. '"A fair striking clock", that is what he called it when it was presented to me. See how it stands upon a silver base, chased with flowers and garnished with gilt and aquamarines and pearls? The crystal in the top is as clear as the clearest glass. I have seen nothing like it in Scotland.'

'We have clockmakers here,' I said. I had never met one, but certainly there must be at least one.

'Oh, yes, I am sure there are clockmakers here, but never such artists as created my *horloge fleurie*.' She began to shiver again. She had come back from her reverie of France to the cold south-west tower of Crichton Castle. 'Nothing is the same here. It is so cold. Sometimes I wish I had never come back to Scotland.'

'Do not say that, Madame. You are Queen of Scots. You were born here. You belong here.'

'I do not want to be queen tonight. Go and tell the Earl of Bothwell to carry on with his sister's wedding – I am not well. I will stay here.'

She pulled the plaid up around her shoulders, flung herself down on the stool, and stared moodily into the fire.

'Remember the fire at Stirling,' I said. I had to change her mood again, and I knew how the business there had affected her. 'Remember the prophecy. You are the Queen of Scots who was foretold a thousand years ago.'

She straightened a little and looked up at me through the shining web of her hair. 'Prophecies,' she said. 'There are prophecies in my mother's silver casket, too, or so James tells me. Your husband sent him a letter, offering to sell him the casket.'

'I did not know what Alexander was doing. I was wrong to show him the casket, Madame, I know that now.'

'But you have it safe? The casket?'

'I do.'

'There are secrets in it, James says. Things my mother knew, and no one else. I am sure there are some evil-starred secrets about James himself, which of course will be the first thing he will destroy if he gets the chance.'

'I did not look inside, Madame.'

'I do not believe you. You had the casket and you had the key – how could you resist? Do not lie to me, Marianette.'

I hesitated for a moment. Then, with a sense that I was casting dice blindly into a void, I said, 'Very well, you are right, Madame. I did open the casket. But the pages your mother wrote were all in cipher. I could not read them, and I am sure Alexander could not. Whatever the secrets are—'

'I have my mother's ciphers, all of them.'

'She meant the pages for you, so I am not surprised.'

'Marianette.' She stood up, still wrapped in the plaid, her magnificent hair glimmering like a faery's in the firelight. I could feel the glamour she was casting over me like a golden net. 'Give it to me now. I swear to you, I will do everything you ask – bring your husband's murderer to justice, confirm your estates to you as a royal fief, protect you from any marriage you do not want. Give me the casket, so I can learn my mother's secrets and put James in his place and keep him there. So I can control the Lords of the Congregation. So I can have the power she wanted me to have, and be more than just a puppet with my brother pulling my strings.'

If I'd had the casket in my hands at that moment, I would have given it to her.

Fortunately I did not.

'And the prophecies . . .' She leaned towards me, her voice soft and coaxing. 'Tied up in scarlet cords, your husband's letter said, and sealed with Monsieur de Nostredame's own seals. *Les quatre maris*. That was what was written on the outside. Four husbands. Eventually I must choose one, and with the prophecies I can choose rightly. It will make all the difference.'

She grasped my wrist. I sucked in my breath as she sank her nails into my skin.

'Give it to me now,' she said again. Suddenly her voice was sharp as a blade. 'Who are you to keep from me what is mine?'

The change in her startled me, and brought me back to myself. She was like Proteus, ancient shapechanger of the sea. And like

Proteus, she would keep none of her sweet promises unless she was forced to do so.

'We have a bargain, Madame,' I said in a steady voice. 'I will keep my side when you have kept yours.'

She threw my wrist from her and cast off the plaid. 'We shall see,' she said. 'Call Fleming and Seton. I will prepare for my brother's wedding.'

The ceremony was performed in the long banqueting hall of Crichton Castle, according to Protestant rites. Who could tell any more, from one day to the next, what form of religion any given person professed? The Earl of Bothwell was nominally a Protestant, although he had supported the Catholic Mary of Guise and was high in favour with the young queen as well. Power, that was what Bothwell worshipped – I always saw him wreathed in his comfrey leaves like the Green Man of the Picts. All sorts of strange things were whispered about Bothwell's religion – or lack of religion – and some even said he practised witchcraft.

A thousand candles blazed and the sweet golden-honey scent of beeswax floated up to the high hammerbeam roof. The huge fireplace at the far end of the hall crackled and glowed; I could smell rosemary and marjoram in the smoke, the herbs of love and marriage. The queen sat next to the fire in a fine chair under a cloth of estate; there were warming-pans at her feet and heated stones tucked into her sleeves. She was wrapped in a cloth-of-silver mantle embroidered all over with more silver and lined with white fur. I, on the other hand, stood far off at the back of the hall in my own less glittering gown and mantle – no fur for me, sadly, and my hands were stiff with cold. The court had gone back into colours following the anniversary of the little French king's death in December, and the queen had arbitrarily cut short my own year of mourning black; she wanted no black crows around her, she said. Tonight my dress and sleeves were spring green, the colour of new leaves. I longed for spring. Last spring, I thought, I was with you, my Alexander, my garden by the sea was flowering, and Màiri was still safe under my heart.

I felt tears sting. I blinked fiercely.

Mr Willock was preaching on endlessly about the evils of idolatry and I wondered what the queen was thinking. After all she had suffered for her Catholic mass in the five months she had been in Scotland, after the humiliating street demonstrations, the tearful confrontations with Mr Knox, the shaven-headed cats and plundered chapels, it was surpassing strange to see her smiling and to all appearances giving her close attention to a Protestant sermon. Lord James stood close at her right hand, looking unbearably smug. Was she simply trying to conciliate her brother and the rest of the Lords of the Congregation? Or could she be seriously considering—

'Look at Randolph. He is measuring her for Elizabeth Tudor's shoes, and she knows it.'

I did not have to turn around to know who it was – the light, edged voice and the bittersweet scents of nightshade and myrrh were unmistakable. He was right. Thomas Randolph, the English queen's agent, was indeed eyeing our queen with an appraising expression. I said, 'To the best of my knowledge, Monsieur de Clerac, Elizabeth Tudor is still wearing them.'

'Queens' shoes have been treacherous in England since the day Elizabeth's mother first cast eyes upon her father.' He stepped up next to me, a long-legged angular peacock in blue and gold damask, his feathered cap worked with pearls the size of a nightingale's eggs. Why was it that no matter what flamboyant finery he wore, there was always that thread of darkness woven in with the gold and silver? It was not crude violence or menace as it was with, say, Rannoch Hamilton – although I was well aware Monsieur de Clerac could be dangerous enough when he chose to be – but a shadow of asceticism that no jewels and laces could quite obliterate.

'I see Master Wetheral is also here with the English delegation,' he said. 'He is an acquaintance of yours, is he not?'

It took me by surprise at first. Then I remembered that he had come up behind me when I was speaking with Blaise Laurentin at the masque of Apollo and the muses. Laurentin had mentioned Richard Wetheral then. Monsieur de Clerac, it seemed had long ears to go with his peacock colours and pearls.

'I would not call him an acquaintance. I have spoken to him once.'

He said nothing for a moment. Mr Knox was reading scripture, something about a woman named Maachah who was removed from being a queen because she worshipped an idol in a grove.

'If I am to help you in your quest for justice,' he said at last, 'you will have to tell me the things you learn. I promise you I will do the same.'

He was right, of course. I did not trust him and I was reasonably sure he wanted to help me only for his own hidden motives, but if he thought to use me, I could use him as well. I said, 'You already know Alexander sent letters, offering the silver casket for sale.'

'I do.'

'One of them went to the court of England – perhaps to the queen herself. Master Wetheral claims to have met Alexander twice in Aberdeen, and actually to have concluded an arrangement with him.'

'If that is true, one of the other prospective purchasers could have killed your husband to prevent the arrangement from going forward. Is Wetheral now attempting to make a new arrangement with you?'

'He is.' Suddenly I realised what he meant. 'You think the assassin may try to kill me as well?'

'Possibly. It depends upon whether he – or she – wants the casket itself, or wants only to keep it from the hands of the others.'

'There was a letter sent to the French court also. That is what Laurentin was telling me, at the masque.'

'And one to Lord James, who of course shared it with his mother Lady Margaret. The English, the French, and the Lords of the Congregation – who else do you think he would have written to?'

'You are asking a good many questions, Monsieur de Clerac, and answering none. Have you discovered anything useful?'

'One thing,' he said. 'There was someone in the church the afternoon you discovered the ruby, and it was not a ghostly Augustinian monk.'

I felt a lurch of apprehension. 'How do you know?'

'After I saw you safely back to your rooms, I searched the church carefully. The choir has been unused since the Abbey became the Protestant church of the Canongate. Yet there were fresh footprints in the dust.'

'So someone else knows about the ruby.'

'Someone knows.'

Was he telling the truth? I could not be sure.

'Is there anything else?'

'Nothing for now. I must be very careful, of course, how I ask my questions.'

'We must both be careful.'

'Then let us talk about the wedding.' There was a glint of humour in his eyes. 'Let us enter into the spirit of the thing, and tell tales about the bride and groom.'

How silken-tongued he was. I would have walked away, but the hall was crowded and I did not want to make a scene. Grudgingly I said, 'The bride is lovely. It is unusual for a woman grown to have such fair hair.'

'Her father was called the Fair Earl for his light-coloured hair. But of course you would have known him – he swore Mary of Guise promised to marry him, not once but twice.'

'I knew of him. He put aside his perfectly faithful wife on trumped-up grounds to court the old queen. Even today Lady Bothwell is immured in her tower at Morland and not here to celebrate her own daughter's wedding.'

'So you knew Lady Bothwell too?'

'No, I did not know her, other than in the tales the other ladies told. I was kept much apart from the rest of the court when I was in the old queen's household.'

'I remember. You were like a virgin in a secret bower, untouched by the world.' When he smiled like that he softened all my spikiness. 'This bride, on the other hand, has been all too touched by it. Master Randolph knew the scandal, and called it a merry story, worth repeating.'

'Well, I do not wish to hear it repeated,' I said. 'Not on her wedding day.'

'You are good-hearted, *ma mie*.'

'Do not call me that – I am not your dear one.'

He smiled again and said nothing more. Mr Willock at last finished his sermon; the rings were exchanged and the marriage was done. I thought of Alexander and pushed the thought away.

The queen rose. Her ladies clustered around her with baskets of dried flowers, rose petals and forget-me-nots, and they all began pelting the bride and groom, laughing. Janet Bothwell's rich fair hair, falling loose and twined with emeralds and amber, made green and gold flashes in the candlelight. Pipers began to play, and the crowd surged toward the archways, probably to avail themselves of the necessaries. Servants came in and began setting up trestle tables for the wedding feast.

'Will they be happy, do you think?' Nicolas de Clerac said. For once he sounded perfectly serious. 'They do not know each other well – the marriage is simply to bind Bothwell to the queen's interests, his sister to her brother.'

'Or to bind the queen to Bothwell.'

'A different thing, I agree. He'd marry her himself, if he could. She could make worse choices, if she wishes to remain in Scotland.'

I looked at the queen thoughtfully. She seemed to glow in her cloth-of-silver, reflecting the candles and the firelight; impromptu dancing had begun and she was matched with the Earl of Bothwell as her brother was matched with Bothwell's sister. The earl, in mulberry-coloured velvet, was half-a-head shorter than she was; she was so exquisitely slender and gossamer light and he so broad-shouldered and thick with muscle that they might have been different species altogether. The fragile long-stemmed peony and the hairy, black-rooted comfrey with its grasping fingerlike flowers – I could see no possible point of connection between them.

'Fortunately she does not wish to remain in Scotland,' I said. 'I suspect she will be on the throne of Spain before the year is out.'

'Perhaps,' said Nicolas de Clerac. 'I know it is what she hopes for, but she has been married to one frail child-king already, and Don Carlos is said to be mad as well as in delicate health. Not the most prepossessing of bridegrooms.'

'You sound as if you think she should actually be happy in her marriage.'

He smiled. 'A great weakness in me, I know. Rinette, if she does leave Scotland, you must give her the silver casket whether your conditions have been met or not. She will require its contents to be safe.'

I had begun to feel – not friendliness, exactly, certainly not real affinity, but the slightest sense of a rapprochement with him. I felt it no longer. I said in a hard voice, 'And what do you know of the casket's contents, Monsieur?'

For quite some time he said nothing. The pipes and rebecs played on, and the dancers wove in and out among the harried servitors trying to lay out the long banqueting trestles. At last, all seriousness gone from his voice, Nicolas de Clerac said, 'Oh, only what gossip whispers, mademoiselle. Magic amulets. Charms and relics. Secret writings. A fortune in jewels.'

Again I could not tell if he was lying or not.

I knew. In my heart I knew. But I did not want to believe it, so I pretended it was only my dislike for Nicolas de Clerac that made the brilliance of Crichton's grand hall turn dark.

12

Later we flocked around the trestles for the marriage feast; I saw a few couples slipping away into the shadows, perhaps inspired by the thought of the bedding to come. I wanted nothing to do with such illicit pleasures and certainly no more to do with Nicolas de Clerac; I pressed my way to the head of the room so I could sit among the queen's ladies. Mary Livingston was there, as was Mary Fleming who was called Flaminia; it was a merry conceit of the queen's to surround herself with young women who bore her own name. One who was not young and not a Mary was Lady Margaret Erskine, who looked at me narrow-eyed and turned away. Malice exuded from her, rank as the scent of the wild arum; but it did not seem to be directed particularly at me as it was at the queen and Lord Bothwell and the bride and the groom and everyone who stood at the centre of the celebration, eclipsing her beloved half-royal son.

My poor breasts ached. Màiri had been left behind at Holyrood with Tante-Mar, Jennet and a wet-nurse from Granmuir village named Annis Cairnie, a cousin of Wat's. I wished I were with them, eating a basin of warm porridge by the fire, and not here at the queen's brother's glittering wedding.

Servitors brought in platters of sliced venison stuffed with cheese and chestnuts, plus rabbits cooked in savoury pies with eggs, honey and spices. These were followed by whole partridges, plovers and moor fowl, then ducks and several enormous geese, roasted with ginger, pepper, cinnamon and salt. Lady Janet ate next to nothing – my own wedding supper at Granmuir had been much smaller and humbler but I knew exactly what she was feeling: excitement and anticipation and an absolute certainty she would never eat again. Lord John, on the other hand, ate heartily and laughed as he was doing it. The feast proceeded to cakes stuffed with fruit and drenched with brandywine, and ended with an astonishing maritime subtlety – the Earl of Bothwell was the Lord High Admiral of Scotland, after all – in the shape of three ships painted with gold leaf, silver sails furled as they scudded over a blue-green ocean with white sugar seafoam.

After the subtlety was served there was more music and more dancing. The younger men – and some of the more daring ladies – began to play raucous and openly suggestive games. Many wagers were cast, both on the games and on the sports that were to follow the next day. Several fights broke out; I caught a glimpse of the Earl of Rothes' man Rannoch Hamilton brawling drunkenly with a man in the colours of Clan Forbes. It was all just a prelude to the most keenly anticipated entertainment of all – the bedding of the bride and groom. I found a shadowy corner and kept to myself. The queen certainly did not need me and it was too soon . . . much too soon. I wondered if I would ever wholeheartedly join in a wedding celebration again.

'It is time for the bedding.' Mary Livingston skipped up beside me. She was flushed and panting and a string of fine pearls was hanging dangerously loose from one side of her elegant little French hood. She loved to dance and young Master John Sempill, who had played Terpsichore in the Apollo masque, had become her favourite partner. 'What are you doing standing here all by yourself, Rinette? Gather up some cakes – we must have something sweet made of wheat flour to crumble over Janet's head once she is settled in the bed.'

She danced away again. Reluctantly I made my way to one of the tables and collected a few spice-and-honey cakes in a napkin – how sticky they would be in poor Lady Janet's hair! But at least she would be fertile, as the grains of wheat that made up the cake had been fertile, or so the old wives' tale said. Surely the poor wheat's fertility had been long lost in the grinding and baking it had undergone.

I could not stop thinking such dark thoughts. How little any bride would want me near her as she was undressed for her wedding night – I was like an evil fairy in a folk tale with my sorrows. I spent a great deal of time wrapping the cakes just so, and fortunately when I followed the rest of the women up the tower stairs to the bedchamber Lady Janet was undressed and safe in the great bed with its topaz-coloured velvet hangings. The queen sat on the bed beside her, laughing like a child. Cold and unhappiness seemed entirely forgotten.

'Here are the cakes, Madame,' I said. 'I will just—'

The gentlemen burst in behind me, and someone – the Earl of Bothwell? Lord John himself? – put large strong hands either side of my waist and lifted me bodily out of the way. When my feet touched the stone floor again, I stumbled and dropped the napkin full of cakes.

'Heigh-ho! Take care, my pretty lassie.' The same hands steadied me. It was Lord John, the groom himself. Once he had me on my feet he slapped my buttocks in a shockingly familiar manner. 'What have you there? Cakes! Gather them up, sweeting, and let's give Lady Janet a good pelting.'

'Is that what you call it?'

'Swiving, I'd call it!'

The men all laughed and shouted other suggestions, each one more obscene than the last. The women squealed and blushed – or tried to look as if they were blushing – and Lord John began to throw the cakes. Lady Janet caught one and threw it back, to the cheers of the other ladies. The queen, not to be outdone, picked up two or three cakes of her own and began to break them in pieces over Lady Janet's fair hair and her naked breasts; the honey stuck to her fingers and she licked it off, laughing. Three or four men caught hold of Lord John, lifted him bodily by his arms and legs, and slung him on to the bed like a log on to a fire.

In the shrieking and thrashing that followed I stepped backward, meaning to slip away upstairs to the quiet and solitude of the queen's chamber. To my surprise – I had thought I was on the outermost fringe of the crowd – I collided with another person behind me, and when I turned to ask pardon I was grasped hard around the waist and jerked outside on to the stairway. The smell of wine and rutting male made my stomach convulse. I screamed.

Which did no good at all, of course, considering the hubbub in the bedchamber.

'Jealous of that naked slut in the bed, witch-girl?'

It was Rannoch Hamilton, and he was vilely drunk. I did not waste my breath arguing with him, but stamped my foot down hard on his. He grunted with pain but did not let me go.

'I should have done this in that tumbledown church at Granmuir, before the very eyes of your pretty young lover and the old priest. I'll show you I'm not afraid of that woodbine-goddess of yours . . .'

He tore off my cap and grasped a fistful of my hair. I screamed again. He swung me around so my back was against the rough-cut stone of the tower, then leaned against me, pinning me with his weight. With his free hand he jerked at the neckline of my bodice, tearing the fine gauze of my partlet. It hurt – how it hurt, with my breasts so swollen and tender. I could not get my leg free of my twisted skirts to jolt my knee up into his groin as Jennet had taught me. I clenched my teeth against his wine-rank mouth and drove two stiffened fingers into his right eye.

He jerked back with a bellow of pain and let me go. I could not get past him to run up the stairs to the queen's chamber so I turned to fling myself down into the grand hall again – and instead flung myself straight into Lady Margaret Erskine.

'What is this?' she said. Her fingers closed around my arm like a hawk's claws. 'Master Hamilton, what is this girl about with you?'

'What am I about with him?' I cried. 'I am about getting away before he rapes me on the stairwell. Let go of me!'

'Be silent.' She shook me hard. Aged and ruined in her beauty she may have been, but Lord James Stewart's mother was strong and her nails were hard and sharp. In her dark eyes I could see plots forming patterns, one then another, as she considered and discarded them. 'Master Hamilton, where is the Earl of Rothes?'

'Up there, with the rest of them, putting the queen's brother to bed with his new wife.' Rannoch Hamilton had one hand over his eye; shock and pain had sobered him and made him ten times as dangerous. *If you kick them in the balls or poke them in the eyehole, be sure to do it hard enough to knock them down*, Jennet had said. *Otherwise they'll hurt you all the worse for hurting them.* 'This is no concern of his, nor of yours, my lady.'

'Oh, but it is.' She caught hold of my other arm and pinned my elbows behind me. 'Take out your dagger, if you please, Master Hamilton, and cut the lacings of her dress.'

Rannoch Hamilton had taken his hand away from his face. His eye was reddened and swollen but intact, for which I was passionately sorry. 'If you touch me, I'll kill you,' I said. 'Lady Margaret, are you mad? Let go of me.'

'I am not mad and I will not let go of you. The queen may have thought to set you aside from any marriage, but she will sing a different tune if Master Hamilton has you in public for everyone to see. Are you going to strip her, you milksop coward, or must I do it myself?'

I kicked at her but what with my skirts and her skirts I could not manage to hurt her. 'What does it matter to you if I am married or not? For the love of Saint Ninian, let me *go*.'

Rannoch Hamilton suddenly came out of his trance. He drew his dagger and slashed the neckline of my bodice. I felt a hot streak of pain and knew he had cut my skin as well, but I would be naked and damned before I would give him the satisfaction of screaming again.

'It matters that you are married because my son requires control of your estate and the silver casket you are concealing.' Her voice was cruel and singsong, lessoning me as if I were a child. 'He is the Earl of Rothes' overlord, and Rothes is Master Hamilton's overlord, and when you are married to Master Hamilton, you and your Granmuir and your casket will all be in my son's power. And then we shall see what the queen has to say.'

'What the queen has to say about what?'

A musical, French-accented voice, still a little breathless with laughter.

The queen herself, framed in the wedding bedchamber's doorway a few steps above us on the stairs. Behind her clustered a mass of glittering gentlemen and ladies. The aura of wedding-night sensuality hung over them all; the ladies' eyes were heavy and their lips soft. The gentlemen, by contrast, seemed sharpened and predatory.

I recollected myself first. 'Madame!' I cried. 'Help me!'

Lady Margaret let go of my arms and embraced me with all the sweet protectiveness of a mother. 'I have you, my dear,' she said. 'Shush, shush. Do not cry.'

Her terrible arum-lily aura dizzied me. Could the queen not see what had been happening? 'I am not crying,' I said. 'Let go of me.'

'I came upon her, Madame, in Master Hamilton's arms.' Lady Margaret said to the queen. Her voice seemed to come from far away. 'All the wine and celebration – they seemed to be playing a small game with Master Hamilton's knife, and it went a bit awry.'

I wrenched myself away from her. 'That is a lie,' I said. I was shivering all over and my teeth were chattering. I probably sounded exactly as if I actually had partaken of too much wine and celebration, and it made me shake even more with sheer fury.

'Marianette, I am surprised at you,' the queen said. 'I do not care for such improprieties in my household.'

'Perhaps you should reconsider your edict regarding Mistress Rinette's marriage.' That was Lord James, coming up beside his sister. His eyes flicked over my shoulder to his mother, then returned to me. 'A husband would steady her.'

'And Master Hamilton would be an excellent choice.' That was the Earl of Rothes, toadying to his overlord. They were all there, Rothes, Lord James, Nicolas de Clerac, goggling at me with my arms crossed over my breast to hide my slashed bodice. 'He is loyal and a good Protestant, and there would be no further question of Granmuir falling to the Gordons.'

'You would have to bind and gag me and drag me to the altar,' I protested. 'I will not marry again, and most particularly I will not marry Rannoch Hamilton.'

Rothes glowered at me. He was my clan chief, after all. 'Binding and gagging can be arranged,' he said.

A moment of utter silence. I could hear Rannoch Hamilton breathing hard. One of the women laughed, high and excited.

'Forced marriages are against the teaching of your own church, my Lord Earl,' Nicolas de Clerac said, in his silky diplomat's voice, to all appearances untouched by any genuine emotion. 'Not to mention the queen's and Mistress Rinette's own.'

'And we gave our royal promise she would not be compelled to wed,' the queen said. She put one hand on Nico's arm with possessive affection, and I saw black hatred pass over Lord James' face. 'However, Marianette, if we continue to find you in stairways in such déshabillée, perhaps we shall reconsider our promise.'

'I did not choose to be here in déshabillée,' I said.

The queen only laughed. She said, 'Go upstairs, if you please, and remain there – you may build up my fire and see that my bed is aired and warmed. Lady Margaret, Master Rannoch, you may come downstairs with the rest of us. I wish to resume the dancing.'

Lady Margaret curtseyed. Rannoch Hamilton, who had clearly recovered his senses far enough to practise self-preservation, bowed. I could see he was flushed – did he have sentiment enough to feel shame that he had been caught out in his attempted rape, or was it simply the wine? I flattened myself against the wall as they all swept past and went downstairs. I wondered – if I had a dagger in my hand right now, which one would I stab first? Rannoch Hamilton, or Lady Margaret, or the queen herself?

A dagger in my hand—

A dagger with a missing ruby—

I should have looked at Rannoch Hamilton's dagger when I had the chance.

Upstairs the fire was out and the queen's chamber was icy cold. I threw myself down on the bed – how furious she would be if she could see me! – and pressed my face into the velvet coverlet. I wanted to go home. I wanted to collect Màiri and Tante-Mar and Jennet and Wat Cairnie and my white mare Lilidh and ride home to Granmuir and never see the court again. Why did I care what happened to Mary of Guise's silver casket with its mysterious writings, pages in cipher with the names of Scotland's greatest lords at the top of every page? With its strange packet wrapped in red silk cords, sealed over and over with Nostradamus' seal, with *les quatre maris* scribbled on the outside in Mary of Guise's own hand?

I tried to cry. I could not.

I got up. Why lie in the queen's bed if I could not cry? I collected her wardrobe-woman's sewing box, took out a needle, and threaded it with pale green silk thread.

Action. Any action, however small.

It was time to stop hiding myself away in my grief, stop feeling sorry for myself, and start acting. The queen's royal inquiry had accomplished nothing so far. The only person who had asked questions at all was Nicolas de Clerac, and I did not know if I could trust him.

It was time for me to make my own list of the people who would have benefited from Alexander's death. Time for me to find a way to examine every dagger in every person's possession for a missing ruby.

13

I decided to start with the Earl of Rothes. There on the stairway
he had said for all to hear that he did not want Granmuir to
fall to the Gordons; thus he had a perfectly good reason, from
his point of view, to kill my Gordon husband. And he would still
be expecting an apology for my insolence.

I bided my time until we returned to Edinburgh, and then I
sent Wat Cairnie with a suitably humble request for an interview.
I was not surprised when Wat returned with the answer that I
was to wait upon the earl after dinner, at Leslie House in the High
Street.

He was anticipating self-abasement, and he would get it. I had
watched the queen and learned the power of a woman's tears
against a man's self-importance. I would get nowhere if I accused
Rothes outright of Alexander's murder and demanded to see his
dagger. I might well get his dagger into my own hands if I sobbed
prettily and begged to show him just what Rannoch Hamilton
had done to me.

I did not like some of the things I was learning at court.

I stayed in my tiny room at Holyrood and ate bread-and-milk
for my own dinner – the queen was occupied reading Latin with
Master Buchanan so I was free. Then with Wat escorting me, I
made my way out through the palace gardens and the Abbey

Strand, into the Canongate and the High Street. It was cold and the air was dripping with mist so thick I could not see two steps ahead of me. As I walked I rehearsed to myself what I knew about Rothes – he was the fifth earl, his given name was Andrew Leslie, he was about ten years older than I was, and his grandfather and my great-grandfather had been cousins.

I left Wat at the doorway with the earl's own man and went into the house. A dour housekeeper took my wet mantle and led me to the earl's private chamber.

'Good day to you, my lord,' I said, with a polite curtsey.

Rothes was seated in a fine carved chair by a window, with a table placed beside him in a square of winter sunlight. There were no other chairs, and so I remained standing. He said nothing, but sat unmoving, looking at me with an expectant expression. Give him what he wants, I said to myself, however bitter it may taste. He will be potter's clay in your hands.

I took a breath and said, 'I wish to speak to you, my lord, about what happened at Crichton.'

'I am sure you do.'

'I humbly beg your pardon for speaking to you as I did.' I did my best to copy the queen's winsome tone. 'You are the chief of my clan and I owe you all deference and respect.'

I saw him soften, before my very eyes. 'I understand that you are still grieving for the Gordon boy,' he said. 'But if you are to live at court, you must put that aside and act with suitable respect for your betters.'

I bit down hard on my tongue. This served two purposes – it stopped my hot words of unsuitable disrespect, and brought tears to my eyes.

'Now, now, do not cry,' he said. 'We shall put the matter aside and start afresh.'

'He was forcing himself upon me,' I said. I had put away my memories of Rannoch Hamilton, his wine-sodden breath, his rough hands, his heavy weight, shut them safely in the stone bubble-chamber inside me. Letting them come out, even a little, closed my throat and made my heart pound. 'Lady Margaret was mistaken, my lord – it was not play between Rannoch Hamilton and me. He intended to hurt me.'

I would not accuse Lady Margaret to Rothes – he would never believe it. I would wait, and find another way to pay her out for her treachery.

'There was a great deal of drinking and carousing,' Rothes said. 'And you are a very pretty girl. Master Rannoch is a man like any other, ready to steal a kiss.'

'But it was not just a kiss. Look—' I pulled down the neckline of my bodice to show the healing cut on my breast. I saw his eyes darken and knew I had won him. I swung one hand in the air, as if warding off an imaginary dagger. 'I would show you – if I had a dagger of my own, my lord, I would show you exactly what he did.'

Without taking his eyes from my breasts, slowly and inevitably as a sailor charmed by a mermaid's song, he took his dagger from its gilded and embroidered sheath and put it on the table. The blade glinted in the sunlight. I reached out just as slowly – I did not want to break the spell – and picked it up. The hilt and guard were worked with the buckles and rue-leaves of Rothes, fashioned out of silver inset in gold. It was smooth and well-worn – probably his father's, or even his grandfather's. Rich enough, but no missing ruby – in fact, no jewels at all. It was not the dagger that had killed Alexander.

I acted as if I were suddenly coming to my senses. I looked at the dagger as if I were surprised to see it in my hand. With a gasp, I put it back on the table and rearranged my bodice.

'Oh, my lord, forgive me. It was just so terrible – when Master Rannoch drew his knife I was taken back to the moment when – when my husband—'

All my playacting evaporated as if it had never been and to my shame and horror I began to cry in earnest.

'Hush, hush,' Rothes said. He had come back to himself as well and I could see a faint flush of embarrassment over his cheekbones. He rose. 'Here, be seated. Compose yourself. Catriona!'

The housekeeper looked in. I could see Wat Cairnie's freckled face behind her. 'Yes, my lord?'

'Another chair. And some wine.'

'Is owt amiss?' That was Wat's voice.

'Mistress Rinette is overcome with distress over her disrespectful actions, that is all. She is perfectly safe.'

There was a flurry of activity, and at the end of it Rothes and I were both seated with a pitcher of wine and two goblets on the table between us. Wat and the earl's housekeeper went out of the room. The earl poured some wine for me as if we were old friends.

'As we are here,' he said, 'there is something else I would like to discuss with you.'

I took a sip of the wine and let it calm me. No longer was I pretending to be anything but myself. 'What is that, my lord?'

'This business of the silver casket belonging to the queen regent.'

I was surprised, because I had been expecting him to talk of marriage again. Cautiously I said, 'What about it, my lord?'

'You are playing a dangerous game, hiding it away and demanding an investigation into your husband's death before you produce it again.'

I said nothing.

'You would be safest if you placed it into responsible hands. The Gordon boy was killed because of it, and you could find yourself with your throat cut as well.'

I drank another swallow of wine, and had a horrible flash of my own throat slashed as Alexander's had been, and the wine spilling down the front of my dress with my blood.

'I do not—' My voice deserted me for a moment. I started over. 'I do not understand what you mean, my lord. Why do you think the old queen's casket had anything to do with Alexander's death?'

I knew the answer to that, of course. But I wanted to know what Rothes knew, and how he had learned it.

'He was attempting to sell it. To my own certain knowledge he had offered it to Lord James and to Huntly here in Scotland, as the leaders of the Protestant and Catholic parties. He also offered it to Elizabeth Tudor in England, and to both the Catholic party of Catherine de' Medici and the Huguenot party of Admiral Coligny in France.'

He seemed so matter-of-fact about it. Nico de Clerac and I had guessed at Lord James, Queen Elizabeth, and Queen Catherine, but not the Earl of Huntly or the Huguenots. I swallowed and said, 'How can you know all this?'

'He wrote it to Lord James in a letter, and Lord James told it to me. Each party was told of the others to increase the price they would offer, and each, I believe, was willing to kill him to keep him from selling the casket to any of the others.'

And there it was. Not just whispers and suppositions, but the truth.

I had taken the casket from my childhood hiding place behind the stone in the Mermaid Tower at Granmuir, never dreaming my secret would be anything but safe with Alexander. Flesh of my flesh, heart of my heart. He had betrayed me and he had died for it.

'And which party,' I said, as steadily as I could, 'actually ordered the assassination? Lord James, or the Earl of Huntly, or the English, or the French?'

'I do not know. No one knows. And there is yet another party involved.'

We looked at each other. I wondered why he was telling me this. Did he think I would break down in tears and give him the casket to save myself? Perhaps he did – with my playacting to get my hands on his dagger, I had certainly given him every reason to think I was a fool.

'Another party?' I said.

'It was Mary of Guise's casket. Who would want it more than the Guises themselves? Not the Duke of Guise or the cardinal, but the old duchess, Antoinette, at Joinville. She is our queen's grandmother.'

'I know who she is. In fact, I have met her.'

And I had, in the course of that one dreamlike year in France when Mary of Guise went to visit her daughter and took all her household with her. The year I was eight years old. The year that divided my life in two and changed everything for me.

She was already old then, of course. Her husband was dead and her son had succeeded him as Duke of Guise. He had a wife of his own, a daughter of the Duke of Ferrara, and so the old duchess had become the dowager. Mary of Guise was her eldest child, the first of twelve. Twelve children! I had always had my mother and my father and my household all to myself and could not imagine having to share them with eleven brothers and sisters. She dressed like a nun, did Duchess Antoinette, and people said she kept her own coffin propped up in her bedroom at Joinville.

As a child I was in awe of her because of the twelve children and the coffin, but she had always been kind to me. She would want her daughter's silver casket, yes, if only to keep it out of the hands of Catherine de' Medici. The Guises and the Medici queen were bitter enemies.

'Well, then,' the Earl of Rothes was saying, 'if you know her, you will know she has spies everywhere in the French court. She could well have found out about the offers to the Medici woman and to Coligny, and taken action to prevent the casket falling into any hands other than her granddaughter's. She has an agent here in our own court, you know.'

'No,' I said. 'I do not know.'

'It is Monsieur de Clerac.'

I felt perfectly detached at first. *Well, yes, of course, who else would it be?* Then I felt an odd little quiver of denial. *No, he is not a spy, I do not want him to be a spy.* Then anger and disappointment blotted out all the other feelings. I thought: So that is why he offered to help me. That is the hidden motive I knew he had to have.

Not only that, he had been there the night Alexander was killed. Seared into my memory – flashes of torchlight off the guard and pommel of a sword, gilding, scrollwork, silver inlay. A hand in a black leather glove. Hair like fire—

'He was in the queen regent's household.' Rothes' voice jolted me back to the room in Leslie House, with the cold winter sun streaming in. 'After her death he accompanied her body back to France. Then as if by magic he appeared in the young queen's retinue.'

'Perhaps she simply wanted him close by, because he knew her mother.'

'And perhaps he is a spy, placed by her grandmother.'

I did not want to believe it. It made me feel a little sick and shaky, and at the same time irked – no, not just irked, furious – with myself that I cared one way or the other. What was Nicolas de Clerac to me, or me to him, that I should care whether he was a Guise spy or not? He had happened upon the murder of my husband and had saved me from the trampling crowd in my terrible extremity.

Or he had murdered my husband himself with a jewelled dagger, then swept out his sword to protect me. With Alexander dead, he needed me alive, because I was the only other person who could lead him to the casket they all wanted.

'I hate the court!' I burst out. 'There is no one to be trusted there, no one.'

'You can trust me,' Rothes said. 'I am your clan chief. Give me the casket, Mistress Rinette, and I will give it to Lord James. He will use its secrets properly – better than the queen ever could.'

And what will you gain, I thought, from Lord James' gratitude?

'You will be safe then,' he went on. 'You will be allowed to go home to Granmuir with your child and your people. Huntly and his Gordons are out of favour, so he will have no power to meddle with you. I myself will not press you to marry, I promise you that.'

'Fine promises, my lord Earl,' I said. It was hard to keep my voice from shaking. 'What of Alexander Gordon's murderer?'

'It has been five months, Mistress Rinette, and the truth will never now be known. Let the boy rest. Give up your inquiries, trust the casket to me, and you will be free.'

Is it shameful to say that for a moment I wavered? I missed Granmuir so much, my Granmuir, my garden by the sea, my home. I missed Màiri – I hated the fact that I had been forced to give her over to a wet-nurse, that she knew Tante-Mar and Jennet better than she knew me. I hated the court and how it was changing me. But I knew I would be as much a fool to trust Rothes as I would be to trust Lord James, or Nicolas de Clerac, or the queen herself.

I stood up. My knees shook. I took a breath and steadied myself.

'I thank you for your offer, my lord Earl,' I said. 'But until Alexander Gordon's murderer is discovered and tried and hanged outside the Tolbooth, I will not give up the silver casket.'

14

8 February 1562
Edinburgh

Would the weddings never end?

On Sunday the eighth day of February, the queen's half-brother and closest advisor Lord James Stewart married Lady Agnes Keith with great splendour – well, as much splendour as Master Knox would permit – at Saint Giles' Kirk in Edinburgh. Easter was to be early this year and so Lent began early as well; the next Wednesday was Ash Wednesday and that left the court only three days to celebrate. We started out to make the most of them with a magnificent banquet that night in the long gallery at Holyrood Palace.

Lord James – newly created Earl of Mar, which had been a royal title since James II – presided with the queen at his right hand and his new countess at his left. Also at the high table was Lady Margaret Erskine, Lord James' mother; she was alight with pride and for once it was easy to see how she had entranced the king, Lord James' father. On her other side, and somewhat to my surprise, sat the Earl and Countess of Huntly. Huntly had lately been out of favour with the queen for his agitation on behalf of his Highland Catholics, but his wife Elizabeth Keith was the bride's favourite aunt – everyone in Scotland was related in some way to everyone else, by blood or by marriage or both – and so there they were, at the high table with the rest of the queen's inner circle, eating peacocks in galantine sauce and a pie of wine-seethed figs, pine nuts and salmon, seasoned with cinnamon, pepper and ginger.

I had begged the queen to allow me to remain in my apartments with Màiri and my own little household. I would have been better off begging for a place at the feast, because then she would certainly have denied me – after everything that had happened at Crichton, I was more out of favour than ever. As it was, I stood behind her in my mended green dress, providing a basin of warm scented water and a clean towel whenever she lifted her imperious white hand.

I was invisible, as all the servitors were, and at least it gave me a good opportunity to study the Earl of Huntly. He himself could not be the murderer – he was old and slow-moving and as slabbed with fat as a grizzled bear in the wintertime. But his son, young Sir John – Sir John, with his father's dash of royal blood – was wild and reckless and aimed high: some said as high as the queen's own person and the crown matrimonial. If Rothes was right and Alexander had offered the casket to the Earl of Huntly – his own clan chief? Would he have had such audacity? – Sir John would have known. And like the French and the English, the Lords of the Congregation and the Huguenots, he might well have wanted to prevent the casket's falling into enemy hands almost as much as he wanted it himself. Perhaps more than any of the others – if he dreamed of marrying the queen he might not have wished her to read Monsieur de Nostredame's prophecies of her four husbands.

Unless he was one of them.

The sweetmeats had been served: winter fruit baked in almond milk, little rosewater-flavoured bridal cakes spiced with cloves and mace, and stacks of gilded gingerbread. The queen had rinsed her hands and dried them one final time then risen – there was to be dancing and she always loved dancing. Sir John Gordon, meanwhile, was bending over his father's chair, whispering in his ear, but all the while his eyes followed the queen; she was perfectly well aware of it and preened herself for him like a long-necked swan. I took a step to one side, where I could observe Sir John more closely. He was richly dressed and wearing a gilded leather belt with a painted dagger-sheath; I could see the glint of jewels. If I could only work my way closer—

'Mistress Rinette.'

I jumped, and almost spilled the water in my basin. I knew the voice, of course. A man's hand, long-fingered, perfumed and glittering with rings, steadied me.

'Monsieur de Clerac,' I said. I felt a rush of contradictory feelings – resentment, fear, pleasure, anger, caution.

He lifted the basin from my hands, put it gently on the table, and stepped up beside me. 'The queen is wrong to relegate you to such menial tasks,' he said. 'What is it that interests you so about Sir John Gordon? If I notice you staring, others will as well.'

'It is only that—' I stopped myself. If Nico de Clerac was a Guise agent, I certainly did not want to share further information with him. What else could I say about Sir John? I went on, as if it did not matter in the least, 'One hears the most scandalous gossip about Sir John – supposedly he has married the widow of Alexander Ogilvie, and yet he courts the queen quite openly.'

'So he does.' Nico had a trick of looking at a single person while appearing to gaze carelessly out over an entire room. He was dressed in a velvet doublet of crimson so dark it appeared black until he moved and the candlelight caught glints of colour; the sleeves were cut away to reveal tight undersleeves of golden-scarlet silk, slashed and ribboned. His trunk hose were rich watered silk and velvet in a darker scarlet colour. All the crimson and scarlet should have been painfully mismatched with his red-gold hair, but somehow they were not.

His eyes were outlined with kohl. He wore more *maquillage* than I ever did, more jewels, more silks, more perfumes . . . so much so that he seemed to be making a deliberate effort to appear effeminate.

For me, at least, he did not succeed. I remembered him standing over me with a sword.

'It is the dagger, I think,' he said. 'You are looking for a missing ruby.'

'Perhaps.'

The tables had been carried out and the musicians had begun to play; the queen had gone out to dance a galliard with Lord James while Lady Agnes was partnered with her father, the Earl Marischal. The queen was a bravura dancer, her height and slenderness giving her striking elegance as she performed the steps; Lord James was stiff and sober beside her. Nico and I both watched Sir John Gordon for a moment as he stood by, awaiting his own opportunity to dance with the queen.

'He is hungering for her,' Nico said at last. 'And not only because she is queen.'

'He will be disappointed.'

'I hope so. A Catholic marriage would be a disaster for her. Do you dance, Mistress Rinette?'

'No,' I said shortly. In truth I loved to dance, although I had never truly appreciated the intricacies of court galliards and pavanes, stylised high dances and low dances – my arms and legs always seemed too long and I could never manage my skirts correctly. I preferred the country dances I had learned from Jennet and Wat in Granmuir village, and I certainly could not picture myself, in my mended dress, dancing with Nicolas de Clerac in all his finery. I, a seaside windflower, and he, the trailing night-shade, dark and rich, sweet and poisonous.

'A single dance? It is only courtesy to the bride and groom, to show our good wishes for their happiness.'

The galliard was finished, and the musicians were playing an interlude while the dancers chose new partners. Lord James and Lady Agnes chose each other, of course; Sir John Gordon and the French poet Pierre Chastelard appeared to be arguing over which one of them would next partner the queen. She herself was drinking wine proffered by Mary Seton and laughing at the two gentlemen.

Nicolas de Clerac put his hand under my elbow. I felt urgency in his touch.

'Dance with me,' he said. 'Listen to the music – the next figure will be a pavane, and what better way to talk a bit with no one paying attention or listening at the keyhole?'

'Why would I want to talk to you?'

He looked at me thoughtfully. 'We are no longer allies, then, in your search for your husband's murderer?'

I was already sorry I had been so sharp with him. If he was a Guise agent and had a hidden motive for pretending to help me, I should be encouraging him with soft words and learning what I could, while keeping my own secrets to myself.

'Forgive me,' I said. 'It is difficult, being out of favour with the queen. Of course I will dance with you.'

He took my hand. His skin actually touched mine, and I felt a sense of shock – his hand was warm when for some reason I had expected it to be cool. Of course he had touched me before – he had carried me from the High Street to Holyrood on the terrible night of Alexander's murder. But that was a different matter. I had been a different person then. This was the first time he had touched me as I was now, palm to palm, nightshade to windflower, and I knew with the absolute certainty of the flowers that he was to be important in my life.

Important how?

Friend? Lover? Betrayer? Murderer?

We stepped into our places in the procession. The consort of musicians halted for a moment, and then the flutes and the plucked strings, the viol and the tabor, launched into the music for the pavane itself. The queen had chosen Sir John as her partner, and they had taken their places at the head of the dance figure.

We stepped forward. A pavane was to be danced, the books and dancing-masters taught us, with decorum and measured dignity. I had performed it many times under Mary of Guise's exacting eye, and Nicolas de Clerac paced off the steps in perfect time and with grave stateliness as well.

'I have nothing new to tell you,' I said, under the cover of the music. 'I spoke to the Earl of Rothes, and tricked him into allowing me to examine his dagger, but other than that he could tell me nothing.'

Nothing but that the Earl of Huntly and Admiral Coligny, the leader of the French Huguenots, had also received letters from Alexander. Nothing but his suspicion that you yourself, Nicolas de Clerac, are an agent of the Guises.

Single step. Single step. Double step.

'I see,' he said. 'Well, it is something, to prove Rothes himself is not the assassin.'

His fingers remained warm and firm around mine. The other

dancers, in front and behind in the procession, paid us no particular attention.

'He could have hired someone,' I said. 'Or sent one of his vassals. It could have been Rannoch Hamilton, who seems perfectly willing to perform any sort of evil deed.'

'A hired bravo would not have a jewelled dagger.'

That was true. I said nothing.

After a moment he said, 'Has Master Wetheral called upon you again? Or Monsieur Laurentin?'

'No.'

'You suspect Sir John Gordon – you were craning your neck like a bean goose to look at his dagger earlier.'

Single step. Single step. Double step.

'I suspect everyone,' I said. 'Even you.'

He did not say anything for a long time. I wondered what he was thinking. We reached the end of the hall and performed the conversion, the series of steps that reversed the direction of the dance.

'I was there,' he said at last, 'because I had heard rumours that one Alexander Gordon had Mary of Guise's casket and was offering it for sale, and I wished to see this foolhardy fellow for myself. When you left Holyrood that afternoon, I lost track of you in the crowd, and so I went to Huntly's house and waited outside. I was fairly certain you would eventually come back there, and you did.'

'Were you one of the potential buyers?'

'I was not. I am not. I had heard the tale and I was curious, nothing more.'

The dance came to an end, and in the final figure after the music stopped the gentleman was to execute a deep bow and the lady a low curtsey. I tried to perform the curtsey but I was so shaken I lost my balance. Nicolas de Clerac steadied me and at the same time bowed to me as if I were the queen herself. Fortunately the queen was too absorbed in charming Sir John Gordon to notice.

Palm to palm, nightshade to windflower.

The flowers were wrong sometimes. At least, sometimes I interpreted them wrongly. Perhaps I was misreading them now.

'There is something more,' he said. 'You are the one—'

''Sieur Nico!' It was the queen. Sir John and Monsieur Chastelard were trailing behind her like hopeful ducklings but she clearly had her eyes on Nicolas de Clerac. 'I wish you to be my partner for the next dance. It is to be a galliard again, and I desire you to perform *la volta* with me.'

The ladies all screamed in mock surprise and indignation. *La volta* was considered scandalous for the close way the gentleman held the lady, lifted her, and actually for a moment touched his thigh to hers. Of course, we were celebrating a wedding, and soon the bride and groom would be put to bed – perhaps that was what put the idea into the queen's head.

'It is my delight to oblige you, Madame,' Nicolas de Clerac said. Whatever he had wished to tell me would have to wait. 'Mistress Rinette, you will excuse me, of course.'

'Of course,' I said.

They went off to form the dance. I withdrew to the shadows along the wall, and slowly made my way to the west end of the gallery where I could slip out of the door and make my way to my own apartments, where my dear Màiri would be sleeping, warm and soft and smelling of milk and soap. The queen would never miss me at the bedding, or when she decided to retire to her own bed. Nicolas de Clerac would certainly not come looking for me as a partner again, with the queen begging him so prettily to dance *la volta* with her.

I reached the door. The music had begun again. No one saw me.

I ran down the maze of west passageways. The darkness and cold were salutary after the light and heat and scents of sweat and perfumes and lust in the gallery. Narrow windows cast pale oblongs of moonlight over the stones. Halfway to the end I ran straight into some drunken fellow sprawled on the floor. I stumbled and barely caught my balance; there was something wet and sticky on the wall above the spot where the man lay.

I looked at my hand. It was dark and shiny. It looked black in the faint silver moonlight but I could smell the salty, rusty smell I would never forget.

Blood.

I went to my knees and ran my hands over the man's face. A low forehead and thick sleekit hair, brushed back. No neck—

I jerked back with a cry. Master Richard Wetheral may have had no neck to speak of, but now he had a single deep cut under his chin, from ear to ear.

The English agent Thomas Randolph was called at once, of course, and directed the queen's guards in the removal of Master Richard's body. A cadre of the queen's servants scrubbed the stones of the passageway. I was given a basin of water to wash my hands. The wedding party was warned, apparently, to take a different corridor when they escorted the new Earl of Mar and his countess to the rooms set aside for their ceremonial bedding. I could hear music and laughter, far off, like a procession from Elfland making its way into the heart of a green hill.

Master Thomas asked me one or two cursory questions but clearly did not suspect I knew anything of value. I did, of course, although I had the wit not to say so and further entangle myself.

I had seen a cut like that before, deep and sure, ear to ear. Across Alexander's throat.

Was this the work of the same assassin? If so, why?

Who would be next?

One of the guards took me back to my own rooms. By then the shock had begun to overtake me; I felt icy cold and my hands were shaking. Jennet, Tante-Mar and Màiri were abed, and I did not want to wake them. There was no way to lock the door so I sat on one of the chairs in the main chamber, facing the entrance, staring into the darkness.

Was I expecting the quiet scratch on the door? I was not sure.

Nicolas de Clerac stepped in and closed the door noiselessly behind him.

'Rinette,' he said.

He pulled me up from the chair and put his arms around me. I did not resist him; in fact, I pressed my face against his shoulder to muffle the sound and sobbed, once, twice, three times. I was so shocked and so frightened, and in some way I could not understand his presence made me feel safe again. The scents of bitter orange and myrrh – I knew I would never smell them again for as long as I lived without thinking of him.

Then I realised what I was doing, and pulled away. He stepped away at the same time. We looked at each other. I am not sure which one of us was the more surprised.

'You are not hurt?' he said.

'I am not hurt. Only shocked, and sorry for Master Wetheral's death.'

'Tell me.'

I went back to my chair and sat down again. He crouched in front of me, just far enough away not to touch me. The room was too dark for me to see his expression clearly.

'There is not much to tell. I was walking – I was running. I wanted to be away from the bedding. I wanted to be here with Màiri. I ran straight into him – he was lying in the corridor. I think he was standing when – when his throat – when the assassin attacked him. There was blood on the wall.'

'You believe it was the same man?'

'The wound was the same.'

He rocked back on his heels. 'It was the shortest way,' he said. 'For you to walk from the long gallery to your rooms here. The obvious way. I believe the assassin guessed you would walk there, and left Master Wetheral's body for you to find.'

'But how did he know I was there, at the wedding?' It was becoming more and more difficult to keep my voice to a whisper.

'Because he was there as well.'

I swallowed hard and breathed for a moment before trying to speak again. 'If he was there, he must be attached to the court in some way.'

'It was a great celebration, with a large attendance – he could have slipped in. But he knows Holyrood well enough to know the passageway you would take, and he carries a jewelled dagger. Yes, I believe he is attached to the court, at least on its periphery.'

'Nico,' I said. 'Why? Why did he kill poor Master Wetheral, and leave him for me to find?'

I heard someone stirring in the other room. Màiri began to whimper.

'He cannot have believed that killing Wetheral would stop the English effort to obtain the casket – Randolph will find someone else quickly enough, or step into the negotiations himself. I think it was a warning to you, Rinette. He is telling you he does not want you speaking to anyone else about the casket.'

'Holy Saint Ninian! Nico, everyone speaks to me about the casket. He cannot kill them all.'

'We must hope not.' He turned his head, listening to Tante-Mar's voice in the other room, comforting Màiri. 'I cannot stay, Rinette. I beg you to take every care – there are a dozen conspiracies afoot, and you are the person at the centre of them all. And I also meant to tell you, before the queen called me away – I am going to France for a little while. I do not know how long. But I will come back, I promise you.'

'Going to France?' I repeated. 'Why?'

I could see the corners of his mouth curl down. It was a strange expression, half sorrowful, half wryly smiling. 'A family matter,' he said. 'I would tell you to do nothing more but keep yourself safe until I return, but I suspect it would do no good.'

'No,' I said. 'It would not.'

15

I t was not easy to search for a murderer when one was a queen's lady.

My every moment was accounted for. Queen Mary was wooing the English queen with letters and gifts – she said she wanted to be recognised as the heir to the English throne, but of course in Catholic eyes she was already the rightful Queen of England. She sent Elizabeth Tudor a ring with a heart-shaped diamond, some verses, and a fine portrait of herself, and even told us all that if the Queen of England were a man, she would marry him forthwith. When she said that, she laughed and laughed. At the same time, secretly, she was negotiating with the King of Spain to marry his poor mad son and declaring she felt it was her destiny to be Queen of Spain and wrest England from Elizabeth Tudor with Spanish gunships.

She went so far as to plan a meeting with the Queen of England for the summer, at York, and we were all given new dresses for the occasion – mine was blue sarcenet trimmed with silver and tiny crystals, and I also received new velvet trimming to cover the mended place on my green dress. Who knows how different all our lives might have been if this great meeting had taken place? But it did not.

In March the Duke of Guise, the queen's favourite uncle, attacked – was attacked by? – a congregation of Huguenots at a

French town near Joinville called Vassy. So many conflicting stories were told that no one knew the truth of the matter, but it was like a spark to dry tinder. France went up in the flames of open war between Catholics and Huguenots, and the Queen of England decided she had best remain in London to see what advantage she could gain from the conflict. Our queen took to her bed in tears, and once again the whole court lurched from a mood of sunny anticipation to the blackest gloom. I wondered where in France Nicolas de Clerac was, and if his mysterious family matter had taken him into danger.

I stumbled over no more bodies. I danced with the gentlemen of the court – *he knows Holyrood well enough to know the passageway you would take, and he carries a jewelled dagger* – and made a list of the ones who did not have daggers with faceted rubies. It was a long list. As often as I dared, I asked the queen about the royal enquiry into Alexander's death, and each time she assured me sweetly – too sweetly – that it was continuing.

In July there was a new scandal. Handsome young Sir John Gordon, he who had danced so blithely with the queen at Lord James' wedding in February, wounded a member of her personal household in a street brawl. The queen was furious. She was looking for a scapegoat, I think, someone upon whom to take out her anger and frustration over the collapse of her meeting with the English queen, and her fears for her Guise relations in France. Sir John's defiance of her royal authority was a spark, and Lord James, who hated the powerful Catholic Earl of Huntly and his Gordons, energetically fanned the flames.

So by August we were off on a progress to the north, to confront the Earl of Huntly once and for all. We would pass by Granmuir on our way to Aberdeen, and I decided to take Màiri and all my household with us and settle them at Granmuir castle.

With its high walls and narrow causeway to the mainland, it was a hundred times more secure than Edinburgh, and however much it would break my heart to be separated from them all, they would be safer there.

I was so tired and more than a little afraid. The Frenchman Blaise Laurentin had tried once to force his way into my chambers and received a beating from Wat Cairnie for his pains. The Earl of Rothes spoke to me often, asking me if I was well in a way that implied he expected me not to be, and Rannoch Hamilton lurked behind him like a black-haired, black-eyed wolf. Lady Margaret Erskine missed no chance to speak publicly of flower-witchcraft and the power of a husband – any husband – to control a wife.

We left Edinburgh on the eleventh day of August, and made our way first to Stirling – *I was burned here!* the queen cried, and told us the story over and over again – then to Perth and Glamis. When we rode out of Glamis north-east towards Granmuir, I left the progress with my little party. The queen had not only agreed to my riding ahead – the long train of the progress was slow, and would catch us up in a day or two – but graciously allotted me two royal men-at-arms to accompany us. She also reluctantly allotted me Monsieur Nicolas de Clerac, who had reappeared at court as mysteriously as he had disappeared. It was obviously Nico's own idea. Perhaps he had something to tell me.

All I could think of, though, was home. For the first time in over a year, I turned Lilidh's head towards the sea. I could smell it, taste it, the tang of salt, the briny scent of minuscule sea-creatures living and dying, of ancient rocks and sea-plants and seabirds. The fields were intensely green – it had been a wet, cool summer – and there were flowers everywhere, white and purple heather, wild roses, thistles and sweet briar and sops-in-wine. Jennet rode beside me with Màiri in her arms; the baby was laughing with delight and reaching out her tiny hands as if she could catch the flowers out of the air. She had never seen Granmuir. My own heart welled up with joy and I knew I was doing the right thing in taking her there.

We reached the castle rock in the early evening. I had sent one of the queen's men ahead, and so when we trotted out on to the causeway I saw Norman More and the boys at the top of the gatehouse flying Granmuir's blue-and-gold colours to greet us. We had no colours to wave in return but Lilidh was as good as any pennon, white as the crest of a sea-wave, her mane and tail touched with rose and gold by the setting sun.

'My lady, my lady!' Bessie More cried as we drew rein in the courtyard. 'And your precious bairnie! And Jennet, my girl! Thanks be to Our Lady for bringing you home.'

They crowded around, Bessie and Norman and the boys, old Robinet Loury, even Père Guillaume, frailer than ever but radiant with holy joy. Jennet and Tante-Mar and the wet-nurse Annis Cairnie handed Màiri around, and to my amazement she did not fuss or cry but happily embraced them all. The queen's men had the good sense to see to the horses and leave us alone; I caught only a glimpse of Nico de Clerac, stroking Lilidh's neck and looking as if he wished he himself could be the next to be handed the laughing baby. It was so unlike him I stopped and looked again; he had turned away to lead Lilidh to the stable block. I was gathered up into Bessie More's capacious arms and the moment was gone.

Home. We were home.

How could I help but think of Alexander, of how hopefully we had set off for Edinburgh the year before, and of everything that had happened between then and now? He would never come home. His tomb was at Glenlithie so I could not even lay flowers over his grave.

I started to cry, and I could not stop.

By the next afternoon I had cried myself out at last. My eyes were swollen and my throat was raw and my nose was red as fire, but for the first time since Alexander's death and Màiri's birth I felt – I am not sure – as if I was no longer crammed full of grief and anger and vengefulness. I ate an oatcake and drank a cup of buttermilk and went out into the gardens, my beloved gardens by the sea. The windflowers were blowing, my own flowers – the ancient stone walls protected them from the salt air of the sea and they always blossomed from Annunciation Day to Michaelmas, unlike ordinary windflowers which bloomed only in the spring. The scents of thyme and honey-sweet woodbine, the glowing colour of sea-pinks and masses of red campion, brought back my childhood with Grannie and Gran'auntie, and the endless summer days when Gran'auntie sat with me in the garden and told me the flowers' stories and taught me how to listen to their voices.

I leaned on the wall and breathed, taking in the scents of the sea, the living stones and the flowers. I said a prayer for Gran'auntie, who had been Marina Leslie like me. After a while I knew the moment was right. The flowers would speak to me, and tell me what I should do.

I crouched down beside the mass of windflowers, each with seven white petals, a heart of green velvet and stamens like threads of golden silk. The flowers themselves were scentless but I could smell the distinctive foxy scent of their leaves. I did not have to say anything – only listen.

You cannot stay here, not yet, the windflowers whispered. *Go back, go back – there is danger at the court but you must face it there or it will follow you here.*

'I do not want to go back,' I whispered.

You began this. You wanted vengeance.

'I do not want it any more. It is too much for me to bear.'

You wanted vengeance and you will have it. But you must pay the price.

'What price?'

The flowers did not answer. I was never entirely sure if what I heard was truly the flowers, or just my own secret thoughts and hopes and fears rising up out of my heart when I stilled myself to listen. Perhaps I was only arguing with myself.

After a while I said, 'What must I do?'

Go back. Take care. In the end you must put the silver casket into the young queen's hands, whatever it costs.

'Will Màiri be safe here?'

She will be safe while she is here, but only if you go back to the court and lead the danger away from her.

I felt a chill. 'I will go, I swear it – I would go to Hell itself to keep her safe. What is the danger, can you tell me? Is it a person?'

It is two men and a woman. Beware, beware.

'Which two men? What woman? Tell me. Help me.'

You will marry again, not once but twice, and you will know despair.

I crouched there, holding my breath, waiting. I did not want to marry again, and I hoped these marriages were far into the future. Two? Why two? Were the two men I would marry the same two men I was to beware of?

The windflowers blew gently in the breeze. It came in from

the east, over the sea, over the walls, and swirled gently in the walled space of the garden. Time passed, and the flowers said nothing more.

'Thank you,' I whispered. 'I will go back. I will be careful.'

I stood up. In the south-east corner of the garden there had been a stand of yellow irises, Alexander's flower, their ruffled golden flags traced with a diamond shape of reddish-brown veins. The veins had been the colour of blood – why had I never seen that before? I had planted the irises when I first fell in love with Alexander, as a wilful child of twelve. Grannie had told me I was being silly, that a twelve-year-old girl could know nothing of love. But I knew. He was like a young golden god to me. When Grannie shut me up in the Mermaid Tower I found a way to squeeze out on to the window ledge and creep down, using the ancient stones as handholds and footholds. What a fool I had been – I could have fallen into the sea, and if I had no one would ever have known what had become of me.

Last spring, when Alexander and I had been so happy together, the yellow irises had flourished. In the autumn there had been no one to cut them back and tend them, and this past spring no one to weed them or cut the flowers when they had finished their blooming time. I wondered if they had bloomed at all. There was nothing left now but dried and spotted leaves.

I bent close and listened.

The irises were silent. All I could read, very faintly, was the earth itself telling me they would not bloom again.

'May God go with you,' I said softly. 'May the Green Lady of Granmuir watch over you, my dear love, even as far away as you are in Glenlithie.'

I stood up. I felt tired and drained of life, like an old woman. Would I ever be a girl again? I was making my way to the gate when I heard footsteps on the gravelled path outside the garden wall.

I did not want to talk to anyone. I knew who it was and I particularly did not want to talk to him.

It is two men and a woman. Beware, beware.

Was Nicolas de Clerac one of the two men?

16

He stepped into the garden and bowed to me as if he were in a great salon full of blazing candles, rich tapestries, queens and kings, and not a simple garden with an old stone wall, looking out over the sea.

'Mistress Rinette,' he said, with grave courtesy.

It had been four months since I had stood face-to-face with him, and he looked different. Older? No, not really, although there were shadows in the hollows of his eyes. Something he had seen or heard or done, in France or wherever it was he had been, had changed him profoundly.

He was dressed for riding, in plain breeches of russet-coloured leather and hose, a white shirt and black doublet. His head was bare and he wore no jewels, no earrings or *maquillage*. I had never seen him dressed so simply; it fitted the strange streak of austerity I always sensed in him, even when he had been outrageously costumed as the Greek muse of astronomy. Outwardly, I thought, he seems as changeable as the queen, but at his heart he is as fixed as the North Star. Whereas the queen is like one of Master Copernicus' planets, brighter than the other stars but wandering, always wandering, from place to place in the sky.

I said, 'Monsieur de Clerac.'

'I am sure you have guessed that I asked the queen to send me with your escort.'

'I have.' I walked along the garden wall again, back to the patch of windflowers among the campion and thyme. I wanted to be among my own flowers, for whatever strength they might give me. 'I hope you found your family well in France.'

He walked along the opposite wall. There was an ancient bittersweet vine clinging to the stone, covered with hanging clusters of purple flowers; it was still too early for the scarlet berries the birds loved so dearly. He seemed to belong where he stood, which puzzled me at first. Then I realised that the bittersweet and the trailing nightshade were closely related. He might as well have been surrounded by his own flower, as I was surrounded by mine.

Bittersweet stood for truth, which was always both bitter and sweet.

'They are well enough.' The tone of his voice made it clear – *I do not wish to talk about that*. 'And you? I have feared for you . . . partly that you would put yourself in danger with your inquiries, and partly that Lord James and Lady Margaret and their faction would have their way and I would come back to find you married, whether you wished it or not.'

'I am as well as I can be,' I said. I was grateful, at least, that he made no comment on the state of my face after all my tears. 'And no, I am not married, although Lady Margaret Erskine would have me so if she could. She will do anything, I think, to put the silver casket into Lord James' hands.'

'She believes it will put the queen in his power, and make him regent in the end.'

The thyme had crept up into the niches and crumbled mortar of the stone wall. I broke off a few stems and breathed the smoky-sweet, slightly astringent scent. Thyme gave one heart and courage. I said, 'I am so tired of the court. I am glad to be home.'

Neither of us said anything for a while. The seabirds wheeled and called on the wind, gulls and guillemots and terns. The slow, rhythmic wash of the waves swept back and forth below them, like the heartbeat of Granmuir. I felt as if we were outside time, the two of us together. I had never felt that way with Alexander. How strange that I should feel it now.

'I feel as if I have come home as well,' he said at last. 'I grew up in a place very like this – ancient and silent but for the sound of the sea.'

It was not what I had expected him to say, but Granmuir affected people that way. It stripped them down . . . changed them. I asked, 'Is that where you went, in France? Your home?'

'No. I have no home to speak of, although I have a small estate at Clerac which supplies my material needs. The place I grew up – it is a great Benedictine monastery called Mont Saint-Michel, on the coast of Normandy. From birth I was intended for the church.'

So that was what I had been seeing – the shadow of the monk under the extravagant affectations of the courtier. If he had been placed in a monastery as a baby, he was either an orphan or a great man's bastard. 'Obviously,' I said, 'the intention was not fulfilled.'

He turned his head and looked at the bittersweet thoughtfully. Again I was struck by the fact that his face looked different, pared down to its essentials, its surprisingly beautiful bones, wide-set eye sockets and elegant angles of jaw. What had happened to him in France?

'Oh, I ran away from the monastery when I was twelve or so, and after that I was put into the charge of more worldly tutors.

Even so, the monks had indoctrinated me so deeply with their Benedictine rule that I have never wholly escaped it.'

'Why did you run away?'

He broke off a branch of the bittersweet and began stripping it of its leaves. He did not seem to want to go on, but with the branch in his hands and the scent of its leaves on his skin, what could he do but tell the truth?

'I wanted to save a beautiful princess from a terrible fate.'

'You were only twelve, and a novice monk, and you had a princess for a lover?'

'You are too literal.' He tore a bittersweet leaf in half. 'The beautiful princess was my mother. As you might have guessed, I am a bastard.'

The word *mother* hurt me. It always did. 'My own mother is a natural daughter of the Duke of Longueville,' I said, making an effort to keep my voice steady. 'Such things are not uncommon. What was the terrible fate?'

'She had been forced to marry a man she hated and feared. I managed to find my way to Rouffignac where he had taken her, and confronted him – needless to say, I received nothing more than a beating for my pains. I was not allowed to return to the monastery, and within the year my mother was dead of her husband's mistreatment.'

What could I say to that? If his mother was dead and he did not know who his father was, what were the family matters he claimed to have gone to France to attend to? Who had his worldly tutors been? How had he come by his name and estate of Clerac?

'Do you understand now?' He threw down the bittersweet branch and looked at me directly, his gaze suddenly and shockingly angry. 'That is my experience of forced marriages. I have tried to forget it, but it was brought home to me again in France, whether I wished to think of it or not – I learned who my father is, Rinette, and why my mother was forced to marry.'

'Why?'

'My father wished to marry a great man's daughter. Because of my mother's refusal to take a husband, a tale had grown up that she and my father had been married secretly. To demonstrate that this was not so, she was forced to marry another man.'

I learned who my father is . . .

Do not ask him, the bittersweet whispered. *It is too hard for him now. Later, perhaps later, he will tell you. Later he will tell you other things as well, things you may or may not wish to hear.*

'The Earl of Rothes is privy to Lady Margaret's marriage plots.' His voice had changed. There would be no more personal revelations. 'Did you know that?'

'The queen has promised to protect me.'

'Do not trust the queen. She means well but she is as inconstant as mercury, and she is entirely subject to Lord James at the moment. It is not my place to advise you, Rinette, but if it were, I would urge you to stay here with your household, and let the queen and her progress go on their way.'

He had thrown down the bittersweet branch and so I no longer knew if he was telling the truth or not. Was he truly concerned for my safety? Had he made such a point of coming to Granmuir to speak to me out of pure selflessness? Or was he an agent of Duchess Antoinette of Guise, as Rothes had suggested, and was that why he had gone to France?

'I have pursued my inquiries,' I said. 'No one has threatened me openly, although the court has been full of dangers and intrigues of its own. I can tell you one thing: Sir John Gordon does not have a dagger set with faceted rubies.'

He smiled. Did he realise I was offering him one tiny crumb of what I knew, in the hope he would give me anything that he knew in return? Apparently he did because he said, 'I can tell you two things. First, Monsieur Blaise Laurentin is not connected to the French royal family by blood or by loyalty – he is a mercenary, and follows wherever gold leads him.'

You might say that I am in the French ambassador's household, he had said, *although I am not exactly in the employ of Monsieur Castelnau himself.*

'So he could be working for anyone.'

'And the person he is working for today might not be the person he is working for tomorrow.'

'And yet the assassin has been consistent. He murdered Alexander to stop him from selling the casket. He murdered Master Wetheral to warn me not to sell the casket.'

'True. Although there are a good number of people who share that same aim – stopping you from selling or giving the casket to anyone but themselves. He could be serving two masters with the same desire.'

I picked at the thyme again as I thought about that. The stems were as tangled as the mystery of the assassin's identity. At last I said, 'What is the second thing?'

'I spoke with Monsieur de Nostredame.'

'You *what*?'

He smiled. 'It is not so difficult as you might think. He does not spend all his time at court – he has a house in Salon-de-Provence, with a rich Salonaise wife and six children. And I had a letter from Queen Mary to serve as my introduction. She is deep in marriage negotiations with the King of Spain, as you know, and desperate to know what the *quatre maris* prophecies predict for her.'

It had never occurred to me that someone might go to France and simply ask Nostradamus what the prophecies were. If he had told Nico, and Nico had told the queen, the value of the silver casket had suddenly dropped precipitously.

My mouth dry, I asked, 'Did he tell you what they were?'

'He claimed he himself did not know – that he writes his predictions in a sort of reverie, and seals them up and sends them off without making copies. It is part of his mystique. As long as the seals on that packet are not broken, no one knows what is inside.'

'Why did Mary of Guise write *les quatre maris* on the outside, then?'

'There would have been a covering letter. He gives cryptic hints. It is hard to say what is real and what is false about him, but for the moment he is the most famous seer in Europe, and kings and queens believe whatever he says. Queen Catherine de' Medici—'

He broke off. I too could hear voices calling in the courtyard, the whinnies of horses and striking of iron-shod hooves against stone. I went to the garden gate and looked out.

It was the queen, with a little company of ladies and men-at-arms. Clearly she had ridden ahead of her own progress, looking for amusement and distraction. Wat Cairnie and Norman More were helping them all dismount, and poor Bessie More was curt-seying as if her life depended on it.

'Nico,' I said. 'Please go down to greet her. I do not want her to come upon us like this, alone together in the garden.'

He bowed. It effectively hid his expression, and when he straightened again he was smiling pleasantly. I recognised that smile. It was his court mask. I could almost see the jewels and the kohl reappearing.

'Of course. Prepare yourself – she will demand you read your flowers for her. She said as much, before we even left Edinburgh.'

'I cannot promise the flowers will speak.'

He laughed. 'Create something. She wishes to hear that she will prevail against the Earl of Huntly, marry Don Carlos of Spain, and with him add the crown of England to the crowns of Spain and Scotland when Elizabeth Tudor dies – oh, say, in a fall from a horse. Tell her that.'

'I am not a tinker at a fair who makes up tales for pieces of gold.' It angered me that he would make light of the flowers. 'If the flowers speak, I will tell her what they say. If they do not, I will tell her nothing.'

'Peace, peace, *ma mie*. I am sorry. I will bring her back with all due solemnity.'

'I am not your *mie*,' I called after him.

He only laughed.

'But how do you do it?' the queen demanded. 'Do you hear voices? See visions? It is a very serious thing, you know, to read the future for a queen.'

'Yes, Madame, I know,' I said. 'But I cannot tell you exactly how I do it. Sometimes it is simply that a certain flower presents itself in answer to a question. Sometimes it is a sympathetic flower – a correspondent – which seems to speak to me. Everyone has a correspondent flower of their own.'

Even as I said it, I remembered the black emptiness I'd felt when I looked at Rannoch Hamilton. I knew he was part of the progress but fortunately he was in the Earl of Rothes' train and not one of the queen's personal party.

'Almost everyone,' I amended. 'If I were to see—'

'What is my flower?' the queen said.

I hesitated. Should I tell her the truth – that she was a peony, a country-garden flower which did not belong in palaces and throne rooms, and was easily damaged by wind or rain or too much sun?

Nicolas de Clerac had suggested I lie, and I had been angry. I could not lie now.

'You are a peony, Madame,' I said. 'Gorgeous and delicate.'

'But I love them, *les pivoines*,' she said. 'They are much cultivated in the gardens of Touraine. That is my jointure, you know – in France I am Duchess of Touraine in my own right.'

'Perhaps that is why I see them so vividly surrounding you, Madame.'

'Well, there are certainly no peonies here,' she said. Her little court laughed like a chittering flock of sandpipers. 'These other flowers – I do not recognise them all – what can they tell you about me?'

'Choose one, Madame, and we shall see.'

She smiled and began to walk around inside the wall of the garden. With her long legs and graceful neck she called to mind a silver heron, an *aigrette*; I had seen herons tilt their heads at just the angle the queen liked to affect. Her women watched her breathlessly. In the background Nicolas de Clerac stood with the two gentlemen-at-arms who had ridden with the queen to protect her, watchful and indulgent. I had a strong impression of wrongness – none of them believed the flowers had any force or virtue, and they were simply amusing themselves at my expense.

The queen crouched down. Her back was to me. 'This one,' she said.

She straightened, turned and thrust it towards me – a single long stem, spotted purplish-black, with slender, deeply notched leaves and a tassel of yellow flowers at the top. I recoiled – for a moment I saw a wasp, yellow and lacy-winged, poised to pierce us all and suck us dry. Then I realised the flower was yellow cock's-comb, which some people called rattle grass. Beautiful in its way, as all the flowers were, but it was an incubus-plant – its roots sucked the life from those of grasses and other flowers unlucky enough to intertwine with it.

'What is it?' the queen asked. 'What does it mean?'

'It is yellow cock's-comb,' I said slowly. 'You should take care if you meet a tall, slender, fair-haired person. It could be a woman or it could be a man, I am not sure, but the cock's-comb represents a person who feeds on others for life and power, and it appears to have called to you.'

'Well, it certainly cannot be the Earl of Huntly, as he is short, fat and grizzle-haired,' the queen declared. All the ladies tittered again. 'I would like to know what Huntly is planning to do. Will he submit himself to my royal command?'

'Please walk around the garden again, Madame,' I said. 'Walk close to the wall, so you are actually stepping through the flowers.'

The rest of us pressed back against the gate. The queen paced slowly around the garden, as if she were dancing a pavane. She was positively glowing with satisfaction at being the cynosure of everyone's attention. When she had made a complete circuit she performed a *révérence*.

'There,' she said. 'Now what do the flowers say?'

I went out into the garden again. Scrambling over the south wall with vines of germander and woodbine was an ancient mass of rock ivy, and rock ivy was part of Huntly's Gordon badge. I looked at where the queen's foot had pressed. There were two ivy leaves there, both of them already lifting themselves defiantly from the flattened undergrowth. I crouched down and closed my eyes, focusing all my senses on listening.

Women's voices. Three – no, four. Some sort of chanting, faint as the wind, with the smoky scent of black witchcraft.

Attack, my lord, attack. You will prevail. You will lie safe in bed afterwards, in Aberdeen city, without so much as a scratch upon your body.

Lady Huntly's voice.

I straightened and returned to the queen.

'Well?' she said.

'The Earl of Huntly will not submit himself or his son to your judgement, Madame,' I said.

Her eyes narrowed and her golden brows slanted down over her eyes. 'We shall see about that,' she said. 'Huntly may call himself the Cock of the North, but even he must obey his sovereign.'

'There is more, Madame.'

She was angry, and it was clear as clear that suddenly she was tired of flower-readings. 'What more could there be?' she said.

'Beware of Lady Huntly. She is encouraging him to attack you. She is using black witchcraft, and she is also looking into the future.'

'Lady Huntly? But she was a friend of my mother's.'

'Nevertheless, Madame, take care.'

'Madame.' It was Nicolas de Clerac, who had stood by silently as I read the flowers. The queen turned to him with a sudden smile, like a sunflower turning to the sun.

'Lady Huntly is known to have tame witches in her household,' he said. He glanced at me – the tiniest flicker of his eyes – and then smiled back at the queen. She stepped up to him and put one long white hand possessively on his arm.

'I care not for witches, tame or wild,' she said. 'And it is the Earl of Huntly, not the Countess, whom I intend to bring to heel.

Come, let us go back to the progress, 'Sieur Nico. Ride with me. Tomorrow we will be in Aberdeen.'

They went away, laughing and talking. No one spoke to me or wished me farewell. I stood in the garden alone, and I wondered if Nicolas de Clerac thought I was a tame witch. If he did, he was wrong. When the flowers spoke to me it was not witchcraft at all but something much older – old, perhaps, like the magic bubble in the living rock under Saint Margaret's Chapel. In those days the earth itself had a voice, the rock had a voice, the flowers had voices. Anyone could hear them if they knew how to be silent and listen.

I had listened to the windflowers and they had whispered, *Go back, go back. Lead the danger away.*

I brushed the grass and soil from my skirt, then I left the garden and went down into the courtyard. Wat would saddle Lilidh for me; only he and Jennet would accompany me back to the progress of the queen and her party. Màiri and her nurse and Tante-Mar would stay here where they would be safe, and one day, God willing, all of us would come home from our exile and be happy at Granmuir forever.

17

21 October 1562
Aberdeen

'Lady Huntly was a friend of my mother's,' the queen said. 'She would never wish me harm.'

'Sister,' Lord James replied, 'you caused one of her sons to be hanged at Inverness. You outlawed her husband and another of her sons, just five days ago. She has every reason to wish you harm.'

We had been on progress now for almost two months. From Granmuir we had gone to Aberdeen, then after a few days started for Inverness. Sir John Gordon and a troop of cavalry followed us all along the way, occasionally showing themselves and performing great feats of horsemanship. The queen was convinced Sir John meant to abduct her; she swore she would have vengeance on all the Gordons for their outlawry, but I could see the spark of exhilaration in her eyes. In her mind she was making a romantic *conte-de-fée* of it all, and she loved being the heroine, the object of a wild Highlander's passionate desire.

At Darnaway Castle on the road to Inverness, Lord James Stewart was publicly invested with the great Earldom of Moray, the revenues of which had long been a Gordon perquisite. This was clearly as much to punish Huntly and the Gordons as it was to elevate Lord James himself; the result was not unexpected. The Sheriff of Inverness, another of Huntly's sons, refused us entry to Inverness Castle. More excitement, although it ended tamely enough; the sheriff changed his mind, opened the gates, and was promptly hanged from the battlements for his pains.

At Inverness we rested for a while; the queen hunted, feasted, dressed herself in plaids and received representatives of the Highland clans. She would have remained there forever, I think, but after a week or so we started back to Aberdeen along the seacoast. With every step the new Earl of Moray grew in self-importance, and spoke with more familiarity to the queen. Once we had settled in Aberdeen again, Lady Huntly had sent a messenger begging for an audience.

'I myself did not hang the Sheriff of Inverness, brother,' the queen said. 'Nor did I personally declare the Earl of Huntly and Sir John Gordon to be outlaws. My privy council consulted together and decided.'

'You are right, Madame, I am certain, about Lady Huntly,' Nicolas de Clerac said in his silky diplomat's voice, before Lord James could reply. 'I am sure she means you no personal harm. But the countryside is unsettled, and it would be dangerous for you to leave the safety of Aberdeen just now. Perhaps Lady Huntly can be persuaded to come into the city.'

'There is no point in seeing her at all,' Lord James said. Or, rather, the Earl of Moray. He was quite touchy about being addressed with every possible respect for his new rank. 'Either she is going to beg for clemency, which we are not prepared to grant, or she has some trap in mind, which we do not wish to give her the opportunity to spring.'

'We,' the queen said, making a point of the royal plural, 'will make up our own mind about the matter.'

'There is something to be said for meeting her,' Nicolas de Clerac put in, once again clearly attempting to smooth over the conflict. 'Who knows what information might be gained about where Huntly is and what he has planned? It is too dangerous for the queen to go, I agree, but I am willing to go in her place, with just a few men. I may be able to read Lady Huntly's intentions, which would—'

'Read her intentions!' the queen interrupted. She turned and looked straight at me, her heavy-lidded golden eyes glinting with a combination of inspiration and malice. 'But of course, 'Sieur Nico, that is just the thing. You do not have the special talent for such reading, though – it is Marianette who should go, and look at the flowers around this Saint Mary's Chapel where Lady Huntly says she is waiting. She chose the place – the flowers there should tell us what she intends. Is that not what you told us at Granmuir, Marianette?'

'It is late in the year and cold for flowers.' To be so suddenly singled out surprised me and made me uneasy. I had been standing quietly with the queen's other ladies, effacing myself; in the past two months of travelling, hunting, feasting and earl-making the queen had said barely ten sentences to me. I had spent every day looking over my shoulder, wondering if the assassin would strike again. 'She wants to see you, Madame – she will turn me away before I come close enough to read anything.'

'That is not what I meant at all, Madame.' Nicolas de Clerac was as surprised as I was, and clearly distressed as well. 'Such a reading is a matter for diplomacy, not floromancy.'

'I agree,' put in the Earl of Moray. He did not often agree with Nicolas de Clerac, and from his expression the words were sour on his tongue. 'If anyone is to meet Lady Huntly, it should be an experienced man, not a trifling girl.'

That made me want to run to the stables and saddle Lilidh on the spot. 'I am no trifling girl, my lord,' I said. 'I simply do not believe Lady Huntly will be willing to see me when it is the queen she desires to meet.'

'Be silent, all of you.' The queen was smiling, delighted to have set us all at each other's throats. 'Marianette will wear one of my cloaks – it is pouring down with rain and no one will know who she is until she is safely arrived at Saint Mary's Chapel. I will send a dozen of my men with her. They will protect her, and at the same time add to the impression that it is actually me riding out upon this commission.'

'I absolutely forbid it,' Moray said.

'I beg you to reconsider,' Nicolas de Clerac said. 'At least permit me—'

'I will do it.' I stepped forward. I was tired of effacing myself, tired of being afraid. A ride in the bracing Aberdeenshire rain, a secret mission spiced with danger – the prospect made my blood quicken for the first time since we had left Granmuir. 'I ask only that I be allowed to ride my own mare, and take my own man Wat Cairnie as well as the royal men-at-arms.'

'Done,' the queen said. 'Go and fetch your man, and ask him to saddle your mare for you. Livingston, find one of my heavy mantles . . . the blue one, I think. You shall go with the party as well, for appearance's sake. My Lord Moray, please arrange for the men-at-arms to be assembled. Lady Huntly's messenger will have to be kept from riding ahead to warn her, so see he is guarded. 'Sieur Nico, you and I shall have some music to while away the time until dinner.'

She put one hand on Nicolas de Clerac's arm, caressing him

quite openly. The Earl of Moray's frown was angry enough to curdle new milk, but he could do little but bow and obey his sister's direct command. I curtseyed politely and turned to go as well.

'Take care, Mistress Rinette,' Nicolas de Clerac said. From his voice one would never have known it made any difference in the world to him that he had suggested this in the first place, or that his suggestion had turned out so unexpectedly. 'The going will be – dangerously slippery – in this rain.'

And so I rode out of Aberdeen towards the north-west, rain and all, my beautiful Lilidh tossing her head and dancing like the windblown white lily she was named for. The queen's blue mantle wrapped me warmly and rippled like a pennon over Lilidh's haunches. Wat Cairnie rode beside me, with Lady Huntly's messenger on a discreet leading-rein; Mary Livingston rode on my other side, her own cheeks flushed with excitement. Twelve of the queen's men-at-arms followed, armed with halberds and with the red lion of Scotland on their coats. If Lady Huntly had posted spies along the way from Aberdeen to the chapel of Saint Mary's at Stoneywood, they would certainly have returned to her with the news that it was the queen herself on a lily-white mare, trotting beside the River Don.

We came up to the chapel after an easy hour's ride. The rain had stopped and I saw a group of women standing in the corner of the churchyard. I had a quick impression of grass, yellow and brown, starred with a few white gillyflowers and a surprisingly late blue violet or two; moss on the walls, ancient and velvety, golden-green. A gnarled plum tree overlooked the wall, its blossoms long past and its fruit mostly fallen. I felt a wave of affection, fidelity, loyalty – but not from the women. Not human, even. Frightened—

They all turned at the sound of riders. I recognised the Countess of Huntly by her rich clothing and her light-coloured, protruding eyes. I had seen her from a distance at Lord James' – the Earl of Moray's – wedding, although I had not been presented to her and so she would not know me. The three women with her were in plain dark dresses and muffled up around their necks and faces with shawls, although all three of them had their heads bare and their hair loose to the wind and rain. They looked like witches out of a folktale. One of them was holding a terrified hound puppy by the scruff of its neck.

That was the source of the fear. That was the love and loyalty. The puppy whimpered and it felt like an arrow straight into my heart.

'Madame!' Lady Huntly cried, seeing only the blue mantle and the red lions and Mary Livingston. She swept a magnificent curtsey, no easy thing considering the wet, muddy ground of the churchyard. It was a signal, because a good dozen men came swarming out of the little chapel, two of them grasping for Lilidh's bridle while the rest brandished dirks and cudgels at the queen's men-at-arms. The men-at-arms levelled their halberds.

Lilidh threw her head back. I could feel her muscles bunching under me and hear the angry swish of her tail.

'Hold!' I cried. 'I am not the queen. Call off your men.'

Everyone froze. I put back my hood.

'Holy Mother of God,' Lady Huntly said. She sounded more exasperated than angry. 'I told Huntly the queen would not fall into so simple a trap. And who are you, young woman? You look familiar. Donal, Calum, all of you, stand back.'

'I am Marina Leslie of Granmuir. The queen asked me to—'

'The Leslie girl. Of course. The one who was married to Glenlithie.'

'Yes.'

'The one who thinks to trade Mary of Guise's silver casket for her husband's murderer.'

'So the gossips say.' She might think the silver casket worth a random bit of prisoner-taking in itself, so I did not dismount immediately. I said, 'Swear me safe passage, my lady, in front of my men and your own.'

She looked up at me for a few moments, and I could see the calculation in her eyes. A formidable woman, Elizabeth Keith, Countess of Huntly – I was reminded unpleasantly of Lady Margaret Erskine. Lady Huntly did not have the remnants of great beauty as Lady Margaret did but perhaps she was all the more dangerous because of it; she would have learned to win her battles without the easy weapon of good looks. She was waiting for me to move, look away, show fear in any way. I sat straight and still in my saddle and stared back at her.

'Very well, I swear it,' she said at last. 'Hear me, all of you – Mistress Marina Leslie and her train are to have full safe passage back to Aberdeen, after they bide here a while.'

The men murmured and nodded. One or two struck up conversations with their erstwhile opponents, the queen's men. They probably knew each other, and more than likely some of them were cousins. I glanced at Wat – *I will keep my een upon them all*, his expression said, *never you fear* – and then slid out of my saddle. I was as safe as I would ever be, and I stepped forward boldly to face Lady Huntly.

'Alexander Gordon of Glenlithie,' I said. 'You knew him. He was blood kin to the Earl of Huntly.'

'I knew him,' Lady Huntly said. I could see she was wary; she had expected me to launch into a message from the queen. 'And yes, he was kin to the earl.'

'Do you know who killed him?'

'Now why would I know that?'

'You were in Edinburgh for the queen's arrival. You and your husband.'

She turned and walked away from me, towards the three women by the wall. I followed her. Once I got close enough I realised there was a wellhead there, built up against the wall. It was made of a single half-circle of stone, carved with what might have been faces. Saints? Angels? Pictish goddesses? They were so ancient it was impossible to be certain. The well was full, and the water's surface glassy as a mirror but for where it was pocked every few moments by a raindrop.

'Do you know what this is?' Lady Huntly said.

'This? The well? No. I know the chapel is called Saint Mary's of Stoneywood.'

'This is a Holy Well. There is a spring that feeds it – it has been here since the days of the Picts, at least, and certainly long before the chapel was built. There is an old tale that if you give it a sacrifice, it will show you the future.'

I did not like that word *sacrifice*.

'It is not the future I wish to learn about, my lady,' I said. 'It is the night Alexander Gordon of Glenlithie was murdered, a little over a year ago.'

'There is little I can tell you. Question the queen's servants at Holyrood – they will tell you Huntly and I arrived at the palace with the queen and stayed through the night. We were not out in the city, either one of us.'

She sounded so scornful she was almost certainly telling the truth. I would, however, question the queen's servants when we returned to Edinburgh.

'What, then, do you wish to tell the queen?' I asked. 'That your husband and your son have reconsidered their outlawry?'

She laughed. The witches laughed with her, like three eerie echoes.

'Certainly not,' she said at last. 'Listen to me, Mistress, and repeat what I say to the queen, word for word. She is just a girl, and a Frenchwoman in all but birth – she understands nothing of Scotland, and has allowed herself to fall too far into the power of her bastard brother and his Protestant Lords. Here in the north we are true Catholics and true Scots. She would be better off taking advice from Huntly, and making James Stewart the outlaw.'

'He is the Earl of Moray now.'

'He is not. Moray has belonged to the Gordons for a hundred years, and we will not give it up. We will fight for it, and for Huntly's rightful place as the queen's chief advisor.'

'Fight!' cried one of the witch-women, a gnarled creature with a single glittering eye. 'There is fighting coming, war and blood and death.'

'Blood and death!' the others echoed.

'I see!' This was the woman with the trembling puppy. 'There will be a battle, and afterwards the Earl of Huntly will take his rest without a wound upon his body, in a soft bed in the heart of Aberdeen.'

'Make the sacrifice, Beathag,' Lady Huntly said. 'I would see this thing for certain. We shall show Mistress Leslie as well, so she can describe it to the queen.'

The woman lifted the puppy by the scruff of its neck again. It yelped with pain and fear. The sound jolted me into action. That poor puppy, skin and bones, huge dark eyes, four freckled white paws flailing helplessly, was to be the sacrifice. I leaped forward and caught it in my arms just as the witch-woman threw it into the well.

In its terror it bit me.

I cried out, surprised more than hurt.

The witch-woman screamed invective at me in old Scots and reached out to take the puppy back. Her nails were long as a cat's claws, yellow and filthy. I tried to hold on to the puppy, but it was squirming and struggling and yelping – definitely hound blood, I thought inconsequentially, from the sound of it – and managed to wriggle out of my arms. It landed on the rain-softened ground, already running.

I felt a rush of sadness so intense it made me dizzy. I wanted to run after the poor little creature. I wanted to feed it, bathe it, dry it with soft cloths, keep it warm, give it a fine leather collar with a silver plate engraved with the sea-wave badge of Granmuir. I wanted it to be mine. But it was gone.

At least it was free.

'I want nothing to do with your witchcraft,' I said. I was panting, my thumb was throbbing where the poor pup had sunk in its teeth, and anger made it almost impossible for me to form coherent words. 'How dare you – how dare you!'

'You are as much a witch as they are,' Lady Huntly said calmly. 'Enough, Beathag, you have seen what you have seen. Huntly will take Aberdeen city from the queen, by force of arms if need be. He has a thousand Highlanders at his back, and we will make Scotland a Catholic country again. Go and tell her that, Marina Leslie.'

'You cannot seriously believe you can take Aberdeen, even with a thousand men?'

'The queen's forces will abandon her. Beathag has seen that. Janet and Meggie One-Eye have seen it as well. Now go. Do not think it is impossible for you yourself to become a sacrifice, here at the Holy Well.'

For a moment there was nothing but silence. Even the horses were still, and the birds in the trees around us.

'I'd like to see ye try it.' That was Wat Cairnie, edging his rough brown cob between us so that Lady Huntly was forced to step back. 'I'll cut ye in collops first, my lady, and your spaewives as well, and the queen's men will back me. Mount up, Rinette, and we'll be off.'

The queen's men-at-arms had lifted their halberds again, and Lady Huntly's men fell back, guarding their own mistress. I chirruped to Lilidh and she came up behind me, thrusting her velvet nose under my hand. I turned to mount and saw a flicker of red-and-white in the brush.

'Stand, Lilidh,' I said. I chirruped again. The filthy, emaciated hound puppy with its freckled white paws and russet ears crawled out of the brush and over the grass, its belly close to the ground. I crouched down and held out my hands.

'Come, little one,' I said.

It sniffed my fingers and looked up at me with liquid dark eyes. I wrapped it in the queen's blue mantle, mud and all. It pressed close to me, trembling, its heart beating fast. One of the queen's men offered me his interlaced hands, and I stepped up into Lilidh's saddle one-handed.

'It is meant for a sacrifice!' It was the witch-woman Beathag, in her high keening voice. 'It will be bad luck to you, girl. Leave it here, or you will rue it.'

'You are wrong,' I said. 'Here I see a plum tree for faithfulness, and gillyflowers for devotion, and a blue violet out of season for loyalty beyond measure. That is what this little dog will bring me.'

'You are a fool, Marina Leslie,' said Elizabeth Keith, Countess of Huntly. 'A tender-hearted fool. Take the puppy, and see what tomorrow brings.'

'I will take it,' I said. Lilidh needed no reins; I could guide her with my knees. 'I will tell the queen what you have said. And do not trust what your familiars have told you about tomorrow.'

* * *

The puppy was a male. When he was washed, he turned out to have long silky ears of a russet colour, a black marking on his back, and the freckled paws that had melted my heart. Other than being half-starved, he seemed healthy enough, and probably of a good bloodline of hunting hounds; how he had come into the hands of Lady Huntly's witch I would never know. I tied a blue ribbon around his neck to mark him as my own until I could have a proper leather collar made. Wat, who for all his size and rough appearance was soft-hearted as an old woman with animals of any sort, named him Seilie, which he said meant 'lucky' in his grannie's Fifeshire dialect, with connotations of 'innocent' and 'blessed' – perfect for an innocent creature saved from drowning in a Holy Well. Lucky the puppy was in both senses – he himself was fortunate we had come along when we did, and despite the witch's threat I felt he would bring good fortune to me one day as well.

I left Seilie with Wat in the stable: clean, dry, stuffed with meat and bread, and sound asleep on a warm blanket. I tidied myself as best I could with Jennet helping me and scolding me for my recklessness, then went to wait upon the queen.

Mary Livingston had arrived before me, and was still recounting the tale of Lady Huntly's three familiars, the Holy Well, and my rescue of Seilie. The women were breathless with excitement. When I made my curtsey before the queen, she called me closer at once and commanded me to tell the whole tale again, from the beginning.

'It would be better, I think, sister,' said the Earl of Moray from a carved chair on the other side of the room, 'if Mistress Rinette told us exactly what Lady Huntly had to say about this business of battles and armies and our own men turning their coats.'

'Oh, very well,' the queen said. 'Beaton, more wine, please.

We shall put aside witches and puppies and converse seriously about war.'

'None of it seemed to have any basis in fact, Madame,' I said. 'Lady Huntly clearly sets great store by her familiars, and it was only in their visions that the Earl of Huntly won a battle for Aberdeen, with the royal troops deserting to join him.'

'What did the flowers say?'

'There was a plum tree, past its flowering, and a blue violet out of season—' I broke off. All the flowers I had seen had been related to Seilie. I could not remember one flower, one leaf, one stem,that might tell me whether Lady Huntly and her witch-woman familiars were right or wrong.

Or were the flowers amusing themselves with double meanings at my expense?

'What does it mean?' the queen persisted.

'The plum tree stands for fidelity,' I said. 'And the blue violet for loyalty. I believe your troops will be loyal, Madame. As for the rest, the prediction that the Earl of Huntly will lie tomorrow night here in Aberdeen – I cannot tell you.'

'There is more than one way to interpret that.' It was Nicolas de Clerac, stepping into the supper-room with a lute in his hand. 'And as for fidelity, and loyalty—' He looked at me. I could see that he had been afraid for me, and was relieved that I was safe.

'Fidelity and loyalty,' he said again, 'are very good things, wherever one might find them.'

18

T he queen had put on her favourite boy's clothes, her purple velvet doublet and long silken hose and feathered hat, and was ready to go to war.

'Madame,' said Nico de Clerac, his face carefully expressionless. 'It is cold. Raining. Your velvet will be spoiled and the colour of your hose will run.'

'Fetch me a proper leather jacket, then,' she said. 'And a broadsword and a buckler.' She made imaginary sword-passes in the air, turning and pointing her toes as if she were dancing a courante. 'And boots.'

'You could not even lift a broadsword,' Mary Fleming said. She always begged off when the queen went masquerading in boy's clothes, but then her lush feminine figure did not show to its best advantage in doublet and hose. "Sieur Nico, please do not encourage her. It is bad enough that the men must go out in the rain and kill each other over who gets to call whom by what title.'

'You have a refreshingly simple view of war, Mademoiselle Flaminia,' Nico said. 'I assure you, I am not encouraging the queen to risk her lovely neck on the battlefield. Her loyal troops—'

He paused and smiled at me. I was also dressed in boy's clothes, and although I did not have the queen's graceful height, I thought

I carried off the jacket and breeches reasonably well. I had no desire to be anywhere near a battle but the queen could not possibly go out among the soldiers without some other ladies present. Seilie lay at my feet with his muzzle resting on his freckled paws.

'Her loyal troops,' Nico said again, 'as foreseen by Mistress Rinette, will manage the fighting for her, and bring her back the Earl of Huntly and his sons in chains.'

'But I want to see the battle.' The queen put her hand on Nico's arm and pulled until he turned to face her. 'I have never seen a battle, and I am Queen of Scots – it is my *devoir* to ride on to the battlefield at the head of my army.'

'God forbid.' Mary Fleming crossed herself.

'I am ready to ride with you, Madame,' I said.

'I am as well.' Mary Livingston's clothes were more practical than the queen's, being chequered wool in the Livingston colours of red and green. She made a stout-looking boy. 'Monsieur de Chastelard will be waiting for us in the High Street.'

'Not Chastelard,' Nico said.

'But of course Chastelard,' the queen said. Her eyes sparkled. 'He has only just returned from France, and made his way instantly to Aberdeen. He wishes to see me ride with my soldiers, so he can compose true songs about it.'

'Madame.' I could tell Nico's patience was wearing thin. 'You may observe. From a distance. That is the Earl of Moray's order, and the order of all your council.'

'I could outride you.'

'You could attempt to do so. Please do not compel me to commit the very great *lèse-majesté* of binding you and conveying you back to Aberdeen on a leading-rein.'

The queen looked at him through her eyelashes. 'You would do it, too, would you not, 'Sieur Nico?'

'I would.'

'Let us go, then.'

She went out, striding like a man. She was certainly correct about one thing: a doublet and hose were much more comfortable than the endless stays and bodices, partlets and sleeves, underskirts and overskirts, we women were compelled to wear. She knew her long legs were slim and straight and perfect, and that every man in the army would be looking at them. Chastelard would compose songs to her beauty and courage, and that was enough for her.

The Earl of Huntly and his Gordons had taken the high ground on a rise called the Hill of Fare, overlooking Corrichie Burn. I kept Lilidh well back, but the queen rode boldly to the front and stood in her stirrups, straining to pick out the figure of Sir John Gordon: so handsome, so gallant, such a lusty dancer. The royal forces, commanded by the Earl of Moray, were ranged on the other side of the burn, on a rising ground.

'When will it start?' the queen cried. ''Sieur Nico, can I not go closer?'

'You will stay where you are, Madame,' Nico said. His voice was sharper than I had ever heard it, at least in addressing the queen. 'Do you understand men will soon fight and die on that hill? They will die in truth, with all their sins unshriven, and not come back when the battle is over to bow and accept your compliments for their fine performances.'

'How disagreeable you are, 'Sieur Nico,' the queen replied sulkily.

She turned to Pierre de Chastelard, who was at her other side, mounted on a fine sorrel gelding which had been her own gift to him. He was not looking at her, but deeply engaged in conversation with the wiry pale-eyed Frenchman Blaise Laurentin. They had their heads together like lovers, and I could not help but wonder how Chastelard would write odes to the queen's gallantry if he was devoting his attention to another.

'What say you, Monsieur de Chastelard?' the queen asked sharply. 'I would like to see Sir John Gordon call out my brother in single combat – you could write a great ode about the two of them, in the style of Ronsard.'

Just then there was a shriek of pipes and a sudden shouting, and one group of horsemen broke away from the Earl of Moray's forces, charging over the burn and up the hill towards the Gordons. The queen cried out, 'For Scotland! For Scotland! For your queen!' Her horse threw up its head and skittered from side to side; Nico reached out and caught its rein.

Moray's men engaged the Gordons only briefly, then retreated, galloping back down the hill. The queen cried, 'No! No! Do not run away! Cowards!' But it soon became clear that this was a deliberate tactic. The Gordons unwisely gave chase, and in doing so not only lost the advantage of the high ground, but flung themselves straight on to the lances of the Earl of Moray's vanguard.

From that point it became a mêlée of swords and spears and arquebus-fire; it was impossible to pick out individuals or tell whether the screams were from men or horses. There was no way to be sure who was winning or losing. Nico was white-faced and grim, clearly wishing he could be swinging his own sword with the men; Pierre de Chastelard, on the other hand, was flushed with – what, excitement? Surely he was only delighting in the couplets he was composing in his head, to the gallantry of a queen who rode out to battle.

I could watch it for only a few minutes. It was terrifying – there was so much blood. The horses, the horses . . . for some reason that broke my heart even more than the deaths of the men. They at least knew what they were doing and had chosen to do it – they were Highlanders and Lowlanders, Catholics and Protestants, Gordons and royalists. The horses were innocents, high-hearted and willing for their riders, galloping unknowing into butchery.

I put my head down against Lilidh's neck. 'Not you,' I whispered. 'Never you. Do not look, my Lilidh.'

I pulled on one rein to turn her, and we rode off a little way. I realised I was crying.

Behind me I heard the queen shriek, 'Moray! Forward, Moray!'

I scrubbed my hand across my eyes. My tears did no good. Slowly I guided Lilidh back to the queen's party. She was looking away from the battle – I could read the telltale expression on her face. She was losing interest.

After a moment she said, 'What will happen next, 'Sieur Nico?'

'Next?' Nico smiled at her, showing his teeth. A scowl would have been less frightening. 'There is no "next", Madame. These men will continue to kill and maim each other until the day is over, and one side or the other has prevailed.'

'Over? But it is only midday. I am hungry and thirsty.'

'So are they.'

'It does not matter who wins, does it?' The queen's voice was turning shrill with the effort of making herself heard. 'I will still be queen, no matter which side wins.'

No one said anything to that. We all just looked at her. I wanted to slap her, slap her hard.

'Well, it matters, of course.' The queen tightened her reins and turned her horse back towards Aberdeen. 'The Earl of Huntly would make himself head of my council, and bring back the Catholic church, and the Lords of the Congregation would be outlawed. He would try to marry me off to Lord John, but he would have a surprise there — I will never marry at anyone's bidding but my own. I wish to go back to the city now.'

She set spurs to her horse and cantered away. Nico followed her at once with his cadre of guardsmen. Mary Livingston glanced at me and followed; I turned Lilidh and started after them. Halfway back to Aberdeen a sorrel gelding came up beside me.

'Madame Leslie.' It was Pierre de Chastelard. I looked around for Blaise Laurentin, but could not see him. 'Hold up a moment. I would like to speak to you.'

I drew up. Lilidh danced in a circle. 'I hope you will write fine verses about the battle today,' I said. My voice shook. 'And the queen's bravery.'

He took my words literally and not with the bitterness I'd intended. 'I will,' he said. 'The queen is wonderful. Her favour, however, makes it difficult for me to speak privately with other ladies.'

Holy Saint Ninian. Was he going to declare his love to me?

'You have in your possession a silver casket, do you not, which once belonged to Mary of Guise? I have a commission, from a certain important personage in France, to—'

'Stop!' I said. 'Are you mad, Monsieur? Men are dying in Corrichie Burn. Pray for their souls, and do not dare speak of something so meaningless as the silver casket.'

I saw a flash in his eyes of something calculating, cruel, which one would not expect to see in a poet. 'It is not meaningless,' he said. 'And time is short. I take my opportunities where I find them.'

'I will tell you only what I have told everyone else — Mary of Guise's silver casket is not for sale. Not to anyone.'

'Perhaps one day soon you will change your mind.'

'Perhaps one day soon these hills will cast themselves into the sea.' I wheeled Lilidh round and, touching her flank with my crop, galloped away.

'I forbid this execution to take place.'

The queen was seated before a window on the first floor of the Earl Marischal's town house on Castle Street in Aberdeen, facing the Tolbooth. A low scaffold had been set up in the square, with a wooden block heaped all around with straw. A Protestant minister stood beside the scaffold, reciting verses of Scripture from memory; at intervals the crowd shouted responses. It was cold and rainy, but in general a holiday mood prevailed.

Mary Livingston and I sat on either side of the queen, doing our best to calm her. Her sleeves were disarranged where the Earl of Moray had held her arms to compel her to sit here at the window where everyone in the square could see her. The fact that he had actually laid hands upon her royal person showed how far up in his own estimation he had vaulted.

'I forbid it,' she said again. 'I am the queen.'

'You are a fool, sister,' Moray said. 'Now be silent.'

It had been five days since the battle by Corrichie Burn. Moray's forces – the queen's forces, actually, although clearly he thought of them as his own – had crushed the Gordons and their Highlanders. The great Earl of Huntly himself, the Cock of the North, had been saved from an ignominious traitor's death only by falling down dead of an apoplexy while still in his armour – I had heard the story from Mary Livingston, who had heard it from her sweetheart John Sempill, who had been present to see it. Young Sir John Gordon, the gallant, the dancer, the brawler, had been captured and condemned to die, here and now for everyone in Aberdeen to see, for his own rebellion and his father's.

'I will not be silent,' the queen said. 'I wish I had never made you Earl of Moray. I can unmake you, brother, remember that.'

'Try it,' Moray said. There was dismissive scorn in his voice. 'You may find I can unmake you as queen just as easily.'

She began to cry again. Anyone could see her tears were from anger and frustration and outrage that she was being compelled to do something she did not wish to do. Death at a distance, in a battle, with flags flying and faces unrecognisable, was one thing; death up close, of a handsome young man she had known and danced with and flirted with, was a different thing entirely.

'My Lord Moray,' I said. I tried to sound humble. 'Please be gentler with the queen. You want her here so the people can see she condones the decision to execute Sir John, do you not? If she is in tears and hysterics, it will hardly prove your point.'

'It will in fact prove,' said Nicolas de Clerac, who was standing a little distance behind the rest of us, 'that you have ordered this execution, my Lord Moray, upon your own authority and without the queen's agreement.'

'I do not agree to it,' the queen said through her sobs. 'Imprison Sir John if you must, strip him of all his lands and titles, exile him – but spare him his life.'

'He took up arms against the crown,' Moray said. 'People say he wished to marry you, sister, and that you encouraged him because he is a Catholic. We must show them this is not true, that you do not care for him, and that you do not intend to marry a Catholic and force them all back to the old Church.'

'Surely he does not have to be executed, to prove that.'

'Surely he does. Some whisper that you lay with him.'

The queen's tears stopped between one sob and the next. 'That is a lie,' she said. 'How dare you—'

At that moment there was a wail of pipes, and a company of men wearing royal badges on their coats stepped out of the Tolbooth and into the square. Sir John Gordon walked in their midst, dressed all in black and with his head bare. His hands were tied behind him with thick rope, which was also looped several times around his chest and upper arms. He looked up and immediately saw the queen at the window.

'Madame!' he cried out. 'It is for you I am to suffer – for the sake of the delights we shared, will you not pardon me?'

The crowd immediately began to whisper. The queen stared at Sir John, frozen with humiliation and horror. I thought, He is using the moment to take his revenge upon her, in the only way left to him.

'There were no delights,' she said. 'It is a lie. There were only dances, nothing more.'

Moray gestured to the men, who dragged Sir John up on to the scaffold. The minister spoke more loudly than ever, exhorting the prisoner to repent of his Catholic faith and embrace the true church of God. Sir John waved the man away – he said something we could not hear, but which left a shocked expression on the minister's face.

The soldiers forced Sir John to his knees in the straw, in front of the block. He managed to lift his head one more time and look straight into the queen's eyes.

'It gives me solace,' he cried loudly, 'that you are here, for I am to suffer for loving you, Madame. Pray the prayers of the True Church for me!'

With a grand gesture – a gallant and a showman to the last – he laid his head down upon the block. The executioner, who had come up the other side of the scaffold, swung back his axe. The crowd screamed; the blade came down in a huge gleaming arc and sank into Sir John's shoulder, flesh and bone, with the ghastly chunking sound of a butcher's cleaver splitting a loin of beef in half. There was no blood at first. The executioner swore and jerked the axe free and bright red blood gushed out.

The queen lurched up from her chair, her hands pressed to her mouth, screaming.

Sir John's body shuddered and strained to one side – his eyes were open and he seemed to look directly at the queen one last time. His lips moved.

The executioner swung the axe again and it made a clean crunching slice through Sir John's neck. The head bounced into the straw; the bound and wounded body dropped behind the block, the neck spurting thin streams of blood out over the crowd.

The queen screamed and screamed. I held her hands, trying to drag her away from the window. Nico put his own hands over her face, covering her eyes. The Earl of Moray stood impassively. The contrast between his kingly composure and the queen's hysteria was so pronounced it might have been planned that way.

'Madame, Madame,' I cried. I was so sickened myself I could hardly hold her. 'Come away, Madame, do not look.'

The queen fainted. Nico caught her up in his arms. I could not help remembering he had once lifted me in the same way, when I had been screaming and fainting and covered with my husband's blood.

'Can you make calming remedies from your flowers, Mistress Rinette?' he asked.

'Yes.'

'Then do so. We will need them.'

19

The best anodyne for the queen's collapse would have been her own flowers, but needless to say there were no peonies blooming in Aberdeen in November. In the kitchen garden of the Earl Marischal's house I found a few remaining green leaves of marjoram, thyme and valerian; pounded together with honey and steeped in wine, they made a soothing drink.

She refused it.

For two days she spent her time either crying and throwing things, or huddled under the coverlets in her bed with her eyes squeezed shut, refusing to speak to anyone. Eventually I burned the herbs in a copper warming pan, so a faint blue haze of sweet smoke filled her room, and tucked sprigs of thyme under her pillow to give her restful sleep and ward off nightmares. The leaves whispered to me that most of the queen's frenzy was play-acting, although a strange kind of playacting that she herself half-believed to be real. I think she needed to convince herself that she had not been complicit in Sir John's terrible death.

The Earl of Moray, meanwhile, calmly went about the business of dismantling the Huntly family's possessions and powers in the north. He stripped Strathbogie Castle of its riches and bundled it all into carts, some to be taken to Edinburgh in the queen's name but most to be sent to his own newly acquired castle of

Darnaway. The Earl of Huntly's body was not decently entombed among his ancestors at Elgin Cathedral but packed in spices and vinegar like a ham and sent off to Edinburgh by sea. Our ancient law called for him to be present, living or dead, at his trial before Parliament for treason against the queen.

I wondered what had become of Lady Huntly and the rest of her children – the Earl Marischal, in whose town house we were staying, was her brother; presumably he had provided for her. I wondered what had become of the three witch-women. They had been right in at least part of their prediction – the Earl of Huntly had lain in Aberdeen the night after the battle, without a mark upon his body. Dead, of course, from his apoplexy – but unmarked.

Seilie was happily unaware of such great matters. He followed me everywhere, and was beside me in the garden, watching me pick more thyme, at the moment Nico de Clerac came to join me. We had not had a chance to speak together since the execution and the queen's collapse. I was not sure how I felt about him – we had found a strange closeness in the garden at Granmuir, and yet since he had returned from France he had been distant, clearly focusing all his energies on re-establishing his influence over the queen.

I wondered if I should tell him about Chastelard's hasty offer on the road from Corrichie. I was not sure if he wished to continue helping me or not.

'She seems a little better,' he said.

'I believe she is.'

'I wish you had not been forced to witness the execution. Or the battle. You have seen too much blood, Rinette.'

I crossed myself. He was right. And at the same time the way he said my name told me he still cared what became of me, still wanted to help me.

'Something happened on the battlefield,' I said. 'Or at least, as we were riding back to Aberdeen.'

Nico crouched down and scratched Seilie's silken ears. The puppy rubbed his face against Nico's knee and made a happy little groaning sound.

'What happened?' he said. 'I am sorry you were left behind – I did not dare let the queen out of my sight.'

'Chastelard the poet . . . He tried to bargain for the silver casket. We were riding away from a battlefield, and he tried to bargain with me.'

Nico picked up a fallen twig and tossed it across the garden. Seilie bounded away after it. 'I wonder who his patron is. There are two parties in France with reason to seek the casket – Queen Catherine de' Medici, of course, and the Huguenots. The casket would be of little value to them in itself, but Queen Catherine wants it desperately – it would give them something to bargain with.'

He did not mention the third party vying for power in France: the Guises. Of course, if he himself was a Guise agent, he would be reasonably certain that Chastelard was not.

'He said only that he represented a certain important personage,' I said. 'And that time was short. The Huguenots have just lost Rouen to the Catholics, have they not? It makes sense they would be urgently in need of some way to put pressure on Queen Catherine.'

Seilie brought back the stick. Nico took it and threw it again. 'You are well informed,' he said.

'The Earl of Moray and the council have been holding their meetings at the queen's bedside. One learns all sorts of things.'

He smiled. 'I am sure one does,' he said. 'Very well, so we can add the Huguenots to our list of possible murderers. That would mean either Coligny or Condé, and neither one of them would draw the line at assassination if it furthered their cause.'

'Have you anything new to add?' I asked. I had collected enough thyme for the moment, and I rose to my feet. The herb's leafy, astringent scent surrounded me. Seilie had kept the stick this time, and was running around the garden holding it, his tail straight up with triumph. 'I must get back to the queen.'

'I have nothing new,' he said. 'But I shall look into this business of Chastelard. If he is under pressure enough to approach you as he did, you can be sure he will try again.'

On the third morning the queen grew bored with herself, for she sat up, called for bread sopped in wine, and a bath and clean clothes, and took up her life again. We arrived back in Edinburgh in time for the Octave of Saint Martin on the twenty-first day of November, and had only just settled in when the queen took to her bed again, this time suffering from a real sickness – fever, coughing, fatigue and wretched aches and pains. Several people in her close circle had the same symptoms. It instantly became the fashion to be sick with what people wryly called the New Acquaintance.

I did not have time for fashion. The queen was a difficult patient and kept all of us running back and forth, up and down her tower stairs, for soups, syllabubs, embroidery silks, clean night-gowns and basins of scented water. Mary Fleming soon fell sick as well, then Mary Beaton, then even stout Mary Livingston. Mary Seton spent most of her time in the royal chapel praying to Saint Geneviève and Saint Pétronille, two French saints who were unfailing proof against fevers; this may have made her feel better but did little to make things easier for the rest of us. Doctor Lusgerie, the queen's French physician, recommended bleeding and purging of the bowels to remove the excess humours that were causing the fever and ague; the queen agreed to the bleeding but refused the purging, for modesty's sake.

It was cold, grey and damp. Flurries of snow left a lacework of white in the gardens. The windows froze shut so it was impossible to get any fresh air. I was lonely – I missed Màiri and Tante-Mar. Jennet More and Wat Cairnie watched over me faithfully, first the one, then the other. My one other companion was Seilie; he was still a puppy and only beginning to learn proper indoor manners, but fortunately his enormous brown eyes, velvet-soft russet ears and freckled paws melted every heart. Even the queen welcomed him on her embroidered counterpane.

As the days passed I myself began to feel stiff and sore and alternately hot and cold, but who would not feel hot and cold, going in and out of the queen's oven-like bedchamber with its three fires, and the icy corridors of Holyrood Palace with no heat at all? One morning – I think it was a morning, although it may have been an afternoon – I found myself so overcome by vertigo and headache that I had to sit down, and sit down I did, on the floor halfway along the corridor between the kitchen and the queen's tower, with a bowl of manchet bread and sweetened milk in my hands. It did not seem strange to me. Seilie was happy at first and gobbled up all the bread and milk; then he began to whimper. The sound took me back to Saint Mary's of Stoneywood. I wondered what Lady Huntly's three witch-women were doing at Holyrood, and I was particularly determined they would not drown my precious Seilie in their holy well.

'Go away,' I said. 'You cannot have him. He is mine now.'

'You stole him from us.' It was the woman Beathag, her voice like the crackling of dead leaves underfoot. 'If the sacrifice had been made the Cock of the North would be king in all but name, and Sir John would be wedded and bedded with the queen instead of mouldering headless in his grave.'

'One puppy?' I said. 'To make such a difference?'

'One life. 'Tis the life that makes the spell, and it matters not if it's a wee hoond-dog or a man full-grown and in his prime. You stole the life and you changed it all.'

I could feel Seilie struggling in my arms. I could feel the presence of another person.

'Go away!' I screamed. 'Seilie, no!'

He wriggled free. I heard his claws click on the flagstones, then silence, as if someone had picked him up. I began to cry. I felt so hot that my tears felt cold on my cheeks.

'Shush. It is all right, *ma mie*. Your little hound is perfectly safe. But I think you should be in bed, and that the physician should see you.'

I knew that voice. I knew who called me his *mie*. I felt so dreadful that it was actually a comfort to be someone's *mie*.

'Nico,' I said. 'I think I am going to die.'

'You are not going to die.' I heard Seilie's claws clicking on the stones again, and was glad the witch-woman had let him go.

'Lady Huntly's familiars are here,' I said. 'They want to sacrifice Seilie.'

'They are gone.' Hands, light but strong, hooked themselves under my arms and pulled me to my feet. I staggered and the arms lifted me, cradling me at shoulders and knees. I sighed and curled myself against an embroidered doublet and a shirt that smelled of bitter orange and myrrh.

'I am going to die,' I said again. 'I thought I was going to die before and you were there, too. You lifted me up just like this.'

'So I did.'

'Why are you here? How do you always know where I am?'

He began to walk. Seilie clicked along beside us.

'Rinette, *ma mie*, I always know where you are. Do you think I have not watched you, since that first terrible night? I have seen you cry with the most heartrending anguish over your husband's dead body, and I have seen you defy the queen to demand justice for him. I have seen you with your daughter, and the love devouring you like a flame. I have seen you dance, and I have seen you ride, and I have seen you with your flowers, in your garden by the sea. My beautiful girl. My beautiful, beautiful girl.'

He bent his head and I felt his lips touch one corner of my mouth, so gently, so softly, I might have imagined it.

'You are burning up with fever,' he said. 'I am bound by a holy vow and have no right to say it, but you will not remember. *Je t'aime, ma mie.*'

'I will remember.' His words were running together and I could make no sense of them, but it made me indignant that he thought I would not remember. 'I remembered when you carried me before, in the High Street.'

'Shhh! I will find the physician, and take care of your little hound for you. Better that you forget that night in the High Street forever.'

I was back in the High Street of Edinburgh and Alexander was walking beside me. The August night was warm and humid . . .

'Make way!' Alexander cried. 'This lady is ill. Make way—'

He broke off with a strange sound, half-shriek, half-exhalation. His arm fell away from my waist and he lurched to one side. I staggered and opened my eyes and saw a flood of glistening black in the torchlight, spurting, bursting from his throat . . .

'I must bleed her. She is full of choleric humours.'

'No. She is too weak.'

Jennet. Faithful Jennet. I could also hear the high yaps of a puppy. Long russet-red ears and freckled paws. My Seilie. The witch-women hadn't taken him.

'A purge, then.'

'You fool of a physicker, she's been vomiting for three days! She needs water, only water, a few drops at a time so she can retain it. Meat broth if we can coax her.'

Were they talking about me? Vomiting for three days? Was that why my back ached and my belly hurt?

I staggered and opened my eyes and saw a flood of glistening black in the torchlight, spurting, bursting from his throat. Slow, slow, everything was unnaturally slow. I could see the hand with the dagger, and I could see the dagger's guard, gold worked in a design of outspread wings. The pommel was in the shape of a falcon's head with faceted rubies for eyes. As I watched, one ruby broke free and traced a shining, tumbling arc into the deep terrible wound the blade was slicing . . .

'You must ask her where she has hidden the casket.' A woman's voice. Not one of the witch-women, someone else.

I felt so sick, so sick.

'She is too weak to be questioned, Lady Margaret.'

'She is dying, Monsieur de Clerac. The physician has given her up. There is not another living soul who knows where she has hidden the casket and unless someone gets the truth from her soon it will be lost forever. Question her. My son will reward you richly.'

'No. If she is to die, at least she can die in peace.'

The torch rolled and struck flashes of light off the guard and pommel of a sword, slicing through the air in a circle and creating a magic space of safety around me. Gilding, scrollwork, silver inlay. A hand in a black leather glove. Hair like fire. Angel or demon?

Somewhere a bell rang. It was all so slow this time that I could actually listen to it. It was the third watch. Midnight.

The pain in my belly was tearing me apart . . .

I opened my eyes. Blessed Saint Ninian, but I was thirsty! I did not have the strength to turn my head or lift my hand. But the fever was gone, the terrible ague was gone, my head was clear and I was alive.

I waited a while, collecting my strength. Then I turned my head a little. Sitting in a heavy carved chair beside the bed was Jennet More.

'Rinette!' she cried. 'Oh, Holy Mary be thanked!'

She jumped up and poured wine into a cup. Gently she lifted my shoulders and held the cup to my lips. The wine was watered, tepid and stale, but nothing, nothing had ever tasted so ambrosially delicious before.

'We despaired for you,' she said. 'You've been out of your mind with the ague for days.'

'I heard—' I began. I swallowed more of the wine and tried again. 'I heard you – arguing with the doctor.'

'He's a fool, and 'tis a good thing I was here to argue with him.'

'Who else – here with me?' I remembered other voices but could not sort them out. I remembered being told I would not remember something, and being quite indignant about it. But whatever I had vowed to remember was gone.

'Well, the doctor, of course. Wat came up every day. We would've sent to Granmuir for Madame Loury and little Màiri, but the weather's been so bad it would not have been safe for them to try the journey. You had some grand visitors – Lady Margaret Erskine for one, and the Earl of Moray with her. Moray is out of favour with the queen now over the whole business of forcing her to execute Sir John Gordon in Aberdeen. That Chastelard fellow, the poet, when the queen would let him out of her sight – very grand he's become. Oh, and even Monsieur Nico de Clerac, who brought Seilie with him. He said he thought the wee doggie would do you more good than all the doctor's medicines, and he was right.'

I tried to put the names together with the voices. It was all so jumbled.

'I had such dreams,' I said.

'That's the fever. Do you think you can eat? A little meat broth or some plain custard?'

'Dreams,' I said again. 'I dreamed of the night – the night Alexander was killed. Something reminded me. I saw it all again. It was as if it was happening again. I remember things now, things I'd forgotten before.'

'Oh, Rinette. I'm so sorry.'

'Do not be sorry.' I could see the assassin's dagger clearly, the guard etched with the design of outspread wings, the falcon's head on the pommel with its missing ruby eye. And I remembered the bells I'd heard – the bells of the third watch. A time. If anyone could account for himself in some other place at midnight on the night the queen came home, I would know he was not the murderer.

'I will eat,' I said. 'Where is Seilie now?'

She laughed. 'He's with the queen,' she said. 'You know how she loves him. She has to keep him on a leash, though, because he wants nothing but to find you and be with you.'

'I want him.'

'I'll get him, and fetch you some decent wine and a custard to eat. Rest now.'

She gave me another swallow of the wine in the cup, then ran out; I could hear her calling to someone in the corridor. I closed my eyes and thought about my fine visitors. Lady Margaret Erskine would have wanted to know where the casket was hidden; she had asked me the same question when I had lain, sick and weak, after Màiri's birth. The Earl of Moray would have come with his mother. Perhaps he had thought the gift of Mary of Guise's silver casket would be a fine way to regain the queen's favour. Chastelard – yes, he wanted the casket too.

So the Earl of Moray was out of favour for forcing the issue of Sir John's Gordon's execution. Good. I would use his misfortune against him. In the queen's own presence I would ask him to show me his dagger, and account for his whereabouts at the moment when Alexander was murdered. He would hardly be able to refuse me without appearing guilty and floundering even deeper into the morass of royal displeasure.

To my horror I was as gaunt as poor Seilie had been when I snatched him from the witches' sacrifice. My bones stuck out, my skin was colourless, my hair was dry and thin – much of it had fallen out, Jennet told me, in the course of my fever. I struggled to eat as much as I could – the richest stewed broth with capons, bread-and-ginger sauce with rabbit, sweet Lombard-style rice with chicken and eggs. I was dispensed from Advent fasting and I took the fullest possible advantage of this freedom. Seilie, bless him, never left my feet, which of course might have had something to do with the fact that I was always eating.

After a week or so I felt well enough to rejoin the company of the queen's ladies. Jennet helped me fasten up my bodice; I was still so much thinner that she had to sew me into it. I braided my hair loosely and covered it with a red velvet coif sewn with garnets and crystals, which I borrowed from Mary Beaton. I did not ordinarily wear red but I hoped the rosy colour would reflect a healthy flush on my face.

Jennet and I, with Seilie close behind, made our way up the staircase to the queen's private chambers in the north-west tower. Two tiny round rooms were attached to the inner chamber; from one of them there issued glowing firelight, music and laughter. I went to the doorway.

The queen was seated in a fine carved chair heaped with cushions, plucking the strings of a rosewood-and-ivory lute. Her head was tilted and her lips parted a little in concentration; by the light of the candles and the fire she was as beautiful as a goddess. Mary Livingston and Mary Beaton stood behind her; on her right was the poet Chastelard, dressed in ruby-coloured damask and velvet, leaning over her shoulder and singing in his pleasant tenor voice to her accompaniment. On her left was Nicolas de Clerac. He looked up at once, as if he sensed my presence.

'Mistress Rinette,' he said. His eyes met mine. *I am happy to see you up and about*, they said without words. *You do not look quite so thin. The red headdress becomes you.* All this passed in the space of a breath, and then he retreated behind his courtier's mask. 'Madame, shall we welcome Mistress Rinette back to life, and give her a part to sing?'

I sank into a respectful curtsey. The queen laughed and said, 'Come in, come in. Marianette. They tell me you tended me faithfully when the rest of my ladies could not, and took the New Acquaintance from me – you ended by being the sickest of us all, and I am pleased to see you better.'

It was the most genuinely friendly thing she had said to me since she had returned to Scotland, and for the first time I felt for myself her celebrated allure. I said, 'Thank you, Madame,' stammering a little, and then hated myself for being so easily ensnared.

She only laughed, and turned her attention to her lute again. 'Do you think a chord in C for this next phrase, 'Sieur Pierre?' she said to Chastelard. I was surprised to hear her call him by his Christian name. 'Or perhaps a passage in three-part counterpoint?'

'Sister.'

I jumped. I had not seen the Earl of Moray in the shadowy corner on the other side of the fireplace. Sir William Maitland was with him. The division between the queen's two lives could not have been more vividly expressed – the queen herself in the golden firelight, playing her lute, with ladies to tend her and two handsome gentlemen hanging on her every word, while Moray and Maitland, the two mainstays of her existence as a political figure, were hidden away in darkness.

'We have matters of importance to discuss,' Moray went on. 'Your lute-playing is all very well, but it can wait until tomorrow.'

'I shall play my lute when I please,' the queen said. 'You are quite free to leave our presence, brother, if you are not interested in music.'

So the Earl of Moray had not insinuated himself back into the queen's good graces, and for the moment at least I was high in her favour. I might never have a better opportunity.

'Before you go, my Lord Moray,' I said, 'I would ask you two questions.'

The queen lifted her fingers from the lute's strings. The room fell silent but for the crackling of the flames. They all looked at me.

'With your permission, of course, Madame,' I said.

She laughed. Her eyes glinted in the firelight. 'Ask what you like, Marianette.'

I stepped further into the room, so I was facing Moray. He remained seated, looking up at me with his dark, hooded eyes, so utterly unlike the queen's. Scots he was, down to the bone, Stewart and Erskine without the golden strain of Guise blood that gave the queen her seductive charm. But he was royal, too, for all his bastardy, and he had his own presence.

He frightened me. I would not let it show. I could feel Seilie pressed up against my ankles and it gave me strength to know a living creature loved me.

Loved me . . .

Something fluttered into my mind and out again, a whisper in French, but it was gone before I could capture it. Real? Part of my fever dreams? I could not stop and try to remember it because what was more important was the guard and pommel of a dagger in the shape of a falcon with a missing ruby eye, and the sound of the bells ringing the third watch.

'My Lord Moray,' I said. 'I would like to see your dagger, please.'

Whatever he was expecting, that was not it. His heavy brows drew together in a frown and he said, 'My dagger is none of your concern, Mistress.'

'Show it to her, brother,' the queen said. There was no way she could know why I wanted to see it – only Nicolas de Clerac knew that, and surely he would not be fool enough to say anything – but she was unerring in her sense for the theatrical. 'I command it.'

Moray looked past me at the queen, then back at me. There was no trace of guilt in his expression, just anger that I had trapped him into a humiliating acquiescence. I had made an enemy.

I did not care. I held out my hand.

He removed his dagger from its sheath and gave it to me.

I could see at once that it was not the dagger the assassin had used. The guard was squared off at either end, and decorated with lions' heads in gold. The pommel was gold as well, worked in the shape of a crown. It bore no jewels, and needed none.

'It was my father's,' he said. 'You, Mistress, would do well to remember that the queen's father and my father were the same.'

I handed the dagger back to him.

'Where were you, my lord, at the third watch on the night the queen arrived home from France?'

'Oh!' the queen said. She sounded delighted. 'You believe James murdered your husband! Well, speak up, brother, and tell us where you were.'

Moray's expression grew so black that he could have knocked crows from the sky with his eyes alone. 'I was with you, sister, as you well know.'

'I do not know. You were at Holyrood, yes, but you could easily have gone out and come back.'

It was impossible to tell if she remembered, did not remember, or was simply taking pleasure in taunting her brother.

'I remember,' said Mary Livingston. We all turned and looked at her.

'Well, I do.' She looked defensive. 'We were all awake because of the piping. I was standing beside Lord James – he was not the Earl of Moray then, of course – and I recall him saying that he could barely hear the bells of the third watch because of the clamour.'

Mary Livingston had no reason to lie. That exonerated the Earl of Moray, although I wondered about his mother. If Lady Margaret had been thirty years younger and a few inches taller I would have suspected her of wielding the dagger herself. As it was, though, if she had hired an assassin, he would have used a plain dagger, without gold and jewels.

'I beg your pardon, then, my Lord Moray,' I said. 'Madame, if it pleases you, I shall withdraw.'

'No, no,' the queen said. 'Let my brother withdraw if his pride is wounded by honestly giving an account of himself. Come and sing with us – you have a pretty voice, and low enough to sing the alto part.'

The Earl of Moray stood up and left the supper-room without a word. I watched him go, feeling nothing, thinking only, Very well, Rothes and Moray have been eliminated. Sir John Gordon was eliminated and Lady Huntly vouched for the earl, although now both Sir John and the earl are dead. Next I must address the English and the French. Master Thomas Randolph will have stepped into poor Master Wetheral's shoes. Blaise Laurentin the mercenary could be in anyone's pay. And Chastelard – as he sang with the queen he watched me, his dark eyes uncomfortably intent.

He had been in Edinburgh the night Alexander was murdered, in the Seigneur de Damville's train. He had remained in Scotland for a while, then gone home to France, and then come back – why had he come back? Was he a Huguenot agent, as Nico suspected? I had never seen him attend mass.

'You have made an enemy, Mistress Rinette,' said Nicolas de Clerac. The tone of his voice was mildly jesting but his expression was intent and serious. I had seen him before with just that expression, in my fever, but I could not remember exactly how.

'Nonsense,' the queen said. 'Marianette is under my personal protection. Now, let us sing it again from the beginning.'

20

I struggled to regain my strength throughout the Christmas season. The queen's penchant for Pierre de Chastelard burgeoned; at the same time Master Knox thundered from his pulpit about the sins of the court, the dancing, the music, the lustfulness, the abomination of the mass. The queen, defiant, spent all the more hours with Chastelard, setting his poetry to music, dancing with him, resting her cheek on his shoulder. No one was surprised when he found the bean in his slice of cake on Twelfth Night and was crowned King of the Bean for the rest of the celebrations.

People began to whisper that he had dreams of becoming King of Scots as well. That was perfectly ridiculous, of course. The queen was still negotiating with the King of Spain to marry his poor mad son; her Guise uncles in Paris were putting forward the twelve-year-old King Charles IX of France, with a suitable dispensation for the fact that he was her brother-in-law. Nicolas de Clerac had been abruptly sent off to Austria to negotiate with the emperor's brother Archduke Karl of Austria; the court did not seem the same without him. Letters and gifts arrived from the widowed Duke of Ferrara, who had known and admired the queen as a girl in France and whose sister was married to her beloved uncle Duke François of Guise. All very well as far as it went, but these royal suitors were far away and Chastelard was present in the handsome, charming, poetical flesh. Surely the queen was only amusing herself and making a gesture of rebelliousness at Master Knox, but who could blame poor Chastelard for dreaming?

The Epiphany passed, and Candlemas Day. It was icy cold in Edinburgh, and everything was grey – the sky, the Firth of Forth, the buildings of the city and its spiky church towers, the mass of Arthur's Seat rising up behind Holyrood and the outline of Edinburgh Castle on its rock at the other end of the High Street. When night came, all turned black, with only a few sparks of light here and there in the city.

I longed for Granmuir. I longed for Màiri. Every day I weighed the two things I desired – justice for Alexander, or Granmuir and Màiri? Every day I wondered if I was becoming like my own mother, who had abandoned me to spend her life in a French convent, praying for my father's soul. At least some day, I told myself, I would be with Màiri again.

I felt the Earl of Moray's eye upon me, waiting for a way to take his revenge.

I missed Nico more and more.

One night in February I was in the queen's bedchamber, filling her silver-and-copper warming pan with coals from the fireplace. Somehow I had become the mistress of the warming pan over the past few weeks, and I welcomed the task – I welcomed any warmth, and it gave me a brief interval of solitude each day. I was grateful to Jennet and Wat for watching over me whenever I was not on duty with the queen, but knew it was as wearing to them as it was to me. Still, I treasured that nightly quarter-hour of being entirely by myself.

By myself but for Seilie, of course. As I began to pass the pan over the queen's sheets he whined. I was surprised. He was not a noisy dog, and had learned manners better than those of many courtiers.

'Seilie,' I said. 'Hush.'

He whined again, then barked once. He had his nose under the queen's bed. My first thought was for a rat or some other vermin. They did find their way into the palace to escape the winter cold.

I went back to the fireplace to put the pan on its rack and collect a poker to investigate under the bed. When I turned around again the poet Chastelard was standing beside the bed, fully dressed in hose and shirt and a luxurious velvet jacket, with a dagger at his belt. Seilie knew him, of course, and was clearly pleased to have flushed him out of his hiding place.

'Blessed Saint Ninian!' I said. 'You startled me. I do not know what you think you are doing here, Monsieur de Chastelard, but you had best be off before I call the guard. This is the queen's private bedchamber.'

To my utter astonishment he stepped closer, drew his dagger and pressed the blade against my side. 'I will go,' he said. 'And you will come with me. Put down that poker, Madame, and call off your little hound if you do not want his throat cut.'

'If you touch him, I will kill you.' It was all so unreal that I was more afraid for Seilie than I was for myself. I put the poker down. 'What do you want with me? I thought it was the queen you loved.'

He laughed. 'So she thinks as well! Oh, I grant you, there is something to be said for being a queen's favourite. But my master in France is pressing me, and I fear it is now time to leave all that behind. Come along quietly, Madame. You have no idea how difficult it has been to catch you unguarded.'

He came closer and grasped my arm. Seilie growled and backed away, the hair standing up in a ridge along his neck and back.

'But what do you want? Surely you cannot mean to ravish me, in the heart of Holyrood Palace with the queen's guards everywhere.'

'*Dieu me sauve*, no. And in fact, Madame, if you will take me to the place where you have hidden Mary of Guise's silver casket, I will set you free entirely unharmed.'

'What do you intend to do with it?'

'That is my affair. Come now. Walk with me and act as if you are willing, or I will slide this dagger between your ribs and be gone before anyone realises what has happened.'

Would he do it?

'Run, Seilie!' I cried out suddenly. 'Guards! To the queen's chamber!'

Chastelard froze, as I had gambled he would. I jerked my arm away and ran after Seilie, who had begun a full-throated hound's baying. The guards stormed in, blades drawn.

'He was under the bed!' I cried. 'He was lying in wait to ravish the queen!'

They took hold of the poet roughly. His dagger clattered to the floor. I was cool-headed enough to take a good look at it – no wings or falcon's head, no eye missing its ruby – before I scooped Seilie up in my arms.

'He was under the bed,' I said again. I had begun to shake. Now that it was over I was more frightened than I had been with Chastelard's dagger against my side. One thing, however, I was certain of. If I told the guards the poet had secreted himself in the queen's bedchamber to abduct me, I would instantly fall under suspicion myself. Better to let them think the queen was his object.

Chastelard himself would say nothing. I was certain of that.

* * *

The poet was taken into the queen's presence the next day, but it was a private meeting and no one knew for certain what they said to each other. When he came out of the queen's inner chamber he left Holyrood without a word to anyone. The palace hummed with whispers. The queen herself was in one of her dark humours, and by ten o' clock she had decided to ride to Queensferry and cross the Firth of Forth to Fife. She took Moray with her, and Mary Livingston and Moray's wife Agnes Keith as attendants, and that was all. The rest of us were left scrambling to pack up her household goods and clothing and follow her. I kept close to Wat and Jennet and saw nothing of Chastelard. If he had any sense at all, he was already on his way south to England, and from there to France.

Once across the firth the queen galloped on along the Fifeshire coast to Rossend Castle. We struggled after her, slowed by pack horses and carts, swearing under our breaths at the frozen roads. I carried Seilie in a blanket-lined basket tied to Lilidh's saddle. It was past dinner-time when we at last arrived at Rossend, and we were stiff with cold, sore and hungry.

The queen, who had arrived some hours before, had been warmed before the fire by Rossend's laird Sir John Melville and his astonished wife. She was dressed in clean clothes, then served a leisurely hot supper of capon in rosewater-scented almond milk, and a pear-and-custard pie. We followers barely had time to snatch a piece of bread and dip it in the leftover juices of the chicken before we had to go up to the bedchamber set aside for the queen, to prepare it.

It was a well-proportioned wainscoted room in an old square tower, with walls thicker than the height of a man, a window covered with a tapestry, two small adjoining closets, and — what we wanted most of all — a fine fireplace. One of the grooms set to work at once to build up the fire. Fortunately there was already a suitable bed, and I checked underneath it carefully before Mary Seton spread it with the queen's favourite feather bolsters, sheets, and thick quilted coverlets. I filled the queen's warming pan with coals and set about warming the bed; the fire crackling in the fireplace warmed my own hands as well.

Around midnight the queen came in, followed by Mary Livingston and Lady Moray. Her dark humour had passed; she was in high spirits again and full of plans for a further journey on to Saint Andrews and a visit to the university there. The groom went out; we ladies undressed the queen and helped her into a clean shift with long sleeves. She took Seilie up into her lap to pet him as Mary Seton took down her hair down preparatory to brushing it. I turned to pick up the warming pan again and jumped back with a cry.

There in the doorway of one of the closets, like a recurring nightmare, stood Pierre de Chastelard.

The four of us – Mary Seton, Mary Livingston, Lady Moray and I – jumped as one to form a barrier between the poet and the queen. Lady Moray said in a voice icier than the sea outside, 'Monsieur de Chastelard, are you mad? The queen has been undressed for the night. Get you out of this room at once, or we shall call the guards.'

The queen put Seilie down and rose. Tall as she was, she looked over all our heads; I saw Chastelard's face flush and then go pale as he met her eyes. She put out her hands and pushed Lady Moray and Mary Seton aside. Her nightshift was perfectly modest, being full and thick for warmth's sake and tied at her neck and wrists with strings. Still, it was a nightshift. She wore it as if it were a robe of state.

''Sieur Pierre,' she said. 'How come you to be in that closet?'

'There is a stair,' he said. He was white-faced and his voice shook. What demands had been made upon him, and by whom, that he would dare a second entrance into a bedchamber occupied by the queen? 'It leads down to the seashore. I followed you from Edinburgh and paid one of Melville's men a silver penny to show me the way.'

'I told you this morning to leave Scotland,' the queen said. Her voice was soft. She had her head tilted to one side in her favourite beguiling pose. Modest nightshift or no, she radiated sensuality. 'I told you I would overlook your presumption and give you freedom to go. You break my heart, 'Sieur Pierre, that you desire me so much you will disobey me.'

'Do you think I am here because I desire you?' His voice was hoarse. 'I assure you that is not the case. It is Madame Leslie I want.'

I did not see the queen's immediate reaction to that, and it is probably just as well. Chastelard stepped straight up to me, grasped my wrist, and dragged me into the closet. He had no weapons; presumably the queen's guard had stripped him of his dagger and sword the night before. I struggled with him grimly, kicking him, stamping his feet, trying to reach his eyes with my nails. He pushed me, and I would have fallen into the stone stair-well if I had not managed to catch myself with my hands on either side of the door. He pushed me again, and I stumbled down a few steps. I was still weak from my long siege with the New Acquaintance and I did not know how long I could keep fighting him.

'I know who murdered your husband,' he said in a harsh whisper. 'Come with me, give me the casket, and I will tell you the name.'

'*What?*'

'I know the murderer. I will tell you.'

'I do not believe you.'

'Nevertheless—' He grunted when I thrust an elbow into his side. 'It is true. Did you see the dagger he used? It is made with the head of a falcon.'

I stopped struggling. Mary Livingston was screaming. Lady Moray was shrieking for her husband. Mary Seton was sobbing. Even Seilie was howling like a mad thing. The queen – I did not hear the queen's voice at all.

I said fiercely, 'Then tell me.'

'Only when I have the casket in my hands.'

'I will show you,' I said. 'But you must tell me—'

Two guards crashed on to the stair. They grasped Chastelard by the arms and neck and dragged him back up into the closet. No, no – I could not lose it, not when I was so close. I scrambled after them, crying, 'Tell me! Tell me quickly!'

The poet, manhandled by the guards, probably did not even hear me. Back in the queen's chamber, the Earl of Moray was taking charge.

'In the name of God,' he said. 'What broil is this?'

I stood there helplessly, panting and dishevelled. I did not dare look at the queen. She had not called out for help. She would happily have seen me dragged away; she had shown softness to Chastelard and he had rejected her to take me instead.

'This man,' the queen said, her voice quite different from its previous tone, 'has trespassed in my private bedchamber. It does not matter what his reason was. Kill him, brother – stab him straight to the heart for his presumption.'

'Are you safe?' Moray said.

By now Maitland had come in, and Sir John Melville and his wife. The room was suddenly full of people.

Moray took the queen by the shoulders and shook her. '*Are you safe?*'

'We are all safe.' Mary Livingston spoke up stoutly. 'Chastelard is mad, that is all. There is a secret stair up into that closet there, and he found his way here because he is mad in love with the queen. Is that not right, Rinette?'

Seilie had found his way to me and I picked him up, holding him close. I was shaking. 'Yes,' I said. I knew she was trying to help, trying to soothe, publicly at least, the queen's wounded vanity. 'He is mad in love with the queen.'

'Kill him,' the queen said again. She had begun to cry with anger.

'Have you anything to say for yourself, poet?' Moray demanded.

I hugged Seilie tight and held my breath.

Perhaps Chastelard thought he would be treated with leniency if he was considered mad. Perhaps he thought he could soften the queen's outrage. In any case he said, 'Yes, I love her. She is more beautiful than any goddess. I am out of my senses with love.'

Moray made a scornful sound. 'Lock him up securely,' he said. 'We will take him to Saint Andrews in the morning, and put him in the prison there. No, I will hear no more talk of killing him now, sister. He will be tried.'

The guards took him away.

At that moment I began plotting a way to speak to him again.

The queen cried and cried. The men, discomfited by her tears and suddenly realising they were in her bedchamber and she was dressed in nothing but a nightshift, fell over each other to get out. Mary Seton began to say her rosary, and even the Protestant Lady Moray did not stop her. Mary Livingston plied the queen with scented handkerchiefs and hot wine mulled with sugar and spices.

I stood there, and held Seilie, and plotted.

'Marianette,' the queen said at last.

Everyone froze. The room became deathly quiet.

'Yes, Madame?' I said.

'Get out. Do not come into our presence again unless you are bidden.'

I said again, 'Yes, Madame.'

I left the room without another word.

The queen and her party went on to Saint Andrews the next day after she broke her fast. Chastelard had been taken away earlier – in chains, it was whispered – and I followed separately in the baggage train, with Jennet, Wat and Seilie. From the height of favour I had fallen into the deepest disgrace; even the grooms avoided speaking to me. At Saint Andrews the queen was warmly welcomed and lodged in a large and comfortable merchant's house on South Street.

I managed to find pallets for Jennet and myself in a tiny room next to the kitchen; Wat and Seilie slept in the stables. Mary Livingston, bless her, was the only one to search me out; she told me the queen's moods changed from hour to hour, from black despair to an almost euphoric energy. With Chastelard gone she had transferred her mercurial affections almost entirely to Nicolas de Clerac, who had returned from Austria as abruptly as he had departed. I felt a twinge of – well, it could not be jealousy, now, could it? But he had come back to Scotland and had gone straight to the queen, without so much as a word to me.

Chastelard was sentenced to death. It seemed an excessive punishment for entering the queen's bedchamber without so much as laying a finger upon her, and I wondered if he had been tortured, if he had confessed the truth about his mysterious master in France and his secret mission in Scotland. There were whispers that he was a papal agent, and other whispers that he was a tool of Admiral Coligny and the Huguenots. I had to speak to him before they cut off his head, and I would have to hurry. His execution was set for the twenty-second, which was only a day away.

'You cannae just walk into a prison and confabulate with a condemned man, Rinette,' Wat said. 'And even if you could, 'tis dangerous.'

'Surely gold will buy us a few minutes,' I said. 'I am not such a fool as to try to go alone, Wat. Come with me. Please.'

'So far all the clack's been about the queen,' Jennet said. 'The ladies who were in the room will never breathe a word about Chastelard wanting you instead, not after seeing what she's done to you. Leave it alone. In a month everyone will believe what everyone else is saying, good as gospel, and no one will recollect what really happened.'

'The queen will.'

'The queen's changeable as the moon. Just wait. She'll remember soon enough that she wants her mother's casket, and that to get it she needs to find Sir Alexander's murderer for you.'

'Chastelard already knows. He said he would trade the name for the casket. I will promise to give the casket to his master in France, if he tells me now – at least he will know that his mission has been successful. If Wat comes with me, I'll be safe enough.'

'We'll both go with you,' Jennet said, with resignation. 'The cook will watch over Seilie for an hour or so. I've got a dirk, and I can fight good as Wat here.'

'Fight snaikie, you mean. That's the only way I'll do it, Rinette – if we all go. You put your boy's breeches on, and a dirk up your own sleeve same as Jennet.'

So once it was dark we made our way up to Saint Andrews Castle on its headland, which served as both the bishop's palace and the prison for the town. I had dressed myself in the boy's clothes I had worn at Corrichie, and had my face well muffled up with a scarf; I had one dagger at my belt and another in my sleeve. Every time we encountered a guard, Wat spoke with him first and pressed a coin into his hand. Each guard seemed amused rather than indignant, and took the money readily.

We were directed to the seaward tower, where there was a sort of vaulted inner courtyard. A short man in a dark cloak and hood stood in front of a heavy wooden door banded with iron; he was speaking into an angled hole in the wall next to the door. The way he was leaning forward with his hands pressed flat against the stone conveyed a sense of longing – there was love and sorrow, held back by a will of iron, in every line of his figure. At the sound of our steps he looked up and I recognised the Frenchman Blaise Laurentin.

'Monsieur Laurentin,' I said, surprised. 'What are you doing here? Where is Monsieur de Chastelard being held?'

'You!' he said. 'At first I thought it might be the queen, come in secret, but you are not tall enough. Pierre——' He spoke into the hole again. 'It is Madame Rinette Leslie, come to gloat over your fall.'

'Tell her to go away.' The poet's voice was muffled.

'That is not true,' I said. I stepped up closer to the hole beside the door. Wat and Jennet stayed close behind me, with their eyes on Laurentin. 'Monsieur de Chastelard, you told me on the stair – you told me you knew who murdered my husband.'

There was no answer. Blaise Laurentin leaned back against the wall and looked at me, his eyes like burned holes in his face, his expression unreadable. I turned away from him and leaned closer to the hole in the thick stone wall.

'Tell me the name,' I said. 'I will take the casket to your master, I swear it. Just tell me who your master is, and who killed Alexander.'

Again there was no answer.

Blaise Laurentin had gone very still. After a moment he shifted his position, then again leaned close to the hole. 'So you told her?' he said. 'Tell her everything then, Pierre. Tell her the name. I would like to hear it as well.'

Silence.

'Monsieur de Chastelard,' I said desperately. 'You described the dagger correctly. Was it you who killed my husband?'

More silence.

'It could not have been Pierre,' Laurentin said. 'He and I – we were together, all afternoon and all night. We were at Holyrood until morning. Is that not true, Pierre?'

'It is true,' the poet said. His voice was very hoarse and soft. 'I was with Blaise all night. I did not kill your husband.'

'Then tell me who did. Give me some evidence, some proof. I will see the murderer hanged and give the casket to your master.'

'Tell us, Pierre,' Laurentin said. His voice was soft and sing-song, as if he and Chastelard were speaking memorised parts in a play they knew and I did not. 'Or was it all a lie, the business about knowing young Gordon's murderer, to get Madame Rinette to give you the casket?'

'Yes. It was all a lie.'

And he would say no more, no matter how much I begged.

I was not sure what I believed. He knew about the falcon's head on the dagger; he could not know that unless he himself were the killer, or unless the true killer had shown off the blade and confessed to the crime. He had taken enormous risks to capture me and force me to give up the casket, and he was about to pay

214

the price with his life. Why was he now claiming it did not matter any more, and that everything he had said was a lie?

'Do you know who his master is?' I said to Blaise Laurentin. We had stepped a little way away from the hole in the wall, so Chastelard could not hear us. Laurentin's eyes were red-rimmed, almost as if they had been bleeding. He looked at me in such a way that Wat and Jennet moved closer, their daggers close at hand. I put my own hand on the dagger at my belt.

'Of course I know.'

'There is a story being told that he is connected to Coligny and the Huguenots.'

Laurentin shrugged and said nothing.

'If that is true,' I said, 'then you must be the queen's man. Queen Catherine de' Medici.'

He bowed to me slightly, although still he said nothing. Did that mean yes or no?

'So you are enemies, you and Chastelard. And yet you were with him all through the night, the night the Queen of Scots came home? You are here now to be with him?'

'Our employers are enemies.' His voice was without emotion; I could tell it was not because he did not feel emotion, but because he did not wish to show it. 'We are not.'

'Did he tell you? I do not care who has the casket in the end. I only want to know who killed my husband, and to see the murderer hang.'

'He did not tell me,' Blaise Laurentin said. His strange bleached eyes looked directly at me. Bryony, I thought. The devil's turnip. Do not trust him.

He said, 'You say he described the dagger correctly. Is this it?'

He took the dagger from his own belt and offered it to me, hilt first. It was of plain steel with no jewels or ornamentation, the sort of ordinary blade one could buy at half a dozen shops in Edinburgh's High Street.

'No,' I said. 'That is not it.'

He put the dagger away. 'Then neither he nor I is the man you are looking for,' he said. 'I only wish I could give you what you want and take the casket home to Queen Catherine. She would reward me richly. I would be willing to share the reward, if gold interests you.'

'No,' I said. 'Gold does not interest me.'

The next day Chastelard had his head struck off at the Mercat Cross. They said he refused prayers from both the Catholic priest and the Protestant minister, and went to his death bravely, reading aloud from Pierre de Ronsard's 'Hymn to Death'.

> *When it is my time, Goddess, I beg you,*
> *Do not leave me to linger long in sickness,*
> *Tormented in my bed. No, if I must die,*
> *Allow me to encounter you suddenly*
> *Either for the honour of God,*
> *Or in the service of my prince.*

I was not there; I could not bear to see another execution. The queen was not there either, and this time Moray did not try to force her. Chastelard turned to face the house where we were staying, they said, and died with the queen's name on his lips. But then, they said so many things. Most of them were lies.

It was the lies, though, that people remembered.

21

I was out of favour while Nico was high in favour at court, and because of it we might have been living in different worlds. Once we were back at Holyrood I waited for him to approach me, because I had never yet told him about the dagger-pattern I now remembered, or the fact that Chastelard had known what the dagger looked like. I wanted his ideas, his knowledge of the world. But he did not come. I wondered if he had become the queen's lover in truth, and was with her day and night. Finally I sent Jennet with a message. She returned to tell me the Earl of Moray in his enmity had set spies to watch me, and Nico was avoiding me so as not to risk sinking me deeper than ever into the queen's displeasure.

Courts. They glitter when you are outside. Inside, they can be ugly things.

'He says you must dress in my clothes,' Jennet said, 'and go out to the bakeshop just as I do every Wednesday. He will ride out the night before, with a packet of letters for a French ship in the harbour at Leith. On his way back he will go secretly to the back door of the bakeshop. It will work, Rinette. Finella the baker and I are friends, and I'll speak a wee word in her ear.'

'Does he think it is really necessary? All this disguising and sneaking around?'

'Unless you want Moray telling the queen you're Master de Clerac's lover, or even worse that you're plotting some devil-ment with him, yes, it seems to be. For your sake and for his, too.'

So we did it all, just as he suggested, and on the following Wednesday I found myself sitting in the tiny, yeast-smelling kitchen of Finella MacBain's bakeshop, dressed in Jennet's cap and apron. I felt ridiculous. When Nico de Clerac slipped in through the back door, dressed in dark blue silk and velvet-soft leather, with a sapphire clasp on his cap and kohl around his eyes, I felt more ridiculous still.

'Rinette,' he said.

I wanted to stare at him coldly. I wanted to fling hot words at him for his neglect. I wanted to jump to my feet and throw myself into his arms. Oh, I surprised myself, with the contradictory things I wanted to do.

I think he read some of it in my face, because he said, 'Forgive me. Please believe me when I say I have been trying to protect you.'

'Protect me from what? The queen's jealousy?'

'I am not her lover, if that is what you mean.' There was a wry deepening at one corner of his mouth. 'But for the moment I am her close advisor, and yes, she desires all of my attentions. I have vowed to support her, and it is a vow I cannot break.'

'A vow?' I said. It surprised me, and yet it did not. Had he told me about the vow before? When? Where? Why could I not remember? 'Do you mean a religious vow? I thought you ran away from the Abbey, Nico, before you actually became a monk.'

He hesitated. I could see him considering a light answer, consid-ering it and rejecting it. Slowly he said, 'Not a religious vow. It was a promise in blood, over true relics of Saint Louis, for a secular purpose.'

I was more and more bewildered. 'To whom? What blood? What did you promise?'

'I cannot tell you any more, Rinette. I am telling you about the vow itself because it binds me to support the queen and remain in her favour, even when – even when I do not agree with her or do not wish to support her.'

'That is why you have arranged this elaborate masquerade, then. Because the queen is angry with me, and will be angry with you if you see me? Not because Moray is watching you.'

'It is perfectly true that Moray is watching me,' he said. 'He would happily use you to damage my standing with the queen.'

'You are all like children.' Much as I disliked and distrusted the court, I felt resentful at being outside the charmed circle of favourites. 'Vows and plots and favours and disguises. A smart smacking would do you all good.'

He smiled. I held my mouth stiff at first, and then gave in and smiled back at him.

'Dangerous children,' he said. 'I have missed you, *ma mie*.'

'I have missed you too. I understand you are walking a very narrow path with the queen. It is just that there are things I have to tell you. Things I have learned.'

He sat down on the bench beside me. 'Tell me,' he said. 'Start with Chastelard.'

'For it to make sense, I have to start with the dreams.'

'Very well. The dreams, then,'

'When I was sick,' I said, 'I dreamed about it. Over and over, I think. The night Alexander was killed.'

He put his hand over mine, where it lay on the rough trestle table. 'I am sorry,' he said. 'You should not—'

'No,' I said. 'It was good. It helped me remember things – things that were in my mind all along, but that I had forgotten.'

I saw the spark of interest in his eyes. He did not take his hand away. 'What things?'

'The bell,' I said. 'I remembered the bell, but I did not understand what it was. Now I do – it was the bell for the third watch. Anyone who can account for himself at the time of the third watch that night cannot be the murderer.'

'You asked Moray about the time, in the queen's supper-room – that is one of the reasons he is so determined to have revenge on you. I wondered why.'

'The other thing is the dagger. Of course I saw it, but it happened so fast, and afterwards – afterwards Màiri came. When I dreamed it, it was as if it was happening very slowly, and so I could look at it carefully and remember what I saw.'

'You saw the jewel broken free.'

'Not only that. I saw the design of the dagger. It was unusual, Nico, and it would be easy to identify even without the ruby. A golden falcon with ruby eyes and outspread wings. The assassin had his hand around the hilt, but the falcon's head was clearly visible, and the design of the wings was engraved on the two sides of the guard.'

He was staring at me as if I had said something astonishing.

'I did see it,' I said. 'It was not magic, the dream, just a way of remembering—'

'Can you draw it?'

I was taken aback. 'I suppose I can. We can ask Mistress Finella if she has paper and ink.'

She did not, of course. She did have a stack of clean towels, however, and I spread one out flat on the table. With a piece of charcoal from the fireplace, I tried to sketch the dagger as I remembered it. The lines smudged together and I could not make them represent what I had seen.

'I can see it so clearly.' I pushed the towel away, angry with myself and my clumsy fingers. 'None of this looks right.'

'Let me try. I was trained to do lettering and illumination at Mont Saint-Michel.'

He spread out a clean towel and lightly drew in the outline of a plain dagger. I was surprised at his skill.

'Now. Here, at the top of the hilt, tell me exactly what the falcon's head looked like.'

I told him. He sketched very lightly, and only when I was satisfied did he draw over the lines and shade in the hollows. The falcon's head sprang to life before my eyes. He drew the two wings on the guard more confidently, adding some of the details before I even described them.

'You know the design,' I said. 'Nico, have you seen a dagger like this before?'

He put the charcoal down and sat back, wiping his fingers with a clean towel. 'Yes,' he said. 'I have. Rinette, this tells me a great deal more about the assassin.'

I was mystified. 'What?'

'Have you heard of the *Escadron Volant* – the Flying Squadron of Queen Catherine de' Medici?'

'Only in gossip. It is a group of beautiful women, is it not? Spies and seductresses who serve the Medici queen?'

'It is that, yes, but there is more. There is said to be another arm of the *Escadron*, very secret, very dangerous: assassins. They also serve the queen as she requires them, but lately they have become more independent – an *Escadron Volant* assassin can sometimes be hired if a person has sufficient gold.'

'And this dagger – the falcon's head and the wings – it is their sign?'

'Whispers say it is. Rinette, there are very few people in Scotland who could pay to hire an *Escadron Volant* assassin. The queen herself has a virtually empty treasury, and uses the income from her properties in France to meet many of her expenses.'

'So it is one of the nobility, or a foreigner?'

'Yes, I think so. Elizabeth Tudor's spymaster Walsingham – he has the sort of connections which would be necessary. The English queen can be miserly, but consider what she would gain by securing the casket for herself. She would thwart Catherine de' Medici personally. She would checkmate any attempt by the Huguenots to coerce the French queen into a peace. At the same time she would increase her power over Scotland – with all the secrets of our noblemen in her hands, she will call the tune and they will dance. Queen Mary will become nothing more than a figurehead.'

'So you think it is the English?'

'There is just as much reason to believe it might be the French. The *Escadron* began, at least, under Queen Catherine's aegis. As for the Huguenots, Coligny and Condé together could likely meet the *Escadron's* price.'

He stopped. After a moment I said, 'And the Guises?'

He picked up the linen towel with its sketch and threw it into the fireplace. The flames blazed up brightly, and the towel was gone. I would have to give Mistress Finella a copper penny to buy more towels. 'Better not to leave this where it might be seen,' he said. 'Yes, the Guises are another possibility.'

'And the Scots? I think I would suspect Lady Margaret Erskine, first of all.'

He smiled. 'If Lady Margaret were thirty years younger, she might have been *Escadron* herself. But yes, she has access to Moray's resources, and her other son's as well.'

'What about Moray himself?'

'Also a possibility.'

'So what do we do next?' I said.

'You will not like my advice, Rinette.'

'You think I should give up. You think I will never find an assassin who is a member of this – this *Escadron Volant*.'

'You never will. He will not use that dagger again unless he is paid to perform another assassination, so your ruby will not help you. That is part of their ritual, their mystery – the falcon daggers are used only when they kill.'

'Do you think it is Blaise Laurentin?'

'Possibly. What about Chastelard? You said you had something to tell me about him as well.'

'You suspect Chastelard? He was only a poet.'

Nico smiled. 'He represented himself as a poet. He was a grandson of the Chevalier de Bayard, did you know that? The knight *sans peur et sans reproche*. There was more than poetry in his blood, and he could well have been secretly a member of the *Escadron Volant* himself.'

'Laurentin said that his employer and Chastelard's were enemies, but that he and Chastelard personally were friends. Possibly more than friends – I suspect they may have been lovers.'

'*Sainte-grâce*, Rinette. When did Laurentin tell you this?'

'The night before Chastelard was executed.'

'I think you had best tell me the whole story.'

I picked up a clean towel from the top of the stack and unfolded it. I needed something to do with my hands. 'There is not much to tell. Chastelard was found in the queen's bedchamber, not once but twice. He was using his supposed passion for her as a pretence – what he truly wanted was the casket.'

I folded the towel again, with the edges perfectly aligned, and picked up another one.

'And that means he wanted you,' Nico said. 'No wonder the queen is so furious with you – she thought he was mad with love for her, and he wanted you instead.'

'Yes. Nico, he told me he knew who killed Alexander.'

'Perhaps he did. If he was *Escadron Volant*, and the assassin was also, they would have known each other, even if they were in the service of bitter enemies.'

I folded the second towel and put it down. Then I stood up and walked back and forth in the little room. All this was so new. It changed everything. It made me edgy, restless.

'Do you think I am in danger?' I said at last.

'Not in the way you are thinking. An assassin will not slip up behind you in the darkness and slit your throat. But you could be abducted, forced to give up the casket. I am glad your little girl is safe at Granmuir, because your hand could be forced by a threat to someone you love.'

'Holy Saint Ninian . . .'

He caught my hand as I walked close to the table. 'Rinette,' he said.

I stopped and looked at him.

'I must go back. The queen has been beside herself for the past few days. The archduke has decided to angle for the Queen of England instead of our queen, so that opportunity is gone. Maitland is in London with instructions for secret negotiations with the Spanish ambassador there, and time is running out for the Spanish match to be made. Last year the Spanish prince fell down a flight of stairs, it is rumoured, and cracked his head open.

He has been more and more difficult ever since, and King Philip may decide he is not fit for marriage at all.'

'A fine husband for our queen.'

He smiled wryly. 'She wants the crown of Spain, and the husband who comes with it is of no importance. That is another thing, Rinette.'

'That husbands are of no importance?'

'No, of course not. The queen's determination to make the Spanish marriage. She has been talking endlessly about the *quatre maris* prophecies. She takes Monsieur de Nostredame very seriously, and she believes the prophecies will predict her future with each of the possible husbands she might marry. She has a new plan of some kind to force you to give them up, so take care when you are around her.'

'I will.'

He ran his thumb lightly over my knuckles and then let go of my hand. 'You would be safest if you would give her the casket now, with no conditions.'

I drew back. 'Is that you speaking, Nico, or your mysterious vow?'

He stood up. 'It is both,' he said. '*Que Dieu te bénisse et te garde, ma mie.*'

When he spoke the French words I once again experienced the disconcerting sense that he had once said something similar to me in French and I had forgotten it. I grasped at it – I almost had it. It was connected somehow with his vow. *You are burning up with fever*, he had said. *You will not remember this*. And then—

But the rest was gone.

22

14 April 1563
Lochleven

'I have sweetened Master Knox's temper considerably, do you not agree, brother?' the queen said. She was alight with self-satisfaction, and did a dance-step all by herself in the centre of the Great Hall of Lochleven Castle. 'We had quite an excellent debate yesterday, and today at Kinross I begged for his help in settling the scandal between Argyll and Jean. Oh, how prettily I begged! And I gave him a watch in an eight-sided crystal – he may preach against vanity but he took the gift quickly enough.'

'I doubt much of anything will sweeten Knox permanently,' Moray said. He cut a candied apricot into four pieces with his royal dagger and ate one of the quarters. 'But you argued well, sister, and showed marvellous self-control.'

As the queen danced down the hall, delighted with her own cleverness, I knelt by the hearth like a kitchen maid, grating sugar to mix with cinnamon, galingale and grains of paradise in the wine I was mulling. We had been at Lochleven for a week, guests of Sir William Douglas and his wife Lady Agnes Leslie – she was the Earl of Rothes' sister and so a distant cousin of my own.

Sir William was Lady Margaret Erskine's son, by her long-dead husband Sir Robert Douglas; this made him a half-brother of Moray's.

In addition to her audience with Master Knox, the queen had sung and danced and feasted every night, and hawked on the mainland every day – the weather could not have been more perfect for April, crisp and sunny, with the waters of Loch Leven reflecting cloudless blue skies. The shallows along the shore were spangled with colt's-foot and celandine, daisies and primroses, blue bank-violets and masses of windflowers.

Moray was back in favour, just as suddenly as he had fallen from it; Sir John Gordon's death had been forgiven and forgotten. Nico de Clerac, however, was highest in favour of them all; Moray, Rothes and the rest of the queen's council were said to be disliking him more and more for his influence and his foreignness.

In addition to Moray and Nico, Rothes was there in the Great Hall with us, seconded by his brutal kinsman Rannoch Hamilton; I avoided the man's devouring black gaze and wondered what he was doing here, at the queen's light-hearted gathering. Mary Fleming and Lady Agnes attended her. I was still in deep disgrace, but as Jennet said, the queen was changeable as the moon and who knew what tomorrow might bring? So I clung grimly to my place and my determination to solve the mystery of Alexander's murder. It might be more difficult to find an assassin of the *Escadron Volant* brotherhood, but I refused to believe it was impossible.

'One thing you could certainly do to encourage Master Knox's favour,' said Lady Margaret when the queen had danced back to where the rest of them were sitting, 'is cleanse your household of witchcraft. He specifically said you have witches in your household.'

'I did not pay attention to that part,' the queen said. 'I have no witches.'

'There is Lady Atholl, who is said to practise sorcery.'

'Do not be ridiculous. She is Flaminia's sister.' The queen gave Mary Fleming a kiss on the cheek and sat down beside her.

'Lady Reres.'

'She is Beaton's aunt, and far too fat to be a witch.'

'And then—' Lady Margaret turned her head and looked straight at me. Malice crackled almost visibly in the air between us and I felt myself pinned to the fireplace like a butterfly with the sugar-grater in my hand. 'There is Mistress Rinette, here in this very room, who keeps a little hound as a familiar and reads the future in flowers.'

They all turned and looked at me, the queen and Moray and Nicolas de Clerac, Rothes and Rannoch Hamilton, Lady Agnes and Mary Fleming. I felt myself blushing hot as the fire behind me.

There was a strange expression on the queen's face. It was as if she were thinking, *Now, this is perfect. Now is the time to spring the trap.*

What trap?

Nico's voice, at the bakeshop: *She has a new plan of some kind to force you to give them up, so take care when you are around her.*

'Seilie is not a familiar,' I said. My voice shook. 'He is a pet, nothing more.'

Lady Margaret smiled. I could see she had expected me to jump to the defence of my little dog even before defending myself. 'There! You do not deny that you use floromancy.'

'It is an amusement, my lady, that is all,' said Nicolas de Clerac in a lazy voice. '*La floromancie* . . . it is no more witchcraft than casting a horoscope.'

'Astrology is a science,' Moray said. 'Sister, my lady mother is right. Mistress Rinette must be made to give up her flower-reading, or be sent away.'

Sent away?

Seilie, who had heard me say his name, had come to sit beside me. He leaned against me and pushed his head under my arm. He was trembling. Or was it I who was trembling?

'I will not send her away,' the queen said. 'Not even for Master Knox. She has not yet given me my mother's silver letter casket, which she promised to do. When she gives it to me, with the *quatre maris* prophecies of Monsieur de Nostredame, she may go off to her sea-rock and read her flowers every day if she likes.'

That was so outrageously unfair that it jarred me out of my shock. 'I was not the only one who made a promise, Madame,' I said. 'You swore you would find my husband's murderer, and exercise your fullest royal justice upon him, and you have not done so.'

'I told you at the time, I could make no promises.' The queen's high spirits had evaporated; she stalked back to her own chair and seated herself under her cloth of estate. 'It has been almost two years since your husband was killed, Marianette, and whoever the killer was, he will never be captured now.'

'I agree, sister,' said the Earl of Moray. 'I believe it is time for Mistress Rinette to give up her search for her husband's murderer, surrender the casket and go, particularly as her presence here adds fuel to Master Knox's flames.'

'I will not give it up,' I said. I could feel panic rising in my throat. How had it come to such an ultimatum so suddenly? I still had the sugar-grater in my hand, and the wine was still simmering gently over the fire, half-sweetened. 'I will not go until my husband's murderer pays for his crime.'

Nicolas de Clerac stepped over to the queen's chair and knelt on one knee, leaning towards her but careful not to touch her; she was the queen, after all, and no one touched her but by her direct invitation. She smiled at him and tilted her head in her favourite coquettish way, then reached out and placed one hand on his arm. Her long slender fingers were like white ribbons against the dark green velvet of his doublet sleeve.

'What say you, 'Sieur Nico?' she said. 'Should the silver casket and the prophecies of Monsieur de Nostredame be mine?'

'In the end, Madame, they are meant to be yours,' he said gravely. 'But I have pity on Mistress Rinette as well, who loved her young husband and longs to see justice done.'

'One cannot help but wonder, Monsieur de Clerac,' said Lady Margaret, in a voice like poison, sugar-sweet, 'if selfless pity is the only reason you have for coming to Mistress Rinette's defence.'

The queen withdrew her hand suddenly.

'It is my only reason,' Nico said, without moving. 'Pity, and sorrow for her loss.'

'Then it should please you to know,' the queen said, 'that a new husband has been chosen for her.'

I dropped the sugar-grater. It clattered against the hearth stone. Everyone else in the room was suddenly silent.

'No,' I said.

'A stout Protestant husband,' said the Earl of Moray, 'who will satisfy Master Knox's objections to Mistress Rinette's presence by putting an end to her flower-reading. And such a husband will also – persuade her – to give up the casket and the prophecies to you, Madame, so you can choose your own next husband rightly.'

'No,' I said again. I felt a sudden sinking terror. Please, Saint Ninian, let this not be why he had brought Rannoch Hamilton to Lochleven. Green Lady of Granmuir, protect me!

'That is an excellent solution, brother,' the queen said. She was looking straight at me and I saw a glitter of knife-edged amusement in her eyes. This was all planned in advance, I was sure of it. 'Who have you chosen?'

'My Lord Rothes?' Moray said. 'Will you tell us?'

'A kinsman and loyal man of my own, Madame,' Rothes said. He would not look at me. 'And through me a vassal of my Lord Moray. Master Rannoch Hamilton is a good Protestant and will brook no nonsense from a wife. He is also much enamoured of Mistress Rinette, and has been since the first moment he saw her.'

The first moment he saw me, in the chapel at Granmuir.

When I threatened him with the vines of the Green Lady.

Enamoured was not a word I would have used to describe Rannoch Hamilton's feelings for me.

I said, dry-eyed and hard-voiced, 'I will die first. I will tear Granmuir down stone by stone and throw the stones and myself into the sea.'

'How very impassioned of you, Marianette,' the queen said. 'But impractical. You will not be the first woman to marry a man chosen for you by your betters, nor will you be the last.'

'A moment.'

It was Nicolas de Clerac. He had risen to his full height; one of the reasons the queen loved dancing with him was that he was one of the few men at the court who was taller than she was. His russet hair shone like fire in the flickering light. His eyes were narrowed, the flat muscles beneath them drawn tight. He wore no *maquillage* tonight, but a fine square-cut emerald flashed in his left ear.

'Marriage is a sacrament in your church, Madame,' he said. 'And a covenant in yours, my Lord Moray – Master Knox himself calls it a blessed ordinance of God. Would you now besmirch this sacrament, this covenant, with force?'

Silence.

I remembered what he had told me in the gardens of Granmuir – how his mother had been forced into marriage, and how he had run away from the Benedictine monks, who were the only family he had ever known, to try to save her.

How he had failed.

Lady Margaret Erskine was the first who dared break the silence. She-wolf though she might be, she had courage. 'I will ask you again, Monsieur de Clerac,' she said. 'What is your interest here, and why do you argue that Mistress Rinette should not be married to the man her clan chief has chosen?'

'Is it perhaps,' the Earl of Moray said, 'that you wish to marry her yourself?'

My heart stopped. Everything stopped, for the space of a breath.

'That is ridiculous.' The queen had come to her feet again, anger flaming from her as heat radiated from the fire. 'What are you thinking of, brother? 'Sieur Nico is speaking out of the pity of his heart, and no other reason. Is that not so, 'Sieur Nico? The pity of your heart.'

Everyone began to talk at once.

Nicolas de Clerac was the only one who said nothing – the only one, that is, other than I myself. He looked at me. I looked at him. His face looked naked, down to the bones.

It was a promise in blood, over true relics of Saint Louis. It binds me to support the queen and remain in her favour, even when I do not agree with her or do not want to support her.

Nico moved at last. He turned to face the queen.

How much alike they were, with their height and slenderness and bright hair – the queen's slightly more golden, Nico's more red. They might have been brother and sister, much more so than the queen and Moray who was shorter, more thickly made, dark-eyed and dark-browed. I wondered why I had not noticed it before.

'I would see no lady forced to marry,' Nico said. It was his courtier's voice again, smooth and practised, warm with emotion that might or might not be genuine. 'Not Mistress Rinette – not even you, Madame. Even a queen should be permitted to follow her heart.'

He held out his hand. After a moment the queen put her beautiful white fingers in his, and he lifted them very gently to his lips.

'Even a queen,' he repeated.

I wanted to strike him. I wanted to strike her. I felt panicked and desperate as a wild doe surrounded by hunting hounds.

'I do not want to marry anyone,' I said. My voice sounded unnaturally loud. 'Not Rannoch Hamilton, not Monsieur de Clerac, not anyone. Even if I am dragged to the altar in chains, I will refuse.'

'You misunderstand, Mistress Rinette,' Lady Margaret said. 'No one is proposing you be dragged to the altar in chains. Is that not so, Madame?'

The queen withdrew her hand from Nico's – reluctance was clear in every line of her body – and seated herself. She stopped being a woman and made herself into a queen again. Nico himself did not move.

'Indeed it is,' she said. 'If Marianette does not freely agree to the marriage, she will certainly not be compelled.'

'Good,' I said. My voice was thick with tears I would never, never, never shed. 'Then I will not marry Rannoch Hamilton.'

'However,' the queen went on, 'there is your daughter Mary to consider. She is my godchild.'

'It is Màiri,' I said. 'None of this has anything to do with her.'

'Oh, but it does. If you are to continue as you are, unmarried and practising your witchcraft, my godchild must be removed from your malign influence. It is perfectly legal – she can be made a royal ward and brought up in one of the castles far from the court. Perhaps even here, at Lochleven, with Lady Margaret as her guardian.'

'No,' I said. 'She is safe at Granmuir, in the care of my own people, and at Granmuir she will remain.'

'Your own people,' said the Earl of Moray thoughtfully. 'They should be questioned. They themselves may be practising witch-craft as well, or may be your familiars.'

'That is an outrage.' I turned to the queen. 'Madame, I beg you.'

She looked at me. Her eyes were half-closed, heavy, and she was smiling. 'I cannot help you,' she said. 'Unless, of course, you wish to give up the casket. The casket would change every-thing.'

I looked at them, each of them. The queen would not help me – she wanted the prophecies and to get them she had planned this device with her brother and Lady Margaret. Nicolas de Clerac – he was bound by his unfathomable vow. His face did not even look like his own, more like an enamelled mask. Lady Margaret was smiling. The Earl of Moray was smiling, too, the same smile – how alike they looked, mother and son. The Earl of Rothes' bony face with its light eyes and narrow moustache was avid, as if he were about to make the last move in a game and win a rich prize. Rannoch Hamilton – no. I stopped there. I could not look at him. He had no flower in his heart and soul, nothing but black emptiness, and he would make me pay for what I had said to him at Saint Ninian's. Pay, and pay, and pay.

And Màiri. Màiri, and Tante-Mar, and Jennet, and Wat, and all my household. Even Seilie, accused of being my familiar.

I had no choices left. Alexander's assassin was beyond my

reach. I had to keep my daughter out of Lady Margaret Erskine's clutches, and myself out of Rannoch Hamilton's bed.

'Leave Màiri and my people safe at Granmuir,' I said aloud. 'Let me go home in peace. I will give you the silver casket.'

'Do you have it with you?' the Earl of Moray said. 'Is it here?'
'No.'

I was numb. I felt as if some vital part of me had been cut off.
'Is it at Granmuir?'

'No. It is in Edinburgh.' I turned to the queen. 'Madame, the casket is for you, not for the Earl of Moray or the Earl of Rothes or anyone else. I will put it into your hands alone. And I ask you to swear on your word as queen that I will then be allowed to go home in peace and my daughter and my household will not be mistreated or interfered with in any way.'

'I swear it,' the queen said. She was as excited as a child. 'In fact, we shall write a bond, and we will sign it – all of us. Brother, will you draw it up?'

Moray exchanged glances with his mother. 'When she tells us more about where the casket is. Just to say it is in Edinburgh means little.'

I nodded. He was right. He was nothing if not hardheaded and practical, the Earl of Moray. 'I will tell you this much – it is hidden in a secret vault within the castle rock, under Saint Margaret's Chapel. I will not tell you how to find the vault, not yet. That I will show you when we have returned to Edinburgh, and when I have the bond in my hands.'

'I know there is a maze of old vaults under the castle,' Moray said thoughtfully. 'Can you draw a map, Mistress Rinette?'

'No. I only know – where the entrance is, and what signs to follow to reach the vault.'

Even if I had been able to draw a map, I would not have been fool enough to do so. Not until I had the bond in my hand with the queen's own signature upon it.

'We will leave for Edinburgh in the morning, then,' the queen said. 'And you will show us. Come, let us have some wine and some music to celebrate such a happy conclusion to this business. 'Sieur Nico, I would like to dance. Marianette, finish mulling the wine, if you please.'

Nicolas de Clerac was looking at me with an indescribable expression on his face – surprise, anguish, mystification, comprehension, regret, all at once. What had suddenly broken the polished surface of his mask? I wondered if he wished, as I did, that we could go back to the beginning of the evening and start again. I wondered if he wished he had never bound himself to the queen with a mysterious secret vow, on true relics of Saint Louis.

She tugged at his sleeve and he turned away to give her his full attention.

Moray and Lady Margaret withdrew slightly and whispered together. The Earl of Rothes danced with Lady Moray as Mary Fleming played on her lute. It was an evening just like all our other evenings at Lochleven. Had anything happened at all? If I closed my eyes, could I pretend that everything was back the way it had been?

Rannoch Hamilton did not dance, or sing, or drink wine. He left the Great Hall without a word, and to my great relief no one called him back.

23

We started for Edinburgh at first light the next morning. The loch was deep under a spring mist as we crossed to the mainland in two boats, the queen with the Earl of Moray, Mary Fleming and me in one, the Earl of Rothes, Rannoch Hamilton, and two of the queen's gentleman-ushers in the other. Lady Margaret Erskine remained behind with her legitimate son William Douglas and his wife, and Nicolas de Clerac had sent word by one of the household servants that he was unwell and would follow us in a day or so. I did not believe that for a moment – I could not imagine Nico unwell, and in any case he had been in perfect health the evening before. I wondered if Lady Margaret had entrapped him somehow, or if Moray and Rothes had contrived some way to keep him away from the queen. Perhaps he simply could not face me, after abandoning me for the queen the night before. I nursed my resentment against him, because it was the only way to keep from admitting to myself that I felt isolated and terrified without him.

The sun was just rising behind us, silhouetting Lochleven Castle in gold and blue, burning off the mist even as we watched. Our horses were in Sir William Douglas' stables in Lochleven village; Wat Cairnie had been staying there with Lilidh. He saw at once that something was wrong but Moray and Rothes were keeping a very close watch on me – did they think I would somehow escape? Where did they think I would go? – and I did not have a chance to explain to him. I wondered what he would think of my capitulation. I wondered if I would ever actually tell him and Jennet and Tante-Mar that I had surrendered in part to save them from imprisonment or worse.

We rode straight south, pressing our horses, and reached Queensferry by noon. From there we crossed the firth and went to Holyrood Palace, where the queen refreshed herself with dinner and clean clothes. I could not eat – my hands were shaking and I felt sick to my stomach at what I was about to do. Moray and Rothes repaired to the west tower, where the queen kept her library, in order to draw up the bond we were all to sign before I led them to the secret vault and the casket. I stood behind the queen's chair like a condemned prisoner as she ate with the greatest of relish.

We all watched as the queen signed both copies of the bond with her characteristic signature MARIE, all the letters separate and of an even height. Moray and Rothes had also signed it and placed their seals; I had signed my name as well. The queen dusted the papers with sand from her silver pounce-box, then handed one copy of the bond to me.

'There,' the queen said. She sounded smug as a child who had won a game of jig-ma-handie. 'Take it, Marianette. Keep it safe. I will keep the other. Now you must do your part.'

'I will, Madame.' I still felt sick. I clutched the paper tightly, thinking, This is my freedom. This is Màiri's freedom, and Tante-Mar's, and Jennet's and Wat's and everyone's. This is Granmuir. I am sorry, Alexander. You betrayed me. Now I have betrayed you as well.

I folded the paper, taking care not to break the seals, and put it in my sleeve.

'Let us go, then.' Moray went to the door, with Rothes beside him. I wondered if Moray thought the queen was going to share the contents of the casket with him, and if Rothes thought he would get a share as well. I hoped the queen would keep it all to herself.

We rode up the High Street two by two, the queen with Moray, me with Rothes. The horses' hooves made hollow clopping sounds on the paving stones. People stopped what they were doing and gaped, and I felt as if I were riding to my execution. Perhaps in a way I was – execution by my own hand, the deliberate execution of the young and passionate Rinette Leslie I had once been, who believed she could checkmate a queen and bring a murderer to justice for the sake of the golden boy she'd loved.

When we reached the castle we rode through the gate and into the lower ward, where we left our horses. Rothes blustered and pleaded but in the end only the queen, the Earl of Moray and I climbed the long steps to the upper ward. The servants at the royal palace within the castle itself were ordered to bring lanterns and then sent away, and the three of us were left alone in the Great Hall.

'Now,' the queen said. 'Show us your secret entrance.'

I took a deep breath. I thought of Màiri, and Granmuir, and my household. I said good-bye to Alexander for good, I think, in that moment.

'Here.' I stepped over to the fireplace. My fingers went straight to the little cross saltire; this time I needed no measuring up or to the side. I pressed. The panel turned. The queen cried out with delight. The Earl of Moray swore.

'As many times as I have been in this room,' he said, 'I never knew.' He took a lantern for himself and handed one to me. 'Lead on, Mistress Rinette.'

I slipped through the opening easily, so easily. But of course I was thin, still recovering from the New Acquaintance and with no baby under my heart. The stone steps spiralled down, just as they had on that night. I could see the marks of my skirt, and here and there footprints in the ancient dust. Alexander's footprints, of course. Two years had not been long enough for the dust to thicken again.

As I looked at those marks in the dust, some of them still sharp and clean, some with a fine film of new dust beginning to soften them, all of a sudden it did not hurt any more. Perhaps it had all hurt too much and cauterised my feelings like a hot iron pressed into an open wound. Whatever it was, I found myself without pain. My hand was perfectly steady as it held the lantern.

'We must go down,' I said. 'There is no handrail – take care, Madame.'

I started down. The queen followed me, exclaiming at everything: the dust, the rock, the patterns the lantern light made. The Earl of Moray followed. I could only imagine his thoughts – the slightest slip, and the queen could fall. With the queen dead and the silver casket in his hands, could he claim the crown for himself, bastard or no?

I did not care. What would that be to me?

'There are crosses,' I said. 'See? They mark the turnings in the maze.'

'Who made this?' the queen asked. 'The crosses are Christian, but the passageways seem so old.'

'It is surely older than the Great Hall itself,' Moray said. 'Much older. There was always talk that the quadrangle was laid out over ancient vaults. The tunnels may have existed long before someone carved the crosses.'

'Lady Margaret said it was a royal secret.'

The queen traced a carved cross with one elegant fingertip. 'Someone should have told me.'

We passed on. I touched each cross as we reached it. I had expected to feel the presence of the casket as I came close to it, or at least the presence of the flowers I had left to guard it. They would be withered now, falling to dust themselves. Even so, I should have felt them.

I did not.

We came out into the chamber.

'It is like a bubble!' the queen exclaimed. 'How extraordinary! And look at the stone underfoot. It is like crackled glass, an old window or a broken mirror.'

'There are no other tunnels, Mistress Rinette,' said the Earl of Moray. His voice was cold. 'This is the end of the maze. Where is the silver casket?'

'It is there,' I said. 'In the niche, straight across the chamber.'

He held up his lantern. I held up my lantern. All three of us looked.

The niche was empty.

The flowers were gone.

The casket was gone, too.

I do not remember how we got out of the vaults and back up to the Great Hall. The Earl of Moray shouted and swore at me all the way, accusing me of having accomplices who had moved the casket to another hiding place, of having moved the casket myself and led them down to the vaults as a trick, to convince them I did not have it after all. The queen cried her easy tears of anger and disappointment and shouted at me that my accomplices were familiars, and that I had used witchcraft to move the casket from its hiding place. I stumbled along between them, numb with shock, protesting over and over that the casket had been there and that I did not know what had happened to it. It was a miracle I did not fall from the ancient spiral stairs. My sleeve tore as Moray pushed me back through the secret panel.

'Call my ladies at once, brother,' the queen said. She shook dust from her skirts. 'Call for wine. Call the guard – I want Marianette shut up at once in the Tolbooth and charged with witchcraft. Her little hound and that white horse of hers – confiscate them. They are her familiars – we will burn them with her.'

'No!' I cried in a panic. 'Oh, no, not Seilie. Not Lilidh.'

'One thing at a time, sister,' the Earl of Moray said. He had me by the arm and was holding on tightly enough to leave bruises. 'Ho, ladies! To the queen!'

Mary Beaton, her aunt Lady Reres and Margaret Carwood rushed in at once. They had certainly been waiting and listening at the door.

'Brush this dust off my skirts,' the queen said. She would not even look at me. 'Carwood, fetch me wine, and a chair to sit on. This is proof, brother, that Marianette is a witch – she has made the casket, *my* casket, *my* prophecies, disappear. . . and after we went to such lengths to write and sign a bond to give her what she desired! She must suffer the penalty of the law for witchcraft, and her familiars with her. It is Master Knox's own law and you are bound to enforce it.'

'Women, bring two chairs,' Moray said. When the chairs and the wine had been brought, the queen flounced into the larger chair and grasped at the golden cup. Moray let go of my arm and seated himself more sedately – I noticed he did not wait for the queen's permission, although she was too much beside herself to notice or care. I stood there rubbing my arm, feeling sick, shaky and cold. How could the casket be gone? Who else knew about the secret panel, the crosses, and the mysterious bubble in the rock under Saint Margaret's?

Was it magic – not the benign white magic of my own floromancy, but an ancient power in the living rock, left over from the days of the old ones?

No. It could not be. Someone else knew about the secret passageways. Some of the footprints had been sharp and clean – too sharp and clean.

Who?

I could not think.

'Now,' said the Earl of Moray. He took a sip of his wine. 'What is your explanation for this, Mistress Rinette?'

'I do not know,' I said. My voice shook and tears stung my eyelids but I would not . . . *would not* . . . give them the satisfaction of seeing me cry. 'I left it there, the day the queen came home from France. Madame, your mother told me about the vaults and the crosses as if it was the greatest of secrets, and the only person who went into the vault with me was Alexander, and Alexander is—is— '

I choked on my own words. Alexander knew. He had written to people describing the contents of the casket, asking what they would offer for them in gold and land and titles. Had he also given away the secret of the vault under Saint Margaret's, and the crosses that were the key to the maze of passageways?

No. He would not be such a fool. He had wished to sell the casket, and so he would not have given away its hiding place.

'You damn yourself with your own words,' the queen said. 'No one else knew of the passageway but you and your husband,

243

and your husband is dead. So did you move the casket to a different place with your spells? Or did you make it invisible? I know how sorcery works – I grew up as the *belle-fille* of Catherine de' Medici, and she is a mistress of the magical arts.'

'It was not sorcery,' I said. 'Not witchcraft. I did not move the casket, or make it invisible. Someone took it. It is *gone*.'

'Sister.' The Earl of Moray was sitting back in his hair, sipping his wine, to every appearance enjoying the queen's ungoverned passion. 'There is no magic here. There is only a deceitful girl who lied to us from the beginning. The casket was never in the secret vault at all, was it, Mistress Rinette?'

'It was.'

'I think it was not. I think you found yourself trapped by the intrigues you created, and contrived this entire elaborate charade to convince us you no longer have the casket. Did you hope we would go chasing after this imaginary thief who somehow knew Mary of Guise's secrets? Did you imagine we would reward you for your presumed honesty and send you home to your castle by the sea?'

'No,' I said desperately. 'No and no. None of that is true. The casket was there, in the chamber under Saint Margaret's. There were flowers there. Everything is gone.'

'It was never there.'

'There were footprints – marks in the dust. That proves Alexander and I were there.'

'It proves only that someone was there, at some time. Perhaps it was the queen regent herself, when she retrieved the casket from its hiding place. She told you the secret, and trusted you to put the casket back in the chamber, but you did not. You took it to Granmuir with you – you claim you put it in the secret chamber only after the queen returned to Scotland. But you never brought it back to Edinburgh at all, did you?'

'I did.'

'And when you were finally trapped, you remembered the queen regent's secret, and used it to attempt to deceive us. You even coerced the queen into signing a bond, by deception. That could be construed as treason, Mistress Rinette. Certainly as *lèse-majesté*. Recall what happened to Monsieur de Chastelard, for a similar transgression.'

I stared at him in speechless horror. I could feel the stiff folded paper of the bond inside my sleeve, lying along the skin of my forearm. I had thought it would save me. Would it now condemn me to death?

'I will give it back,' I said. 'I will—'

'No.' The queen cut me off. She had finished her wine and was holding out her cup for more. In a characteristic volte-face, she said, 'Brother, I cannot bear another trial and execution, and in any case, if she is executed, we will never find the casket. I want those prophecies, and I want them quickly.'

'True.' Moray was smiling a thin smile, as if he knew what she was going to say next.

'Let us instead proceed with our original plan – marry her to Rothes' kinsman. He is a brutish-looking fellow and will have no qualms about beating the truth out of her, whether she has hidden the casket by her sorcery or has it secreted away in some other hiding place. I will promise him a knighthood and Granmuir as a royal fief, in exchange for the casket.'

'An excellent plan, sister,' Moray said. His smile had deepened into smugness. He wanted her to have the *quatre-maris* prophecies. He wanted her married to the Spanish king's mad son, married to some foreigner somewhere, and gone from Scotland – who else would she appoint as regent but he himself? 'Much better than simply burning her as a witch, or striking off her head for treason.'

'I would rather burn,' I said. 'I would rather you strike off my head. I will never marry Rannoch Hamilton and he will never, never be master of Granmuir.'

Moray finished his wine, handed the empty cup to a waiting-woman, and stood up. 'We shall see about that,' he said. 'Sister, let us return to Holyrood. Mistress Rinette can spend the night shut up in the Tolbooth to meditate on the stake and the block, and what might happen to her daughter and her household if she continues to be contumacious.'

The queen drank off the rest of her own wine. 'I would like some music,' she said. She acted as if I were not even there. 'Some dancing. A little supper. Tell the Earl of Rothes to arrange for the marriage at Saint Giles' Kirk, in the morning.'

24

They took me to the old Tolbooth. I expected chains and rats and dripping stone, but ended up locked in a tiny but perfectly ordinary front room on one of the upper storeys. There was a small window covered by a rusted iron grille, a pallet with a single dubious blanket, a stool and a necessary-pot. I dragged the stool to the window and sat there, looking out to the west at the castle on its rock.

'Where did you go?' I whispered to the silver casket. 'How long have you been gone, and why has no one come forward to announce their possession of you?'

The casket, of course, did not answer.

The darkness fell quickly. Stars pricked out in the clear black sky. A gaoler brought me an oatcake and a reasonably clean cup of cider; I ate and drank because there was nothing better to do, and because whatever happened I would need all the strength I could muster.

Would Moray really carry out his threat to have me executed if I did not submit?

Probably not. The queen had said she did not want any more executions, and now that he was back in favour Moray would not again make the mistake of offending her sensibilities. But the queen was like a gilded weathercock, pointing this way one moment and that way the next.

Moray believed I knew where the casket was. Another reason his threat was empty.

So if I continued to refuse to marry Rannoch Hamilton, what would happen?

I would stay here, of course. Or perhaps I would be moved to a cell where there actually were chains and rats and dripping stone. Moray would find a way to take Granmuir for the crown, and Màiri would be made a ward of the queen. Lady Margaret Erskine had threatened to take her to Lochleven, and the thought of my beautiful little daughter, Alexander's golden child, in Lady Margaret Erskine's spiteful hands made me blind with anger.

Tante-Mar would be left helpless and beggared. Surely Norman More would take her in . . . Jennet would see to it. But what would happen to Norman More and his family if Granmuir were no longer mine? He would lose his place, lose his home. And old Père Guillaume and my mother's elderly man-at-arms Robinet Loury, what would happen to them? What would happen to the people in Granmuir village?

If I agreed to the marriage, at least I would be alive, out of prison and still Lady of Granmuir. I would be able to fight for my daughter and my people and my home.

Or would Rannoch Hamilton kill me, taking his revenge for what I had said to him in the chapel at Granmuir, and how it had unmanned him?

No. He would not dare kill me. He would believe I still had the casket hidden somewhere, because Moray believed it. He would have to keep me alive and in my senses as long as he believed I knew, and as long as I did not tell him.

And of course I would not tell him. I could not tell him, because I did not know.

A fine jest that was.

So I had – how long? Until the person who had truly taken the casket made it known that he – or she – had the sealed packet of prophecies from Nostradamus, and the ciphered pages with Mary of Guise's secrets? Too many people wanted them. Someone would eventually reveal where they were.

What would I do then?

I did not know.

Even if I could escape this moment, even if I could make my way to Holyrood, even if I found Wat and Jennet and Lilidh and Seilie there – and I did not even know if they had followed us from Lochleven or not – even if we found a way to flee to Granmuir together, what then? Granmuir Castle, on the seaward side of its narrow causeway, could be defended until the end of time. Or at least until we all starved.

I did not know what to do.

The thought of being Rannoch Hamilton's wife made me sick and shaky.

I longed for Alexander. I longed for – but I would not even admit to myself who else I longed for. I longed for Seilie, at least, faithful Seilie with his solid warm body and his satin-soft ears and his freckled paws.

I looked out at the stars, and I wept.

Morning came.

Two men wearing the Rothes badge took me to Saint Giles'. I had been given no water to wash with or even a comb to tidy my hair. I was wearing the same plain grey-blue fustian riding-habit I had put on at Lochleven – could it have been just yesterday morning? It was stained and wrinkled and hardly suitable for a wedding, but I did not care. Even if I had been offered a gown of scarlet Venetian silk with slashings and couchings and pearls, a shift of the sheerest lawn and chains of rubies and citrines to wear in my hair, I would not have worn them.

We stepped into the church through the great rounded arch of the west door and passed through the nave, the western part of which had been partitioned off by the Reformers as a meeting place for Parliament and the Lords of the Session. It was early morning on a Friday and everything was empty and dark and smelled of stone. No candles, no incense for Master Knox and his Protestants. Further on in the nave of the old church itself there were many small chapels, and in one of them a group of men waited. Moray. Rothes. Rannoch Hamilton. A man I did not know, small and fat, in the black gown and cap of a Protestant minister. Half a dozen men stood outside the chapel wearing Moray's badge. They wore their swords and daggers too, even inside the church. The queen was not present, nor were there any other women at all.

'Mistress Rinette,' the Earl of Moray said. 'I take it you have decided in favour of godly marriage instead of the fire or the sword.'

I looked straight into Moray's hooded dark eyes and said to the minister, 'Master Minister, you hear what the Earl of Moray says. I am being constrained into this marriage by threats, which is against the law of your church.'

The poor minister said nothing. I had not expected him to.

'There have been no banns,' I said.

Still nothing.

'I have no women to support me, and no witnesses of my own.'

Rannoch Hamilton himself stepped forward. He was well dressed in a brown wool doublet and black hose, his shirt spotlessly white, his dark hair short and neat under a plain brown velvet cap; beside the Earl of Moray and the Earl of Rothes he might have been a rough-coated, wild moor stallion among refined and domesticated coursers. If I had not known him, had never faced off against him in Saint Ninian's Chapel, I would not have found him uncomely. But there was nothing behind his eyes, no flower, no symbol of life. The black emptiness of him made me dizzy.

He said, in a terrifyingly reasonable tone of voice, 'Be silent, woman. Our marriage has been arranged by the Earl of Rothes, clan chief of the Leslies, and by the Earl of Moray, the leader of the Lords of the Congregation. No other witnesses are required.'

We faced each other. His expression was controlled. The deep cleft between his brows made it look as if he was scowling, but he was not. I tried to breathe but I could not seem to suck the air into my chest. What was I going to say? What?

'Beloved brethren,' the minister began. He gabbled through the exhortation. He was sweating despite the chill inside the church and I knew he wanted only to be done with this hole-and-corner marriage and gone as quickly as he could be.

I still did not know what I was going to say when the moment came for me to speak.

'I require and charge you,' the minister said, 'as you will answer at the day of judgement, when the secrets of all hearts shall be disclosed, that if either of you do know any impediment why you may not be lawfully joined together in matrimony, that you confess it.'

I made up my mind all at once and said, 'Stop. I am not willing, and that is the—'

Rannoch Hamilton drew back his hand and with no change of expression at all struck me hard across the mouth.

I staggered back, tasting blood, covering my mouth with my own hands. One of Rothes' two men caught me from behind and pushed me back to my place. I stood there. I felt tears welling over and streaking down my cheeks. I hated the tears but I could not keep them back. My mouth stung.

'We know of no impediments,' Rannoch Hamilton said calmly.

The minister swallowed, looking from Moray to Rothes and back to Moray. Moray nodded, a small tight nod. The men-at-arms standing outside the chapel shifted their positions slightly, the leather of their belts creaking. One man put his hand on the hilt of his sword.

'If you believe assuredly these words which our Lord and Saviour did speak,' the minister said very fast, 'then may you be certain, that God has even so knit you together in this—'

'I know of an impediment.'

We all jumped. One of Moray's men-at-arms drew his sword with a rasp of metal against metal.

Outside the chapel, in the dark empty nave of the church, one man stepped forward as if he were materialising out of the shadows. He wore plain black riding-clothes covered with dust, and unlike the Earl of Moray's men he had respected the church enough to leave off his weapons. His head was bare and his russet hair glimmered with gold as if it had been touched by an illuminator's brush.

'The lady is unwilling,' said Nicolas de Clerac. He did not speak loudly or harshly but with four words he commanded the attention of every single one of them.

I shivered all through my body, as if I were suddenly both cold and hot at once.

The Earl of Moray broke the spell. 'This is none of your affair,' he said. 'The marriage is being made at the queen's own command.'

'So she told me, the very moment I arrived back at Holyrood.' I could see him shift his weight forward, to the balls of his feet;

he had done it so often in dancing and in masques. The blade of a man-at-arm's sword was pointed straight at his heart, and his hands were empty. 'Even so, someone must say it. A marriage is not a marriage if both parties do not consent.'

'Nico,' I said. I could still taste the blood on my lips as I said it. 'There are six of them, and they are all armed.'

He smiled. 'So they are, *ma mie*,' he said. 'But that does not—'

The sword-blade sliced through the air; it made a sound like a great bird's wing. Steel rang as the rest of them drew their blades. I screamed – I could not help myself – and struggled frantically to escape the hold of Rothes' two men. Rannoch Hamilton himself grasped my arms from behind and held me.

Nico did not move. There was a slash in the black fabric of his doublet. The six men with their naked blades surrounded him.

'This is God's house,' he said. His voice was perfectly steady. 'Would you profane it with spilled blood, my Lord Moray, as well as with a forced marriage?'

Moray made a gesture. The men stepped back and lowered their weapons but they did not sheathe them.

'The marriage will go on,' Moray said. 'It is the queen's will and by the queen's command. If blood is spilled, Monsieur de Clerac, it will be by your choice, not mine.'

'I support the Earl of Moray,' said Rothes. 'I and my men.'

'A pox on all this fine talk,' Rannoch Hamilton said viciously. 'I'll meet you blade to blade, Frenchman, just the two of us, once I've married your witch-girl and—'

'Master Rannoch,' Rothes interrupted him. 'Remember your purpose here. You are marrying Mistress Rinette for the good of her soul and in support of the Lords of the Congregation.'

Rannoch Hamilton's fingers tightened on my arms until the pain forced a gasp from me, however hard I tried to suppress it.

Nico stepped forward. Moray's men raised their swords again. Rannoch Hamilton laughed.

'That's nothing,' he said. 'She'll soon be—'

'Master Rannoch.'

He said nothing more. I clenched my teeth together. If I could grasp one of the men-at-arm's blades, could I thrust it into his black heart before they stopped me? I would be willing to have my own head struck off, willing to burn – But of course that was not true. I could not leave Màiri behind.

'Now, Monsieur de Clerac,' Moray said, in his most unctuous voice. 'Would you like to remain and witness the marriage between Mistress Leslie and Master Hamilton? You are quite welcome to do so, if you wish.'

Nico looked at me. He was thinking the same thing I had been thinking – *If I could grasp one of the men-at-arms' blades* – I could read it in his face. But if he did, even if he killed one or two or three of them, the other five or four or three would cut him down. And I would be married anyway. I would be left with no one, no one.

'Go away,' I said. I made my voice cold. 'I do not want your blood on my hands. If you want to help me, see to Màiri and my family. See to Seilie and Lilidh.'

He stepped back. 'Rinette,' he said. He did not sound like himself. 'Rinette, forgive me.'

I said, 'It is not your fault.'

'Yes,' he said. 'It is.'

He turned and went out of the church.

The marriage went forward. When Rannoch Hamilton was asked for his protestation of consent, he answered firmly. When I was asked for my protestation, I said nothing. No one cared. He forced a plain gold ring on to my finger. I tried to clench my fist but he squeezed my wristbones together until my whole arm turned numb, and I surrendered and opened my hand.

'Therefore,' the minister said, 'apply yourselves to live a chaste and holy life together, in godly love and Christian peace.'

Both the Earl of Moray and the Earl of Rothes listened to this without so much as a flicker of expression at its irony. I did not look at Rannoch Hamilton's face and so I do not know if he found it incongruous or not. All I could think was: They have threatened them all. Everyone I love. Màiri. Tante-Mar. Jennet and Wat and the Mores, old Robinet Loury and Père Guillaume, everyone at Granmuir. Granmuir itself, Lilidh and Seilie. Even Nicolas de Clerac.

Even Nicolas de Clerac.

And the moment I realised that, realised I loved him whether I wished it or not, the memory I had been struggling to capture clicked into place, neat as a pebble in a cup – the corridor at Holyrood, me collapsing with the queen's bread-and-milk in my hands, and then Nico pulling me up. I remembered his soft deep voice as he cradled me in his arms.

You are burning up with fever.

I am bound by a holy vow and I have no right to say it, but you will not remember.

Je t'aime, ma mie.

I love you, my dear one.

As I heard Nico's words in my heart, the minister said, 'The Lord sanctify and bless you; the Lord pour the riches of his grace upon you, that you may please him, and live together in holy love to your lives' end. So be it.'

And it was done. There was no sanctification, no grace, no holy love about it. Rannoch Hamilton still held me by my arms as if I were a captive. I was a captive. I wanted to die.

'Get you to your rooms, Master Rannoch,' Rothes said, 'and make this marriage complete before someone else attempts to meddle in your affairs. We shall talk later about the business of Granmuir and your new rights and title there.'

'Granmuir,' said Moray. 'Yes. And, of course, the silver casket.'

25

Rannoch Hamilton was quartered in rented rooms on the upper storey of a tavern on the Cowgate, down the steep south slope from the High Street. He kept hold of one of my arms and I did not resist him. All I could do now was cling to whatever dignity I had left. I prayed – why did I remember the night Mary of Guise died, the night we all prayed fine Latin prayers? It was the night she gave me the silver casket with her last breath. That night changed everything, and ended with me here, walking with Rannoch Hamilton, married to him, a man I hated and feared. The prayers the minister at Saint Giles' had read were in Scots, not Latin. Protestant prayers. There was no help for me from either the Catholics or the Reformers; as I walked I prayed silently to the Green Lady of Granmuir.

Help me, Lady, help me.

Help me endure.

Help me forget what I should never have remembered.

We reached the tavern and went upstairs. A few early-morning drinkers stared at us. My new husband pushed me ahead of him into his rooms, and when he came in he locked the door behind him and put the key in his pouch.

'Now,' he said.

I walked across the room to the window. It overlooked a tiny garden laid out alongside the stable block. In the garden I could see herbs, a row of berry bushes, a few flowers, and a single stunted pear tree – pear blossom symbolised separation and loneliness but when I reached out to them with my thoughts I could not touch them. The window faced east, towards Holyrood, and the sun was just coming up. I wondered what the queen was doing. I wondered what Nico was doing, where he had gone.

Rinette, forgive me.

Why had he said that? What did he mean?

Je t'aime, ma mie.

Heavy hands came down over my shoulders and turned me around. Not exactly rough, just hard and deliberate. 'Never again,' Rannoch Hamilton said, 'are you to turn your back to me when I speak to you. Do you understand?'

My mouth was still painful from where he had struck me. My lips felt swollen. I shut my mind to any thoughts of Nico and said carefully, 'I understand.'

'Good.' He jerked off my cap. My hair was braided and pinned. He threw the cap on the floor. 'Take down your hair. Then take off your clothes. Do it slowly.'

I looked at him. Again I was struck by the neatness and newness of his own clothes, the cleanliness of his person. He thought to rise in the world, did Rannoch Hamilton, and keep company with Rothes and Moray and even the queen. I could see only his narrow dark eyes, the deep slash between his brows, the curl of vengeful self-satisfaction at the corner of his mouth.

I said, 'I would like to wash myself.'

He laughed. 'You can wash yourself afterwards,' he said. 'Now be silent, take down your hair, and strip yourself.'

My hands felt cold. I unpinned my hair and put the pins on

the table, and then began to untwist the braids. All the time I was doing it I was thinking of ways to escape. But of course there was no way to escape. The door was locked and the window was mullioned into diamond-shaped panes no larger than my hand.

Rannoch Hamilton unbuckled his belt as he watched me, and put his sword and dagger aside. Then he began to unfasten his coat. His breathing had quickened.

'Go on,' he said. 'The mantle, the dress. All of it.'

I unhooked the mantle, slipped it off my shoulders, and began to fold it.

'Drop it.' He took off his doublet and began to unlace his points. 'Now the dress.'

'Master Hamilton,' I said. I could not bring myself to form the sounds of his Christian name. 'It is morning. The sunlight is shining in. Can we not put a curtain over the window, at least?'

'No. It pleases me to look at you in the light. I would take you in the middle of the High Street for everyone to see, if I could. Now drop the damned mantle on the floor and take off your dress, or I will cut it off you.'

I dropped the mantle. 'You want to shame me,' I said.

'I have dreamed of it, since that day in the chapel on your godforsaken rock. You shamed me that day, Marina Leslie, in front of my men.'

'So you admit it.'

'Why would I not admit it? I would cry it from the rooftops – this woman dared to threaten me with her pagan goddess and I will make her pay for it. She belongs to me now and I will have her on her knees, crying and begging.'

'I may cry,' I said. My voice shook. 'But I will never beg.'

'So you say now. The dress, wife.'

The riding-habit was made in two pieces, a short, tight-fitting jacket with the sleeves attached, and a separate skirt. The jacket fastened in the front with corded loops and carved ivory buttons. I began to pull the loops free. There was no point in resisting, and if he cut the riding-habit to pieces what would I wear to leave the room?

If I would ever leave the room.

Màiri, I said to myself. My household. Granmuir. Lilidh and Seilie. I am here in this room now because I will do anything to keep them safe.

In that one year I had spent at the French court as a child, I had seen amazing mechanical devices, animals and nymphs and gods that moved their arms and legs, turned their heads, almost as if they were alive. I held that image in my mind, and moved my arms and legs to do as he asked. I kept my eyes open but I did not look out through them.

I took off the jacket and dropped it on the floor. I unhooked the skirt, let it fall, and stepped out of it. That left me in my laced bodice over a thin linen chemise tied at my neck and wrists, a full, long petticoat, my gartered stockings and my shoes. I unlaced my bodice, took off my underskirt and chemise, crouched down and unbuckled my shoes. Stepped out of them. Stripped off my stockings. Then, naked as a clockwork sea-nymph, my hair hanging loose and the April morning sunshine warm on my bare skin, I straightened and looked at a point somewhere over Rannoch Hamilton's shoulder.

I remembered my wedding night with Alexander. I wanted to cry, oh, how I wanted to cry.

'You're a gey beautiful woman, I'll give you that,' he said. 'Like a wild white Barbary filly with long legs and a silk mouth and a mane all brown and gold. Do you remember what you said to me, at Granmuir?'

'No,' I said. It was a lie – I remembered every word.

'*Take care for the goddesses.*' He repeated it word for word, with the exact tone and inflection I had used. It was eerie. How many times had he said it over and over to himself to remember it so well? '*You take pleasure in binding? There is a Green Lady of Granmuir, who will come in your sleep and wrap her woodbine around your cock and balls and pull it tighter and tighter until they turn black and fall off.*'

He was mad. He had to be mad. I felt genuine fear melting my belly and making my knees shake. I struggled to keep the image of the mechanical devices in my mind but I could not. I felt sick with horror.

'She never did,' he said, in his own voice. He stepped closer. I did not look at him, although I could feel the animal heat of his flesh. 'She never came and never bound me. I've still got my cock and balls, wife, and I've waited for two years to show you just how well and how hard I can wield them.'

We were there in that room all day. He did things to me I knew I would never forget. I tried not to fight him because I knew he wanted me to fight, and I did not want to give him that satisfaction. Mostly I succeeded. Once or twice I did not. Those were the worst times, because although I fought like a wild thing he compelled me to do what he wanted, laughing.

About midday he called for wine and bread and meat. A boy brought them, not a ragged street urchin but a servant wearing a badge I did not know. Rannoch Hamilton called him Gill and asked after two horses by name, and I realised for the first time that Rannoch Hamilton of Kinmeall had a life of some kind outside his position as one of the Earl of Rothes' men. Servants of his own, horses, a home. Did he have brothers and sisters?

Were his father and mother still living? I was not even entirely certain where Kinmeall was.

'Eat, wife,' he said, when the boy Gill had gone. He seemed to have expended his anger and vengefulness for the moment; at the end I had hidden away inside my clockwork-self and surrendered to him in everything, and it had seemed to satisfy him. 'I think you need the strength of it.'

'I am not hungry.'

I saw the crease between his dark brows deepen.

'I am desperately thirsty, though,' I said. 'If you would give me a little of the wine it would be very welcome.'

He refilled his own cup – he had only the one – and handed it to me. I forced down my queasiness and drank. The wine stung my bruised mouth. I handed the cup back to him.

'Thank you,' I said.

He liked that – when I thanked him. He took the cup and filled it two or three more times for himself as he ate the bread and meat. When he had finished and relieved himself, he took hold of me again.

I did cry, in the end. I cried from misery and hopelessness and shame and pain and sheer exhaustion. He licked the tears from my cheeks, revelling in them. He stroked my hair, a little awkwardly, almost gently, as I cried.

But I never begged.

Not one word.

26

The next morning I woke before he did. There was no need to slip quietly out of the bed; he was sleeping like a felled ox. I wanted to wash myself. Sweet Lady, how I wanted to wash myself.

There was something else, though, I had to do first.

I wrapped myself in my petticoat and went over to the table where Rannoch Hamilton had left his sword and dagger.

No, I did not intend to do away with myself; I was not such a coward as that. I wanted to see his dagger and examine it for a falcon's head and a missing ruby.

It was plain workmanlike steel with a haft wrapped in leather. The leather was scuffed and the steel, though polished, was worn.

So I had one piece of evidence, at least, that I was not married to Alexander's murderer, an assassin of the *Escadron Volant*. I had not really believed it, but I had to be sure. The other piece of evidence would be credible testimony as to where Rannoch Hamilton had been at the third watch on the night the queen came home.

The water in the jug was cold and there was no soap, but I scrubbed myself as best I could, working gently around the bruises and the reddened teeth-marks. It was not as bad as it could have been. Not as bad, in a physical sense at least, as I had expected.

Once he had expended his first vengefulness he had been gentler. I could not help wondering if he thought to wheedle the casket out of me for himself, and betray Rothes and Moray.

I dressed myself quickly and quietly, in my chemise and habit only, leaving off my laced bodice and stockings. The boy Gill had to be somewhere nearby, probably in the stable block beside the garden where the horses would be kept. I stepped into my shoes and wrapped my mantle around my shoulders, concealing my face as much as I could. The key was in Rannoch Hamilton's pouch and easy to retrieve. Downstairs the tavern was deserted – it was only just dawn. I went out of the back door into the garden, and through the garden to the stable.

The horses were awake, warm and snorting. The earthy, familiar smell of horses and cut straw and oiled leather gave me a pang, thinking of Lilidh; I wondered where she had been taken when I was led off from Edinburgh Castle as a prisoner. Seilie, too – Jennet and Wat had presumably ridden south from Lochleven with the queen's household, and I prayed they had both Lilidh and Seilie safe. I prayed they were safe themselves. The boy who had brought Rannoch Hamilton's bread and meat and wine was down at the end of the stalls, talking quietly to a big bay with a star on his forehead. The horse seemed to be paying close attention, his ears pricked forward. I stepped through the door and stumbled, my foot sinking into a straw-covered hole in the earthen floor. My ankle twisted and I fell against the flimsy wall. The whole building shuddered, and the horse threw back its head.

Gill jumped, and when he saw it was me he ran to help me up. 'Mistress,' he said. 'You gave me a fright, you did. Are you all right?'

'Yes, yes, I am sorry – I am perfectly well, I did not see that hole.'

He went back to the horse's head. 'Shush, shush, my laddie,' he said. ''Tis only the mistress, come to meet you. I should have raked up the straw, mistress. Please dinnae tell the master.'

He calmed the bay with words and a touch. The horse settled immediately. Seen close to, Gill was only twelve, fourteen at most, but clearly he was good with horses. He did not seem at all surprised to see me, or uncomfortable with what he had seen the day before.

'I will not tell,' I said. My ankle was throbbing but I was embarrassed to have been so clumsy. 'What is his name?'

'Diamant. For the mark on his face. He's the master's favourite riding-horse, and fast! You should see him run.'

'I have a horse, too. A white mare. Her name is Lilidh.'

'Where be she?'

'At Holyrood Palace, I think. I hope – the master – will have her brought here, and I know you will take good care of her.'

'Never had a white horse to tend before. Lilidh, that's a good name.'

I stepped closer and held out my palm to Diamant. He snuffled at it, his whiskery muzzle like velvet stuck with pins. 'Gill,' I said. 'Have you served your master for long?'

'All my life, mistress, and my da before me.'

'Did he come to Edinburgh, when the queen came back from France?'

'We all did, mistress, master and my da and me. The Earl of Rothes called all his people to come, and we're the earl's men, we are.' He seemed pleased to have someone to talk to, and I kept quiet, wanting to learn as much as I could. 'My da, he died last year, but he always said he was glad he lived to see the young queen come home. He never gave up the old religion, though the earl is reformed and so is the master.'

'So you saw the queen on the first day? You saw her ride from Leith to Holyrood Palace?'

'Nae, mistress, not that part. We was a few days late arriving. But the master stood with the earl the day she entered the toun ceremonial-like, pretending it was the first time, with fifty men dressed up like Moors and wine a-pouring out from the spouts on the Mercat Cross. I was standing right behind them that day, the master and the earl.'

'Then your master was not in Edinburgh on the queen's first night here?'

'Nae, mistress, we hadna even left Kinmeall on that day.'

So Rannoch Hamilton had not killed Alexander. In a way I was glad, but in a way almost disappointed. If he had been Alexander's murderer, I could have found a way to kill him and free myself. My conscience quivered a little at the coldness of the thought. I pushed it aside. I had no more need of a conscience.

'Thank you, Gill,' I said. 'I will come and talk to you again, if the master allows it.'

'He's nae so bad, mistress, long's you dinnae cross him.'

I felt myself turning red, and pulled the hood of my mantle closer around my face. I wondered if there were bruises other people could see. I had no mirror, and I would never ask. 'Good day to you,' I said.

'Good day, mistress.'

I limped back out into the garden. The sun was coming up over the roofs of the tall narrow houses, and the sky was a cloudless April blue. I would have to go back upstairs to that terrible room – the Green Lady help me, I would have to live in that room now, away from the queen and the court, with no one but Rannoch Hamilton for human companionship – but I would steal a few minutes, at least, to speak to the flowers, the herbs, the pear tree.

I touched its trunk. The bark was rough and scaly – it was an old tree, then. It had begun to blossom. I wanted to know what it would say, whether its meaning of separation and loneliness would cling to me forever.

It was silent. I could touch it, I could smell the sweetish, slightly musky scent of the flowers, but it was only a tree. It did not speak to me.

I walked over to the herbs. There was mint and mallow, rampion and rosemary, clary and thyme, all grown together cottage-garden style with pinks and daisies and columbines. I crouched down – how strained and sore my muscles were, how bruised I felt – and ran my hand over the leaves, releasing their scents. Sweet, spicy, fruit-like, resinous. Their textures velvety, crisp, spiky, smooth. And that was all. They were only plants.

I cried for a moment or two, all alone in that tiny courtyard behind a seedy tavern in the Cowgate. I longed desperately for Granmuir and the sea and my gardens there, for Màiri and Tante-Mar, for Seilie and Lilidh, and yes, to be completely and humiliatingly honest, for Nicolas de Clerac, who had saved my life that night in the High Street, who had helped me search for Alexander's murderer, who had told me the secret story of his mother's tragic forced marriage, who had whispered *je t'aime, ma mie* and then abandoned me to be wed to Rannoch Hamilton at the queen's command. I wanted to cry in his arms. I wanted to kill him.

Forgive me, Rinette.

For one blinding blood-red moment I wanted to kill them all.

Fortunately the moment passed. At least it burned the tears from my eyes.

I had cried enough.

Now I had to keep a cool head, and think, and plan.

First . . . It was foolish and dangerous to think about killing Rannoch Hamilton, no matter what he did to me. I did not want to hang at the Tolbooth myself, so for now he held the upper hand. Very well. I would bend beneath that hand and wait for Fortune's wheel to turn. Because turn it would. And perhaps I could even find a means of pushing it on its way.

Second . . . Everyone believed I still had the casket, or at least still knew where it was, hidden away in some secret place. Very well, let them believe it. I would stop denying it and find ways to use their belief against them. I could turn Rannoch Hamilton against Rothes, Rothes against Moray, Moray against the queen herself. I could do it because the only person who knew the truth was the person who had taken the casket.

If that person had taken it in order to sell the contents, the truth would come out quickly. But if the person who had taken it meant to use the contents to gain knowledge and power inside Scotland – well, then, they would be keeping their possession of the casket as secret as secret could be, and I would have some time, at least, before any whispers began.

So who had taken it?

Who had known about the secret vault?

I could eliminate the poor doddering Abbot of Dunfermline in France. Mary of Guise – had she told someone else? Could she have written the secret to her own mother, Duchess Antoinette of Guise in France?

King James would have known. Lady Margaret had known. If it was Lady Margaret who had the casket, she would keep it the deepest and darkest of secrets. She would use it to make Moray regent, then to make him king, and she would let him believe it was his own worthiness, his royal blood, effecting his rise.

I passed my hand over the plants again. If they had spoken to me then, would I have heeded them, softened my heart, done anything differently?

I will never know because they did not speak. I drew myself up to my full height, scrubbed the tears from my face with the backs of my hands, and went inside.

When Rannoch Hamilton finally awakened, I was sitting by the window, gazing out at the sun rising. I heard him stretching and yawning, then heard the uneven floorboards creak, and I turned my head.

He had a fine, powerful body, I would grant him that, long legs, heavy shoulders and arms, the shape of each muscle clearly delineated. His skin was swarthy even where it was not exposed to the sun; the hair on his chest and arms and legs was thick and gleaming as a black wolf's pelt. He made no attempt at all to cover himself.

'Well, wife,' he said. 'What say you now about your pagan goddess and her woodbine?'

'I would say you have escaped her.'

He laughed. If a vicious wolf could be said to preen itself, he preened.

'I would also say she has lived at Granmuir for a thousand years, and will live there for a thousand more, and that if you think to take Granmuir for your own you had best make peace with her.'

'I make peace with nothing female, goddess or human. This Green Lady of yours is the one who will surrender to me, just as you have done.'

'A forced surrender is no true surrender.'

He laughed again. 'I'll force it until you forget anything else but the fact I'm your master, and in the end you'll crawl to me and beg me to take the old queen's casket.'

'I will never give you the casket.' As I said it I looked at him and made my eyes say, *I do have it and if you betray Rothes and Moray perhaps I will give it to you, who knows?* 'And I will die before I crawl to you, or anyone else.'

He laughed. I could see he had understood my wordless suggestion and it had excited him.

He went to the door and shouted for hot water and food. I turned away and looked out of the window again. Behind me he splashed in the water and pulled on his clothes. I heard metal clink as he buckled on his belt with his sword and dagger. I had put the key back in his pouch and with luck he would never know I had gone downstairs.

'I'll spend the day attending upon my Lord Rothes, as usual,' he said, as he gobbled up coarse oatcake and drank ale. 'Stay here. I'll have the room watched, so don't think to slip away. Try it and I'll beat you within an inch of your life, casket or no casket.'

'I will not try to escape. Where would I go?'

He looked at me. I wondered if he himself felt the emptiness I saw in his eyes, or if he thought everyone was as empty as he was. 'You can call for hot water if you like,' he said. 'Women always seem to want hot water and soap. And Gill will bring you food.'

I said nothing. The crease between his brows deepened and he went out.

Hot water. The Green Lady be thanked. Hot water and soap. I waited just long enough to be sure he was away, then went to the door and called for Gill. He willingly brought me clean hot water, a little pot of rosemary-scented soft soap – where had it come from? I was not going to question it – and clean towels. I stripped myself and washed, then washed again, washed my body and my hair and kept washing until the soap was gone and the water was cold. The rosemary scent was medicinal and comforting. I sponged my riding-habit and underclothes, too, as best I could, and towelled my hair. Then I dressed myself and pinned up my hair and called for Gill again. He brought me hot fresh oatcakes, an egg custard, and wine caudle.

'Gill,' I said. 'When I have eaten, I would like to sleep. Can you send someone to warn me before – the master – comes up to the room?'

'I'll try, mistress. I'll watch for him myself, and send Bel up to wake you.' He did not seem at all puzzled as to why I did not want Rannoch Hamilton to come upon me unawares.

'Thank you, Gill.'

For the rest of the morning and most of the afternoon I slept.

A soft knock on the door woke me. I had been dreaming of the ancient garden wall at Granmuir, overgrown with nightshade and— But it was gone before I could make sense of it. I scrambled up out of the bed and went to the door.

'Master be coming, mistress.' It was a scrawny, dirty little girl of ten or twelve. 'Gill askit me to wairn ye.'

'Thank you, Bel,' I said. I wished I had a penny to give her. She did not wait, but ran down the stairs and disappeared.

I settled myself in the chair by the window, just as I had been when he went out. A few minutes later he came in the door, shouting for wine as he came. He looked pleased with himself.

'A fine thing it is,' he said, 'to come home to a wife. I have news for you.'

'What news?'

'The Earl of Moray and my Lord Rothes have assigned me an apartment in Holyrood. Two rooms and space in the stables, and—'

Gill came in with a beaker of wine and two cups.

'We're going to live at the palace, Gill,' Rannoch Hamilton said. 'What do you think of that?'

'All o' us?' the boy said. 'Horses 'n' all?'

'Horses and all. In fact, you'll have another horse to look after – your new mistress's mare.'

I closed my eyes and prayed the boy would not say anything about Lilidh that would reveal we had spoken together that morning. He was obviously cleverer than I gave him credit for, because he made a great show of pouring the wine without spilling it. Then he said, 'That's guid, master, and I'll wager the stables at the palace are better than the ones here.'

'That they are. Now off with you. Bring some supper in an hour or so.'

'Aye, master.'

Rannoch Hamilton gave me one of the cups and drank off his own in a single draught. 'So are you pleased?' he said. 'You'll be back among your fine folks of the court with barely a day away, and I'll be knocking elbows with them as well.'

I took a sip of the wine. It was cheap and sour. 'I do not want to be back among them,' I said. I could not face them, the queen and her court, and see in their eyes they knew I was Rannoch Hamilton's possession.

'I thought you'd be pleased,' he said. The line between his brows deepened.

'Very well, I am pleased.' I took another swallow of the wine. 'What about my own people? Jennet More and Wat Cairnie? Are they back in Edinburgh from Lochleven, and safe? And Seilie, my little hound?'

'They're there. The woman's moving your clothes and chests to my rooms tonight. The dog's been a-whining, she says, and pacing in the night, looking for you.'

'Thank you,' I said.

His brow smoothed a little. Good.

'The Earl of Moray will be regent in a year or two, you watch – the queen will go traipsing off to Spain to marry the king's daft son and one day be queen there.' He poured himself another cup of wine. 'Then my Lord Rothes will be higher than high, and I'll be at his right hand, wife's kin to him. That's why he wants me close by.'

'He wants you close by because he does not trust you. Neither one of them trusts you. They are afraid you will find out where I have hidden the casket and keep it for yourself, and they want you close where they can watch over you.'

He drank the second cup of wine. I could see doubt in his expression, and felt a grim pleasure that I had sown it.

'I'll prove myself to them,' he said.

'Perhaps.'

'You'll tell me where the casket is and I'll place it into my Lord Rothes' own hands.' He began to unbutton his doublet. 'You'll tell me.'

'I will not.' I looked away, and glanced back at him from the corners of my eyes. *Maybe I will. Maybe you can be higher than high on your own merits, if you think twice before placing the casket in Rothes' hands. Earl of Kinmeall, how do you like the sound of that?*

'You will,' he said. 'And you'll give up your talk about Green Ladies and woodbine and doing magic with flowers.'

Little did he know I had tried to do magic with flowers that very morning, and failed. The flowers had abandoned me. Little did he know that even so, I'd be praying to the Green Lady with all my heart and soul, every time he laid his hand upon me.

I said nothing more. I had planted enough seeds for one day. I drank my wine, made myself into a fanciful mechanical device with no feelings or fears, and took off my clothes again.

27

Nine days later – and I knew it was nine because I counted them, day by joyless day – Rannoch Hamilton brought me a court dress, bodice and sleeves, skirt and overskirt, all in dark blue velvet slashed and trimmed with pale turquoise silk. The velvet was embroidered with gold thread and trimmed with pearls and crystals; there was a headdress in the same dark blue velvet sewn with tiny pearls in the shape of my own device, the sea-wave. There was also a long gauzy white veil in the same style the queen affected.

It meant I would have to go back to court.

'Where did you get the money for all these things?' I asked.

'I am not a pauper,' he said. 'I have a strongbox full of gold at Kinmeall.'

Probably stolen, I thought. 'When are you taking me to court?'

He grinned at me. He knew it would be agony for me, and he was looking forward to it. 'Tomorrow,' he said. 'And I expect you to smile sweetly at the queen and tell her I am the best of husbands.'

The Earl of Rothes escorted us into the queen's little supper-room.

'Madame,' he said formally. 'I present to you my wife's kinsman Master Rannoch Hamilton of Kinmeall, and his wife Marina Leslie, daughter and heir of Patrick Leslie of Granmuir.'

I looked straight into the queen's eyes. I would not show fear and I would not show deference and I would not show the shame and misery that prickled all over my skin as I felt everyone in the room looking at me.

The queen smiled. 'Good day, Master Rannoch,' she said. 'Good day, Marianette.'

Rannoch Hamilton bowed. He had shaved himself and cut his hair and bought fresh clothes for himself as well; they had not yet settled to fit his body. He moved like a wild animal, a wolf or a wildcat, every step smooth, collected and wary.

'Good day to you, Madam,' he said.

I curtseyed, my dark blue skirts belling out around me. I kept my head up and my eyes fixed upon hers. 'Good day, Madame,' I said.

'Tell me, how do you find married life?'

Rannoch Hamilton said nothing. He could probably think of nothing to say that was suitable for refined company. After a moment I said, 'It is as you might imagine, Madame.'

The first shock of humiliation was over. I had survived it. Little by little I let myself look at the other people in the room.

On either side of the queen stood Nicolas de Clerac and a small dark man – I had seen him about the court but I could not remember his name. Nico was looking down at a lute, fingering a chord with great care. I could not look at his face; I looked at his hands, the smooth sun-browned skin, the courtier's nails trimmed and buffed to a shine, the light and decisive way he placed his fingertips on the lute's strings. Nico, Nico. Silently I thanked the Green Lady he was not looking at me. I could not have borne it if he had looked up into my eyes at that moment. Did he know that? I suspect he did.

In a carved chair by the fireplace sat the Earl of Moray. It was easier to look into his eyes because I hated him and he hated me. The hatred gave me strength.

Behind the queen stood Mary Beaton, Mary Fleming, and Agnes Keith, Countess of Moray.

I would be all right. I would be able to bear it. As long as Nico did not look up, I would be able to bear it.

'I do not wish to attend the trial of the Earl of Huntly,' the queen said.

Clearly she was picking up the thread of her previous conversation. Rannoch Hamilton squeezed my forearm, causing a jolt of hot pain, and pulled me to one side.

'He has been dead since last November,' the queen went on. 'Why does his poor body have to lie in its coffin in the court? You cannot tell me it will not stink, however hard the embalmers may have worked on it.'

'It is Scots tradition, sister.' Even coming into the conversation in the middle as I was, it was easy to tell that the Earl of Moray's patience was wearing thin. 'A peer of the realm to be attainted must face his accusers.'

'He is *dead*. He cannot face anyone. I will open the Parliament and I will make a very fine oration, but I will not stay for the trial. What say you, 'Sieur Nico? Signor Davy? Do you believe a queen should be forced to sit face-to-face with a rotting corpse?'

Signor Davy. Of course. David Riccio. Rannoch Hamilton had railed against him – another foreigner, another Catholic to encourage the queen in her heresies, a papal agent even, some whispered. Another foreigner. Another *Escadron Volant* assassin, perhaps, placed at the court by the French or the English or even the pope himself?

He was small, dark and simian, and looked like a sad-faced monkey next to Nico's fair-skinned, elegant height. I was surprised to see him so intimate with the queen, although he was said to be a charming conversationalist and a singer with the most glorious deep bass voice imaginable. Perhaps the queen liked the contrast between the two men, Nico and Davy. They were like midnight and noon, Vulcan and Helios.

'You should not be forced to do anything you do not wish to do, *Vostra Maestà*,' David Riccio said. 'You are too fine, too delicate, to be subjected to such unpleasantness.'

'On the other hand,' said Nico de Clerac gently, still avoiding my eyes, 'because you are the queen, Madame, you are honour-bound to abide by the ancient traditions of your people. Remember, the world is watching you here in Scotland, and taking note of how you discharge your royal obligations.'

''Sieur Nico, how is it that you can tell me what I do not wish to hear, and at the same time make it sound so sweet?' The queen tapped him playfully on the arm with the enamelled case she used to hold her embroidery scissors. 'The world is watching! What a diplomat you are. But I suppose you are right. Very well, I shall preside over the Earl of Huntly's trial next month. Livingston, you shall keep me liberally supplied with pomanders.'

All the ladies giggled.

The queen set another stitch in the piece of embroidery she was working. I could see the device was a French anagram of her name. MARIE STUARTE. TU TE MARIERAS. *Mary Stuart. Thou shalt marry*. That, of course, was why the world was watching. Who would she marry? Who were the *quatre maris* in Nostradamus' prophecies? Were they four men she should marry, or four men she should not?

I wondered if either one of us would ever know.

'*C'est cela*, then,' the queen said in a bright voice. She turned to me again. 'Marianette, you have had enough of a *lune de miel*, I think. I wish you to return to my service, married or not — I myself will marry again soon, and I think it will be a good thing to have more married women around me.'

I was not sure I wanted to take up another position at the court. Face Nico every day? Did I have the strength to do it? On the other hand, a place at court would take me away from Rannoch Hamilton's presence, and that was certainly a good thing. Most important of all, if I wanted to find out who had taken the casket, I had to be at court.

If I appeared to want to be there, Rannoch Hamilton would almost certainly forbid it.

I said, with every appearance of meekness, 'That is for my husband to say, Madame.'

'Surely he will not gainsay me.' The queen looked at Rannoch Hamilton and smiled. 'You will be much occupied in the affairs of the Earl of Rothes, is that not so, Master Rannoch? I understand he has installed you and your wife in rooms here at Holyrood, so you will be close at hand.'

Once again Rannoch Hamilton said nothing. He looked as if he wanted to say, *I'll do what I please with my own wife, Madam, and I'd do it to you, too, if I had the chance.*

'I had intended,' Rothes put in hastily, 'for Mistress Rinette to serve my own wife.'

'Surely the countess can find someone else,' the queen said in her sweetest voice. 'Very well, it is settled. Marianette, you and your husband shall move back into the rooms you occupied before you were married, which will be more convenient for me. You had a maidservant, I believe? Where is she?'

'She is here, Madame. So is my groom.'

'And your little Seilie?'

'He has been staying in the stable, with my groom and my mare Lilidh.'

'Bring him back into the palace, so I can enjoy his company as well. I always found him particularly charming.' The queen smiled. '*Voilà*. All will be just as it was.'

At that moment Nico turned his head and looked at me for the first time. I knew he had to do it eventually but that did not make it easier. It was as if he had struck me. I felt shame and anger and misery scald me, from my pearl-embroidered headdress to the tips of my toes.

Shame and anger and misery and hopeless, hopeless love.

To the queen I said only, 'All will never be as it was, Madame.'

28

All will be as it was.

Was she mad? Nothing was as it had been.

Although that is not entirely true. Jennet and Wat were back in attendance upon me; Wat took the boy Gill under his wing in the stables. Seilie was back as well, following me up and down the corridors of Holyrood Palace with his little claws clicking, sitting close at my feet, delighting all the ladies as he had always done.

At night Rannoch Hamilton hovered over me like a hawk with its prey, stooping and grasping me as darkness fell. He could not seem to get enough of his dominance over me and the Green Lady. Sometimes he spoke to me, taunted me when he had me pinned beneath him, as if I actually were the Green Lady in the flesh. Jennet loathed him and kept out of his way as much as possible.

I missed Màiri so much. It was coming up to the end of May, and in August she would turn two. She had taken her first steps for Tante-Mar, not me. She had spoken her first word – *oatcake*. Tante-Mar had sent me a length of ribbon to show me how tall she had grown, and an ivory ring with the marks of her tiny teeth – she had twelve now, six on top and six on the bottom, and one back tooth was beginning to come in. Every night I prayed for her. I still had the ruby from the assassin's dagger, and I had not given up hope of finding the truth and seeing justice done and going home. For the time being, however, all I could do was endure.

Today we were clustered around the queen as she sat under her royal cloth of estate in the Great Hall of the new Tolbooth, presiding at the ceremony of attainder to be performed over the Earl of Huntly's corpse. All the estates of Parliament were there, sitting solemnly. The galleries above were packed with city folk in serviceable browns and greys and a few bright holiday colours; in the front rows were such representatives of foreign governments as happened to be in Edinburgh. The preserved remains of the dead earl lay in a wooden coffin under a banner worked with his arms and escutcheons.

'Say you,' cried out the Lyon King of Arms, 'that said Earl of Huntly's treason has been declared proven, and that his forfeiture is good, and that his arms shall be riven off and deleted forth of memory?'

The Lords of the Articles, the queen's council, and everyone else in the three estates who had packed into the Tolbooth out of ghoulishness or curiosity, shouted their agreement. The Earldom of Huntly was no more; the banner was pulled off the coffin and taken away. There was a cry of fascinated horror as those closest to the front saw what remained of the earl himself.

'I wish to withdraw.' The queen rose suddenly. 'I cannot bear this.'

'You must bear it,' the Earl of Moray said. He had directed his servants to place his chair quite close to the queen's, so his left arm at least was under the cloth of estate. 'There are more attainders still to be pronounced. You must be present.'

'Delay them. I will return in an hour or so, when I have refreshed myself.'

She swept out, with all of us scrambling to follow her. I was not quick enough, and the crowd around the door blocked my passage. When I turned to search for a different way out I found myself facing a short, compact man in black with cropped grey hair and bleached-bone eyes.

'Madame,' he said. 'A moment, if you please.'

'Monsieur Laurentin.' I was surprised to see him; by his own admission he had no official standing with the French ambassador. 'I must follow the queen, Monsieur,' I said. 'Will you let me pass?'

'You follow her like a lap dog, after what she has done to you?'

I should have smelled the miasmic scent of wild white bryony, the devil's turnip, but I did not. Married to Rannoch Hamilton, I had no connection with the flowers, no floromancy any more. Perhaps it was all sucked into the empty blackness inside him.

I said, 'You are offensive, Monsieur.'

'I do not mean to be. It is common talk about the court that you were unwilling to marry Rothes' bastard brother-in-law. As well you should have been – you are a granddaughter of a Duke of Longueville. You would be better treated in France, Madame, where your blood would be appreciated.'

I felt a surge of – what did I feel? I was gratified, of course, that he thought me too good for Rannoch Hamilton. I was pleased to be reminded that my grandfather was a great duke in France, so high that his legitimate son had been married to Mary of Guise herself. But I disliked and distrusted Blaise Laurentin, and I knew he was saying these things deliberately to produce my feelings of gratification and pleasure.

'My blood,' I said, 'and my possession of Mary of Guise's silver casket.'

He leaned forward. I could have sworn his ears actually swivelled slightly and pointed towards me, like a demon's ears. 'You admit that you have it, then.'

I had to be careful – I did not know who really had the casket. I did not want to be caught in an outright lie.

'Perhaps,' I said. 'Perhaps not. You believe I have it, however, and that is why you are flattering me.'

All around us people milled and swarmed, chattering about Huntly lying half-rotten in his coffin, his titles stripped away. No one paid us the slightest attention.

'I am not flattering you,' he said. 'Is it not true that you are the Duke of Longueville's granddaughter? Queen Catherine herself is perfectly well aware of this, and of the fact that your marriage was a Protestant ceremony, performed without your consent. If you were in France, under Queen Catherine's protection, an annulment from the true church would be a simple matter. You could choose your own husband from the flower of the French nobility, or resume your status as a widow with a fine estate of your own. In Normandy, perhaps, beside the sea.'

'These annulments and noble husbands and fine estates depending,' I said, 'upon me putting the silver casket into Queen Catherine's hands.'

He smiled and spread his hands apart. 'But of course.'

'And if I did not wish to leave Scotland?' I said. 'If I required gold instead? What price, do you think, would Queen Catherine place upon what I have?'

He stepped closer. I stepped back involuntarily.

'A very high price,' he murmured. 'I should have to consult her.'

'Do so, then.'

'I would have to be certain that you are telling the truth. Perhaps

284

you could show me the casket? It is the prophecies of Nostradamus that Queen Catherine particularly desires to have.'

'I am afraid you will have to depend upon my word alone.' I felt a quickening of panic as he continued to move close to me, pressing me towards the edge of the crowd. 'Monsieur Laurentin, step aside, if you please, so that I may go out and rejoin the queen's party.'

'I think not,' he said. 'I think you will be much more willing to show me the casket if you and I are alone together, *n'est-ce pas?* Let us just go down this passageway. I have horses waiting—'

I threw back my head and screamed.

The expression on his face would have been funny if I had not been so genuinely frightened. Perhaps in France ladies were too elegant or too polite to scream like a farm-wife when men threatened them at public gatherings.

'Is this fellow a-batherin' you, mistress?' It was a stout townsman, easily twice the size and half the age of Blaise Laurentin. Two or three more men had turned their heads and started towards us.

'I cede the day to you, Madame,' Laurentin said. 'But Queen Catherine will have that casket and all it contains, one way or another.'

He looked at the townsman briefly and scornfully, then went off down the passageway alone.

'Thank you, sir,' I said to the townsman. 'I have become separated from my husband in the crowd. I believe he is—'

'Here.'

But it was not Rannoch Hamilton. It was Nicolas de Clerac, richly but severely dressed in black and silver. His eyes were outlined with kohl; he wore diamonds and pearls in his ears, and his fingers glittered with rings.

'Take better care of your wife, me lord,' the townsman said. 'That fellow meant her no good.'

I saw gold coins slip from Nico's fingers into the townsman's palms. They laughed together, man-to-man at the foolishness of women, and the townsman went away.

'I was managing perfectly well by myself,' I said.

'So I see. Even so, I am sorry I could not fight my way through the crowd quickly enough to put a dagger between Monsieur Laurentin's ribs.'

'At which point my real husband would most likely put one between yours, for your presumption.'

I had been avoiding Nico. It had not been easy; the queen called upon him constantly for advice, conversation, companionship, and at the same time she kept me so close I felt as if I would suffocate. Was she sorry for what she had done to me, and trying to make amends? Whatever the reason for my sudden return to favour, I did not want to talk to Nicolas de Clerac. I felt sick and shamed at the thought of him looking at me, face to face, eye to eye, and imagining me in Rannoch Hamilton's bed.

'Your husband has already gone outside with the Earl of Rothes,' he said. His voice was light and gentle, as if he knew what I was thinking. He probably did. 'So I am safe for the moment. What did Laurentin want?'

'Nothing. I must find the queen's party – she will miss me.'

'If she were going to miss you, she would have done so already. Better to stay here, and resume your place after she has returned for the rest of the proceedings. She will be distracted by her dislike of this whole business of the attainders, and forget anything else.'

He was right, of course. I said nothing.

'Come up into the gallery with me,' he went on. 'I would like to talk to you for a moment.'

'No.'

'Please. It is not what you think.'

I wanted to strike him. I wanted to shake him. I said, in an unsteady voice, 'You do not know what I think.'

'Forgive me. Of course I do not. Listen to me – this business with Laurentin disturbs me, and you know why. I want to know what he said to you. Tell me here if you wish. There are plenty of gentlemanly townsmen about to save you if I become too importunate.'

'Do not be ridiculous,' I said. 'Very well, let us go up on the gallery.'

We walked up the stairs. He took exquisite care not to touch me. Even the slashed and embroidered fabric of his paned trunk hose did not touch my skirt. He was right – the galleries were almost empty. There were just enough people to make it clear to anyone who looked that we were not alone.

We stood there for a moment. Then he leaned over the railing, resting his forearms on the wooden ledge. Without looking at me, very quietly, he said, 'Rinette.'

How could there be so much sorrow, so much regret, so much intensity of feeling, in a single word? It struck me to the heart. I felt sick and dizzy, hot and cold. I felt – the loss, the loss. As if I would die, there in the gallery of the Tolbooth, from the emptiness and hopeless sorrow.

I could not have spoken, even if I could have thought of something to say.

After a moment he straightened. His face was drawn tight and blank of any expression. I thought, That is what he will look like if he is ever wounded unto death.

'Tell me what Laurentin said to you.' His voice was quiet and formal. 'Tell me exactly what he thought to do.'

'It is none of your affair.'

'He believes you still have the silver casket, does he not?'

'He does.' Even though it was not a lie – Laurentin truly did believe I had it – I could not look at Nico de Clerac when I said it.

After a moment he said, 'You do not have it, do you?'

I looked down at my hands. My wedding ring felt heavy as a fetter, for all that it was made of polished gold.

'I do have it,' I said. 'Moray was right – I hoped if I took them on a wild goose chase, they would believe someone had stolen it, and would allow me to go home in peace.'

He looked at me. His eyes, golden hazel, so similar to the queen's that if I looked at his eyes alone I might be looking at the queen herself, were steady and clear. 'So,' he said. 'You say you have it. Were you offering to sell it to Laurentin?'

I could feel myself flushing.

'I was not,' I said. It was hard to lie to him – it hurt me to say untrue words, and it frightened me because I knew I was transparent to him.

'Laurentin is a dangerous man. He is almost certainly a member of the *Escadron Volant*. If you attempt to trick him in some way, you could pay dearly.'

'It is not your place to fear for me.'

His hands tightened on the rail. He looked away and said, 'Even so, I do.'

I could not bear this. I had to stop it somehow before it tore my heart out of my breast.

'Leave me alone, Nico.' I struggled to keep my voice low and steady. 'You cannot help me now. I will do whatever I must.'

I felt him flinch. After a moment he said, 'You say you want your freedom and your estate.' His voice was different, harder. 'What of justice for Alexander Gordon – are you abandoning that, despite the love you professed for him?'

'I loved him. He betrayed me.'

More silence. Why did he not just go away and leave me to my anguish?

'I will pursue the assassin,' he said. 'Rinette, forgive me. I could not help you escape this marriage, but I can do one thing for you, and that is find out who killed your Alexander.'

I said nothing. I did not know what to say.

'They are coming in again. You had best go downstairs now, so the queen and your husband do not wonder where you are.'

I went down a step, and then another. Without turning around to look at him I said, 'Nico. I know there was nothing you could have done to prevent the marriage, once the queen set her mind to it.'

'I would have given up my life,' he said, 'if I could have stopped it.'

'I know.'

'I would take you away now, to France, with Màiri and all your people. I would—'

'*Stop.*'

He stopped.

I could taste bitterness like sea-wormwood in my mouth and my heart. When I could speak I said, 'You say you will take us away, Nico? What of your vow?'

He said nothing. There was nothing he could say to that.

'Good day to you, Monsieur de Clerac.'

Very softly he said, 'God go with you, *ma mie.*'

* * *

I slipped into the queen's train in the midst of the crowd, and I was only just in time. Rannoch Hamilton pushed his way through a phalanx of townspeople from the other side of the room and took hold of my arm. I flinched, and he loosened his grasp.

'I did not see you outside the Tolbooth,' he said.

'Nor did I see you.'

'The queen and Mary Fleming started to scream at each other, all of a sudden out of nowhere. I swear by that Green Lady of yours, they almost came to blows. The Fleming wench has been sent away in tears.'

'I did not hear what they were quarrelling about,' I said, perfectly truthfully.

'I didn't hear it either. Stay away from the queen, though – she's going to be looking for another lady to sleep in her bedchamber with her, and I don't want it to be you.'

'That would be terrible.'

He gave me a shake to emphasise his command, then let go of me and went back to the group of men surrounding the Earl of Rothes. I immediately made my way as close to the queen as I could get. She was still angry, high colour in her smooth cheeks and her amber eyes glittering, berating poor Lady Reres about some imagined unevenness in her cloth of state. All the other ladies were hanging back and avoiding the queen's attention, fearing more explosions of royal temper.

'Madame,' I said in my sweetest voice. 'Perhaps I can help Lady Reres adjust the cloth properly.'

'It is past time someone offered to help,' the queen said. She threw herself down in her chair in a very unregal fashion. 'When you are finished, Marianette, fetch me something cold to drink.'

'Of course, Madame.'

For the rest of the afternoon, while the Earl of Huntly's eldest son and other lords who had allied themselves with Huntly's rebellion were attainted and condemned – young George Gordon's life was spared, at least, and he was sent off to Dunbar to be kept in confinement there – I made every effort I could think of to make myself charming and indispensable to the queen. By the time we left the Tolbooth again, I was her new bedfellow. She laughed at the thought of Rannoch Hamilton sleeping alone and disgruntled, deprived of his wife.

I did not exactly laugh, because I knew I would pay for it in the end. But I smiled. I would have some nights, at least, of blessed freedom.

29

'J ust drink the tea, Rinette,' Jennet said. 'It's getting cold.'

I concentrated on folding a coverlet. 'It is too late.'

'There's still time. You taught me the plants yourself, and I picked them careful. Pennyroyal, tansy and rue, steeped gentle-like in fresh-fallen rainwater, long enough to say the *Miserere* three times all the way through.'

'I do not doubt you picked the right plants and made the tea correctly.' I put the coverlet in the queen's travelling chest. 'But it is too late. I could do harm to myself and the—' I could not say the word *baby*. 'I could do harm.'

'Rinette, the tea will bring your courses down. It will not harm you. Do you want the seed of that cluitie-foot Rannoch Hamilton growing inside—'

'*Stop it.*'

She stopped.

I was shaking. I closed my eyes and counted my breaths, deep and even. I did not know what I was going to do but drinking the tea was not the answer.

I opened my eyes.

'Oh, Jennet,' I said. I went across the queen's bedchamber to her and hugged her. 'I am sorry. I know you mean the best. But I do not think I can drink the tea safely. I am so thin, I have been since I was sick with the New Acquaintance at Christmas. I cannot seem to eat properly. And I cannot sleep – the queen sleeps so little herself, and she expects to be amused whenever she awakens in the night.'

'All that's true enough,' Jennet said. She patted my hair like she might pat a child's, although she had a mulish look about her.

'We are to set off for Glasgow tomorrow. I have to ride with the queen. You know the tea will make me sick, and if I am sick they will leave me behind. He—' When Jennet and I were together I never called my husband by his name. 'He will stay behind too, because he will take it as a chance to have me to himself again. Oh, Jennet, I could not bear the next two months here in Edinburgh with no company but his.'

'No, nor I either.' Jennet picked up the noggin of pennyroyal tea and started out of the room. 'I'll be having a wee word with Lilidh, though, and telling her to give you a sair rough ride from here all the way to Glasgow toun.'

We set off on our progress in the morning, riding west along the shore of the Firth of Forth. It was the first day of July, clear and dazzlingly beautiful, the sun climbing behind us, the sky cloudless and endlessly blue. Over the firth the cormorants and kittiwakes and guillemots swooped and glided, shrieking at each other and diving for fish.

The queen's personal party might have been off on nothing more than a pleasure ride. The queen herself was dressed in a scarlet velvet riding-habit with glinting gold-and-pearl embroidery and a jaunty little feathered cap. No one else wore red, or even a bright colour. We ladies were dressed in muted tones of blue and grey, our habits cut out and sewn from fine Flemish cloth provided as a gift from the queen. Mine was a soft speedwell blue that might have been a reflection of the sky – not very practical for a riding-habit, but we wore what the queen directed. The gentlemen tended to browns and russets and dark greens and blues. Thomas Randolph was with the party, as was the French ambassador Castelnau; I caught a glimpse of Blaise Laurentin among the French.

We stayed in Glasgow for three days. There was no trace of my courses, and every time Jennet looked at me I looked away. I kept close to the queen, who received Protestant officials from the College and made them a gift of thirteen acres of land. Most of her council was in attendance, with Moray looking grave and self-important and Rothes hiding a yawn behind his hand. Nicolas de Clerac and David Riccio, the foreign Catholic favourites, were much to the fore, although the Protestants whispered against them. I kept away from Nico as best I could, and he seemed to do his best to keep away from me as well. It hurt me like a knife in my heart every time I looked at him. I wondered if it hurt him in the same way.

From Glasgow we rode on to Dumbarton. We crossed Loch Long and hunted our way through the forests of Argyll, deep and sun-spangled green, with huge oaks that might have been a thousand years old amid copses of willow and hazel, beech and rowan trees. Seilie was in hound heaven, and for the first time I heard the high singing baying that meant he had found a coney or a squirrel. At dusk we crossed Loch Fyne to Inveraray, where the Earl of Argyll and his wayward countess, the queen's half-sister Jean Stewart, received us at Inveraray Castle's gatehouse with blazing torches, ceremonial cups of fine French wine and six pipers playing the great Highland pipes.

'Welcome to Inveraray, Madame,' the Earl of Argyll said, once the horses had been led away and the pipers had finished their piping. 'I have supper prepared for you and all your party. Or would you prefer to retire after your day of riding?'

'Retire?' the queen said. She embraced her sister affectionately – Jean Stewart, for all her wilfulness, had always been one of the queen's favourites. 'Do not be ridiculous, brother. Of course we will eat your supper, and afterwards we will dance all night – assuming you have a proper consort of musicians to play, and not more of that wretched piping.'

Everyone laughed, flatterers that they were. The cups were passed around and each of us drank some of the wine. It was cold – what had it cost the Earl of Argyll to obtain ice in July? – and deliciously, deceptively sweet. I drank again the second time the cup was passed, and felt a wave of lightheadedness.

'Let us go in,' the queen said. 'Brother, sister, lead the way. I would like to wash and change my dress, and then you may serve your supper.'

They went off up the stairs. I could not help but feel sorry for the pipers, and I stopped to exchange a word with them.

'I am Marina Leslie of Granmuir, on the coast of Aberdeenshire,' I said. 'So I cannot claim to be a Highlander. But the great pipes always thrill my blood, and your piping was wonderful.'

'Thank ye, lassie,' said the leader of the group. 'Ye have a kind heart to go with that sweet face. The earl, he loves the pipes, being a Campbell and all, but o' course he couldnae say so in front o' the queen.'

'It was, as the lady says, quite wonderful.'

A familiar voice, behind me.

Nicolas de Clerac.

The wine was singing its way through my veins, to my fingers and toes, and however much I had been avoiding him since the progress began, I was happy, so happy, to hear his voice.

'Thank ye, me lord.' The piper bowed, quite creditably. 'I dinnae blame the queen, poor lassie – 'tis nae her fault she was brought up in France.'

'A great handicap for her,' Nico agreed gravely, 'in terms of her musical education. Mistress Rinette, will you walk in with me?'

I could hardly refuse him in front of the pipers. I said, 'Of course, Monsieur de Clerac.'

I had enough sense left not to put my hand on his arm, and he made no attempt to touch me. We walked across to the stairs, close enough to speak to each other, but separate in every other way. He was dressed in hunter's green, the colour of the forest, with a russet leather belt and breeches; a diamond brooch the size of a gull's egg was carelessly pinned in his hat. It was his only jewel; no earrings or rings or trinkets today. No *maquillage*. He was playing the part of the queen's huntsman, perfectly contrived down to the bow and quiver slung over his back.

'I have been attempting to find out if there was an *Escadron Volant* assassin placed in the queen's household when she returned to Scotland,' he said. 'Or perhaps sent to Scotland ahead of her, while your Alexander was writing his letters. As you may imagine, such questions are dangerous.'

'Very dangerous,' I agreed. 'Have you learned anything new?'

'There were, at one time, three separate *Escadron Volant* assassins in Scotland, in service to three separate persons.'

'Three,' I said. 'I did not think so many. Were they all—?'

I could not finish the sentence.

'Were they all sent to assassinate Alexander Gordon?' he said gently. 'I am not yet sure. I am not even certain of their identities, although I believe poor Monsieur de Chastelard was indeed one of them.'

'Oh, Nico,' I said. I fought with the effects of the wine, which made me want to put my arms around him and lean against him and cry until I could cry no more. It was hard, so hard. I kept hearing what he had said in the gallery of the Tolbooth in Edinburgh.

I would take you away now, to France, with Màiri and all your people . . .

And my bitter response: *What of your vow?*

Stiffly I said, 'Be careful, I beg you.'

'I will.' He was remembering too. I was sure of it. 'You had best run up by yourself, *ma mie*. The queen said she wished to change, and you know she will be looking for you.'

There was a great deal more wine that evening, a lavish supper, and music and dancing. Inveraray Castle was a tower house, new compared to Granmuir – it had been built by the first Earl of Argyll and was only about a hundred years old. The Great Hall was enormous, with a huge fireplace at one end and a high barrelled ceiling painted with pictures and Gothic characters. Hundreds of candles blazed up and down the length of the hall; music was provided by a consort of fiddles, lutes and viols who certainly made up in enthusiasm for what they may have lacked in fine technique.

The queen had put on what she called her Highland dress – a bodice, sleeves and vasquine of embroidered black and white silk, with a headdress and a looped-up overskirt made of the striped material the Highlanders called tartan. She was romping like a child, laughing and singing with the music as she danced. She did not know or care, I was certain, where each of her ladies happened to be at any given moment.

In the confusion, noise and drifting candlesmoke it was easy to separate myself from Rannoch Hamilton as well; he was much more interested in acting the lackey to the Earl of Moray and the Earl of Rothes, and certainly had no intention of dancing. I made my way around the edge of the hall and finally came upon the English agent Thomas Randolph, making conversation with young John Sempill of Beltrees, Mary Livingston's sweetheart. Master John wasted no time in taking advantage of my approach to extricate himself and go in search of his lady. So easily it was arranged, then, for me to have my talk with the representative of the English queen.

'Good evening to you, sir,' I said politely. 'I trust you are finding the progress agreeable?'

I did not like Randolph; he was a Protestant and had encouraged the Lords of the Congregation to rebel against Mary of Guise. He was brown-haired and brown-eyed, with arched brows that always gave him a look of surprise; he combed his hair down over his forehead as Julius Caesar was said to have done, to hide his balding pate.

'Indeed I am.' He smiled with a remarkable lack of sincerity. 'I might ask you the same, Mistress Rinette, regarding your new estate of marriage.'

I imagined myself striking him, disarranging that fringe of hair he seemed so proud of. As I did, I smiled. I suppose I looked just as insincere as he did.

'Very agreeable,' I said. 'Although as I am sure you know, there are always some things a wife does not entirely give over to her husband.'

His eyes sharpened. I saw him glance over my shoulder, and to the left and right. He lowered his voice. 'Or to her queen, I understand.'

'You understand quite correctly.'

He rocked back on his heels for a moment. I could almost see the plots and conspiracies forming themselves in his head. 'It occurs to me,' he said, 'that a wife who is married against her will might seek asylum far from her unwanted husband. In another country, perhaps, where the husband and his law could not touch her.'

'Perhaps. She might be more likely to wish to stay on her own lands here in Scotland, and use good hard gold to purchase a divorce and protection from her enemies.'

Enemies such as you and Blaise Laurentin, I thought. Even as I thought it I kept my expression frank and earnest.

'All the better. My queen is particularly interested in the ciphered notes of the former Queen Regent of Scotland, although she also wishes to obtain the prophecies of Nostradamus for her own astrologer's consideration. And to keep them out of the hands of – another lady, you understand.'

'I understand.'

He rubbed his hands together. 'Very well,' he said. 'Let us be frank. How much do you think—'

'Trying to buy my wife's favours, Englishman?'

We both jumped. People say their hearts sink when something frightening happens, but it is not the heart, it is the stomach. I suddenly felt so sick I feared I might disgrace myself there in the Great Hall of Inveraray Castle, in front of everyone.

'Not at all, Master Hamilton.' Here I had been, thinking what a deceiver I was. Thomas Randolph put me to shame with his cool-headed craft. 'I was asking your lady how much she thought it had cost the Earl of Argyll to purchase ice in July, to cool our wine tonight.'

'I have never had ice-cold wine in the summer,' I added faintly. 'It must be very expensive.'

Rannoch Hamilton looked at me, then at Thomas Randolph, then at me again. 'The queen is asking for you, wife,' he said. 'Come with me.'

He jerked me away without any polite word of farewell to Thomas Randolph. The Englishman's eyes met mine briefly but he said nothing. I knew he would find another way to speak to me. Difficulty might even make the prize richer.

'Stay away from him,' Rannoch Hamilton said under his breath as he dragged me across the hall. 'You belong to me and I don't want other men's eyes upon you.'

'I am not a piece of furniture to belong to you or anyone. And I can hardly avoid men's eyes altogether. You are hurting me, Master Hamilton, and people are looking.'

'Let them look, Green Lady. They will see a husband properly taking charge of his wife.'

I felt that unpleasant sick sinking feeling in my stomach again. Someday I will be free of you, I thought. I will wash every trace of you off my skin and out of my hair. I will burn every piece of my clothing you have ever touched. I will take Gill with me, and that is all. In every other way I will be free of you, and I will never, never—

A shocking high shriek of terror cut short my thought. I turned towards the sound; everyone in the Great Hall turned towards the sound. It was Mary Seton screaming – Mary Seton? Meek and pious Mary Seton, who never raised her voice? She stumbled towards the queen. The front of her carnation-coloured gown was wet, darkened. Had she spilled some water? Why would she scream so about spilling water?

Then I saw her hands, red and shiny, and I realised the dark wetness was blood.

'Madame, Madame,' she cried. She threw herself at the queen's feet. The queen drew back, surprised and uncertain; at her side the Earl of Argyll put his hand on the hilt of his dagger.

''Sieur Nico,' Mary Seton sobbed. 'I found him. Holy Mother, the blood . . .'

My heart stopped.

'Blood?' the queen said. 'But I only sent him to bring me a book of music. You must be mistaken.'

'It was 'Sieur Nico, Madame, I swear it. I found him in the passageway. He was—'

'He is perfectly well.'

Our heads all jerked around at once. Nicolas de Clerac stood just inside the Great Hall with one hand pressed to his throat. He looked unsteady but he was on his feet. There was a great deal of blood on his white shirt and his elegant hunter's-green jacket. On the jacket it looked black. On the shirt it was bright red. In his other hand he carried a music book, bound in soft violet leather and stamped with the queen's monogram.

'I had hoped,' he said, 'to avoid creating a sensation. Madame, I have brought your music book.'

He took a step forward and fell full-length on the paving stones.

The queen herself tended him that night. I was frantic with terror that he would die, as Richard Wetheral had died, as Alexander had died, but no one would tell me anything, I had no opportunity to speak to Nico alone, and I could not let Rannoch Hamilton see my distress. The queen's physician and the Earl of Argyll's chirurgeon consulted together through all the next day; the queen remained by Nico's side and left the rest of us kicking our heels. On the second day I was finally invited to attend upon her. I found them all sitting perfectly calmly in the solar set apart for the royal household, with David Riccio and the queen herself playing their lutes.

'I am not seriously hurt, you know.' Nico looked at me once and looked away – *I am all right, do not be afraid* – and acted as if he were speaking to the queen. 'I am not such a fool as to walk alone in a dark passageway without being on my guard. The assassin did not expect that.'

He stressed the word *assassin* very slightly. Was he telling me that it was a member of the *Escadron Volant* with a falcon dagger who had attacked him?

As you might imagine, such questions are dangerous.

'Argyll is beside himself,' the queen said. She fingered a difficult chord. 'Such a failure of hospitality, to have a guest's throat cut in his own castle. Well, cut only a little.'

She smiled at him. Clearly it was a *plaisanterie*, a repeated jest, between them.

'Only a little,' he repeated. 'And I will heal. Unlike poor Master Richard Wetheral.'

The queen tilted her head and frowned. Again I felt distinctly that Nico was speaking to me in the only way he could.

'Think you there is a connection?' The queen was dubious. 'That was back at Holyrood, and months ago.'

'Even so, there are too many similarities. I was walking in a dark corridor, and was attacked from behind, pushed against the wall. If I had not been half-expecting it, I would be dead in exactly the same manner as Master Wetheral died, with my throat cut.'

'*Grâce à Dieu*, you were able to fight him off. Whoever he was, I wish you had managed to kill him. Or see his face, so he could be arrested. I do not care for the thought that an assassin is travelling with our progress.'

'You are in no danger, Madame, and in any case you are well guarded, day and night,' Nico said. 'But I think it would be wise for the rest of us—'

He stopped, looked directly at me for a fraction of a second, before returning his attention to the queen.

'Wise for the rest of us,' he said again, 'to look closely at dark passageways before venturing into them.'

Within a few days he was up and about with a bandage under his left ear; he wore elegant high collars to conceal it. I myself was far from elegant. I felt sick more often, and my blue riding-habit was tighter over my breasts. We continued on our progress, riding south along the shore of Loch Fyne and crossing the Firth of Clyde to Ayr, then passing through the Forest of Galloway as we turned to the east again.

We arrived at Saint Mary's Isle in the estuary of the River Dee late one night in mid-August. We were to stay at the priory there, which had been secularised and was now held by a Protestant commendator at the queen's pleasure. For once the queen went straight to the chamber set aside for her. I slept in the same room with her as usual. The next morning, by the time she had dressed and broken her fast and released me, I was dizzy with sickness, and barely managed to find a basin and an isolated corner before doubling over to my knees and vomiting helplessly.

'I'll be looking for a big belly on you in two or three more months, wife.'

He followed me everywhere. He would drive me mad with his following. I tasted the salt of tears with the bitterness of bile.

'No,' I said.

'Yes,' Rannoch Hamilton said, with great satisfaction. 'That's my seed inside you, swelling up and giving you the cowk every morning. What do you think your Green Lady has to say to that?'

'I can cast it out,' I said through my teeth. 'The Green Lady can do that much.'

'If you wanted to do that, you'd have done it already.'

I turned my face away from him. Some of my hair had come loose, and it fell over my cheek. At least it hid my tears.

'Give me the old queen's silver casket,' he said. 'Give it to me, not Rothes or Moray. I'll treat with the queen direct, and I'll be Duke of Kinmeall before I'm finished. Who knows? The queen herself might take a fancy to me. I've seen her look at me, and 'tis said she likes a spice of rough with her smooth.'

'You are mad,' I whispered.

'So you say.' He laughed. 'Give me the casket and I'll divorce you and send you home to Granmuir.'

'I don't believe you.'

'I've had what I wanted from you. Look at you, on your knees a-cowking with your hair hanging down like a scullery maid's. What do you think your gold-headed angel boy would say if he could see you now?'

'Leave me alone,' I said, my voice shaking with fury and anguish. 'I will never give you the casket because I will not give you the satisfaction.'

I will never give you the casket, I thought helplessly, *because I do not have it*.

'You will,' he said. He drew back one boot and, before I could comprehend what he intended to do, kicked me hard in my ribs just under my arm. I cried out once, in shock and pain, then bit my lip hard to keep from making another sound. Involuntarily my body curled itself into a ball to protect my belly.

'I will not,' I said through my clenched teeth.

'I've given you chance after chance to be a proper wife,' he said with vicious bitterness. 'I've tried to be gentle with you but nothing I've done's been good enough. I'm finished with trying.

If you won't give the casket to me, I'll see you don't give it to anyone.'

He walked away.

I did not move, not until I could no longer hear his footsteps.

I hated him, hated him, hated him. I wanted to kill him. I wanted to take a knife and carve his seed out of my belly with my own hands and die there on beautiful Saint Mary's Isle, happy and free.

30

6 September 1563
Craigmillar Castle, outside Edinburgh

The queen closed her eyes, listening. We all listened. David Riccio's voice was so glorious, so deep and true. He might have been Sir Tristan singing to Iseult.

> *An thou were my ain thing*
> *I would love thee, I would love thee,*
> *An thou were my ain thing*
> *Sae dearly I would love thee.*

'Stop,' the queen said said. 'Signor Davy, can you arrange that with quarter notes?' She sang the first two bars in her own pretty voice. '*An thou were my ai-ai-ain thing.*'

'Indeed I can, Madonna,' David Riccio said. He had become so familiar with her that he no longer called her *Vostra Maestà*. He plucked the notes on his inlaid guitar. 'Yes, I like it that way. Messer Nico, what do you think?'

'I like it,' Nico said. 'Perhaps you could write a part for the tenor voice as well.'

We were gathered in a small arched room off the Great Hall

in the central tower of Craigmillar Castle. The progress was over. The queen had declared she would never again plan such a long progress with so many different stops along the way.

'Marianette,' she said. 'My head aches. Give me more of your herbs, please.'

I stepped forward and gave her a fresh sachet of herbs and flowers. I wished I could have had one for myself, and a quiet dark room to rest in. I felt awful. I looked worse – in my mirror I saw a swollen face and lank hair and eyes sunk in dark-ringed hollows. It was as if Rannoch Hamilton's child was sucking the light and life out of me.

'Sing another verse, Signor Davy,' the queen said. 'Marianette, what flowers are in this? Did they speak to you when you gathered them?'

> I would take thee in my arms
> I'd secure thee from all harms,
> For above mortals thou hast charms
> Sae dearly do I love thee.

'There is sweet cicely, Madame, which is calming,' I said. 'Some of the French sorrel you yourself planted when you first came to Craigmillar – sorrel is cooling. A little mallow and comfrey for ease, and some alkanet for its strawberry scent and the beautiful blue colour of its flowers.'

'But did they speak?' the queen said fretfully. 'The flowers?'

'No, Madame.'

'You must pick some more tomorrow. Perhaps they will tell me who this mysterious husband is, that the Queen of England dangles before me.' She pressed the sachet against her forehead. 'I thought I would go mad, listening to Master Randolph with his cryptic messages. "A husband such as I might hardly think she would agree to",' indeed. What good is it to tell me riddles when there are no answers?'

'Someone we would hardly believe she would agree to,' repeated the Earl of Moray. He was cracking hazelnuts on the table. 'Perhaps it is not an Englishman at all. I would hardly believe she would agree to Don Carlos of Spain.'

The queen laughed. All of a sudden she was in a merry mood again, and put aside the sachet. 'Or Archduke Karl of Austria. Or my brother-in-law King Charles of France. Isn't it strange they all have the same name? Carlos, Karl, Charles.'

Sir William Maitland picked up one of the hazelnuts and crunched it. 'Queen Elizabeth did say she could not be your friend, Madame, if you married a connection of either Imperial house. Perhaps the Duke of Norfolk? Or even Arran, which would bring together the Stewart and Hamilton claims to the throne? Of course, Arran is mad as a March hare, but Don Carlos is hardly—'

He broke off at the sound of heavy boots in the hall. David Riccio stopped singing. Nico de Clerac looked up from the notation he was sketching on a scrap of paper. All the ladies pressed closer to the queen.

To my astonishment Rannoch Hamilton appeared in the doorway, dressed in rough clothes for riding and reeking of brandywine. Behind him were five or six men-at-arms, their boots muddy and their hands on their sword-hilts. All the gentlemen in the room came to their feet. David Riccio brandished his guitar like a weapon, with an Italianate flourish. Somewhat more practically, Nicolas de Clerac and the Earl of Moray stepped between the intruders and the queen.

'Madam, I have asked you more than once for an audience, and you have refused me,' Rannoch Hamilton said.

The queen rose; she had the Stuart gift of audacity in a crisis. She held out her hands and swept her brother and Nico to either side.

'It is our royal prerogative to give or refuse audiences as we please, Master Rannoch,' she said with hauteur. 'How do you dare interrupt us like this?'

'I have a piece of news for you, Madam. And I wish to remove my wife from the court.'

Everyone turned and looked at me. I felt the blood rush up into my face, then drain away again to leave me lightheaded. Seilie pressed close against my skirt, hackles raised in a bristling line from his scruff to his tail.

'And why do you find it necessary to tramp in here with soldiers and swords to do that, Master Rannoch? Could you not simply direct your wife to go wherever you want her to go?'

Rannoch Hamilton shifted his gaze to me. His eyes were like pieces of black stone, hard and empty.

'She won't obey me in anything,' he said, 'unless I force her. And you, Madam, have encouraged her in her defiance.'

'If Marianette will not obey you,' the queen said, 'perhaps she has good cause. In any case, I will not allow you to carry her off to your estate, wherever it is – she is to remain here until I hold my mother's silver casket in my own hands.'

'The queen is right.' The Earl of Rothes finally stepped forward. 'It was our agreement that you would compel her to reveal the casket's true hiding place, in exchange for the marriage and her estates. You have not fulfilled your part of the bargain.'

Rannoch Hamilton laughed. It had an ugly sound. 'That I haven't,' he said. 'And I don't intend to. Your promises aren't worth a chip of dung, my Lord Rothes, and I'm tired of being at your beck and call.'

The little room suddenly went very quiet. Moray and Rothes exchanged a look.

Rannoch Hamilton rocked back on his heels and stared at the queen as if she were a barmaid in the High Street. 'I've found the hiding place where my wife was keeping your casket, Madam, and I've burned it all – the French sorcerer's papers, your mother's memorandum book, all of it. Now you'll never—'

'No!'

The queen and I cried out at the same time. She, of course, meant, *No, you cannot possibly have done such a thing because I want those papers for myself.* I meant, *No, you cannot possibly have done such a thing because there was no hiding place and no casket to find.*

I knew as clear as clear why he was lying. If the queen thought the casket was gone, she would let me go as well. Rannoch Hamilton would take me to Kinmeall and there, when I was entirely in his power, he intended to force me to give up the casket he still thought I had.

He had caught me in the net of my own lies.

'That cannot be true, Master Hamilton,' Nicolas de Clerac said. His voice was quiet and perfectly reasonable.

My husband grinned. 'I watched the lot of it burn with my own eyes, Frenchman.'

'You are lying,' I said desperately. 'Madame, he is lying.'

'Do you realise what those papers were worth, you fool?' Moray demanded. 'Do you realise what value they might have had for Scotland . . . what power they might have given us with England and with France?'

'They were my mother's papers,' the queen said. Her voice was shaking. 'I have so few things left of my mother's.'

'You should have given me an audience when I asked you to,'

Rannoch Hamilton said. He was beginning to sound less cocksure. 'Blame yourself, Madam, not me.'

'And so, in a moment of drunken spite,' Rothes said, 'you destroyed it all. Are you certain? All of it?'

'It's gone, that's all I know. And you'll use Rannoch Hamilton as a pawn no more.' He stepped forward and grasped me roughly by the arm. 'Come, wife. No more court for you.'

There is a plant called touch-me-not, which flowers from early summer to the first frost. It is pretty and innocuous-looking, sometimes white, sometimes pink, but it is called what it is because when its seed capsules are swollen they explode when they are touched.

I exploded.

I swung my arm wide and struck at my husband with all my strength; Seilie snarled and showed his teeth. Rannoch Hamilton drove his fist at my face and missed by a finger's breadth. The ladies screamed. Nicolas de Clerac stepped forward and with one neat, vicious kick doubled Rannoch Hamilton over and dropped him to the floor.

'If you strike her,' he said, in a voice I did not recognise, 'I will kill you.'

Je t'aime, ma mie . . .

''Sieur Nico!' the queen cried. 'Hold!'

Rannoch Hamilton scrambled to his feet, gasping for breath, and reached for his dagger. Nico's blade flashed first, in the firelight. That was enough to rouse the rest of the men into action, for to draw steel in the queen's presence was the gravest of offences.

'Both of you, enough,' the queen said. 'Brother, take 'Sieur Nico into custody, if you please. Master Hamilton, you are dismissed. Take your wife with you, and do not come back.'

Rannoch Hamilton made an obscene gesture. Nico stepped forward, his own dagger still in his hand; what I saw in his eyes frightened me. Moray and Rothes caught him by the arms and dragged him back.

Je t'aime, ma mie . . .

'Nico,' I said. 'Stop. It is too late.'

He wrenched his arms against Moray's and Rothes' hold. The queen stared at him in astonishment. My husband took hold of my arm again, and this time I did not resist him.

'Seilie,' I said. 'Seilie, come.'

Seilie followed me, his white-tipped tail tucked between his legs. Behind me I heard the queen say in a shaken voice, 'Call the guard, brother, quickly – I want Monsieur de Clerac locked up at once. Signor Davy, play the rest of the song. Sing! Everyone sing!'

The Italian played a chord and began to sing again. His voice sounded thin.

> *An thou were my ain thing*
> *I would love thee, I would love thee,*
> *An thou were my ain thing*
> *Sae dearly I would love thee.*

'I am ill,' the queen said. 'Oh, I am so ill – my mother's papers, Monsieur de Nostredame's prophecies, gone. I have such a headache, such a pain in my side.'

She began to cry. That was the last I heard.

'Get rid of that damned hound,' Rannoch Hamilton snarled at me. 'If it bites me, I'll drown it.'

I had a horrified flash of Seilie as a puppy, of Lady Huntly's witch holding him over the holy well at Saint Mary's of Stoneywood.

'Go, Seilie,' I said. 'Find Jennet. Quick, quick!'

He looked up at me, his dark eyes liquid with intelligence and fear. He whined and put one freckled paw on the hem of my skirt.

Rannoch Hamilton kicked at him, and he jumped. He looked at me one more time then trotted back down the passageway, turned a corner, and disappeared.

My Seilie, my luck, was gone.

31

5 December 1564
Kinmeall House, Perthshire

When he took Kitte away from me, I knew he was
going to kill me.

My little Kitte. Her full name was Katharine
Hamilton but I refused to call her that. She was not yet a year
old – I had lost track of time, locked away in a tower at Kinmeall
House – and so I knew only that she had been born in the early
days of March and it was now hard winter. My second winter at
Kinmeall.

I had almost died bearing her, I knew that. When we first
arrived at Kinmeall in September of 1563 I had been Rannoch
Hamilton's wife, however much we had hated each other.
Grudgingly – whether he wanted my baby or not, a son would
be a sign of his virility – he had provided warmth, food, clean
water to wash with, the services of a laundress and clean linens
for my bed. There was a girl to wait upon me and be my
companion. Her name was Nan; she had no surname, or at least
none that I could ever find out. We sewed and sewed, making
clothes and clouts for the baby. I taught her to do simple tapestry-
work. Every so often I would look out and see the boy Gill

exercising the horses. He would ride Lilidh under my window, and I knew he knew I was watching.

All through that first winter I was reasonably comfortable, although I was sick with sadness and longed so much for Granmuir and Màiri and my own people that I thought I might die of it. Little did I know then of what I might die.

When my pains started in the spring, there was no one but an old herb-woman to help me. I could not help thinking of the queen's fine French physician, who had attended Màiri's birth; I could remember his face but not his name. The old woman did more harm than good with her leaves and poultices and bitter teas, although I managed to keep my wits about me and nurse Kitte once she was born. No priest came to christen her, nor even a Protestant minister. I named her myself, and prayed to the Green Lady to bless her.

By that time Rannoch Hamilton had sunk deep into drink and black melancholy. Had I wounded him as terribly as he wounded me? Sometimes I wondered, and wondered what he might have been like if he had never broken into Saint Ninian's Chapel to stop my wedding. If I had never flung the curse of the Green Lady at him. Since Kitte's birth the curse had taken hold of him with a vengeance, it seemed, and when he tried to bed me he was incapable. He tried twice, and then shut Kitte and me up like prisoners in these two bare tower rooms.

He tried to take the girl Nan as his mistress and apparently failed her as well – she came to the door and railed at me through the barred wicket, demanding I set him free from the Green Lady's spell – and drank himself into insensibility every night. A different girl brought me food twice a day and took away the slops, all through the wicket in the door. I thought she was deaf and mute – she never spoke or acknowledged anything I said.

To myself I called her Mousie, for her shy ways and quivering pink nose.

Did I go mad, a little, shut up like that? I think I did. I had one window, which looked out over a boggy moorland. In the distance I could see the waters of a loch. I did not see Gill so often, although once in a while he managed to ride Lilidh along the path skirting the treacherous peat. I dreamed of Granmuir and the sea, Màiri and Alexander, Jennet and Tante-Mar and Wat. I dreamed of Seilie and prayed someone had him safe. Sometimes I dreamed of Nicolas de Clerac. I heard him say, *I will kill you if you strike her.* I heard him say, *Je t'aime, ma mie.*

I hoped, at first, he would come to rescue me. I prayed for him to come.

He never did. After a while I stopped praying.

They were like ghosts, all of them. Nico himself. The queen and her four Marys. Moray and Lady Margaret Erskine, Huntly and Bothwell, Maitland and Rothes. The *Escadron Volant* assassins – who? Blaise Laurentin, Pierre de Chastelard, David Riccio, Richard Wetheral? Were there others, shadowy figures I had never identified? Had I ever actually held Mary of Guise's silver casket in my hands?

It was all just a dream.

Kitte did not know she was a prisoner. She learned to lift her head, and turn over, and sit up. She captured her own waving feet with her tiny hands, and played with the sunbeams through the window as summer passed. Mousie was enchanted with her, and began to smile at me sometimes; she would stand outside the door and watch through the bars. Kitte started to crawl, and to pull herself up against my knee when I sat in my one chair.

And then one day Nan came with two men and took her. I

screamed and fought but the men held me and Nan dragged my sobbing baby out of my arms and carried her away.

From that day on, my food tasted bitter. I began to feel sick and weak.

Rannoch Hamilton was poisoning me, I was sure of it. What good was I to him? Kitte he would keep alive, as she was co-heiress to Granmuir. Perhaps he thought when I was dead he would be a whole man again.

If it had been me alone, I think I would have eaten the poisoned oatcakes and haggis and gristly stews, drunk deep of the poisoned sour milk and ale, and escaped that way. But I could not leave Kitte behind, tiny and helpless, at her father's mercy.

So I ate as little as possible, tasting carefully and spitting out everything that tasted bitter or foul. Grimly I fought my way out of the dark hopelessness of my dreams and began to contrive a plan of escape.

There was one person at Kinmeall who might be willing to help me, and that was Gill. It could not be chance that brought him past my window with Lilidh; he knew how much I loved her and he wanted me to see she was safe and well cared for. If he would do that for me, would he risk more – risk his sodden and brutal master's fury, risk his place, risk his life – to help me rescue Kitte and join me in a flight to Granmuir?

Even if he would help me, how could I let him know I needed his help? I did not know if he could read, and in any case I had no paper, no pen. Even if I had them, I had no way to communicate *Gill* to Mousie.

Or did I?

The next morning when she brought my food, I was ready. I knew there would be sour milk, and there was – it was thick with curds. I poured it out on to the floor. That puzzled Mousie, and she gestured towards me. *Eat the food, you are hungry*. I shook my head, and with my finger began spreading the curds out on the floor in the outline of a horse. A fine mare with a proud wedge-shaped head, an arched neck, long legs and a flag of a tail. All in white curds.

Lilidh.

I could see Mousie recognised the white horse.

I crumbled the oatcake and added the stick figure of a boy beside the white horse.

Mousie frowned.

I made my hands into two mouths, facing each other. I had done it many times as a game with Kitte, making one hand sing a lullaby while the other quacked like a duck. This time I just made them talk, opening and closing my fingers and thumbs, first one, then the other. Then I pointed to myself, and to the stick figure of oatcake strips beside the horse of white curds.

Mousie looked at me. I wondered what she was thinking. I wondered if she ever saw Kitte. After a moment she closed the wicket and went away.

I scooped the curds back into the bowl, and the pieces of oatcake. I nibbled around the edges of the cake and sipped a little of the ale – I was famished and thirsty, so thirsty.

Please, Mousie. Please.

It had gone dark when she came back with my food for the night. She opened up the wicket and handed in the bowl. The smell of rank mutton was overwhelming, and this time it had a sickening musty edge – a different poison, some kind of mushroom, but my connection to the plants and flowers had deserted me so completely I did not know for sure what it was. I took the bowl, my hands trembling with hope. Mousie looked at me and turned away.

I wanted to cry. I wanted to throw the bowl of stew.

Then Gill's face appeared at the wicket grille. For a moment I thought I would faint.

'Steady, mistress,' he said. 'Are ye sick? Where's the bairnie?'

'He took her,' I gasped out. 'Oh, Gill, he took Kitte away and he's trying to kill me. Every bit of food and drink he sends is poisoned.' I held the bowl of stew up to the wicket. The boy scrunched up his face in distaste at the smell.

'Since when?'

'Two days ago. Gill, can you bring me some ale? Or even water? Anything I can drink safely – I am parched with thirst.'

'I'll fetch something. Dinna despair, mistress, I'll help ye.'

He vanished.

I put the bowl of stew down on the floor. I felt dizzy.

A little while later Gill returned. Mousie was with him. She showed him how to open the wicket and he handed me a wooden cup of weak ale. I drank it greedily – when had anything ever felt so good, so wet and cool in my mouth, tasted so ambrosial upon my tongue? Even the wine Jennet had given me when I awoke from my sickness with the New Acquaintance had not been so wonderful. I handed him back the cup.

'Is there more?'

'Wait awee, mistress – ye'll be sick. Here, eat a bite of this bread.'

He handed me a quarter of a loaf of coarse oat bread. I wolfed it down.

'Gill, we have to find Kitte,' I said. 'That girl, that Nan, she took her away. I know he wants her because she is co-heiress to Granmuir. He thought to poison me and use my poor baby to take my home and—' I started to cry. I could not stop myself. 'We have to find her.'

'Just take a breath, mistress, and try to quieten yourself. Here, have another cup of ale.'

He handed me the cup, refilled, and I drank it down more slowly.

'Libbet here dinnae have the key to the door,' he said. 'I'll have to steal it from the master. He's rairin' drunk every night, so it shouldnae be hard to do.'

'Kitte,' I said. 'We have to find Kitte.'

'We will.' He handed me another chunk of bread and one last cup of ale. Even though the ale was weak I was beginning to feel lightheaded. 'Eat this and try to rest a wee bit. Lilidh's been a-missing you, mistress, and it's glad she'll be to see ye again.'

That made me smile, even in my distress. 'We will ride for Granmuir, all of us, won't we, Gill? We must take Libbet with us. If we escape and take Kitte, the – the master – will blame her.'

'We'll all go together.'

He and Mousie – Libbet – went off together. I went and sat in my chair and ate my bread and drank my ale, slowly and carefully so my poor stomach would not cast them up again. I tried to remember the terrible ride to Kinmeall – what, fifteen months ago? How could it have been so long? – and how we could find our way from Kinmeall to Granmuir. We had to ride east, around the loch and straight to the sea, then north along the coast. Oh, to see the sea again, even if it was December! We would need heavy plaids and the warmest clothes we could find. Not the best time to be setting out on a journey, but I would rather freeze to death with my Kitte in my arms than die here and leave her to her father's mercies. And surely we could find villages along the way where we could purchase shelter and firewood.

Purchase. We needed gold. In the first weeks I'd been at

Kinmeall, Rannoch Hamilton had shown me his strongbox, hidden under a flagstone in front of the fireplace in the central hall. He was proud of his hoard of gold. I prayed that he had not spent it all on brandywine.

The key turned in the lock with a scraping sound and the door opened.

'Gill!' I jumped up. 'Oh, thank you, thank you! We must find—'

Libbet came in behind him with Kitte in her arms.

My heart stopped.

'Oh, Kitte,' I said. 'Oh, my baby.'

I caught her to me and hugged her fiercely. She twined her tiny arms and legs around me as if she wanted to attach herself to me forever and said in a small frightened voice, 'Mum-mum.'

'Yes, I am your mum-mum, my precious. I will never let you go again, I swear it.'

'We have a little time,' Gill said. 'The master's in bed with Nan, and they're both snoring drunk. I'll be out to the stable and get the horses saddled and a pack horse loaded up with blankets. Libbet—' He made some hand signs to her, something I had never seen before. I could see that he was miming eating food and drinking ale. 'Libbet'll pack as much food as she can. Mistress, do ye know where the master keeps his gold?'

'I do,' I said grimly. 'And I will take every piece of it.'

32

We set out in the dark, along the south shore of the loch. Gill told me it was named Loch Rannoch, and that the moor behind us was called Rannoch Moor. I wondered who Rannoch Hamilton's mother had been, and why she had named her son for the bleak, wild loch and moor. Perhaps it was her way of rebelling against the power of the Hamiltons.

'We must be far away as we can be by morning,' I said to Gill.

The moon was nothing more than a sliver and provided no useful light; we picked our way carefully with the shoreline to guide us. I led the way on my beloved Lilidh; she was surefooted and intelligent and I trusted her instincts absolutely. I had Kitte wrapped against my breast with a thick, warm plaid; she had nursed a little then gone to sleep like an angel. She did not seem unusually hungry; Rannoch Hamilton must have found a wet-nurse for her in the village.

We reached the end of Loch Rannoch and followed a frozen stream to another loch – the Dunalistair Water, Gill called it. At the easternmost point of the water, just as the sky was lightening in front of us, we came upon an abandoned herders' cot. We crowded in, horses and all. No fires, so there would be no telltale smoke. But we ate cold bread and cheese seasoned with freedom, drank ale as delicious as starry wine, and made pallets of blankets.

Lilidh folded herself down to lie in a pile of straw, and all of us pressed close to her warmth. Her muzzle was softer than any velvet. The other two horses drowsed on their feet through the day.

No one found us, may the Green Lady be thanked. When darkness fell we started out again and by morning we were able to lose ourselves in the forest. Under the cover of the ancient trees we rode during the day and slept at night, although every time a badger started from its hiding place or a feather-legged capercaillie took flight I trembled and looked around for Rannoch Hamilton and his men. Were they tracking us, waiting, allowing us to ride far away from Kinmeall so they could kill us without being suspected?

The winter, at least, seemed to be hand-in-glove with us – it was cold but there was no fresh snow. After six more days of riding we found ourselves at last on the coast. We turned to the north and followed the coastline for three more days; still there was no pursuit, and with each day I felt less overwhelmed with fear. In the end, on a mid-afternoon when the sea was silver-grey and the clouds were the colour of pearls and huge feathery flakes of snow were just beginning to drift down around us, we saw the great rock of Granmuir loom out of the mist.

Lilidh might have been made of sea foam, arching her neck and quivering with excitement. My thick warm plaid wrapped me around and around and streamed out behind me like a banner. Gill and Libbet reined their horses on either side of me, my saviours, my unlikely cavaliers.

Granmuir.

Home.

I held Kitte close to my breast and cried.

* * *

Màiri did not know me at first.

I suppose I did not help matters, rushing in and snatching her up and crushing her to my heart until she shrieked. My Màiri, my Màiri. I had not seen her since my visit to Granmuir in August of 1562, more than two years before, when she had just turned one year old. Now she was three years and four months, no longer a baby but a fawn-legged little girl – oh, my Màiri, those years lost to me forever – with Leslie eyes the colour of the sea and Alexander Gordon's curling golden hair.

I let her go. She ran to Tante-Mar, although she did not cry; she tucked herself under my aunt's arm like a kitten and looked at me with great suspicious eyes.

''Tis your maman, *ma petite*,' Tante-Mar said. 'Just like in the tales I've told you every night. Your beautiful maman who sings songs with the queen and dances with all the handsome lords. You know her – we talk to her, you and I, every night before you go to sleep.'

'Maman?' Màiri said. She had the sweetest, clearest little voice, with a trace of a French accent. It was Tante-Mar, of course, who had been teaching her to talk. 'Maman hugs too hard.'

Tante-Mar tried to shush her, but I laughed. She was right. I crouched down and held my arms wide.

'I promise I will not hug too hard, ever again,' I said. 'It is just that I have missed you so much, my bairnie-ba. Will you let me try again, and hug you soft as a robin redbreast's feathers?'

'Robin,' she said. 'I know robins. And gulls.' She lowered her voice as if she was imparting a bit of enormously important secret information. 'They are birdies.'

'Oh, my dear. So they are.'

Tante-Mar pushed her a little, and she lifted her chin and walked across to me. She was brave, my Màiri. I put my arms around her and hugged her again, soft as a robin redbreast's feathers.

'I love you, Màiri Gordon,' I said. 'I am your maman and I will never leave you again, I swear it by the Green Lady of Granmuir.'

'The Green Lady makes flowers.'

'Yes, she does.'

'I have flowers. Would you like to see?'

'I would love to see. Show me.'

She ran off. I sat back on my heels and looked up at Tante-Mar. My vision was watery, as if I were looking up from under the sea. I had been crying, off and on, since that first moment we approached Granmuir.

'Thank you,' I said. 'Thank you, thank you. I never thought to be away so long. I never meant to—'

'Hush, *ma douce*. Do you think your daughter is not as much the light of my life as you are yourself? And your new little one – she too.'

Jennet was sitting with Kitte on her lap, playing clap-hands with her. 'How different they are,' Jennet said. 'Dark and fair. I'm glad you did not – did not do what I suggested, Rinette, back when we were starting out on that cursed progress to the west. This one is not responsible for her da, and we will never let him touch her, will we, hinnie?'

Kitte laughed and waved her hands for more clapping.

Màiri ran back into the room with small carved cherrywood box in her hands. 'I c'lected them,' she said. 'Tante-Mar helped. We made them flat.'

'We pressed them,' Tante-Mar said. 'And dried them.'

Màiri held out the box. I had a sudden vision of a silver casket, decorated with hunting scenes in pouncework on the sides and intricate ribbons of repoussé work on the lid. I blinked, and it was gone. I took the cherrywood box from my daughter and opened it.

And the flowers spoke.

Welcome home, they said. *Welcome home to the gardens by the sea where you were born and where you belong and where you will die . . .*

The box was filled with windflowers, wild roses and maiden pinks. The windflowers were my own flower and the wild roses were Màiri's – the maiden pinks, then, with their spicy clove scent, had to be Kitte's. Even pressed and dried, they whispered to me – faint, faint voices like rustling silk. My heart expanded and drank in the sound. Until I heard it again I had not realised how desperately I had missed it.

Could Màiri hear them too? Somehow she had chosen Kitte's flower before she even knew of her baby sister's existence.

'Pretty flowers.' She shook the box. 'My favourites.'

Windflowers, wild roses, maiden pinks – and as my little daughter shook her box another spray of flowers found its way to the top, the blossoms of rich purple dried to a heathery silver colour. I recognized the bell shapes of trailing nightshade.

You will see me soon, the nightshade murmured. *I will tell you things you will not expect to hear.*

'I like the purple ones,' Màiri said artlessly. 'And see those rose ones? Tante-Mar says those are mine.'

I closed the box and put it back into her hands. 'They are yours indeed,' I said. 'My Màiri-Rose, my little love. I think it is time for us to eat supper now.'

Little by little we learned to know each other again. Everyone learned to know and love Kitte, who blossomed with all the attention. Wat Cairnie took Gill back under his wing in the stable, as he had done in Edinburgh; Bessie More taught Libbet Granmuir's standards of cleanliness in the kitchen, which were far, far higher than the standards at Kinmeall. Père Guillaume celebrated the mass for us in Saint Ninian's Chapel on the last two Sundays of Advent, and we decorated the Great Hall of Granmuir Castle with joyous pagan evergreens from the mainland, and with holly and ivy from our own gardens. *I will protect you from poison from now to forever*, whispered the holly, the prickly green leaves and clusters of bright red berries. *I am fidelity*, sang the ivy, *good fortune and constancy, promises kept*.

The men had laid in extra stores and reinforced the castle gate in anticipation of a seige. In shifts they watched the clifftop road every day, but there was no sign of Rannoch Hamilton coming to take Kitte or me back to Kinmeall. Was he too sodden with drink to care any more? Or did he have some other plan?

I was content enough, although I missed Seilie.

Jennet and Wat told me that after Rannoch Hamilton had dragged me away to Kinmeall, the queen herself had adopted my little hound and refused to give him up. She had a new collar made for him, soft blue leather with gold sequins and sapphires, and tried to teach him tricks. He drooped sadly, Jennet told me, from the first day. Then she and Wat were sent home to Granmuir, and after that they did not know what had happened to him.

I would find a way to get him back. I did not know how, but I would find a way.

I also found myself thinking of Alexander. I did not miss him exactly, but Màiri was such a picture of her father, my golden lover, my tattered and faulty and murdered archangel. I spent hours by myself in the Mermaid Tower, thinking about him, about how we had loved each other, how he had betrayed me, how everything that had happened had sprung from that one betrayal like a poisonous vine from a single seed. I wondered if he had regretted what he had done, in the moment between the thrust of the assassin's dagger and the nothingness of death.

I pulled out the loose stone and looked into my secret hiding place. I do not know what I hoped to find. The only thing left was my mother's hand-lettered and hand-drawn storybook, full of *contes-de-fées* and country folktales her own mother had told her. The silver casket was gone. It was gone from the vault under Saint Margaret's Chapel as well. Where had it disappeared to, and who had it now? Who could have known about the secret vault, when it was Mary of Guise's own secret? Who else had she told?

I cannot say I forgot about the nightshade flowers in Màiri's box. But I stopped myself and turned my thoughts whenever they came into my mind. I began to read my mother's storybook again, curled up in my bed in the Mermaid Tower. There were fairies and witches, unicorns and lions, queens and princes in the stories. My mother had drawn pictures with coloured inks and paints and even touches of gold leaf. The pages were crumbling. I wanted to read the stories to Màiri and show her the pictures, but she would grasp at the book, and it was too fragile.

You will see me soon. I will tell you things you will not expect to hear.

33

On the twentieth day of February, a sunny day with a sky as blue and cold as ice, a single rider trotted out of the forest on the mainland and on to the causeway. Old Robinet Loury raised the alarm and we all flocked to the courtyard wrapped in our plaids like the country people we were.

'Is it a king, Maman?' Màiri demanded. Over Epiphany-tide I had told her the story of the three great magician-kings who had visited the Christ Child with their offerings of gold, frankincense and myrrh. Ever since she had been expecting kings to arrive at Granmuir. 'With gold and – and frank – and those other things?'

'I don't think so, Màiri-Rose. I think I know who it is.'

You will see me soon. I will tell you things you will not expect to hear.

Norman More and Wat Cairnie opened the gates, and as I had expected it was Nicolas de Clerac who rode in on a black Friesian stallion with feathered fetlocks and a mane and tail like crimped silk. He was dressed in brown leather and mallard-green velvet and his head was bare despite the cold; with the sun striking his flame-coloured hair he might well have been a king with a crown. My first impression was that he had not changed at all in the year and a half since I had seen him last, facing Rannoch Hamilton in the queen's supper-room.

I had changed a very great deal – I had only just turned twenty-one years of age and yet there were silver threads in my hair. I had paid for Kitte's birth and the privation that followed it with two of the four back teeth Tante-Mar called *les dents de sagesse*, the teeth of wisdom. I could not bear being in a room with all the doors and windows closed. I wondered what Nico de Clerac would see when he looked at me. I wondered why he was coming now, when he had left me to suffer at Kinmeall for fifteen terrible months.

Loping beside his great black horse was a long-legged red-and-white hound with a black spot on his back and freckled paws—

'*Seilie!*'

He jumped up against me, into my arms like a puppy, although he was taller and heavier than I remembered him and almost knocked me off my feet. I wrapped my arms around him, laughing and crying, as he whimpered with ecstasy and licked my face. My Seilie, my luck, my luck.

'Doggie!' Màiri said. She was jumping up and down with excitement. 'A doggie for Maman!'

'Yes, indeed, it is a doggie for your maman.' At first Nico's voice sounded affected and overprecise; then with a shock I realised it was just as it had always been. My way of listening was what had changed, after so much time in the countryside.

I wondered if my speech had changed as well.

'Down, Seilie,' I said. 'Down, my precious boy.'

Seilie let himself be placed on his own four feet again, although he remained pressed close to my skirt, trembling with delight.

'Welcome to Granmuir, Monsieur de Clerac.' I tried to make my voice formal but it was difficult with my hair loose, my plaid askew and Seilie's kisses still cold and wet on my cheek. 'I thank you more than I can ever say for bringing Seilie home.'

He bowed his courtier's bow. 'It is my privilege to visit your home, Mistress Rinette, and to serve you in any way I can.' He bowed again to Tante-Mar. 'Madame Loury,' he said to her. 'Wat. Jennet. It is my great pleasure to see you all again.'

Màiri's eyes were huge. In a loud whisper she said, 'Maman, are you sure he is not a king?'

He laughed. 'I am not a king, *ma petite*. I have met you before, but perhaps you were too young to remember.'

She scowled at that and drew herself up to her full height. 'I am old enough,' she said. 'I remember.'

I could not help but smile. 'I will just remind you, then,' I said to my little daughter, 'that this is Monsieur de Clerac. You must show him your very best manners, Màiri.'

She performed a curtsey with a sweet perfection that almost broke my heart. So many things Tante-Mar had taught her. 'How do you do, M'sieu Declac?' she said.

Nico bowed to her, one hand over his heart. 'I do very well, Mademoiselle Màiri,' he said. 'Thank you for taking an interest.'

'Now come along,' Tante-Mar said briskly, taking Màiri's hand. 'Jennet, I need you to help me manage dinner. Wat, see to Monsieur de Clerac's horse, if you please. Good day to you, Monsieur. We will leave the Lady of Granmuir to converse with you privately.'

Before I could stop them, they all went away.

'Come inside out of the cold,' I said. I felt awkward and did not know what else to say. 'Would you like some wine?'

'I would like some hot water, if I may, to tidy myself after riding from Wemyss in three days.'

'Three days? From Wemyss, in February? Why were you there, and what could possibly be so important about coming here?'

'I was there because the queen is there, and it is the queen's will that is important – what else? I have a letter for you, and private messages from the queen not committed to paper. Come, let us go in. I will tell you everything.'

We went in, and I called for Annis Cairnie to make arrangements for Nico's refreshment. I myself ran up to the Mermaid Tower, where I hastily washed my face, braided up my hair and put on a fresh coif. The old silver mirror made my skin look blue-green, as if I were a mermaid in truth. A year and a half, I thought, since I saw him last. I look ten years older. With no court dress, no jewels, no cosmetics, with silver in my hair, I look like a different woman entirely.

I am a different woman.

Half an hour later Nico and I settled in a small room on the south side of the Great Hall, which I half-facetiously called my solar. Jennet poured two cups of wine and went away, her expression speaking volumes – *you know why he is here, he loves you, he wants you to go back to the court, he will find a way to get you away from that monster* – although she said nothing. We were left alone.

He handed me a letter. It was sealed with red wax in which was imprinted the royal lion of Scotland.

'Read it,' he said.

I was not sure if I wanted to read it. Slowly I broke the wax wafer and unfolded the paper. The letter was only a few lines long, written in what I recognised as Mary Beaton's handwriting; it was very similar to the queen's and she often dictated to Beaton in a deliberate ploy to make her letters appear personal while evading the effort of writing herself.

Your husband Master Rannoch Hamilton has written to Master John Knox of Saint Giles' Kirk complaining that you have fled

his household with his daughter. Master Knox himself demands
I support your husband in his claim and require your daughter
to be returned to her father. I command you to come to Edinburgh
at once so that you may answer this claim.

MARIE R

'He only wants her because she is co-heiress to Granmuir,' I
said. My voice shook with terror and fury and the paper trembled
in my hand. 'I will never give her up. Never. And I will not go
back to Edinburgh.'

Nico leaned back in his chair and took a sip of the wine. I was
certain he found it thin and sour compared to the fine wines to
which he was accustomed. 'Let me tell you what the queen did
not desire to commit to paper.'

I felt a tremor of uneasiness. 'Very well,' I said. 'Tell me.'

'First, she will help you to obtain a divorce. Then neither
Hamilton nor Knox will have any power over you.'

'A *divorce*?' It was the last thing I would ever have expected.

He smiled. 'We are living in the new reformed Scotland,' he
said. 'A civil magistrate can pronounce a divorce, given suitable
circumstances. The queen has promised to arrange it all – with
Moray's help she can smooth matters over with Knox.'

'Must I see him? Rannoch Hamilton?'

'No. The queen has discouraged him – strongly, she says –
from coming to Edinburgh himself. He is to send a proxy.'

I looked at the letter again. The signature was actually the
queen's, so she had made that much effort, at least. 'Why would
she do this for me?' I asked.

'That brings me to the second thing the queen does not wish
to put in writing. You remember, of course, the day she visited

you here, on her way to Aberdeen to suppress the Earl of Huntly's rebellion. The day you read the flowers for her.'

I remembered. I remembered her walking in the garden like a silver heron, long-legged, long-necked and elegant. I had asked her to choose a flower and she had chosen a yellow cock's-comb.

You should take care if you meet a tall, slender, fair-haired person. It could be a woman or it could be a man, I am not sure, but the cock's-comb represents a person who feeds on others for life and power, and it appears to have called to you.

'She has met the person foretold by the yellow cock's-comb,' I said.

He did not seem surprised that I had grasped his meaning. He said, 'She has.'

'Who is it?'

'It is Henry Stewart, Lennox's son. Lord Darnley, he is called, by courtesy.'

'Is he here, in Scotland?' How easy it was to be sucked back into the intrigues of the court. I remembered Darnley's name being mentioned now and again as a possible husband for the queen – he was younger than she was but he had a Tudor grand-mother just as she did. The same one, in fact. 'I am surprised Queen Elizabeth allowed him to leave England.'

'Perhaps she sent him deliberately. Who knows? Our queen gave him an audience three days ago, at Wemyss, and was imme-diately enamoured of him.'

'What has any of that to do with me?'

'You predicted ill of the tall, fair-haired person the queen was to meet. She wishes to hear only good of Lord Darnley, and so she requires you to come at once to meet him and make a different prediction.'

I stared at him. 'The flowers mean what they mean,' I said. 'I cannot change it to something different, just because the queen wants me to.'

He put the wine cup down and for the first time looked straight into my eyes. I started back as if he had touched me. He said, 'Not even in exchange for a divorce from Rannoch Hamilton, and the confirmation of your own sole wardship of your daughters?'

I looked down at my hands. They had changed too – they were reddened and calloused, and the nails were cut short and straight instead of being shaped and rubbed to a shine. I had thought to leave the lies and plots of the court behind. Not yet, it seemed. Not yet.

'I will do anything for Màiri and Kitte,' I said. 'And you know it. Very well, I will go wherever the queen wishes me to go, meet Lord Darnley, and tell her he is a prince and an angel above all other men. But I will not leave the rest of my household behind, not this time. We all go, or none of us.'

'It will be arranged, just as you like. Lend me that likely looking boy Davy for a messenger, and I will give him a letter to carry to Lord Seton at Holyrood. The queen is returning from Wemyss to Edinburgh in a few days, and Lord Darnley will rejoin her there. She wishes you to be lodged at Holyrood so she can call upon you when it pleases her.'

'You yourself are not returning to Wemyss?'

He stood up and walked to the window. 'If you will allow me,' he said without looking at me, 'I would like to stay here for a few days, and then ride to Edinburgh with you.'

'Stay here?' That made no sense to me at all, and my first thought was that the queen had ordered him to stay to prevent me from escaping. 'Why?'

'Did you ever wonder,' he said, still without looking at me, 'why I did not come to Kinmeall and tear it stone from stone until I could take you away from Rannoch Hamilton?'

At first I was too surprised to say anything. Then I said, 'No.' Then I felt the blood rushing up into my cheeks even though there was no one to see it. For a moment I was back in the tower at Kinmeall, alone and hungry and half-mad with fear. I whispered, 'Yes. I wondered. I hoped. I prayed. Then – you did not come. No one came.'

He stood quite still, silhouetted against the light of the sun and the sea. I could not see his hands or his face and so I could not read what he was feeling. 'I was arrested and put into ward that night,' he said. His voice was without any expression. 'The reason given publicly was that I had drawn my dagger in the queen's presence and endangered her. The real reason, of course, was that I had revealed my – admiration – for a lady other than the queen herself.'

'For me,' I said.

'For you, *ma mie*.'

I could not think of anything to say. After a moment he went on. 'A few days later I was taken to Leith harbour where I was put on a French ship, under guard. When we reached France I was taken to Joinville. It was a luxurious prison, to be sure, but still a prison.'

'Joinville,' I said. It had never occurred to me that he had not been in Scotland at all throughout my ordeal at Kinmeall. 'That is the home of the Guises. The queen's grandmother lives there – Duchess Antoinette.'

'She does.'

'Why did they send you there?'

'I asked them to.'

'Why?'

He turned, and before I could even properly register the fact that he had moved, he was beside the table and grasping my upper arms in his hands, lifting me to my feet. How did he manage to hold me so hard and at the same time so gently? I saw that he had changed after all, that there were threads of silver just like my own in the gleaming russet of his hair, and new lines like fine crescent-shaped knife cuts at the corners of his mouth. There were no jewels in his ears, and no trace of the flamboyant *maquillage* he had once affected.

I thought he was going to kiss me, and turned my face away. I had experienced too many terrible kisses. He hesitated, then bowed his head, his forehead against my shoulder, and simply held me for a moment. I could feel his hands shaking.

'Tell me,' I said.

'Have you ever wondered,' he said, without looking at me, 'why I am so like the queen? In height . . . in colouring?'

I was not sure how to answer that. Of course I had wondered. Everyone had wondered. 'Yes,' I said. 'I have.'

'I told you the tale of my mother, and how she was forced to marry, and her death?'

'Yes.'

'My father was Duke François of Guise, the queen's uncle. I, like the queen, am a grandchild of Duchess Antoinette of Guise.'

I was both surprised and not surprised – great dukes, like my own grandfather the Duke of Longueville, were laws unto themselves. I lifted my hand and touched his hair very lightly. It was crisp as a hawk's ruffled feathers.

'Did you know this before?'

'Duchess Antoinette told me when I went back to France in 1562, the spring before Huntly mounted his rebellion. My – father – had just come from Vassy, where he ordered the burning of a makeshift church with hundreds of Huguenots inside. To him it was nothing – he was a militant Catholic and truly believed he was defending his church. To the world, it was a massacre. To me— There were women and children in that church, Rinette. And at the same time I learned he was my father.'

'Duchess Antoinette told you? Not the Duke himself?'

'I did not wish to speak to him. Nor did he wish to speak to me.'

I stroked his hair again. He lifted his head and pushed me back a little, holding me at arm's length.

'Rinette,' he said. 'It was Duchess Antoinette who placed me in Mary of Guise's household. Duchess Antoinette who recommended me to the queen when she was preparing to return to Scotland. She is my grandmother, and the only true family I have – she took me in when the Benedictines put me out, educated me, gave me a place in the world. She invested me with one of her own small estates at Clerac so I would have a name and an income and some standing at court. Duke François had seven legitimate children with the Duke of Ferrara's daughter and God alone knows how many bastards. I meant nothing to him. He is dead now – you will remember the news of his assassination. We never spoke, not one word.'

I thought about that for a moment. 'So you have been Duchess Antoinette's agent, all along, at the Scottish court. And even the queen herself did not know that you and she are cousins?'

'Even the queen did not know. Or if she suspected, she said nothing. Duchess Antoinette at last gave me leave to tell her when I returned to Scotland two weeks ago. The Guises believe in blood ties, and Duchess Antoinette has reason to be afraid for the queen, caught between Lord Darnley and Moray with no fair-minded advisor.'

I frowned. 'Reason? What reason?'

He looked away from me. There was something terrible. Something that had put those glints of silver in his hair.

'I cannot tell you, *ma mie*. Do you remember when I told you I was bound to the queen by a holy vow? That vow was made to Duchess Antoinette, my grandmother, my closest living blood relative, and it is not yet fulfilled.'

'And yet you want to stay here at Granmuir? Are you here to spy on me, Nico?'

'No. I want to stay because I feel stillness and peace here.'

I looked into his eyes and I knew what he was going to say and I wanted him to say it and I was terrified he was going to say it.

'And because I love you,' he said very gently. 'Surely you know that? I want a few days with you, here at Granmuir – it may be all I will ever have.'

My heart stopped.

'Oh, no,' I said. 'Nico, no. Please no.'

He let go of my arms and lifted his hands away from me. 'What, do you think I am asking you for anything? I am not, other than perhaps your presence, or a chance to look at the sea with you and talk a little. And you need not do that even, if it does not please you. My precious soul, my love, to breathe the same air that you are breathing will be enough.'

I started to cry, as much like a child as Màiri or Kitte. I could not help myself, and I put my hands up to cover my face so he could not see how contorted it was. 'It pleases me,' I managed to choke out. 'I am glad you are here and I want you to stay, if we can – if we can – keep apart from each other. Simply to look at the sea and talk to you sounds like heaven.'

'Then that is what we shall do. Please do not cry, *ma mie*. Did you truly think I would ever hurt or coerce you?'

'No. I am sorry, I just – I thought you were going to kiss me. I could not bear that.'

He smiled a little, with just one side of his mouth. 'Well, perhaps I was,' he said. 'Would it be so distasteful to you?'

I kept my face covered with my hands. I felt hot, as if I had a fever. 'Yes,' I said. 'No. I do not know. Oh, Nico, it is just – there were so many kisses. And I had no choice. Over and over, I had no choice.'

'You have a choice now. You will always have a choice.'

I looked at him through my fingers. Then I took my hands away from my face. 'Will you – not move – if I kiss you?'

'Of course I will not.'

I put my hand against his cheek. I felt roughness. He had not stopped to shave on his ride from Wemyss. I almost stopped there, because Rannoch Hamilton had often gone days without shaving. But Nico's whiskers glinted with gold and red in the sun. They were different. The structure of his bones under my hand was different.

He did not move.

I leaned forward. I felt the warmth of his breath. I was shaking – fear, sickness, shame, and at the same time a tiny spark of – what? I did not have a word for it.

I could not do it. I drew back.

His eyes were steady. They were darkened, but however expanded their centres were I could still see a circle of hazel-gold around the outer edge. No black emptiness. The trailing nightshade was there, strong and alive. It was beautiful and bittersweet.

I closed my eyes. That made it easier. Nico's scent was different, bitter orange and myrrh. Rannoch Hamilton always smelled of sweat and iron.

'Nico,' I said.

He did not move. 'Yes,' he said. 'Shhh. It is all right, whatever you do.'

I leaned forward again and touched my mouth lightly to his.

He did not move, did not put his arms around me, did not bite my lips or force my mouth open or—

I drew back. I was shaking. 'I cannot do any more,' I said.

'You need not do any more. You need never do anything more, if it does not please you.'

'Perhaps – later.'

He nodded gravely. 'Perhaps later,' he said.

34

If I had turned into a countrywoman over my month and a half at Granmuir, Nicolas de Clerac turned into a countryman overnight, with a little help from Wat Cairnie and Norman More. The next day he appeared with a laced linsey-woolsey shirt over his brown leather breeches, and a plaid over his shoulder like a herdsman. This chameleon-like changeability – well, now I knew why he was so like the queen in that. Where he was different was in his inner steadfastness, trained into him by the Benedictines, evidenced by his keeping faith with his mysterious vow. What would the queen have been like, I wondered, if she had been brought up with such discipline?

I wanted to touch the coarse fabric of his shirt, rest my cheek against the checkered wool. It would smell of the sheep's lanolin, of soap and heather, and under that the scent of Nico's own skin, warm and clean—

But no. I could not let myself think these thoughts, not yet. I was not ready.

Bessie More put out oatcakes and buttermilk and he ate his share without complaint. I thought of him breaking his fast with the queen, on fine sweet wine and spiced manchets of bread, and could not help but smile. We might have been lord and lady of the castle, sitting at top and bottom of the trestle table with our household on either side: on the women's side Bessie More and Jennet and Libbet, who had blossomed almost as much as Kitte; Annis Cairnie with Kitte on her lap and Tante-Mar spooning a bit of honey on Màiri's oatcake. On the men's side were Norman More and Wat Cairnie and the boy Gill, with Robinet Loury and Père Guillaume sitting next to each other and talking about the old days. Davy More had ridden off to Edinburgh with Nico's letter the night before.

No, there were no servants' tables at Granmuir. Nico laughed and talked with them all as if he had lived at Granmuir all his life. For the first time since Alexander's death, I felt safe. I could pretend, in my secret heart, that Nico and I were indeed the lord and lady. We could sit together in the solar and look out at the sea and talk to one another, and I could pretend we would never have to leave Granmuir. Once again in a secret bubble of time and space, like the ancient vault under Saint Margaret's. Like the stone bubble within my heart. Were these all I would ever have?

I would not think of that.

'Nico,' I said. Somehow it was easy to call him by his Christian name here, with all of us sitting around the table. 'As you are going to stay here at Granmuir for a few days, there is something I would ask you to do for me.'

'Nico!' Màiri cried. 'Nico, Nico, Nico.'

'Shush, *ma petite*,' Tante-Mar said. 'You must call him Monsieur de Clerac.'

'I will do whatever you like,' Nico said. He was smiling. 'Carry water? Chop wood? Muck out the stables?'

I could not help but smile as well. 'No, nothing so demanding,' I said. 'I have an old book of my mother's, and Père Guillaume, I am sure, has a stock of fine paper and ink and colours.'

'I do indeed, my daughter,' Père Guillaume said. He looked interested. 'I have been saving the paper to make a copy of the Little Office of the Blessed Virgin for you.'

'This is only a book of *contes-de-fées*,' I said. 'But I will buy you new paper and colours in Edinburgh. Nico, I remember how skilfully you drew the – how skilfully you draw. I would like you to copy my mother's book, and reproduce the illustrations if you can. The original is too fragile for everyday reading, and I would like to begin reading the tales to Màiri as my mother read them to me.'

Père Guillaume looked at Nico. 'I mean no offence, Monsieur,' he said with courtesy. 'But the paper is very fine, and the ink and colours costly. Have you the skills to copy a book properly?'

'I am not as useless as I look,' Nico said. There was a glint of humour in his eyes. 'I was, in fact, trained as a Benedictine in the abbey of Mont Saint-Michel in France, until I was so unfortunate as to be invited to depart. In any case, I will take every care with your paper and inks, *mon Père*, and endeavour to give satisfaction to Madame Rinette.'

That afternoon I brought my mother's book downstairs and laid it out on the table in the solar. Père Guillaume brought out his hoard of paper, pots of ink, a rule and a pointed stick for laying out lines, and quills of various sizes. Most amazing of all was a box of colours like a treasure trove: cinnabar and cochineal for reds, saffron for yellows, powders of malachite and lapis-lazuli for greens and blues, flake white and chalk, lampblack, fine strips of gold and silver leaf.

'I had no idea you had these beautiful things, *mon Père*,' I said.

'Your dear mother gave them to me,' he said. His eyes filled with tears. 'I have kept them carefully ever since.'

Nico was turning the pages of the original book very carefully.

'Some of these stories I have heard before,' he said to me. 'Some I have not. Did your mother write them herself?'

'She wrote them from memory,' I said, 'from tales her own mother told her. She made the drawings herself. Look at the expression on the face of this little squirrel. I always loved him when I was Màiri's age.'

'I will copy it all as exactly as I can,' he said. 'It will be *un travail d'amour* for me.'

I drew back. I could not help myself.

'A labour of love for your daughter, your mother, and yourself,' he said gently. 'That is all.'

And it was a labour of love for him too. I could see the ghost of the boy he had been in the care with which he marked out straight lines almost invisibly on the paper with the rule and pointed stick, arranged the spaces for the illustrations, and then copied the letters in my mother's handwriting with eerie perfection. We sat together in the solar and looked at the sea, and I read my mother's stories aloud as he worked. There was always a beautiful girl – sometimes a peasant girl, sometimes a princess. She always faced dangers and monsters. She always won out, by cleverness and honesty and grace, and was always happy in the end. Sometimes she was happy as a queen and sometimes as a farmer's wife. Sometimes she was happy alone.

Would I be happy one day? Would I be the wife of – I was afraid even to think his name – or would I be alone?

Every day Màiri came in and looked at the pages. I cautioned her not to touch them, not yet, and I told her the stories. She was rapt with delight.

Sometimes I talked about my childhood, growing up wild at Granmuir. I told him about my father and mother, Sir Patrick Leslie of Granmuir and beautiful Lady Blanche, how they were like a fairytale prince and princess to me, spending their time at the court of King James V and Queen Mary of Guise, and descending on Granmuir for holidays and quarter-days, with gifts of sweets and pretty dresses. I told him about dear strict Grannie, who had raised me, and half-fey Gran'auntie who had taught me about the flowers. I told him about the year I was eight, when Mary of Guise went back to France and my father and mother and I went with her; about how it had cut my life cleanly in two with my father's death and my mother's self-immurement in her Parisian convent. I told him about Tante-Mar, my mother's legitimate half-sister, who had bravely left her French farmhouse behind to return to Granmuir with me.

I told him about Alexander Gordon, my golden archangel boy who had been part of a hunting party passing through Granmuir, and how he had fallen from his horse and broken his arm. How he had been left at Granmuir to recuperate. How I, twelve years old to his sixteen, precocious and fierce, had fallen so much in love with him I could think of nothing else.

'Did he stay at Granmuir after his arm had healed?' Nico asked. He was copying a sketch of a princess and a prince in a garden; he had laid out threads over the original page in a grid pattern and drawn a matching grid on the paper with his rule and pointed stick. I could see how it made it easier to copy each marked square and thus reproduce the whole. Although Nico's version was identical to the original in every detail, somehow there seemed to be more longing, more intensity, more suppressed desire between the two figures.

Or perhaps I only saw what I myself was feeling.

'He did,' I said. 'His own father and mother were dead. He was a ward of the Earl of Huntly and the earl had pots of his own to stir. Tante-Mar was beside herself, trying to keep us apart. I think that is why Mary of Guise had me taken to Edinburgh when I was fourteen – to separate us while we were still so young.'

Nico drew a leaf and coloured it with malachite. When he put the brush down and reached for a different one, his fingers touched mine, lightly, so lightly. 'And then the *Escadron Volant* separated you forever.'

'And tried to kill you as well.'

'I had asked too many questions, I think. I learned a great deal about the *Escadron Volant* from Duchess Antoinette, though, while I was in France. Her *belle-fille*, the Duke of Ferrara's daughter, is said to have hired them to kill Coligny, in revenge for Duke François' assassination. Some even say Poltrot, the man who assassinated the duke, was himself *Escadron*.'

I leaned closer to look at the drawing. Our faces were close enough that I could feel his breath in the feathery wisps of hair in front of my ears. I said, 'It is like a bryony vine, this *Escadron*, spreading and poisonous.'

Nico finished the leaf and began to draw its delicate veins, his hand not entirely steady.

'The *navet du diable*,' he said. 'A good comparison.'

He placed a highlight on the leaf with a bit of gold. It was a perfect reproduction of my mother's sketch, but for the single tiny imperfection in the veins. I thought, I will always look at that crooked line and remember this moment.

He began to outline the head of the prince.

'However terribly it ended,' he said, 'and whatever agonies you have endured since then, Rinette, you are fortunate to have such a love to remember.'

I was off my guard after our peaceful days together. I said, 'Have you never—'

I stopped.

Have you never had such a love?

'Only once,' he said quietly. 'Only now.'

'Nico.' I took a breath, then reached out my hand and put it over his where it lay on the table steadying the paper. It was the first time I had deliberately touched him since that strange, dream-like half-kiss in the solar, the day he arrived. His skin was warm and I could feel the elegant lines of his fingers.

'What is it, *ma mie?*'

'Will you come up to the Mermaid Tower with me?'

He did not move his hand under mine. I could feel a fine tremor, in the skin and muscles and all the way down to the bone, and I wondered how much effort it cost him to let his hand lie quiescent, subject to my choice. 'I would like to,' he said. 'Very much. Oh, *ma mie*, you must know how much. But only if it is what you wish.'

'I think it is.'

I wanted it to be different. If it was different, perhaps it would exorcise the dark emptiness Rannoch Hamilton had left inside me. If it was not entirely different, I could not have borne it.

'Put your arms around me,' I said. I stood with my back to the door, my hand on the latch. 'Just hold me.'

He put his hands on my shoulders first, very lightly, and after a moment ran them down over my arms. I flinched and he took his hands away in an instant.

'Rinette,' he said. 'You need not—'

'I want to. I want to – wipe it out, all of it.'

He put his arms around me. I could feel the heat of his body, although at first there was a space between us. Slowly, so slowly, giving me every chance to pull away, he leaned against me. I gasped once, and then I put my own arms around his waist. For a long time we stood there, simply holding each other. I breathed his scent, clean and bittersweet.

'Now,' I said at last. My voice did not sound like my own at all. 'Undress. You first, Nico.'

He stepped back, spreading his hands wide in a gesture that said, *I am at your command*. He took off the plaid and folded it with exquisite care. I remembered trying to fold my mantle – But no. I would not let myself remember.

He put the folded plaid on the chair and unlaced his shirt. Every move was slow, and easy for me to predict and understand. He pulled the shirt over his head. He had the milky-white skin of a red-haired man where the sun did not touch him; his throat and arms were brown. His lean, long-muscled fencer's chest and flat belly were only lightly traced with hair; I could see his skin through the interweaving of it. High up on his throat, under his left ear, I could see the scar of the *Escadron Volant* assassin's dagger.

Different. He was different. He was Nico and he was not Rannoch Hamilton. He looked different. He smelled different. I said it to myself over and over as I watched him.

He unlaced the points of his leather breeches and took them off. Under them he wore linen drawers. Fine linen, gathered on a silk cord and embroidered with blackwork. The one remaining piece of clothing that belonged to the other Nico, the Nico of courts and queens.

I clung to the latch of the door.

He took off the drawers.

He was not like Alexander – Alexander's body had been perfect, sculpted and sensuous, the body of a marble angel. Nico's flesh showed the asceticism of his youth in its spareness. He was nothing like Rannoch Hamilton. There was no dark emptiness in his eyes, no sense of the wild animal in his skin or hair. He was alive in every possible way, heart and mind, soul and body, not an animal but a human man with scars and secrets, sorrows and joys, regrets and desires.

He did not speak. He stood lightly, every secret revealed, his palms open to me at his sides.

'Let me,' I said. 'Let me – do what I want. Let me stop, if I want to. Please, Nico.'

'Do you think I would do anything else, *ma mie*?'

I felt more confident.

'I will tell you what to do,' I said.

It took a long time, and twice I stopped him at the last possible moment. God alone knew what it cost him in self-control to hold back. In the end we came together very slowly, very gently. I wrapped my arms around him and cried and cried and cried, until all the shame and misery had been cried away.

'When we have finished what we must do in Edinburgh . . .' I said. We had slept for a while. The moonlight awakened me, and when I opened my eyes I found him awake as well. 'When the queen is satisfied the yellow cock's-comb represents the sum of all her dreams, and when the magistrate has pronounced my divorce . . .'

I stopped. Why, when I wanted to say it so much, was it the hardest thing I had ever tried to say?

He stroked my hair. 'What?' he said.

'When all that is done, will you come back to Granmuir with me? Will you marry me in Saint Ninian's Chapel by the sea, and live here with me and Màiri and Kitte forever?'

He lifted my hand and kissed my reddened countrywoman's knuckles very lightly. I felt that kiss down to the marrow of my bones. My heart had been bleak and blank like a field of wind-flowers burned to the bare earth, and now new leaves, tiny ones, were thrusting up through the ashes like knives. It hurt. It made me wonder if the new growth would be stunted and pale.

'With all my heart, I will,' he said.

'I do not know if I can – feel for you – everything you want me to feel. What I felt for – What I felt when I was young.'

'And now you are so ancient,' he mocked gently. 'It will not be the same, *ma mie*, and it should not be. We will find our own way.'

'And the court? The queen? The duchess in France? Are you willing to give it all up?'

'I must fulfil my vow,' he said. 'In Edinburgh. When that is done— Are you certain you truly want to give it all up forever, *ma mie*? You are, after all, a French duke's granddaughter and the Lady of Granmuir. I have Duchess Antoinette at Joinville, and my estate at Clerac.'

'I would like to see it,' I said, surprising myself.

'In time, you may even wish to visit courts again, both in Scotland and in France. In time, you may wish to visit your mother at Montmartre.'

I drew away a little. 'I will never go to Montmartre,' I said. 'Edinburgh, perhaps. Joinville and Clerac, perhaps. But not Montmartre.'

He stroked my hair back from my forehead. 'Not Montmartre, then.'

'Visits,' I said. 'Short ones. My father and mother lived at the court and visited Granmuir upon occasion. I would like to do just the opposite.'

He smiled. 'We shall do just the opposite.'

In three more days he finished copying the book, and after that we all went down to Edinburgh.

35

2 March 1565
Holyrood Palace

'Rannoch Hamilton is in Edinburgh.'

The brush in Tante-Mar's hand stopped, halfway down the length of my hair. My mouth turned dry. I said, 'Where did you hear that?'

Jennet came into the bedchamber, taking off her shawl. 'In the High Street,' she said. 'There's clack about it everywhere. That Englishman Darnley, the Italian Riccio, the Frenchman Laurentin and Rannoch Hamilton. The four of 'em are roistering together through the wineshops and whorehouses every night.'

'Are you sure, Jennet?' Tante-Mar said. She put the brush down and I knew what she was thinking – *We should not have brought the children*. 'He was to have sent a proxy for the business of the divorce.'

'Didn't see him myself, but stopped a couple of braw fellows and asked them – was it Rannoch Hamilton of Kinmeall they'd seen with all those foreigners? They said it was.'

I turned and looked at Tante-Mar. 'Go,' I said. 'Stay with Màiri and Kitte, and keep Wat and Gill with you. I am almost dressed – I can manage the rest myself, or Jennet can help me.'

We had arrived in Edinburgh the night before, in the midst of a great storm. Nico had immediately gone to the queen's apartments; I did not expect to see him again until I myself was called to wait upon her as well. We had agreed: until the divorce between Rannoch Hamilton and me was handed down and both Màiri's and Kitte's wardships were safely and legally mine, we would not spend time together alone. Surely that would be no more than a few weeks. We would wait, however much we longed for one another, until we could properly and openly pledge ourselves, one to the other.

The rest of us had crammed ourselves into the two rooms provided for us up under the roof of Holyrood, and before we could even get the children settled with the thunder and lightning overhead, a lady came with a message from the queen commanding me to dine with her the next day. Thus this morning Tante-Mar was attempting to make me look presentable in an old gown and skirt of worn black velvet with a bodice and sleeves of black-and-white striped satin. Thus this morning Jennet had gone out into the High Street to hear what the town had to say about Lord Darnley. She had come home with more than either of us had expected.

'Peelie-wallie you're looking,' she said, once Tante-Mar had gone. 'And thin as a bow-saw. That black does you no favours – you need some face paint.'

'I do not have any face paint,' I said. 'The queen will simply have to take me as I am, peelie-wallie or no.'

She twisted my hair up inside an embroidered cap and thrust in a few pins. Over the cap she fastened a starched veil of white linen gauze, forming the shape of a heart around my face and falling down over my shoulders and back.

'That high collar's a blessing,' she said. 'Covers up those scrawny neckbones. Now don't fret about the bairnies – we'll keep them safe. I'll walk with you over to the queen's tower. You need to take care as well, Rinette.'

We walked downstairs, past the entrance and great ante-chamber and through the queen's lobby, and then upstairs again to the queen's outer chamber in the north-west tower. On the last step she said, 'Don't fear. Master Nico will be there, and he'll look out for you.' She kissed me firmly and went back down. The gentleman-usher smiled at me and asked me my name. I hesitated, and then I told him firmly that I was Marina Leslie of Granmuir.

He announced me.

I took a deep breath. How many times had I been banished from the queen's presence and then recalled? I should be accustomed to it by now. I held up my head and squared my shoulders and went in.

'Marianette!' the queen cried. We might have been eight years old again, in France, and best friends as we had been perhaps one day out of four. 'Come in, come sit beside me. *Vite, vite, ma chère*! I wish to make you known to Lord Darnley.'

I walked towards her. She was, if anything, more vivid and alluring than ever, wrapped in silver tissue with pearls and diamonds, and her beautiful red-gold hair braided with more pearls in the Italian fashion. There were so many familiar faces in the room – Mary Livingston and Mary Fleming, the Earl of Moray and the Earl of Rothes, the queen's half-sister the Countess of Argyll, and my dark-eyed, black-hearted nemesis Lady Margaret Erskine, as always watching for any oppor-tunity to move her son a step closer to the crown. I was not surprised to see the Englishman Thomas Randolph, but I was sur-prised to see Blaise Laurentin in the train of the French ambas-sador Monsieur Castelnau. Perhaps Laurentin's wineshop friendship with Lord Darnley had made him welcome in the queen's inner circle.

I could only thank Saint Ninian it did not seem to have done the same for Rannoch Hamilton.

With the queen at the high table lounged an elegant, long-legged, fair-haired man with the face of a Greek demigod, who was clearly already the worse for drink. On the other side of Lord Darnley sat the dark, monkey-like Piedmontese musician David Riccio, and next to Riccio, Nicolas de Clerac.

Nico smiled at me.

For a moment I felt as if I could not catch my breath. Then I steadied myself. It would never do to make my love obvious. The queen was rapt in her own love, I thought, and she would want it to be the only love in the world.

I sank into a deep curtsey. When I straightened I had collected myself.

'Good day to you, Madame,' I said. 'It is my pleasure to come into your presence again, after such a long absence.'

I did not say, *After being brutalised by the man you forced me to marry, and kept prisoner, and almost poisoned, and barely escaping with my life and the life of my precious daughter.*

'We shall see to it that you are not absent again,' the queen said, as lightly as if I had been away by my own choice. 'Harry, *mon cher*, I present to you Marina Leslie of Granmuir. I have known her since I was a little girl in France, where I always called her "Marianette". Marianette, this is Henry Stewart, Lord Darnley, son of the Earl of Lennox. He is my cousin, or I should say, my half-cousin – half-cousin by marriage – it is a very distant relationship.'

She tilted her head and looked at Lord Darnley sidelong, her mouth curling in a sensuous little smile. He leaned towards her, his eyes half-closed, his own lips parting.

He was certainly not looking at me but I curtseyed again. 'It is my pleasure to make your acquaintance, my lord,' I murmured.

And what am I going to tell the queen about you, I thought, when I can feel strongly and clearly that, beautiful as you are, like the yellow cock's-comb you will batten upon her and destroy her?

'We are deep in preparations for a wedding,' the queen said. 'No, no, not my own . . . not yet at least.' Another languishing look at Darnley. 'And not yours, my Marianette, although 'Sieur Nico has hinted to me that once you are divorced, you will quickly become my own *cousine*.' Her eyes sparkled as she looked from me to Nico and back to me again. So much for my attempt to hide my feelings. Since she was in love, it apparently pleased her for the whole world to be in love.

Everyone looked at me. I saw Lady Margaret Erskine turn her head and whisper something to the Earl of Moray. Both of them were looking at Nico. Clearly the news that he was the queen's own blood cousin through the Guises had not been universally well received. Nor had the news that he intended to marry me. Steadily I said, 'Whose wedding, then, Madame?'

'Livingston's. She is marrying John Sempill of Beltrees on Shrove Tuesday, four days from today, and none too soon, I think.'

All the ladies cried out with mock indignation, Mary Livingston herself loudest of all. Young Master Sempill, who had danced so amusingly as Terpsichore in the masque of Apollo and the muses so long ago – could it be almost three years? – took his lady-love's hands and pressed them to his heart.

'None too soon for me,' he said. 'Although only because I love her so dearly.'

The ladies applauded him. Mary Livingston rewarded him with a kiss on the mouth. Three or four of the bolder gentlemen took that as a suggestion to kiss the ladies next to them, with or without invitation. There were high cries of laughter and one smart slap.

They were like children, playing at life as if it were nothing but a masque itself. Had any of them ever suffered or starved or cried or struggled through a ten days' ride in December cold? Had I ever been part of their golden world? I had, of course, but it felt as if it had been in another life. Even so, I went to Mary Livingston and embraced her. She had been my first friend at court, and I wished her well with all my heart.

'I am so happy the queen has invited me to return in time for your wedding,' I said. 'I would have known, even if she had not told me – you are glowing with happiness.'

She embraced me in return and kissed me on both cheeks. 'I am so happy indeed – thank you, my dear. You are just in time to be one of the wedding party – the queen has given me ells and ells of wonderful lady-blush satin for dresses, and hundreds of pearls, and silver embroidery for headdresses. I will ask my seamstresses to send you enough for a new dress.'

'Thank you.' I leaned closer and whispered, 'Tell me about Lord Darnley.'

She widened her eyes at me. 'The queen is mad in love with him. He is the only man, she says, other than 'Sieur Nico, who is tall enough and strong enough to properly lift her and swing her in the dance.'

'He is certainly tall.'

Mary glanced over my shoulder to be certain no one was listening. 'I do not think 'Sieur Nico cares for him. But tell me, is it true? Are you and 'Sieur Nico to marry, once you are divorced from Rannoch Hamilton?'

I hesitated. It still sounded wrong to me, bred up a Catholic as I had been – not only to be divorced, but to be divorced and then at once to marry another man. But my marriage to Rannoch Hamilton had been a Protestant ceremony, supported by civil law and dissoluble by civil law. It was a new world and I had no choice but to live in it.

'I would rather talk about your wedding,' I said, perfectly honestly. 'Or the queen's. Surely she is not serious, hinting at a wedding for herself and Lord Darnley? What does Moray have to say about that, or Maitland? What about the Queen of England – Lord Darnley is an English subject, is he not?'

Mary Livingston laughed, although there was an edge to it. 'None of us likes him, other than Riccio who is his bosom friend. But the queen will hear nothing against him from anyone. Be sure you say he is the handsomest and finest fellow you have ever seen. And—'

'Marianette,' the queen said. Her sweet voice could be sharp and imperious when she chose to make it so. 'That is quite enough whispering with Livingston for now. Come here, and let us arrange for you to read the flowers and tell me my future.'

I gave Mary Livingston one last hug and made my way obediently to the queen's table. 'I am at your command, Madame,' I said. 'Although it is still early in the year. In a few weeks, perhaps, when the spring flowers begin to bloom, I can—'

'We do not wish to wait until spring,' she said, her fine brows drawing together. 'Surely there are herbs, at least, growing in the kitchen gardens where it is sheltered. In France we had such forcing-houses, filled with roses and lilies even in the coldest months of winter.'

'Perhaps, my dear love, it is a sign.' Darnley turned his head and looked at me lazily. His clothing was very rich but there was a wine-stain on his doublet and the lace at one wrist was torn. 'Mistress Marianette cannot practise her art without flowers, and there are no flowers. *Ergo*, as Aristotle would say, you are not meant to look into the future through her floromancy.'

'In this case, *mon cher*,' the queen said, 'Aristotle would be wrong. Marianette's art is quite unusual – she predicted the truth of the Earl of Huntly's rebellion from only a few leaves and blossoms. There is one particular flower—'

Here the queen paused and looked at me.

I saw her in the old walled garden at Granmuir, clear as clear could be.

She thrust the flower towards me – a single long stem, spotted purplish-black, with slender, deeply notched leaves and a tassel of yellow flowers at the top . . .

'—one particular flower,' she repeated, 'which I absolutely require Marianette to look at again, to be certain she has read it correctly.'

'Well, if it is anything to do with marriage,' Darnley said with offhand viciousness, 'I would not believe a word she says. Mistress Marianette is not interested in making marriages, after all, but in unmaking them.'

There was a moment of shocked silence. I could not help looking at Nico, but his practised courtier's expression revealed nothing. David Riccio laughed, too loudly. The two ambassadors, French and English, had pricked up their ears – any discussion of marriage always interested ambassadors.

Once I would have struck back at Darnley – *Perhaps I should apply to the tavern keepers of the High Street, my lord, for instruction on the finer points of marriage?* – but I had learned the hard lessons of court life and swallowed my hot words. Instead I said temperately, 'The marriage of a queen is far above ordinary marriages, so much so that it is an entirely different matter. Would you not agree, my lord?'

The queen, of course, was pleased by that. Darnley looked from her to me and back again, and his cherub's mouth curled down at the corners. 'This business with flowers is witchcraft,' he said. 'I suspect your precious Marianette knows things she has not told you.'

The queen laughed and patted his cheek as if he were a sullen child. 'I am sure she does,' she said. 'I am all agog to hear them, *mon cher*, and you should be as well.'

The queen did not allow me to leave her presence until long after supper. Màiri and Kitte were both asleep when I returned to our chambers up under the south roof of the palace; Jennet and Tante-Mar were fussing over a bolt of rose-coloured satin, a box of pearls and a headdress made of silver embroidery which had clearly been sent over by Mary Livingston's seamstresses. I was tired and lonely, and the last thing I wanted to do was stand in front of the fire for them to measure me and drape the cloth around me to see what effects they could achieve.

I missed Nico. I missed him more than I could ever have imagined.

There was a scratch at the door. I jumped. Tante-Mar was just threading a pin into a pleat and it dug viciously into my shoulder.

It was not Nico, though. It was Gill.

'I has a message for you, mistress,' he said. 'From the master.'

For a horrifying moment I thought he meant Rannoch Hamilton. He must have seen the blood drain from my face because he stepped forward quickly and went down on one knee before me.

'From Master Nico,' he said. 'Not t'other one.'

'Saint Ninian be thanked,' said Tante-Mar, crossing herself. 'Rinette, hold out your arm, you are bleeding and it will stain that beautiful satin.'

I held out my arm. 'Where is the message?' I said. 'Where did you see him, Gill? Why did he not come himself?'

'It was in the stables, Mistress, when I went down to make sure Lilidh and Diamant were fed proper. He said he couldn't bear to see ye and leave ye, so better he didn't see ye at all. He said it like some kind of poetry, though.'

I had to smile. I could imagine Nico quoting love poetry to poor uncomprehending Gill. 'Where is the message?' I said.

'He made me mind it, and say it over and over till I had it perfit. Said he didn't dare write it down, for fear someone would take it from me.'

That frightened me. What could possibly be so dangerous?

Tante-Mar pulled the sleeve off. On the bare skin of my arm I could feel the heat of the fire and the cold of the chamber.

'Tell me,' I said.

Gill took a breath and rattled off, as if it were all one long sentence: 'There is talk that Rannoch Hamilton and the Frenchman Laurentin have some plot against you watch the children go nowhere alone juh temm mah mee.'

I doubled over laughing at his pronunciation of the French. Laughter, fear, laughter. I think I became a little wild. I laughed and laughed, until the tears came.

'There, it's all right,' Jennet said, wiping my bleeding shoulder with a handkerchief. 'Wat and I, we'll take care of you and the babes. You just tell the queen whatever she wants to hear about that yellow-haired tattie-bogle she's taken such a fancy to, and she'll get you free from that black devil Hamilton, and we'll all be home safe at Granmuir by Whitsun.'

'I thought I would be able to see Nico for a little while, at least.' I gulped back my tears and tried to catch my breath. 'I do not know how I will bear never seeing him alone, for weeks and weeks.'

'The time will pass quickly, *ma douce*.' Tante-Mar was folding up the satin. 'It is correct for you to remain separate from him until you are — Until your situation is settled.'

Poor Tante-Mar. She could not even say the word *divorce*.

'Now, you must try to sleep,' she went on. 'Gill, go in the other room, please, where the children are sleeping, and help Wat and Davy watch over them through the night. Jennet and I will stay here with your mistress.'

'I never trusted that French fellow Laurentin,' Jennet said. 'He and that poet, that Chastelard, they had some kind of scheme between them. Just let him try his tricks with me.'

'We have two good sturdy stools,' I said to her. 'We can come at him from either side.'

We both laughed until our stomachs hurt. Then we made wine caudles around the fire and talked about going home to Granmuir.

That night, I slept.

36

Shrove Tuesday was the day of Mary Livingston's wedding. Tante-Mar and Jennet dressed me in my lady-blush satin bodice and sleeves and skirt, with a long dark green overgown from an old court dress of my mother's. I thought of the gowns and mantles I had worn at the queen regent's court as a girl, and later when I had come back to Queen Mary's court with Alexander, and after his death. Who knew where they had all gone? Some of them had been left behind when Rannoch Hamilton dragged me off to Kinmeall; the rest remained at Kinmeall itself, probably worn to shreds by the kitchenmaids.

'I've brought your mother's gold pomander chain,' Tante-Mar said. She fastened it around my waist and let the pomander swing free. It was made in the shape of a scallop shell, its two hinged halves pierced and jewelled. I could smell the dried lavender and thyme Tante-Mar had filled it with.

'And her turquoises,' she went on. '*Regarde-toi*, they are perfect in your hair, the rose-gold and the blue-green stones. They bring out some colour in your cheeks and eyes. Oh, *ma douce*, forgive me, but you look so much like her sometimes.'

I was happy enough that even my bitterness against my mother had faded. I could hear Nico's voice: *In time you may wish to visit your mother at Montmartre*. In response, my own voice, stubbornly saying: *I will never go to Montmartre*.

But perhaps I would. With Nico and the children, perhaps I would.

I hugged Tante-Mar. 'I am happy you brought them,' I said.

With Jennet's help she twisted the jewels in my hair and then covered my head with the same gauzy white veil I had worn to my audience with the queen, freshly laundered and starched.

'Now, stay here, all of you,' I said. 'I shall be perfectly safe in Mary Livingston's wedding-party, and Nico will be in attendance on the queen, I am sure of it. It is Màiri and Kitte I fear for, with Rannoch Hamilton in Edinburgh.'

'Davy will go with you,' Wat Cairnie said. 'No, dinna argie-bargie with me, Rinette. He's a stout boy. Gill and Jennet and I will guard over the bairns, and I'll wager Mistress Loury and Seilie will give a good account of themselves as well if anything threatens.'

'Bar the door,' I said. 'Please.'

'I will.'

I kissed the girls, and then off I went to the Chapel Royal in Holyrood Abbey with Davy More as my gentleman-usher, his eyes the size of dinner plates.

Mary Livingston on her bridal day was magnificently dressed in silver, cloud-grey and gold, with a band of pearls gleaming in her hair. Her *devant-de-cotte*, silver tissue embroidered with frisé silver thread, had been a gift from the queen, as had her vasquine of grey satin bordered with rich gold braid. Her cheeks were flushed and her eyes sparkling; how happy she was with plain John Sempill, the younger son of a lord and nothing more.

'The queen has given her a great bed of scarlet velvet,' said an Englishman's voice in my ear. 'All bordered round with embroidered black velvet, with scarlet taffeta curtains. Can you just imagine what she and young Sempill will get up to, naked in the midst of all that scarlet and black?'

It was Henry Stewart, Lord Darnley. As usual, he looked like an angel, was dressed like a prince, and spoke like a gutter lout. I wondered why he was not with the queen's party, which was gathered on the other side of the chapel.

'She is beautiful, my lord,' I said. 'And the queen has been very generous. Anything more than that is not my concern, or yours.'

'You are a fine one to be prating about the sanctity of marriage, Mistress Marianette.'

I said nothing.

'Your husband is an excellent fellow. Well set up, shoulders like an ox. He must have been a stallion in the marriage bed, even if you did not have scarlet taffeta.'

I clenched my teeth together. I would not let him provoke me.

'He tells me—' Darnley leaned closer. His breath smelled of distilled spirits. 'He tells me there was once a certain silver casket, which was of great interest to the queen. Great interest to three queens, in fact – our own fine Stewart lassie with her sweet lips and golden eyes, my mother's cousin Elizabeth Tudor in England, and that dumpy little Italian sorceress Catherine de' Medici in France.'

No.

It could not all be starting again.

'If he has told you anything,' I said, goaded beyond endurance, 'he has told you that he himself destroyed what was in the casket, out of drunkenness and spite.'

This was not true, of course. The real silver casket and its secrets had vanished into the ancient air of the vault under Saint

Margaret's Chapel. I had hoped and prayed that after all this time it had been forgotten.

'On the contrary,' Darnley said with honeyed venom. 'Rannoch Hamilton says what he told the queen that night was a lie. He says he never had the casket and never destroyed anything.'

At first I did not put the words together with the meaning. John Sempill was slipping a gold ring on Mary Livingston's finger, and appreciative whispers were rustling around us like the sound of the sea. Then it came together and I said, too loudly, 'He says *what*?'

Darnley chuckled, clearly pleased with the fact that he had finally broken through my reserve. 'Shush,' he said. 'Everyone is looking. Step outside a moment, Mistress Marianette. You should know what else your husband is saying about you in the taverns of the High Street.'

The priest was blessing the bride and groom preparatory to offering the nuptial mass. The Protestants were shifting their positions, looking about, preparing to leave before the Catholics practised their idolatry. I gestured to Davy to follow close behind me and slipped through the crush of courtiers and out into the huge, shadowy nave of the Abbey church. To the east, before the altar, Alexander's body had lain, and here in the church I had found the ruby fixed fast in his blood—

But I would not think about that now.

I did not walk more than a step or two from the chapel. Even with Davy to support me, I was not fool enough to go so far that I could not easily call for help.

'Very well, my lord,' I said to Darnley. 'I will go no farther. Tell me what Rannoch Hamilton has been saying.'

He rocked back on his heels, smiling. His fair hair made a halo around his head, and I could almost see the outline of the yellow cock's-comb superimposed over his tall, slender figure. It made me feel sick and dizzy.

'He says you still have the Guise woman's silver casket yourself, hidden away at Granmuir, and are only waiting for the right moment to sell it to the highest bidder.'

'That is a lie.'

'He says he will agree to the divorce only if you give him the casket. He believes it will make him the richest, most important man in Europe.'

'Listen to me, my lord,' I said. I was so shaken and furious the dimness of the Abbey church seemed to have closed in around me, with Lord Darnley and his mirror-image yellow cock's-comb far away in a pinpoint spot of light. 'I do not have the silver casket. I do not know who has the silver casket. I have not seen the silver casket since the day I left it in the vault under Saint Margaret's.'

'All perfectly true.' A different voice, French-accented, heart-sinkingly familiar, directly behind me. 'And yet you are the one person who will put the silver casket into my hands.'

Blaise Laurentin seemed to materialise out of the cold Abbey stone itself, as if he were an effigy come to life. Darnley laughed, high as a girl, said something in quick gutter French to Laurentin, and started back into the chapel. I turned to follow him. I was not fool enough to stand out in the shadowy nave alone with Blaise Laurentin, even if I did have Davy to protect me.

'Do not go,' Laurentin said, in a pleasantly conversational tone. 'If you do, I will strangle your two little girls like unwanted kittens.'

I stopped.

He held out a tiny white linen cap, embroidered with roses. Two or three shining strands of golden hair were caught around the button.

Màiri's cap.

At first I stood immobilised, not believing. Then hot tears of terror and rage flooded up into my eyes and my heart felt as if it would burst into a thousand pieces within my breast. I snatched the cap from him and said, 'I will kill you.'

He smiled. His eyes were like stones, hard and colourless. 'Best not, for the moment at least,' he said. 'Or you will never see them again. Come with me, Madame. No theatrics, if you please, if you want your two little girls to live. Send your boy back into the chapel, and tell him to wait. Tell him to say nothing to anyone, particularly Monsieur de Clerac.'

'Davy,' I said. I clutched Màiri's cap tightly. 'Go back into the chapel, please. Nothing is wrong – I only wish to speak with Monsieur Laurentin for a moment.'

'Wat said I wasn't to leave ye, mistress. Not even for a meenit.'

'I understand. I will explain to Wat. Go back in the chapel, please, and say nothing to anyone, particularly Monsieur de Clerac.'

He looked puzzled and uneasy, but he said, 'Yes, mistress.'

He went back into the chapel.

I said to Blaise Laurentin, 'What do you want?'

'The silver casket, of course.'

'For the love of God. *I do not have it.*'

'I know.' He took my arm. 'But I also know who does. Come with me now. Quietly. I will take you to your children.'

I clutched Màiri's cap hard in my hands and walked beside him. My knees felt like water.

'You know who has the casket,' I repeated. I was determined to work it all out for myself. 'You must think it will help you somehow, to have my babies and me as prisoners.'

'Exactly so.'

'Rannoch Hamilton is part of this, too.'

'Perhaps.'

'He would love to see me dead. Màiri as well. Then he could claim Granmuir in Kitte's name.'

He laughed and said nothing more. I could not imagine who it was he believed had the casket after all this time, or what his plan was.

'How did you get into our chambers?' I wanted to scream for help so badly my voice was thin and shaky. I did not dare. I did not dare. I pressed Màiri's cap to my heart. 'The children were guarded. My people would have protected them.'

'Your people are as susceptible to trickery as any others.'

'Trickery or no, they would have died before they gave up the children.'

'Oh, yes,' said Blaise Laurentin lightly. 'You are quite right about that. They did.'

37

The filthy storage shed smelled like a stable. Màiri was huddled in one corner with Kitte clutched tight in her arms, like a tiny lioness with a single cub. Kitte was curled in a ball, her baby eyes screwed up tight. Màiri's eyes were wide with terror and defiance; her golden Gordon hair was loose and tangled. Her little kirtle was covered with blood.

'Màiri!' I cried. I ran across the beaten earth floor to them and flung myself to my knees. 'Kitte! My precious girls, are you all right? Màiri? Are you hurt? Show Maman where.'

'Maman,' she gulped. Her voice was shaky. 'They hurt Wat and Jennet. Seilie cried. Tante-Mar fell down.'

'Oh, God. Oh, no. Blessed Saint Ninian, no!' I could not think it, I could not bear it. I embraced them both fiercely. 'Let me see. You are sure you are not hurt, Màiri-Rose?'

'Tante-Mar fell down,' she said again. Then she threw herself against me and began to cry in great heartrending sobs.

I held them both close to my heart and looked up at Blaise Laurentin. 'You black-hearted bastard,' I managed to say through my gritted teeth. 'You devil's seed. What have you done?'

'It wasn't him.'

I jerked around in horror. Rannoch Hamilton grinned at me from the corner like a hobgoblin from the blackest pits of hell.

'It was me,' he said.

I would have leaped at him and torn his face like a wild animal, but I could not leave my babies unprotected.

'I killed them all,' he said. 'And now I am going to kill you, too, wife, and Alexander Gordon's spawn, and when I have been invested with the Lordship of Granmuir in my own right, I'll throw the other one off the cliff face into the sea. Stand aside, Frenchman.'

'I think not,' said Blaise Laurentin. He drew his dagger. 'You have served your purpose, Monsieur Rannoch, and for the moment I require Mistress Rinette and her children alive.'

My husband swept his own dagger from its sheath. He was still grinning. He was mad – he had to be mad. 'Play me false, will you?' he said. 'Then I'll kill you too.'

They lunged at each other. I ducked away and put my head down and gathered the girls against my breast so they could not see. Kill each other, I prayed. Saint Ninian, Green Lady of Granmuir, make them kill each other. Màiri and Kitte sobbed against me.

The two men grappled and panted, swearing at each other in French and Scots. One of them cried out. I smelled hot fresh blood.

'Kill each other,' I said aloud, through my gritted teeth.

I heard a grunt of pain, a sickeningly filthy epithet in Scots, the creak of the door's hinges. Footsteps, slow, staggering, then faster. The door crashed shut.

I looked up.

Blaise Laurentin stood with his back to the door, his dagger in his right fist, blood running down his left arm.

'I will find him and kill him later,' he said. 'You are no good to me dead.'

He came up to me. I threw myself down over the babies. He grasped my hair from behind, veil and turquoises and all, jerked it out of its pins, and to my shock and horror began to hack at it with the dagger. I reached up involuntarily – what woman would not reach up to protect her hair? – and felt the knife cut indiscriminately into my fingers and palms. I struggled to grasp hold of it. What did I care if the blade cut my fingers to the bone? If I could wrench it away from him I would kill him inch by shrieking, shuddering, bloody inch.

'There,' he said. He stood back, holding up the tortoise-shell coils of my hair like Perseus holding the head of Medusa. The hair and the veil were bloodied – my own blood – and in the twists and braids my mother's turquoises glinted. My head felt unbalanced, too light and too cold.

'Maman,' Màiri sobbed. 'The bad man cut your pretty hair.'

I clenched my fists to stop the bleeding and held her closer, Kitte along with her. I had to be calm. I had to be brave. If I gave way to my terror it would only frighten the girls all the more.

'Now what are you going to do, Monsieur Laurentin?' I said, with all the scorn I could muster.

'Give me the child's cap,' he said.

I picked up Màiri's cap. At first I tried not to mark it with blood, and then I thought – whoever it is, they should know this monster would hurt a child to get what he wants. I closed it in my fist slowly, letting my blood sink into the fabric, then threw it at Blaise Laurentin's feet.

He laughed grimly and picked it up.

'Excellent,' he said. 'Enjoy this space of time with your children, Madame.'

He went out. I heard the clink of metal – a key, then, and a metal lock in the hasp. We were locked in, but at the same time Rannoch Hamilton was locked out, if he should decide to come back. There were no windows, no chinks in the wooden walls, no possible means of escape. The little room was black dark but for a knife-thin tracing of light around the top and sides of the door.

'Maman,' Màiri whispered. Her voice was shaky. 'Kitte is afraid of the dark.'

My brave, brave girl. She herself was piteously frightened by the dark but she would never admit it.

'It is all right, Màiri-Rose,' I said. 'Monsieur Laurentin will come back for us soon. We must be brave, for Kitte's sake. Will you sing me a song?'

'The counting song?'

'*Bon*. In English and in French, my precious.'

Màiri began in English, her voice tiny and sweet and true. After a moment Kitte joined in with her baby nonsense syllables. I sang with them, straining to be calm, to soothe them, all the while trying desperately to think of some way to save them.

It was the smell that did it, the plant-and-stable smell – horses and oats and musty straw. Even as they mouldered away, the oat grains and the barley and the stalks of the straw spoke to me. *Remember. Remember. Remember the morning after you were married to him, remember the hidden hole, and how you stumbled . . .*

The shed had an earthen floor. If I could dig a hole, just in the spot where Laurentin would step when he returned, dig a hole and disguise it with a few fronds of straw, he would stumble. If he were taken by surprise, and if I was expecting it, I would have a single moment to jump at him and snatch his blade and stab him.

A single moment. If I hesitated, or fumbled, or did not find an immediately vulnerable spot with the knife, I would fail.

I had to try. I would succeed. The thought of sinking Laurentin's own dagger into the pulsing vein at his throat filled me with a sense of unholy anticipation.

As my little ones sang their way through every song Tante-Mar had ever taught them – Tante-Mar, Tante-Mar, *Tante-Mar fell down*, I could not think about that now – I got up and flattened my back against the door and took a step into the room. The placing of the trap had to be just right – since the door was hinged on the right, it should be a little to the left of centre. Since he would be standing outside when he unlocked the door and stepped in, perhaps two-thirds of a step into the room . . . I chose my spot and I began to dig.

My slashed hands made it agony. My fingernails cracked and tore. I barely managed to scrape up an inch or so of the hard earth.

I sat back, panting. A loose strand of raggedly cut hair fell over my cheek and stuck to the sweat and tears. The children had stopped singing and had actually fallen asleep, worn out by fear and shock. My mother's pomander made a clinking sound as it fell to my side.

My mother's pomander.

Mother, I thought. You abandoned me for the nuns of Montmartre and I never forgave you, not for all the years when I was growing up. Help me now. I forgive you – help me now.

With shaking hands I pried the pomander open and began to dig again with the sharp scalloped edges. The scents of the lavender and thyme comforted me, and the halves of the pomander cut easily through the dirt. It did not take long at all for me to create an oval hole, big enough for a man's foot, and a good twelve inches deep. If he stepped in that, all unaware, it would certainly make him stagger, knock him off balance.

I dug the hole deeper, slanted towards the doorway so his unwary foot would slide into it. Then I laid fronds of straw carelessly over it: not enough to look like a pile of straw, but just enough so it would not draw the attention of a man stepping into a dark room, not expecting it. I swept the loose earth into my skirt and carried it to the back of the room.

And then all I could do was wait. I had to keep myself awake, taut, prepared to spring. How much time had passed? It had been just before midday when Blaise Laurentin accosted me outside the Chapel Royal, as the nuptial mass for Mary Livingston and John Sempill was beginning. Had it been two hours . . . three . . . five? I was hungry, thirsty, aching. My hands burned with pain. I flexed them gently. I could not let my fingers stiffen or I would never be able to grasp Laurentin's dagger even if I had the chance.

Tante-Mar fell down.

You are quite right about that. They did.

I prayed to Saint Ninian that it might all be a lie, but I knew it could not be. They would have fought for Màiri and Kitte, all of them, Wat and Jennet and Gill, fragile Tante-Mar, even gallant little Seilie with his freckled paws. I cried, stifling my sobs so as not to wake the children, and I prayed for their souls. I prayed to the gentle goddesses of the fields and the harvest, gave thanks for the oats and the straw, for the scents that spoke to me. I prayed for my precious daughters' lives.

I prayed to the Green Lady of Granmuir for the strength to kill Blaise Laurentin with his own dagger and bathe my hands in his blood.

* * *

The light in the cracks at the top and sides of the door faded, so I knew it was evening. Good. I would not be dazzled by the glare when the door opened. I kept flexing my fingers, and walking from one side of the narrow space to the other. The air was thick and stale.

I heard voices first, a good distance away. Boots then, coming closer. I heard the faint metallic rasp of the key in the lock.

The children were still asleep. I crouched down beside them, as if I had been huddling there all afternoon. I flexed my fingers one last time. The blood had dried in the cuts and I felt it crack.

The door scraped open. It swept all my carefully arranged straw to one side. My stomach lurched; I had not planned for that. Even so I gathered my legs under me and leaned forward on my fingertips.

Blaise Laurentin stepped into the room. He was absolutely confident and smiling at me. His left foot sank hard into my hole, his ankle cracked audibly, and his whole body lurched to one side.

I sprang at him, screaming like a *bean nighe*. He was down on one knee, hurt, off balance and surprised, and I fell on him, biting and scratching like a wildcat. He shouted something at me and reached for his dagger. I sank my teeth into the wiry muscle of his upper arm and he screamed, swinging his other arm to strike at me. His fist slammed into my cheekbone and rocked my head back but I held on grimly. At the same time I got my own fingers around the haft of his dagger.

– and I felt the falcon's head –

I did not throw my arm back to stab at him; he would have caught my wrist and his strength was too great for me. I pulled the dagger free from its sheath at his hip and drove it straight into the vulnerable crease between his thigh and his belly, then with both hands jerked it sideways and up. If I could have gelded him with a single stroke I would have done it gladly. As it was his breeches-lacings and codpiece protected his manhood. But blood spurted high and hard, bright red. He shrieked and let go of me, curling up like a woodlouse to protect his soft parts.

'Màiri!' I screamed. 'Màiri-Rose, take Kitte . . . run, run, run!'

Màiri was awake; my first cry had wakened them both. She lifted Kitte by the waist and dragged her towards the door. Kitte was crying wildly but Màiri was resolute and silent. I knelt over Blaise Laurentin and stabbed him again, aiming for his throat. The blade slipped off his collarbone and left a deep shallow gash in his shoulder. More blood welled and soaked into his shirt. He grunted and flailed at me weakly.

Tante-Mar fell down.

'You fall down!' I screamed. I stabbed him again. He did not make another sound. 'Devil! Coward! Fall down and stay down, and may your black soul go to hell where it belongs and rot forever!'

'Maman!' Màiri cried. Her little voice was thin and high. 'Maman, come out, hurry!'

I lurched to my feet, the bloody *Escadron Volant* dagger still held tight in my right hand, and ran outside. It was cool and overcast and I could smell dung and straw and refuse, and faintly, faintly, the sea blowing in along the Firth of Forth. Oh, Green Lady, Saint Ninian, the sea, the sea, the sea which washed everything clean. I swept the screaming Kitte up under my left arm.

'Hold my skirt, Màiri-Rose,' I said. 'Run, now.'

We ran down the alley. Where were we running? I did not know. I did not care. I had to get away and get my babies away. I think I would have run all the way to Queensferry if my way had not been blocked at the end of the alley by a man wrapped in a black cloak and hood, holding a naked sword which glinted faintly in the light from the street behind him.

I put Kitte down and pushed both girls behind me.

'I have a knife,' I said. I was panting with anguish and terror. 'I have just killed a man and I will kill you, too, if you—'

Then I realised who it was.

'Nico,' I whispered.

His face was white as sea-polished bone. 'Rinette,' he said. '*Sainte-grâce*, are you hurt?'

'No. Only a little. My hands. It is his blood, not mine.'

'And you killed him? Are you sure? Where did you get the knife?'

'Yes, I am sure. It is his knife. I made a trap for him. Nico, what are you doing here?'

'I was coming for you and the children.' Some colour had come back into his face and I saw his mouth twist in a bitter – why bitter? – smile. 'But I see you have rescued yourself quite effectively. Rinette, we must go, quickly. You must not be found here, like this.'

'I do not care. Let them find me.' I started to cry, gasping sobs that hurt my throat and chest. 'He killed them, Nico. He killed them all . . . Tante-Mar and Jennet and Wat and Gill and Seilie. I brought them from Granmuir because I could not bear to be parted from them and Rannoch Hamilton killed them. They were in the plot together, Rannoch Hamilton and Blaise Laurentin.'

Kitte started to cry again when she heard me crying. Màiri just stared at me, her eyes huge. I wished I could take the words back. Had she understood?

Metal rasped against metal as Nico sheathed his sword. 'Did he tell you that? Could he have been lying?'

I choked on my own breath. It had never occurred to me to

378

doubt him. I managed to say, 'He told me. But they would never have let him take Màiri and Kitte.'

Nico swept off the black cloak and wrapped it around me, covering the blood on my dress and the ruin of my hacked-off hair. He was wearing a plain dark doublet and Venetian breeches with riding boots; he had a pair of saddlebags slung over his shoulder so he was clearly prepared for flight. He pulled Màiri and Kitte in under the cloak as well. Kitte's sobs quieted at once. Màiri clung to my leg as if she would never let it go.

'I have been staying at Maitland of Lethington's house in the High Street,' he said. 'Sir William and I both dislike Darnley more than we dislike each other, it seems. I will take you and the girls there, where you will be safe, and then I will go to Holyrood myself.'

'No,' I said. 'I will go with you.'

'Rinette, you cannot take the children there. Would you have them see what your mad husband has done?'

'Surely there is someone at Lethington's house who can watch over them for a little while. I am coming with you, Nico.'

'Let us at least get to Sir William's house,' he said, 'and then we shall see. Rinette, let go of the knife, *ma mie*. You have saved yourself, and defended your daughters bravely, and you do not need the dagger any more. Leave it here, in the close – it is better that no one sees you in possession of it, in case it is identifiable as belonging to Blaise Laurentin.'

I looked down at my right hand. I felt amazement – genuine amazement, and a dizzy lurch of distress to see I was holding the dagger so tightly my knuckles were white. The blade and my hand and wrist were covered with blood. There was something about the dagger, something I had recognised, but my mind was so jumbled—

'I cannot move my fingers,' I said.

Màiri whimpered.

'Just breathe,' Nico said. 'Think them open. I am so sorry, *ma mie*, that you had to do such a terrible thing. I am sorry with all my heart that Màiri and Kitte had to see it.'

'I wish they had not,' I said, 'but I am not sorry I killed him.'

I opened my fingers slowly. It hurt. I could feel the cuts pulling apart again. At last the dagger fell to the stone cobbles of the close.

The falcon's head with its single red ruby eye winked at me in the light from the street.

The dagger I had taken from Blaise Laurentin, the dagger I had used to stab him over and over again in a wild passion of fury and anguish and revenge, was the dagger which had killed Alexander Gordon.

38

I took the dagger with me. Nico tried to convince me to leave it lying in the alley, but how could I walk away and leave it when I had been pursuing it so resolutely, for so long? I cut a strip from my ruined overgown to wrap the blade, and thrust the dagger into the pomander-chain around my waist. I carried Kitte and Nico carried Màiri and we were at Maitland of Lethington's house within half an hour. Sir William himself was at Holyrood, of course, for the wedding celebrations; what his majordomo thought when we descended upon him in the dark, wild-eyed and bloodied, I never knew. He called for maidservants, who in their turn brought hot water, clean nightsmocks, and sugared porridge for the children; I was provided with a proper coif, at least, to cover my shorn head, and one of the majordomo's wife's own mantles.

I did not want to go to Holyrood. Mary Livingston's wedding masque would be in full dazzling progress. Candles would be blazing, the queen's consort of musicians would be playing, a hundred people would be laughing and chivvying the bride and groom with bawdy jests. In the midst of all that, could I bear to walk into the apartments I had left this morning – just this morning! How could it be possible? – and find – and find – unimaginable horrors?

I did not want to go.

I had to go.

Nico put his saddlebags away, wrapped himself in his own dark cloak again, and we set off. It was about a quarter of a mile down the High Street to the Netherbow Port; silver glinted as it passed from Nico's hand to the watchman's. From there we walked straight down the Canongate. We did not say a word to each other. With every step I felt more and more dread. When we reached the palace one of the queen's guards stopped us. Nico spoke to him quietly and another coin changed hands. In that moment when the guard was distracted I ducked under his pike and ran into the palace.

I ran. I could not stop to think because if I did I would fall down on the stone steps and howl like an animal. To the staircases in the south-west corner and up and up and up, panting and sick. Then to my left and down the corridor – another of the queen's guards stood outside a chamber, *the* chamber. I burst past him before he could move or speak.

Tante-Mar sat stiffly upright in a carved wooden chair – where had the chair come from? There had been no chair in the room before. Her head was tilted to one side, resting against the polished wood. Her coif was off – unthinkable. I had never seen her, not once, without her neat linen widow's coif. Her hair was white, cut short. Her eyes were closed and her skin was grey.

Jennet More lay upon the bed. Her bodice and apron were dark brown with dried blood. Her profile was sharp and yellow as freshly hacked wood. Her hands were crossed upon her breast.

There was blood on the floor. Someone had tried to mop it up.

There was a body on the floor as well, laid out neatly and covered with a blanket. Beside it Seilie lay stretched out, his muzzle tucked under the edge of the blanket, his fur wet as if someone had tried to wash him. His freckled white paws were spattered with blood.

The music and laughter of Mary Livingston's bridal masque floated up the stairs and through the corridor.

Everything seemed to get very small and bright. My ears hummed. I felt hands on my shoulders and a voice spoke from behind me but it was all so far away. My stomach twisted and lurched up against the back of my throat.

Then Seilie lifted his head and whined softly.

My world shifted and rushed back to normal size. It came too far, in fact, and I saw Seilie as if he were close before my eyes. I heard some of the words the person behind me was saying.

'. . . Doctor Lusgerie has been tending Jennet, and only stepped out for a moment . . . Madame Loury was stricken with an apoplexy, but she will recover . . . Wat Cairnie is gone, *ma mie*, but he fought bravely, thanks be to God, and saved the others . . . everyone else is safe, even Seilie, his hurts are superficial . . .'

I doubled over and vomited bile that burned my mouth like fire, and that was the last thing I remember.

It was Gill who told us what had happened. He himself was unhurt, but for a plum-sized lump on his forehead.

''Twas Jennet,' he said. 'She went for the master – for Master Rannoch – with a stool, she did, and when she swung it around she caught me a clip that knocked me flat.'

I could not help but smile a little, remembering how we had laughed together over the stools being our chosen weapons. Dear Jennet. Thanks be to God, she would live, despite two serious knife wounds. Doctor Lusgerie had treated them with an ointment of egg yolk, oil of roses and turpentine, instead of cauterising them with boiling oil; it was a battlefield technique he had learned in France, he said, from the famous chirurgeon Ambroise Paré.

'She saved your life,' Nico said. 'Rannoch Hamilton must have thought you were dead in the mêlée.'

'He was stark daft, he was, swinging his dirk and a-swearing,' Gill said. 'And he was mostly going after Wat. Didn't think a boy or a couple of women would be much trouble. It was Davy who woke me up – he came in and started a-screiching for help.'

'I came back here,' Davy said. He was untouched but white as a ghost. 'I didn't know what else to do, mistress, when ye didn't come back to the chapel. I came here and found – all this. Called the guard and they fetched the queen's doctor fellow.'

Doctor Lusgerie had also cleaned the cuts on my palms and fingers, and applied some of his healing ointment. Before he bandaged them, he made me curl and straighten all my fingers, and seemed satisfied. I would have scars, he said, but I would have the normal use of my hands. With that, he had gone out, promising to return in the morning.

The provost's bailies had taken Wat's body away to be examined and embalmed; when they were finished we would take him home to Granmuir. Nico had somehow produced the queen's own priest, Père René Benoist, who had said prayers but at first refused the unction on the grounds that Wat was already dead. Nico took him out into the passageway and spoke to him privately; when he returned he looked frightened, and gave Wat the unction without any conditions. Then he scuttled away.

'How did – Master Rannoch – get in, Gill?' I asked. I was crouched down on the floor with Seilie in my arms. With my bandaged hands I could not pat him and feel the warm silkiness of his ears; instead I rubbed my cheek against his soft russet head. 'Wat promised to keep the door barred.'

''Twas a woman's voice,' Gill said. 'A-screaming and a-crying, and calling out all our names. It was the names, Mistress — she called for Wat and Jennet, and she even said Tante-Mar, French-like just the same as ye would have done, and she sounded like she was hurt, and Wat opened the door.'

'It is my fault.'

I swung around. Tante-Mar's eyes were open. Nico had arranged to have extra pallets brought in and assembled; with exquisite gentleness he had helped to settle her upon one of them. She looked deathly tired but she smiled at me a little, and my heart blossomed.

'I suspect it was just some girl from the street,' she said. 'But he had lessoned her. She said "Tante-Mar" just the way you would have said it, and cried for help. I told Wat to open the door.'

She lifted her hand, as if to cross herself, but could not complete the gesture. Her hand fell back on to her breast and she closed her eyes again.

I patted Seilie one last time, then stood up and went to her. 'It is not your fault, Tante-Mar,' I said. 'Gill was fooled as well, and I am sure Wat would have opened the door regardless. Look, Doctor Lusgerie left a distillation of lily-of-the-valley for you — I will mix it with a little honey and wine if you would like some.'

'Not now,' she said. She opened her eyes again. 'Perhaps when I am ready to sleep. I am so happy you and the little ones are safe, *ma douce*, I simply want to look at you.'

I patted her pillows and made sure she was comfortable. Then I walked over to where Jennet lay in the bed and put my hand on her forehead. Her skin felt hot and moist, and she looked flushed. Doctor Lusgerie had warned us she would experience some fever.

I smoothed her hair back, then walked across the chamber and looked out of the window. It faced south, over the park; the stars of Orion and Gemini were low on the horizon and the silver veil of the Via Lactea divided the dark sky in two. 'Laurentin wanted the casket,' I said. 'Everything always comes back to the casket. We would all be happy and safe at Granmuir, even Alexander, if I had refused to take it from Mary of Guise that night. If I had just slipped away and left them to quarrel over it. It would have been weeks before the Earl of Rothes thought of me, and Alexander and I would have been long married.'

'If you had not taken the casket that night,' Nico said, 'Moray would have had it. The Lords of the Congregation and John Knox would have had it. They would have kept Mary of Guise's secret notes, and used them against the remaining Catholics to consolidate their own power, and suppressed the secrets about themselves. Mary Stuart most certainly would never have come home to Scotland, and might well have been quietly poisoned while she was still Queen of France. The world would be a different place, *ma mie*, if you had not taken the casket that night.'

I turned and looked at him. He was bone-white and his eyes were dark with – what, exhaustion? anguish? guilt of his own? – in the beautifully made hollows of their sockets. It was one of the moments when I could actually see him as a monk, giving up his life in penance for the sins of the world.

'Yes,' I said. 'It would be different. I do not know if the world we have is better.'

He walked across the chamber and took me in his arms. 'It is what it is,' he said. 'Your daughters are safe. Granmuir stands. Rinette, there is something I must tell you.'

'Is it good?'

'No.'

I put my forehead down against his shoulder. 'Then I do not want to hear it. Not now. Not tonight, after everything that has happened today. Please, Nico.'

'Tomorrow, then. It is important, *ma mie*.'

'Tomorrow.'

He pushed back my borrowed coif and ran his hand gently over my hair. What remained of my hair. I had always taken it for granted, because I had always had it – hair past my waist, the glinting dark and gold colours of polished tortoise-shell, pulled straight by its own weight but with a bit of a curl at the ends. Now it was gone. My mother's turquoises were gone. The short pieces at the back of my head were rough and prickly.

'I might as well be a boy,' I said.

He touched his lips to my temple. 'No,' he said. 'Not a boy.'

Out in the city I heard the bell ringing the third watch. Midnight. Had it only been this morning that Tante-Mar and Jennet had dressed me for Mary Livingston's wedding? Was it only now, perhaps, that Mary Livingston and John Sempill were being put to bed amidst the magnificent scarlet draperies, their wedding gift from the queen?

And Wat Cairnie was dead.

Blaise Laurentin was dead. I had killed him with my own hands.

Rannoch Hamilton was out in the city somewhere. Dead? Alive? I did not know.

At least Màiri and Kitte were safe at Maitland of Lethington's house.

I put my arms around Nico's waist and leaned against him. He smelled of bitter orange and myrrh and gold-and-purple nightshade, and he was wonderfully warm and solid. 'I am so tired,' I said.

He leaned down, slid one arm behind my knees, and lifted me. 'Gill,' he said. 'Davy. Fold that extra coverlet, if you please, and my cloak and Mistress Rinette's mantle. Move one of the pallets under the window. Let us make your mistress as comfortable as we can.'

I closed my eyes. I heard the fabric rustling. Then I felt myself being lowered to the pallet. The coverlet had been stored away somewhere with sprigs of rosemary, and kept a trace of their astringent scent. Rosemary for memory, a herb of love and marriage. A cold nose nudged my chin, and then I felt Seilie turning around and around before thumping down next to the pallet. I reached out and rested one hand on his fur. I could feel his warmth and his heartbeat.

'I'll sleep right here in front o' the door,' Gill's voice said, as if from a long way away. 'Anyone trying to get in'll have to walk right over me.'

'And me,' Davy said.

'Good boys.' Nico's voice was close by. I felt him settle himself beside me, his back against the wall. I turned over, wanting to face him, and felt the hard metal shape of Blaise Laurentin's dagger, still thrust in the pomander chain. I rolled over on my back again.

'The dagger,' I said. I sounded fretful as a child. 'I cannot lie comfortably.'

He unfastened the chain and took both it and the dagger away. 'There,' he said. 'Is that better?'

'Yes. Thank you.'

'I wish you had left it there. Will you allow me to dispose of it tomorrow?'

'No.' I opened my eyes. His face was half in shadow, and I could not quite read his expression. 'I want it to be known that a member of this *Escadron Volant* brotherhood has been in Scotland. I want the queen to be warned.'

He had unwrapped the strip of cloth from the dagger's blade, and held it flat with one fingertip under the guard. It was perfectly balanced. The falcon's one red eye was lost in the darkness. 'It was probably Catherine de' Medici who hired him, but we are still not certain of that. You cannot touch her, *ma mie*.'

'I can show the dagger to the queen, at least. Show her how the ruby I found fits perfectly into the socket of the falcon's eye. I can bring the whole network of assassins into the light, and blacken Queen Catherine's name.'

'It is black enough,' he said. 'With sins she did commit, and sins others have committed in her name. Leave it as it is, Rinette, I beg you.'

I closed my eyes again. 'I want the dagger,' I said stubbornly. 'Give it back to me.'

He picked up my hand, taking great care of the bandages, and kissed my fingertips. Then he laid my arm gently over Seilie's warm fur again.

'You will hurt yourself with it, *ma mie*,' he said very softly. 'I will give it back to you in the morning.'

And he did. It lay on the table as I painfully scratched out a letter to the queen, telling her of Rannoch Hamilton's attack on my household and Blaise Laurentin's plot to abduct me. I did not try to explain Laurentin's conviction that the silver casket and its contents had not been destroyed after all, nor did I mention Lord Darnley's involvement in the whole intrigue. I did not write that I had killed Blaise Laurentin, or that his dagger was the weapon that had killed Alexander, or that Nicolas de Clerac had spent the night with us here. These were things better not committed to paper, and with my bandaged hands I could not write easily. As I sanded the ink, I thought wryly that my letter omitted rather more than it told.

As I wrote, Nico arranged for two men-at-arms to guard us and a brisk bedchamber-woman named Una MacAlpin to help me care for Jennet and Tante-Mar. Then he went out to consult the provost about a murdered body in some stable outbuildings; he wanted to be certain I would not be blamed for Blaise Laurentin's death. I gave Gill careful instructions on how to find the queen's tower on the other side of Holyrood Palace, and sent him off with my letter. I was only just dressed when he returned. I could not help but smile at his expression; he looked like a mouse who had come face to face with a lion.

'She actually said words to me,' he said reverently. 'The queen herself. Asked me what my name was.'

'Did she read my letter, Gill?'

'So she did, and gave me an answer, too. Wrote it down, so's I didn't have to recollect it.'

He handed me my own letter again. At the bottom someone – not the queen herself, probably Mary Beaton – had scribbled, *Wait upon me after dinner, MARIE R.*

'Well done, Gill,' I said. 'Now, I have another errand for you. Run down to Sir William Maitland of Lethington's house, if you please, in the High Street. Ask after Màiri and Kitte, and make certain they are well. I do not dare bring them here until Rannoch Hamilton is captured, but we cannot move Tante-Mar or Jennet – for now it is best that they stay where they are.'

'Aye, Mistress,' he said. He turned to go and ran straight into Nicolas de Clerac.

'Nico,' I said. 'Look, I have a letter from the queen—' I saw his expression and said, 'What is it?'

'Laurentin. You did not kill him, Rinette.'

I stared at him. 'How can you say that? I stabbed him over and over, with his own dagger.'

'The provost's bailies said no murdered body had been recovered overnight, so I went back to the stable outbuilding where he held you and the girls. I wanted to make sure he was dead.'

My stomach lurched. 'And you found him alive?'

'No. I did not find him at all.'

'Could someone have taken his body?'

'There was a trail of blood, up the alley to the street. He crawled.'

'But I *stabbed* him,' I said again. I picked up the dagger, despite my bandaged hands, and drove it into the wood of the table. It stuck there, quivering. 'He was *dead.*'

'He was badly wounded, I think, but not dead. At least his death is not on your hands. What does your letter say? Has she asked you to wait upon her?'

'Yes.'

'Go, then, and tell her what Rannoch Hamilton has done. She has a horror of violence, and she will be all the more willing to see you divorced. Or to see Hamilton captured and hanged.'

I tried to pull the dagger out of the table. I could not get hold of it properly. 'What are you going to do?'

'I am going to find Laurentin, and kill him myself.'

It was only after he was gone that I remembered his promise to tell me something. Something I would not wish to hear. Something important.

39

' I will be present when the provost questions Monsieur Laurentin,' the queen said. 'It is a member of my own household, my Marianette, of whom he makes his accusations.'

'All the more reason for you not to be present, sister.' The Earl of Moray had slipped precipitously out of favour with the rise of Lord Darnley and the revelation of Nico's parentage. Once again the wheel of fortune had turned; the queen did not need a bastard half-brother when she had a tall shining fair-haired cavalier and a Guise half-cousin to advise her.

'You have no official standing at the provost's examination,' Moray persisted. 'Your presence at this chirurgeon's house could be construed as pressure to exonerate Mistress Rinette, should she be innocent or guilty.'

'I have no intention of going as myself.' The queen pirouetted around the room, showing off her perfect legs in watchet-green stockings, with paned trunk-hose, a matching green velvet doublet and a soft russet-coloured leather jerkin. With her hair pinned up under a jaunty feathered cap, she made the most beautiful youth imaginable. 'I shall be Harry's friend from France. Say you so, my love?'

'So I say.' Lord Darnley grinned at Moray, triumphant as a

spoiled six-year-old. 'And I must certainly be there – you can imagine how surprised I was when I learned Monsieur Laurentin had dragged himself to my very own doorstep, bleeding like a stuck boar, claiming Mistress Rinette attacked him all unprovoked.'

'Oh, yes,' I said. 'I can imagine how surprised you were.'

I was waiting by the door, plainly dressed in black camlet with narrow white ruffles at my throat and wrists. My head was covered by a linen headdress like a nun's, with a sheer white veil, and my hands were bandaged. Mary Seton had done her best to trim the ruined remains of my hair; even so, without a head covering I looked like a shorn prisoner facing the sword.

'*Alors*, Marianette, we are all surprised!' The queen laughed, determined to make an adventure out of it all. 'Monsieur Laurentin has it backwards, no? It was he who attacked you, and it will do him no good to claim special friendship with Harry. Will it, *mon cher*?'

'Of course not,' Darnley said. 'We met by chance in a wineshop or two, no more.'

'There, you see? And Monsieur Castelnau has disavowed any connection with him as a French agent, so he will not escape by that means. We shall sort this out with the provost, Marianette, and then proceed with your divorce. Although if Rannoch Hamilton is captured, the hangman will make you a widow quite quickly enough.'

'It cannot be too quickly for me, Madame.'

'Indeed,' she said. 'Nico, *mon cousin*, where are you? And Signor Davy? We shall make a very fine coterie of young gentlemen to meet the provost at the chirurgeon's house. Marianette, go ahead, if you please. Brother, send two royal men-at-arms to accompany her. You yourself may attend or not, as you please.'

Moray's expression was black as thunder. 'I do not please,' he said.

Blaise Laurentin was stretched picturesquely on a bed set up in the front room of Master Robert Hendersoun's house in the High Street. Master Robert, a chirurgeon in the occasional employ of the town council of Edinburgh, was best known for raising a dead woman from the grave, wherein she had lain for two days after having supposedly been strangled. After that, saving the life of Blaise Laurentin had surely been little more than child's play.

The provost, Sir Archibald Douglas of Kilspindie, arrived attended by two bailies. He looked around at the crowd. The queen smiled winningly – she knew, of course, that he recognised her, but because of her costume he did not dare acknowledge her as queen. I could tell she liked the feeling, as if she were wearing a cloak of invisibility from an old *conte-de-fée* and because of it could do anything she liked.

Sir Archibald seated himself on a three-legged stool at the writing table provided. His bailies put out paper and ink and sand, and a pen with which to write his notes. When all was arranged to his satisfaction, he turned to the man lying on the bed.

'You are Master Blaise Laurentin?' he said. He spoke the French name with a pronounced Scots accent.

'I am,' Laurentin said. He was pale and there was a sheen of sweat on his face. His unshaven cheeks were grizzled with silver. His eyes were not quite focused; had the chirurgeon given him poppy syrup or nightshade for pain?

'Master Robert,' Sir Archibald said to the chirurgeon. 'Would you detail this man's wounds, if you please?'

'He has been stabbed three times,' Robert Hendersoun said. 'Once, from the hip down to the groin, once again in the shoulder and upper chest, and once again in the side. The wounds could not be self-inflicted. The two things that saved his life are, first, that the attacker did not seem to have the strength to drive the weapon to its fullest depth, and second, that the wounds were not so placed as to be fatal.'

'And what do you deduce from this?'

'That the attacker was a small man, or even a woman, and one without knowledge of how to kill with a knife.'

Blaise Laurentin smiled like a wounded badger. 'Just as I have said. It was Madame Marina Leslie who attacked me, with no provocation.'

The provost turned to me. 'What say you, Mistress? Do you deny this charge?'

I stepped forward. 'I do not deny it,' I said. 'However, I wish to present a charge of my own. Monsieur Laurentin abducted me, with a clear intent to do me harm. I had no weapon, which I certainly would have had if I had intended harm to Monsieur Laurentin. Instead I managed to take hold of his own dagger, and stabbed him only to defend myself.'

The queen whispered in Darnley's ear. He turned his head, stole a quick kiss from her lips – she pretended it was a great surprise – and whispered something to her in return.

The provost said, 'Is this true, Master Laurentin? Did Mistress Rinette stab you with your own dagger?'

'She took it from me by trickery,' Laurentin said. His voice was slightly slurred but perfectly understandable. 'It is a blade with a particular meaning for me, and I desire her to return it.'

I took another step forward and said, 'And is this the dagger you say I took from you by trickery, Monsieur Laurentin?'

With the unbandaged tips of my fingers I reached into the embroidered pouch at my waist, drew out the dagger, and laid it carefully on the provost's table. The feathered curves of outspread wings engraved on the guard shone gold in the morning light. In the falcon's head there was only one jewelled red eye.

The queen bounced up and down on the balls of her neatly booted feet, excited. I did not take my eyes off Blaise Laurentin. Was he weakened enough, drugged enough, to admit the truth?

The provost frowned. 'Is that your dagger, Monsieur Laurentin?' he demanded sharply.

'Yes,' Laurentin said. He looked dizzy and sick and off his guard. 'It is mine. Give it to me.'

The queen squealed with delight. Everyone turned to look at her.

'I think not,' I said. 'You will notice, Sir Archibald, that one of the falcon's ruby eyes is missing.'

'I see,' the provost said.

I reached up and pulled the chain of my silver locket over my head. Slowly, again using only the tips of my fingers, I opened the locket to display the small faceted ruby inside.

'I took this ruby from the terrible wound that killed my husband, Alexander Gordon of Glenlithie. You will see his blood is still upon it. Monsieur Nicolas de Clerac will stand witness to my discovery.'

'I so witness,' said Nico.

'You kept this dagger hidden,' I said to Blaise Laurentin. 'You knew I had the ruby – you were hiding in the Abbey at Holyrood when I found it, were you not? Monsieur de Clerac found your footprints in the dust.'

Blaise Laurentin said nothing. His eyes were fixed upon the dagger.

'You knew the missing ruby would identify your dagger as the weapon used to kill Alexander Gordon. So you concealed it, until you received another commission from the *Escadron Volant* and were required by the *Escadron's* ritual practice to use it again.'

The room was so silent I could hear Laurentin's laboured breathing.

'You told Monsieur de Chastelard you killed my husband. He was a brother in the *Escadron Volant*, was he not? That is how he knew what the dagger looked like, and who had killed Alexander.'

All of a sudden everyone in the room began to talk at once.

Sir Archibald pounded his fist on his table. 'Silence!' he cried. 'Mistress Rinette, the murder of your husband is a wholly different matter, and to pursue it you will be required to bring a separate charge against Master Laurentin. In the meantime—'

'You cannot charge me, even if I did slit the Gordon boy's throat.' Blaise Laurentin's eyes had steadied and his whole expression had sharpened; he was realising his mistake. He looked straight at the queen. No more cloak of invisibility for her.

'I am in the employ of Queen Catherine de' Medici,' Laurentin went on. 'She will insist upon my safe return.'

'But you confess to this murder?' the queen said. 'Marianette's husband?'

'It was three years ago and more,' he said. 'And it was a small thing – Alexander Gordon was a nobody, *un insignifiant*, who jumped himself up into matters he did not understand.'

'A small thing,' I said. I did not speak loudly but every other sound in the room stopped. If I could have killed him with my voice alone I would have done it. '*Un insignifiant.*'

'And Richard Wetheral?' It was Nico's voice, silky and dangerous. 'Was he also an insignificant one? Am I—' He reached up and pulled his own collar open, displaying the scar on his throat, up under his left ear. 'Am I *un insignifiant* as well?'

'You are a murderer, Monsieur Laurentin,' the queen cried. 'A murderer twice over, and you attempted to kill my cousin Monsieur de Clerac, all here on Scottish soil.'

Laurentin's face had flushed, with fear or fury or outrage. His eyes looked like two ancient sun-bleached stones. He said, 'If you attempt to charge or detain me in the matter of these deaths, *Madame la Reine*, I will make public such secrets that you—'

A pistol shot exploded.

Blaise Laurentin's face disappeared in a fusillade of blood and bone and brain. His body toppled over backwards, off the pallet on the far side.

The queen screamed.

'You'll play no man false again, Frenchman.' The figure of the man in the doorway was like a flat cutout in black paper, featureless with the light behind it. He threw the spent pistol aside and drew his sword.

The provost's bailies were immobile with shock. The whole room might have been a painting, unmoving – the provost at his table, his pen in his hand, his mouth open; David Riccio and Lord Darnley on either side of the queen, short and tall, neither one with so much as a hand on the hilt of his blade. I stared at the spot where Blaise Laurentin's face had been. Rannoch Hamilton's sword – and yes, it was Rannoch Hamilton, he had taken a step into the room and the light had changed and he was recognisable now, however much his face might be contorted with hatred – his sword was the only thing moving. It was sweeping towards me, and it would lop off my head with a single stroke. Nothing else moved. Nothing—

Another blade rang against Rannoch Hamilton's. The angle was wrong and it did not stop the thrust entirely, but it deflected it. The room surged into motion again, I stumbled back unhurt, and Nico de Clerac and Rannoch Hamilton faced off against each other in the centre of the floor, sword to sword.

'I've killed one Frenchman,' my husband said between his teeth. 'I'll gladly kill another. Stand aside.'

'You fool,' Nico said. He sounded as if he were making light conversation after supper. 'The queen is in the room. Stand down.'

There was a flash of steel and a ringing crash as Nico's blade parried a sweeping cut from side to side. I heard him let out his breath with the effort of parrying Hamilton's brutal strength. He stepped to one side, putting his back to the door, drawing Hamilton's focus away from the rest of us and directing the light into his opponent's eyes. My husband swung around, squinting.

'Do you mean the slut in boy's clothes?' he said. 'Knox is right about her – she is a harlot, and one of the monstrous regiment of women who have no right to rule over men.'

He attacked. He hacked and slashed with brute strength. Nico de Clerac parried – it looked easy, but I had seen enough sword-play for sport's sake to know how much skill it took to block such a violent advance so elegantly.

'Kill him, *mon cousin*!' the queen cried. She stepped forward and Lord Darnley caught her in his arms to hold her back.

'There's no woman here but the Green Lady,' Rannoch Hamilton said. 'And I'll have her head off before I'm finished. Too bad the brats aren't here as well, to be spitted—'

He jumped back, barely managing to parry Nico's smooth thrust straight to his throat.

'No one will be spitted,' Nico said, 'but you. Darnley, Riccio, for the love of God, will you get the queen out of the room? Rinette, go with them.'

He traversed and ducked under Rannoch Hamilton's swing, high and wild. Neither Darnley nor Riccio moved. The queen was clinging to Lord Darnley, watching the two men fighting, her lips parted, her amber-coloured eyes shining. As the two blades clashed and rang together in the chirurgeon's small front room, I pushed the provost from his place at the table and picked up the stool he had been sitting on. I waited until Nico had grappled Hamilton back against the table, their arms and shoulders straining, their swords guard to guard, and then, bandaged hands and all, I swung the stool in a wide arc and with all the strength I had, all the bitterness in my heart, I struck Rannoch Hamilton's head from behind.

He dropped like a felled ox. The queen shrieked with delight.

'Spit him, then,' I said. My voice did not sound like my own. 'Or give me your blade, Nico, and I will.'

Nico laughed, sheathing his own sword with a rasp and a clang and collecting Rannoch Hamilton's from where it had fallen.

'Let us leave him for the hangman,' he said. 'I think the queen will agree.'

'I agree,' the queen said. She was flushed with excitement. With the fight over, she clearly felt she needed no more protection, so she pushed herself free from Lord Darnley's embrace. 'He drew steel in our royal presence, and threatened our life, before witnesses. A trial is not necessary.'

I looked at her. I could read it in her face, plain as plain. She was remembering Sir John Gordon, and how she had fainted at his execution. She was remembering Chastelard, and how he had gone to his death reciting Ronsard. Her half-brother James Stewart had ordered their deaths, in her name. This time, she would give her own order.

'A trial is not necessary,' she said again. For all her doublet and hose, she was quite capable of radiating royalty when she chose to do so. 'We, Mary, Queen of Scotland, pass judgement upon Master Rannoch Hamilton here and now – he will hang at the Mercat Cross, tomorrow.'

40

B y morning I realised I did not want to watch Rannoch Hamilton hang. In the heat of the swordplay the day before, when he had raved about spitting my precious babies, I would have killed him happily with my own two hands. But my heat had cooled. I was safe. My babies were safe. Blaise Laurentin had confessed to the murders of my Alexander and Richard Wetheral and to the attack on Nico, and was dead with a pistol ball in his face. I would have been happy enough to leave Edinburgh that very morning with my children and my household, and go home to Granmuir. Nico could remain at court long enough to fulfil his mysterious vow, and then follow us.

Rinette, there is something I must tell you.

Is it good?

No.

When we were safe at Granmuir, he could tell me. High in the Mermaid Tower, with the sea breeze blowing through the shutters, just the two of us with my own ancient walls around us — there he could tell me anything, and I would love him all the same.

No, I did not want to watch Rannoch Hamilton hang, but I could not leave Edinburgh, because Jennet and Tante-Mar were not well enough to travel. Nico was in attendance on the queen — he was in the highest possible favour, saving Lord Darnley of course, after risking his own life to defend her with his sword. I had not seen him since the moment when we all streamed out of the poor chirurgeon's house, leaving Blaise Laurentin's faceless corpse for the coroner. Rannoch Hamilton had been imprisoned in the Tolbooth. I wondered if he was in the same room where I had spent the night, before I had been married to him.

Jennet was sitting up, and lucid enough to criticise poor Una MacAlpin's oat porridge as cooked to a pudding. Gill and Davy ran back and forth between Holyrood and Maitland of Lethington's house with news of Màiri and Kitte. It did not surprise me when the queen's favourite page Master Standen arrived with a message, commanding me to attend the queen after dinner, and accompany her to the execution of my husband, scheduled for mid-afternoon. The queen, Master Standen said, was still inflamed with rage over Rannoch Hamilton's epithets addressed to her in the heat of his attack yesterday, and was determined to see him die.

'She says,' Master Standen told me, 'that if Sir John Gordon and Monsieur de Chastelard were required to die for their crimes, she will be certain Rannoch Hamilton dies for his as well.'

So I had been right.

I clearly had no choice in the matter, so I sent Master Standen on his way with my assurance I would wait upon her as she desired. I could only pray she did not have one of her sudden changes of mood and succumb to hysteria as she had at the execution of Sir John Gordon. Rannoch Hamilton, at least, had not danced and flirted with her, and would not cry out to her that he was dying for love of her.

Una MacAlpin helped me dress, again with considerable criticism from Jennet, which she took with a good heart. I did not want to wear black or white, because I did not want anyone to think I grieved for Rannoch Hamilton's death, but on the other hand my blues and greens were too springlike and light-hearted for anyone's execution. We settled on a pearl-grey bodice and sleeves with a skirt of a dark mulberry colour, almost the colour of dried blood.

I was beginning to feel sick and apprehensive. As Una helped me with my headdress and veil I said to myself over and over, like a litany: He married me against my will. He brutalised me. He tried to poison me at Kinmeall. He planned to kill me, and Màiri, and Kitte too, his own daughter, as part of his twisted plot with Blaise Laurentin. He killed Blaise Laurentin and would have killed everyone in the chirurgeon's front room, even the queen, if Nico had not engaged him. He deserves this death, and death a dozen times over.

Even so, I did not want to watch him die.

The queen and her party were downstairs already, gathered at the front door of the palace while her grooms brought up the horses. She was dressed with great magnificence in cloth-of-silver and diamonds, and as such a gown and such jewels were entirely unsuitable for either an afternoon or an execution, was clearly refuting Rannoch Hamilton's words about her boy's clothes and her right to rule. He was dying as much for his vicious tongue as he was for the murder of Blaise Laurentin.

So be it.

'Marianette!' the queen cried. 'Come along! It is time.'

They were making an entertainment out of it. Lord Darnley, of course, was at the queen's side; he looked fretful and pale, and there were two or three pustules on his forehead. Too much fine food and wine, my lord, I thought; too much conspiracy with wineshop companions and fear of what Rannoch Hamilton might say as he stands on the ladder with the noose around his neck. Nico was there, of course, dressed in a black doublet richly embroidered with gold thread in a barred pattern, high-collared and with a narrow white ruffle framing his face; he was grave and silent, and although he smiled at me he did not leave his place at the queen's side. David Riccio sported his usual peacock colours; the queen's secretary, Sir William Maitland of Lethington, and the Englishman Thomas Randolph were more sober in browns and blacks. For ladies the queen was attended by her half-sister Jean Argyll, all four of the Marys – even the newlywed Mary Livingston, looking drowsy-eyed and happy – and Lady Margaret Erskine. For a moment the breeze caught her veil and revealed her hair, dark streaked with white.

Clove pinks, variegated, black at their hearts but with white edging on their jagged red-violet petals. Misfortune. Bad luck. Streaks of white – old age, an old woman with white in her hair, white she covered with jewelled coifs . . .

I remembered thinking that, but I did not remember when or where or why.

The Earl of Moray was conspicuous by his absence. The Earl of Rothes had stayed away as well.

With the queen and Lord Darnley in the lead we rode down the Canongate and through the Netherbow Port into the High Street. The Mercat Cross stood between the High Street and the Lawnmarket, facing the Tolbooth and Saint Giles' Kirk. The gallows had been erected, and two tall ladders leaned against it. A noisy crowd filled the square and spilled down the Lawnmarket. A platform had also been built for the queen and her party, perhaps five feet in height and draped in black cloth. Eight steps led up to it; upon it was placed a fine chair with the queen's cloth of estate draped over it, as well as stools upon which others could sit at her pleasure. The chancy March sun had decided to shine, and the sky over the grey city was a deep saturated blue.

'We are ready,' the queen said, when she was properly situated. 'Proceed, Master Sheriff.'

The sheriff went over to the Tolbooth, followed by the under-sheriff, the provost – who still looked half-stunned from his experience the day before – the hangman with his rope looped over his shoulder, a Protestant minister and two bailies. After a moment they brought Rannoch Hamilton forth. My husband's hands were bound behind his back but otherwise he looked much as he always looked: dark, scowling, and dangerous. He ran his eyes over the people seated on the platform and found me at once; he looked directly at me with such hatred that it seemed to crackle in the air between us. I looked away, my stomach lurching.

'Now we shall see,' the queen said, under her breath. 'Do you still think I am nothing but a slut in boy's clothes, Master Rannoch? Do you still think I have no right to rule? Look upon your queen for your last sight in this world.'

The hangman climbed one of the ladders and threw the rope over the gallows crossbar; he had already made the noose at one end, with its thirteen coils, and it was heavy enough to drop straight and true. He nodded in satisfaction, then tied off the rope around the gallows upright and yanked the knot tight.

Rannoch Hamilton then climbed the other ladder, one rung at a time without the use of his hands to help him. He did not resist or struggle. When he reached the level of the hanging noose, he stopped.

The minister began to read loudly from a black leather-bound book of Scriptures.

'Prisoner,' the sheriff cried, 'you may speak if you wish.'

'I will speak,' Rannoch Hamilton said. His voice was strong and unafraid and carried out over the crowd. 'You, minister. Shut your clack.'

The minister stopped mid-psalm.

'I repent of nothing,' my husband said. 'I fear no god and no man. I fear no pagan spirits. See that woman over there on the platform behind the queen, wearing a wimple and veil like a damned nun? Her name is Marina Leslie of Granmuir, and she's my wife. She's not even a good Catholic – she's the Green Lady of Granmuir in her heart and soul, and she can't wait for me to be turned off so she can marry her lover.'

The crowd stirred and murmured as everyone gaped at me. I felt my face burning. I wanted to scream back at him that he had tried to kill me and my babies. But I had no voice. I felt as if there was a noose tightening around my own throat as well.

'The queen is no better,' Rannoch Hamilton went on. 'She calls herself Mary Stuart – she's no true Stewart, no true Scotswoman, she's a Frenchwoman by raising and a Catholic Jezebel whore just like my wife.'

'Stop!' Lord Darnley shouted. The queen sat frozen in her chair, her lips parted. When it was words and not a sword, Darnley was quick to leap to her defence. 'That is enough. Silence him.'

'Hangman!' the sheriff cried. 'The hood.'

The hangman reached out from his own ladder and jerked a pointed black hood over Rannoch Hamilton's head.

'It was all about a silver casket,' my husband shouted. His voice was muffled by the hood. 'A silver casket full of French witchcraft – she had it, and it disappeared, and they told me to force it out of her. Then it appeared again and I would have had it this time, but he betrayed me, the Frenchman I killed.'

I was disoriented with horror. I had always imagined Rannoch Hamilton with a black void where his face and eyes should have been, because he had no flower correspondent. Now I was staring at my nightmare in the flesh, the black hood with the voice unnaturally powerful from inside it.

The hangman dropped the noose over his head and pulled it tight.

'I curse it in the devil's name, that silver casket – whoever touches it or anything inside it will—'

The bailies on the ground dragged away the ladder the prisoner was standing on, and he lurched off into nothingness. The rope jerked tight with a ghastly twanging sound. Rannoch Hamilton kicked and writhed, twisting slowly. I could see his powerful shoulders straining at the rope binding his wrists.

The queen screamed.

Holy Saint Ninian, he was climbing – trying to climb on air, as if he were straining for steps to support his weight. He almost seemed to be finding – something – something to stand on. His body arched and strained and he twisted, twisted, the rope quivering.

The dark man looked at Alexander for a moment. There was utter silence in the little church. Then with one well-practised and ringing arc of movement he swept his sword from its scabbard, plain workman-like steel with no jewels or fancywork. He levelled it at Alexander's heart. The dying light of the sun through the broken door edged the glittering blade with blood-red.

He was right – if it had not been for the casket, if Rothes had never sent him after me, if he and I had never met, he would not be dying at the end of a rope under a blue, blue sky.

You're a gey beautiful woman, I'll give you that. Like a wild white Barbary filly with long legs and a silk mouth and a mane all brown and gold. Do you remember what you said to me, at Granmuir?

My fault, my fault.

I've found the hiding place where my wife was keeping your casket,

Madam, and I've burned it all — the French sorcerer's papers, your mother's memorandum-book, all of it. Now you'll never—

It had all been a lie. Why? To get me away from court? So he could force the truth about the casket out of me? Or had he actually cared about me, in some twisted, terrifying, empty fashion?

Slowly Rannoch Hamilton's jerking and thrashing became like the swimming of a man in deep water, sluggish and effortful. His muscles began to twitch, his movements became spasmodic, less purposeful. Then he seemed to – lengthen. With sick horror I watched him actually grow longer, as his muscles and sinews lost their tautness and gave way, his straining gave way, his last vestige of control over his flesh gave way.

Hooded and motionless, oh, thank God, motionless at last, Rannoch Hamilton's body turned slowly until it was still, facing the queen's platform.

The queen fainted.

I turned away and vomited.

Darnley threw his hat in the air. 'The queen's justice is done,' he cried, his voice thin against the roar of the crowd. 'God save Her Grace!'

Nico was holding me. Back at the Lawnmarket he had given me a towel and some wine to rinse my mouth, then made me drink a cupful all the way to the bottom. He had lifted me on to Lilidh and walked beside her all the way back to Holyrood, murmuring to both the mare and to me wordlessly, comfortingly. Now we were settled in the queen's little supper-room. The queen herself had changed out of her silver costume into a loose gown, and was eating a *doucette* of cooked almond milk and sugar, thickened with rice. She had recovered herself much more quickly than I. The wine made me drowsy and dulled the edge of the horror.

Mostly I was thinking about how the gold thread worked in rows on Nico's doublet was prickly against my cheek.

'We shall plan your wedding, Marianette,' she said. 'We will have to wait for Lent to be over, but it will give the flowers time to bloom, and you can read them for me then. You can find some more of that yellow flower – what did you call it? – and tell me what it really means.'

The last thing I wanted to think about just now was a wedding. I would stay with Jennet and Tante-Mar, and have my precious babies with me again, and when Jennet and Tante-Mar were able to travel we would all go home. I would marry Nico in the little church of Saint Ninian when I was ready, not when the queen directed. The queen thought she still had a hold over me, but she did not.

'For your wedding gift,' the queen said, 'I will send Monsieur Laurentin's dagger to my *belle-mère* Queen Catherine in France. She will know her assassin has been unmasked.'

'Perhaps there will be a wedding, perhaps not,' said Lady Margaret Erskine in her deliberate voice. She was stirring a cup of hot mulled wine with cream and spices, and the steam might have been the breath of a witch's cauldron. 'Mistress Leslie might choose not to marry Monsieur de Clerac after all.'

I closed my eyes. 'I will,' I said.

'Of course she will,' the queen said.

The slow, calm movement of Nico's breathing stopped. I felt him tense. It brought me back to myself.

'Do you think so?' Lady Margaret said. 'I have a serving-man at Lochleven who tells a strange tale. Perhaps you can explain, Monsieur de Clerac, how it came about that you left Lochleven secretly, the very night Mistress Leslie revealed the hiding place of the silver casket. Perhaps you can tell us the reason you paid the servant to lie, and say you were in your chamber, and not well enough to ride to Edinburgh with the rest of us in the morning.'

I could hear the fire crackling, and Lady Margaret's silver spoon going around and around and around in the cup of mulled wine. There was no other sound in the room.

Clove pinks . . . misfortune . . . an old woman with white in her hair, white she covered with jewelled coifs . . .

I remembered.

I had put the clove pinks in the niche with the silver casket, in the secret vault under Saint Margaret's.

'Could it have been,' Lady Margaret went on inexorably, 'that Mary of Guise told her mother how to find the secret vault under Saint Margaret's Chapel, and that her mother, your own grandmother, passed the secret on to you? Could it have been that you rode to Edinburgh in the night, unknown to us all, and took the casket from the vault? Could it be that you have actually had the silver casket in your possession, from that moment to this?'

I sat up. My head was spinning. Of course it was a lie. Nico was too high in favour with the queen. The Earl of Moray was too deeply in disfavour. Lady Margaret would do anything, say anything, fabricate anything, for the sake of her half-royal son.

'I do not believe it,' I said.

Rinette, there is something I must tell you.

Is it good?

No.

Lady Margaret said, 'My serving-man will testify that what he says is true.'

'Monsieur de Clerac,' the queen said at last. Not *mon cousin*. Not even '*Sieur Nico*. She sounded genuinely shaken. 'What have you to say to this charge? Did you take my mother's silver casket from the secret vault? Have you had it all this time?'

Nico took hold of my shoulders and gently put me apart from him. He stood up.

No, I thought. No, no.

'Yes,' he said. His voice was stark and steady. 'And no. I did take the casket from the vault under Saint Margaret's. I do have it now. I have not had it all this time – it has been in the safe-keeping of your grandmother and mine, the Dowager Duchess of Guise, in France.'

'And did she open it?' Lord Darnley demanded. 'Did she read the papers inside? Have you read the papers inside?'

'The casket was closed and locked when I sent it to Duchess Antoinette,' Nico said. He did not look at Darnley. 'She gave it back to me locked again. Whether she looked at the papers I do not know, but I did not unlock it or look at anything inside it.'

'You will give it to me at once,' the queen said. 'I have waited to open this casket since the day I set foot back on Scottish soil, and I will have it now.'

'I cannot do that, Madame,' Nico said. 'Not until I have Duchess Antoinette's permission.'

'I do not need her permission. The casket is mine.'

'I have written to her. When she replies, the casket will be yours.'

'You may leave the court until that day, then.' The queen's eyes sparkled with anger. 'And I forbid any marriage between you and Marianette.'

'That,' said Nico, with a sudden flash of answering anger, 'is for Rinette herself to say.'

I was lost. The wine was making me sick and dizzy. I was not in the queen's supper-room at all, but in the kirk of Saint Giles, surrounded by Moray and Rothes and Rannoch Hamilton and a dozen men-at-arms with drawn swords.

Rinette, forgive me.

It is not your fault.

Yes. It is.

I never guessed he had meant it literally.

'Rinette,' he said again. It jolted me back. 'I could not break my vow to Duchess Antoinette. Forgive me, *ma mie.*'

I stood up. The effects of the wine and the horror of Rannoch Hamilton's death were gone. I was clear-minded and cold and utterly solitary in my bubble of stone.

'I am not your *mie*,' I said. My voice was shaking. 'And I will never forgive you.'

41

'You must forgive him, *ma douce*,' Tante-Mar said. 'You cannot live with so much sorrow and bitterness in your heart.'

She had suffered another fainting attack, and as Jennet had healed and grown stronger, Tante-Mar had grown frailer. I was terrified she would never come home to Granmuir with us. It had been difficult enough moving her to the pretty little house in the Canongate I had taken after the terrible day of Rannoch Hamilton's hanging and Lady Margaret Erskine's shocking revelation in the queen's supper-room. I could not stay at Holyrood after that. I did not know where Nico had gone, although I knew Tante-Mar knew. She had been sending messages back and forth with him, with Gill's help and Una MacAlpin's.

'I do not have sorrow and bitterness in my heart,' I said. 'I am living perfectly well.'

She smiled. 'You have taken care of us all. Even so, I hear you crying in the night.'

'I do not cry in the night.' It was a lie. 'Perhaps it is Seilie you hear.'

'Ah. Perhaps.'

We sat together for a while. I looked out of the window into the little back garden. There was a plum tree, young and straight, and it was blossoming. I remembered the gnarled old plum tree in the churchyard of Saint Mary's in Stoneywood, where I had rescued Seilie from Lady Huntly's witch-women. Plum blossoms for faithfulness.

Whose faithfulness? To whom?

'I ask you only one thing, *ma douce*.' She put her thin, veined hand over mine. I no longer wore the bandages, but the knife-scars on my palms and fingers were red and tender. 'Imagine you had been brought up in a great religious house, with the significance of holy vows all around you, every day. Imagine you had made a vow upon holy relics to someone you loved, someone to whom you owed a great debt. Imagine this vow would do good for a whole kingdom, and for a young queen who is still struggling to find her way.'

'Why are you—'

'Shhh.' She patted my hand. 'Let me finish. Then imagine – you are forced to choose between this vow, which has been your whole life, and doing great harm to someone you love with all your heart. It was a terrible choice, Rinette.'

'Why are you defending him?'

'He is my nephew, Rinette, just as you are my niece – have you ever thought of that? I have been working it out, since we were all at Granmuir together after Christmas and he told us his true parentage. Your mother, of course, is my half-sister, and the Duke of Longueville was your mother's half-brother. He married Mary of Guise, who was Duke François of Guise's full sister. By marriage, then, Duke François was my half-brother, and Monsieur Nico is my nephew.'

'I am your niece by blood. It is not the same.'

She smiled again. 'No, of course it is not the same, *ma douce*. But it is the business of old women, is it not, to keep account of

415

family ties? In fact, you and Monsieur Nico are related in the second degree of affinity, and cannot marry without a dispensation from the Holy Father.'

'It is a good thing, then, that we will never marry.'

'Perhaps. I am not asking you to do so. Only to see him, and talk to him, and if you can, forgive him.'

'He *knew*,' I burst out like a wounded child. 'He knew all along. Tante-Mar, I *trusted* him. I trusted him so much that I—'

I could not say it. Tante-Mar would be shocked if she knew what Nico and I had done in the Mermaid Tower.

'That you took him into your bed?' she said placidly. 'I am not such a dried-up old maid as you might think, Rinette, and I have eyes in my head. If you could trust him so much then, can you not trust him now, at least enough to talk to him?'

'No,' I said. 'I cannot.'

The plum tree dropped its blossoms and began to unfold its leaves. Everyone in Edinburgh was talking about Lord Darnley being sick with the pox at Stirling Castle, and the queen tending him with her own hands. This was a great intimacy for a queen. Did she intend to marry him? Had Nico had his letter from Duchess Antoinette in France, giving him permission at last to give the queen the casket, and had she read the prophecies of Master Nostradamus about the *quatre maris*? Was Darnley one of them?

My hair grew a little. It felt softer, not so spiky. My bitterness was softening too, however much I tried to hold on to it. I put aside my nun's wimple and wore a little velvet cap, like a boy's. My hands continued to heal, and I began to work in the walled garden, wearing gloves for protection. It was a city garden with worn-out soil, and it had been sadly neglected by the previous tenants of the house; with Gill's help I enriched the planting-beds with manure from the stables, chopped straw, and vegetable leavings from the kitchen. I planted marjoram and borage, fennel and thyme. I planted lily-of-the-valley for Tante-Mar, wild roses for Màiri and maiden pinks for Kitte. The garden slowly came to life. I tried to plant my own windflowers but they drooped and died. I knew I was not meant to stay in Edinburgh much longer.

Then Nico came.

He found me in the garden, kneeling by the bed of rosemary under the plum tree. My apron was grass-stained and my gloved hands were covered with dirt. Seilie was with me, digging a hole of his own, hunting for voles.

'Jennet and Madame Loury allowed me to come in,' he said. His voice sounded worn, as if it had been scoured thin by explanations and confessions. 'But I will not stay if you ask me to leave.'

I sat back on my heels and looked up at him. I opened my mouth to say, *I do not want to talk to you*. But the garden forestalled me, the little garden so newly come back to life, and to my own surprise I said, 'You tried to tell me.'

'I should have told you sooner. I should have told you at Granmuir.'

'Yes. You should have.'

We looked at each other for a moment in silence.

'After you escaped from Laurentin, I should have told you,' he said. 'I did try. But you had been through hell itself that day, and you were so tired. I thought – in the morning. But from that moment there was never an opportunity.'

He did not call me his *mie*. He did not even speak my name.

I thought of that day, and how I had stabbed Blaise Laurentin and then run down the alley with my little ones. I saw it all, and – suddenly I saw it all.

'You were there,' I said. 'In the alley. It was not just chance. Blaise Laurentin found out somehow you had the casket. That is why he wanted me and Màiri and Kitte. It was you he intended to trade us to, for the silver casket.'

'Yes,' he said.

'You had saddlebags over your shoulder. You had the casket with you. You were going to give it to him.'

'Yes.'

'Despite your holy vow.'

He smiled a little. I felt a pang of the feeling I had never thought to have again. 'Yes. Despite my holy vow. Even if I would be damned for all eternity. I have something for you.'

He turned back the flap of the velvet pouch at his belt and took out a chain of jewels – of turquoises! My mother's turquoises!

I blinked, and saw Blaise Laurentin again, holding my sheared hair, with my bloodied veil and the blue-green stones woven and braided into the coils.

'He gave your hair to me,' Nico said. 'And Màiri's cap. As proof. I wanted to kill him then, but I did not know where he was holding you.'

I took the chain. 'What did you do with my hair?' I whispered. It was a foolish question but I was compelled to ask. 'Where is Màiri's cap?'

'I kept them,' he said. 'I was afraid – I was afraid it might be all I would ever have – I was afraid he had hurt you, or would hurt you.'

For some obscure reason I was comforted to know that my poor hair was safe. I ran the turquoises through my fingers.

'I have forgiven her,' I said. 'My mother. I think now I understand a little how she felt when my father died, and why she went to the Benedictines at Montmartre.'

418

He nodded. Seilie went over to him and sat in front of him, looking up at him with a tongue-lolling hound smile. Seilie had always loved Nico. He reached down and stroked Seilie's soft ears.

After a moment he said, 'I will tell you the whole thing, from the beginning, if you will allow me to.'

I stood up and brushed grass and soil and bits of rosemary from my apron. The scent of the crushed rosemary was sharp, astringent, cleansing. I breathed it in deeply. I said, 'Very well. I will listen.'

'After Mary of Guise died, may God rest her soul—'

He crossed himself. I did the same.

'—I realised almost at once the casket was missing. No one knew what had become of it. Later that year, in October, I went back to France with her body, and then to Joinville to report to Duchess Antoinette.'

'And she placed you in the young queen's household.'

'She did. She knew the secret of the vault under Saint Margaret's – her daughter had written it all to her, in cipher, and told her the vault was her hiding place for a special collection of papers. Duchess Antoinette also knew of her daughter's correspondence with Nostradamus. But she did not know there was a sealed packet from Nostradamus in the casket – not until she received a letter.'

He stopped. I said, 'From Alexander.'

'Yes.'

'I suppose I must forgive him, too.' It came out, all in a rush. I could not stop myself. 'Tante-Mar says I cannot live with such sorrow and bitterness in my heart.'

Nico took a step forward, as if he would touch me, even take me in his arms. But only one step. He did not touch me. He said, 'Rinette. There are no words for me to say how sorry I am for all of this. There is no penance I can do that will ever be enough.'

'What Alexander did was not your fault. Go on, Nico.'

'We learned this Alexander Gordon of Glenlithie was married to Marina Leslie of Granmuir. I knew you from the old queen's household, and that is how I knew she had given you the casket. I thought at first you were complicit with your husband, in offering to sell it.'

'I never was. I showed it to him, showed him the hiding place. Oh, I loved him so much. I never dreamed—' I choked on tears. I thought I had cried all my tears for Alexander long ago.

'We knew he had offered it to a number of people, in order to increase the price. Duchess Antoinette required me to swear a vow, on holy relics of Saint Louis, that I would find the casket and give it to her, and that I would support Queen Mary, with my life if need be.'

'And you are monk enough to be bound by such a vow.'

He looked surprised. After a moment he said, 'I suppose I am. We assumed you had it at Granmuir.'

'And that is why you befriended me. Why you offered to help me find Alexander's murderer.'

'Yes,' he said. 'At first.'

'Is that why you made an excuse to come to Granmuir, when the queen rode north to confront the Earl of Huntly? Did you hope for an opportunity to search for the casket?'

'No,' he said. I was hurting him more with every question, but the questions had to be asked and answered. 'I hoped you would tell me, yes. But I swear to you, Rinette, I would never have searched without your knowledge.'

'You hoped I would tell you.'

'Yes. I asked you, do you remember? In the bakeshop.'

I looked down at my gloved hands. I could almost feel his thumb running lightly over my knuckles. *You would be safest if you would give her the casket now, with no conditions.*

'I refused you.'

'You refused me. It never occurred to me to think the old queen had told you the secret of the hidden vault, or that you had put the casket there. Until that night on Lochleven, when you confessed that was where you had hidden it.'

'When they threatened to force me into marriage with Rannoch Hamilton unless I confessed it.'

'Yes,' he said.

'And even so, knowing what they would do, you rode ahead and reached Edinburgh before us. You went down into the vault and took the casket. What did you do with it, Nico? Did you have it hidden at Holyrood when you came to Saint Giles' Kirk to watch them give me to Rannoch Hamilton against my will?'

'No,' he said. His whole body had tensed, as if he were being flayed alive. 'I had already sent it on to France, to Duchess Antoinette, by a special messenger. She did not want the young queen to see what was in it, not until she herself had examined it all – she feared the young queen would simply give it to Moray.'

'At that particular moment, she would have.'

'If I had still had it, Rinette, I would have given it up to them, that day in the church, vow or no vow. I would have done anything to save you from being forced to marry Rannoch Hamilton.'

I remembered him telling me about his mother's forced marriage, in the gardens at Granmuir. *Her new husband mistreated her, and less than a year later she was dead*, he had said. How had he felt, standing there in Saint Giles' Kirk, seeing it all happening again and helpless to stop it?

Tante-Mar's voice: *It was a terrible choice.*

It was. It had marked him.

'I did not die,' I said. Something had changed in my heart. I was not telling him that out of anger. I was telling him to reassure him.

'For which I thanked God on my knees, when Madame Loury wrote to me from Granmuir to tell me you had come home.'

'She *wrote* to you?'

He smiled. Each time he smiled, he seemed a little less sad and tired. Each time I felt another pang of remembered affection. 'She did. Why do you think I came back to Scotland?'

'I thought Duchess Antoinette sent you.'

'She would have sent someone, because with Lennox back in Scotland she knew Darnley would be next. It was time for the young queen to see what Nostradamus had predicted, and what her mother had written. I asked her to make me her messenger, and she decided it was also time to tell the queen I was her cousin.'

'But you did not give the queen the casket, not at first.'

'No. My instructions were to observe the situation with Darnley – Duchess Antoinette has not opened the *quatre maris* prophecies, so she does not know if Nostradamus has anything to say about Darnley, but she herself has great suspicions. I was to be certain the queen would not allow Darnley access to the casket before I gave it to her.'

'She will give it to him. She is beside herself with infatuation – she is waiting upon him with her own hands, at Stirling, where he is sick with the pox.'

'So I have heard as well. Even so, after Lady Margaret forced my hand with the truth, I wrote to Duchess Antoinette. I told her everything – that I wished to leave the court, leave her service. That I would send the casket back to her, or leave it in the vault under Saint Margaret's, or give it to the queen. Today I received her answer.'

I took a breath. 'And what was it?'

He bent down and stroked Seilie's head again. 'I will never be entirely free,' he said. 'I am half-Guise, and I have no other blood connections. But she has released me from my vow, and asked me only one further thing: that I see the casket safely into the young queen's hands.'

I turned and walked around the little garden. I listened to it, newly enriched and planted, whispering with life. I breathed in the scents of fennel and thyme. I stepped on the blue flowers of the borage; it smelled of honey and seawater. *Courage*, it whispered. *Courage and strength and simplicity. Truth, sharp as a knife.*

'Where is the casket now?' I asked.

'It is on the small table beside Madame Loury's bed, in your own front room,' he said. 'Mary of Guise gave it to you, and I give it back to you, so you can fulfil your own promise and give it to the queen yourself. I know it will not take away the pain and sorrow you have suffered, Rinette, but you are alive and safe with your children, and it is all I have to give.'

I bowed my head. He had defeated me. All the love I had ever felt swept back into my heart, and the power of it almost knocked me off my feet. I did not trust my voice, and so I took off my gloves and dropped them on the grass and held out my scarred hands.

He took them. He folded them between his own and pressed them to his heart.

'*Je t'aime, ma mie,*' he said very softly.

We stood there in the garden, in the April sunlight, with the scents of rosemary and borage and thyme surrounding us. After a while, we went indoors. In the front room, I knelt by Tante-Mar's bed. I did not even look at the casket on the table. Such an insignificant thing, to have caused such pain and loss.

'You were right, Tante-Mar,' I said.

She put her hand on my head, brushing back the wisps of my hair as she might have done when I was a child. 'I will write to Père Guillaume, *mes douces*,' she said to me and to Nico at once, 'and ask him to send to Rome for your dispensation.'

42

17 April 1565
Stirling Castle

I was summoned to Stirling Castle on the Monday after Easter, to present the silver casket to the queen.

Her finest gilded chair had been set up in the enormous hall; her greatest cloth of estate, made of golden tissue lined with red satin and embroidered with lions and crowns in red and gold silk thread, had been brought from Holyrood. It was a grey, rainy day, unexpectedly chilly for the middle of April, and hundreds of candles blazed. Fires had been built up in two of the five fireplaces, casting light and shadows over the dais. Outside the large side windows black storm clouds were gathering.

Six trumpeters and six pipers played as the queen processed in, dazzling in more cloth-of-gold and with a mantle and train of crimson velvet trimmed with ermine. On her brow was the crown of Scotland, Scottish gold and gemstones and freshwater pearls, worn as a circlet without the half-arches, monde and cross. I had not seen her since the day Rannoch Hamilton had been hanged. She was beautiful in an unearthly way and I felt as if I did not know her at all.

Lord Darnley was with her, walking by her side as if he were already her consort. His fevers and agues had apparently subsided but his handsome white-skinned face was still disfigured by the lingering red marks of his illness. Edinburgh still buzzed with gossip that he was suffering from the pox and only calling it measles to reassure the queen.

She seated herself under her cloth of estate. The Countess of Argyll and Mary Livingston arranged her train to spill gracefully over the edge of the dais, then stood back with the other ladies and gentlemen. Darnley sat next to her in another chair, quite as splendid as hers, but of course without the royal canopy. He radiated sulkiness.

David Riccio, newly appointed the queen's French secretary after Nico's dismissal and the death of Monsieur Raullet, brought out a small gilded table and set it on the edge of the dais, in front of the queen. Members of the queen's council surrounded her – Moray, Rothes, Maitland and Chatelherault. The English ambassador was present, Master Throckmorton, with his agent Thomas Randolph. Monsieur Castelnau stood on the other side, alone.

'We are prepared to receive the petitioner,' the queen said.

The pipers and trumpeters played another fanfare. I stepped forward with Nico beside me.

Yes, Nico was beside me. After his first visit we had talked every day, and little by little I had let go of my bitterness and mistrust. We had not become lovers again, not yet, although Tante-Mar serenely continued her correspondence in pursuit of a dispensation for us to marry.

Today he was dressed in a black velvet doublet and black hose and stockings, embroidered in silver but plain compared to the costumes he had worn as a courtier. I wore black velvet as well, with a white lace ruffle showing at the edge of my high collar and long oversleeves pinned back with emeralds over tight blue-green silk undersleeves. My hair was mostly hidden by a jewelled net and a velvet cap embroidered with pearls.

Everything was new and fresh, from my shift to my long white lawn veil, with one exception. Around my neck, bright against the black, I wore my mother's chain of turquoises set in gold.

I carried the silver casket in my hands. The candles' light glinted off the repoussé work on the domed lid, and the hunting scenes in pouncework around the four sides. With the casket I carried a stalk of yellow cock's-comb, a single long stem spotted purplish-black, with slender, deeply notched leaves and a tassel of yellow flower-buds at the top. The buds had only just begun to open – Lord Darnley's power over the queen had only begun to blossom. I did not know if I could convince her to repudiate him before his influence came to full flower, but I had to try.

When I was halfway along the length of the hall, I saw him lean forward and whisper to her. His hands were shaking. He was afraid. Good. He deserved to be afraid.

I reached the dais and bent my knees as if I was performing a *révérence* in a dance; I could not perform a full court curtsey with the casket in my hands. Nico stopped beside me, and bowed gravely.

'Marianette.' The queen nodded to me. Then she looked at Nico. I saw her expression soften. She would never be able to look at him without feeling affection for him; they were so much alike that when she looked at him she surely saw herself. '*Mon cousin*,' she said.

'I have brought your mother's silver casket,' I said. 'The murderer of Alexander Gordon has confessed his crime, and is dead. You have sent the *Escadron Volant* dagger to Catherine de' Medici as a royal reminder of her complicity. Is this not so, Madame?'

427

'It is so.'

'You have kept your part of the bargain, Madame, and I am here to keep mine. I have brought you the yellow cock's-comb as well, and I will tell you what it says to me, as you have asked.'

The queen lifted one long-fingered white hand and gestured. 'You may place the casket upon that table,' she said. 'The key with it, if you please. You have the key?'

'I do, Madame.'

I stepped forward and placed the casket on the table. The reflection of the flames licked and flickered over the silver. I laid the yellow flower on top of the casket, and then detached a short chain from my jewelled cincture. The key swung from the end of it. I placed the key beside the casket. Then I stepped back.

'Madame,' I said. 'When you first chose the yellow cock's-comb in the garden of Granmuir, I told you it suggested you would meet a tall, slender, fair-haired person.'

The queen smiled. She looked at Lord Darnley and placed a loving, proprietory hand upon his wrist. 'I have done so,' she said.

I paused for a moment. The queen waited expectantly, her hand upon Lord Darnley's wrist.

'The flowers say what they say, Madame. The yellow cock's-comb represents a person who will batten upon your life and power, suck it away from you, and in the end cause your death.'

'Witchcraft!'

Everyone in the room stopped moving. Lord Darnley jerked his wrist away from the queen's hand, rose to his feet, and snatched up the stem of yellow cock's-comb. He threw it to the floor and stepped down upon it, crushing it.

'Witchcraft,' he said again, this time laughing. 'Mary, my love,

428

you have allowed this woman to take advantage of you with her so-called floromancy. I would never do you harm.'

'Of course you would not,' the queen said. 'Marianette, you are mistaken. Your yellow cock's-comb may indeed represent a tall, fair-haired person, but it could be anyone. Perhaps it is the King of Sweden. He is one of my suitors, and he is certainly fair-haired.'

I bowed my head. I had warned her, and that was all I could do. 'I can only beg you to take care, Madame.'

'Let us open the casket now, and see if the King of Sweden is one of the *quatre maris*. Harry, take the key and open it for me, if you please.'

Darnley stepped forward again and picked up the casket and the key. The crushed flower-buds of the yellow cock's-comb clung to the sole of his leather-and-velvet shoe. He unlocked the casket and threw back the lid.

'*Voilà*, my Mary,' he said. 'The predictions of Nostradamus are yours.'

The queen took out the packet, with its net of knotted scarlet silk cords and its blood-red seals. None of the seals had been broken, and the intricate pattern of the cords was undisturbed. 'It has not been opened,' she said. 'I will be the first, then, to look upon it.'

She thrust her long white fingers into the cords. The wax of the seals broke with an audible cracking sound, and the cords came loose. She opened the folded sheets of parchment. The room was so silent I could hear the rustling sounds, even over the crackling of the flames.

'*Les quatres maris de Marie, Reine d'Ecosse*,' she read. 'Let us see, now, who these four husbands are, and what Monsieur de Nostredame has to say about each one.'

'Madame.' It was Nico. He had not spoken up to this moment. 'The prophecies are for you alone, and perhaps your most trusted advisors. Half Europe has been pursuing them since your mother's death. If Duchess Antoinette were here, she would beg you not to read them publicly, particularly in the presence of the French and English ambassadors.'

'You yourself could be one of those trusted advisors again, *mon cousin*. I know it would please my grandmother if that were so.'

I held my breath.

'I think not,' Nico said evenly. I closed my eyes and breathed again. 'But please put the prophecies away, Madame, and consult your council in private as to what they foretell.'

'Tell me only, my Mary,' said Darnley, 'if I am one of them.' His hands were shaking again. 'Surely I am one of them, as we love each other so truly.'

The queen paused, her gaze running down the parchment. I saw her brows slant together – something made her angry. She said in a clear, diamond-hard voice, 'I shall read them if I choose. This is the first:

> *"The island king and the king from the south,*
> *Vie for a child queen who takes to the sea.*
> *In the white colour of mourning she weds the dolphin prince,*
> *Into whose ear a foreigner pours poison."'*

'That is the little King of France,' Darnley said. 'The dolphin prince – *le dauphin*. Hardly a prediction, as you were destined to be married to him from the time you were a child.'

'But the last line,' the queen said. 'Was the poison figurative or literal? And who was the foreigner?'

'What difference can it make now, my Mary? Read the next one. It is your next husband we all wish to know about.'

'It is longer. I shall read part of it only.

> *"The queen will make a king, and conquer a bastard.*
> *There will be death and birth and death again.*
> *Letters are found in a silver casket,*
> *No signature and no name of the letter-writer."'*

'Make a king!' Darnley was exultant. 'That is me. And the bastard – that is you, Moray.'

'There are many bastards in Scotland,' said the earl. He was flushed with anger. 'Death and birth and death – perhaps you are the one who will die, Darnley, and the king she will make will be a son of her own body with a more suitable husband.'

'The letters in the casket,' I said. 'No signature and no name – those could be your mother's ciphers, Madame.'

'Be silent, all of you.' The queen was revelling in the drama of it all. 'Here is one couplet from the third prophecy, to tantalise you all:

> *"A Lord from the Sea will carry off the Queen,*
> *She will pretend she is unwilling."'*

She smiled. 'There is more. I will keep it in my own heart, and ponder it.'

Darnley tried to snatch the parchment from her; she held it just out of his reach, teasing him.

'You will have no more husbands after me,' he said. 'Nostradamus was probably drunk when he wrote these. Or in bed with his rich wife. Do not even read the last one.'

'The last one, I shall read. It is a single quatrain.

"In a great castle where a king was born,
The Queen will meet the fourth into whose hands she will be given.
In the early morning she will wear a red robe,
And after that she will know no more sorrow."'

The room was suddenly silent. There was something eerie about the fourth quatrain. The queen stood frozen and silent, as if reading Nostradamus' words had put her under his spell.

'Mary,' Darnley said. '*Mary*. You will not have four husbands. You will have only two – the little King of France, and me.'

The queen lifted her head and came out of her trance.

'You are right,' she said. She smiled. '*Bon*. We do not choose to believe or pursue these prophecies, with our council or without them. We have made our own royal choice.'

With one sweeping gesture she cast the parchment into the fire. It went up in a sheet of flame. Whatever strange ink Monsieur de Nostredame had used resisted the fire longer than the parchment did; for the briefest of seconds the words seemed to float unsupported in the heart of the flames. Then the red wax seals exploded in a series of flashes and the prophecies were gone.

'The ciphers,' Darnley said. 'Your mother's secrets. Burn them too, my Mary. Be free from the past, and we will rule together in a new Utopia.'

The queen hesitated. The casket lay open before her. I could see the papers inside. How carefully Mary of Guise had hoarded the scandals and misdoings of the Scottish lords for her daughter's sake. Those same lords surrounded her daughter now, from Darnley and Lennox, his father, to Moray and Rothes and Maitland

and Chatelherault with his mad son Arran. Any one of them would have killed to possess the old queen's secrets for himself; none of them would want their secrets known by the others.

'Burn them,' the Earl of Moray said.

'Yes, burn them,' said the old Earl of Chatelherault.

I was stunned by the thought that no good at all would have come of the pain and death the silver casket had wrought.

'Madame,' I said, 'I beg you . . . do not burn them. Keep them. Put them away safely. Read them later, when you are alone. Do not show them to anyone else.'

'Mary,' Darnley said. He stepped close to her and took her hand; his voice was husky and sensuous. 'My Mary. Burn them, or I will have to leave you – I cannot bear there to be secrets between us.'

Do not listen to him, I thought. It will change everything. Oh, Madame, your whole future will change if you listen to him now. Look down, look down, see the buds of the yellow cock's-comb clinging to his shoe, see how they have attached themselves to both shoes now, and even his stockings . . .

The queen took the papers out of the casket and threw them into the fire.

I cried out with horror. I would have run to the fireplace and reached in with my scarred hands to pull the papers out, if Nico had not held me back.

'It is too late,' he said. Everyone else was shouting, and the rush of sound mingled with the crackling of the flames and the rustle and spatter of rain against the windows. He spoke softly, for me alone. 'They are gone.'

'That means it was all for nothing.' I was crying. I hated it but I could not stop myself. 'All for *nothing*, Nico. Alexander's death. Wat Cairnie's death. Rannoch Hamilton. All of it.'

'No. You kept your promise to the old queen. The young queen has chosen her path, and now she must walk it to the end.'

'That is not enough.'

'I think it is. There may be more – she did not read the entirety of the prophecies aloud. Do you remember how I told you the world would be a different place if you had not taken the casket?'

'I remember.'

'The world may have been changed again, now that the casket has been opened. It is not always given to us to understand the ways of fate, *ma mie*.'

'The casket,' the queen said. Everyone else was suddenly silent again. 'The casket itself was truly my mother's. I will keep it. It must be polished, of course. Perhaps it will serve for my own letters one day.'

'An excellent plan, my Mary,' Darnley said. 'It is very pretty – I will send you letters and poems to put inside it.'

They had eyes only for each other. I curtseyed deeply, and beside me Nico bowed. We went out together, and no one called us back.

43

Tante-Mar still could not manage the long ride from Edinburgh to Granmuir, but we could wait no longer. Nico arranged for a ship to take us all from Leith harbour to Aberdeen, with Wat Cairnie's lead coffin in the tween-deck and the horses, Lilidh and Diamant, stabled in the hold. Seilie stayed with Tante-Mar and Jennet, Una MacAlpin and my babies and me in the women's cabin; Nico and the boys, Davy and Gill, remained on the deck with the men. Once we were all in Aberdeen it would be only a short ride south to Granmuir, and we could take it in easy stages, with Tante-Mar in a litter. Jennet could ride, if we rode slowly.

We crossed the causeway from the mainland on a brilliant June day, the sky speedwell blue, the sun sparkling off the sea. Granmuir Castle stood on its great rock as it had done for four hundred years. The blue-and-gold colours of the Leslies of Granmuir were flying from the gatehouse.

Home. Oh, home.

There was no rush to the church to be married, not this time. Père Guillaume could not marry us until the dispensation arrived, and that could take months – years, even. I had no intention of waiting so long, and neither did Nico, but there were other things to be done first. I saw Père Guillaume and Nico with their heads together, speaking softly in French, and I suspected they were coming to some sort of agreement.

I established Tante-Mar in her sunny room in the south-east tower, and made sure Jennet understood she was to undertake no heavy work until her wounds had completely healed. On the second day we all crowded into Saint Ninian's for Père Guillaume to celebrate the funeral mass for Wat Cairnie; Nico, Norman More and old Robinet Loury dug his grave in the tiny cemetery behind the church. Dear Wat, the closest thing I had ever had to a brother, who had died trying to protect my little girls. I wept until I had no more tears. At least here at Granmuir where he had been born he would rest peacefully, lulled by the endless waves of the sea.

'What did you say to Père Guillaume?' I asked Nico, on the third day.

We were in the garden, looking over the ancient wall at the sea. It had been almost three years since the first time we had stood there, when he had told me about his childhood with the Benedictines and the death of his mother. Everything that had happened – could it really be over? Were we really here safely, the two of us, after all we had come through?

'I suggested he hear our espousals *de futuro* – our promises that we will wed when the dispensation arrives. It will not marry us in the eyes of the church, so his conscience will be clear, but it will create a betrothal. What you in Scotland call a handfasting.'

I put my hand on the wall, and he put his over it. 'So we will be handfasted,' I said. 'That is something, I suppose.'

He laughed softly. 'It is more than something. If we pronounce our promises *de futuro* before a priest, and afterwards live together as man and wife, we have shown consent and in essence, we will have married ourselves. It is irregular but perfectly legal under canon law, and binding unless you later choose to sue for an annulment on the grounds that we are related within a forbidden degree of affinity.'

'You know I will not!'

He laughed again. 'When the dispensation arrives, Père Guillaume will call us before him, hear our confessions, and marry us properly. After that, *ma mie*, you will have no means of escape.'

'I will want none. When can these promises – *de futuro* – be pronounced?'

'At vespers, if you wish it.'

'I wish it.'

He lifted my hand and kissed my knuckles gently, then turned my hand over and kissed my palm. The cuts from Blaise Laurentin's *Escadron Volant* dagger had healed, but I would bear scars for as long as I lived. I wondered what Queen Catherine de' Medici had done when she had received the dagger. I wondered if she had shrugged and smiled and given it back to the leaders of the *Escadron Volant*, to be used by another hired assassin.

'Ugly,' I said, curling my hands closed.

'No. Brave battle-scars.'

'They will always remind me of Laurentin, and of Alexander.'

'Alexander is Màiri's father. You will never forget him, nor should you.'

I put my hand on the garden wall again. The stone of Granmuir, warmed in the sun. 'What will our life be like, Nico? Will we just live here, and be country people?'

'Is that what you want?'

'I think it is. For a long, long time, at least. Although—'

'Although what?'

'Do you remember when you asked me if I would ever want to go to Montmartre? Ever want to see my mother again?'

He looked out to sea, towards the south. Towards France. 'I remember. You said you might go to Edinburgh, to Joinville, to Clerac – but never to Montmartre.'

'I have changed my mind.'

'So you do not wish to be an Aberdeenshire farmer's wife after all?'

I had to smile at the image of Nicolas de Clerac as an Aberdeenshire farmer. 'Perhaps I shall be like Proserpine,' I said. 'Half the year here, and half the year in the world.'

'Barring the fact that if you are Proserpine, I shall have to act the part of Hades, I think that is an excellent plan,' Nico said. He was smiling, too. 'We will make a quiet life here, *ma mie*, with our crops and our sheep and your gardens, and make occasional visits to the world outside. Short ones.'

Visits, I had said. *Short ones. My father and mother lived at the court and visited Granmuir upon occasion. I would like to do just the opposite.*

He remembered.

'Will you stay with me tonight in the Mermaid Tower, Nico? After we make our promises?'

'I will stay with you,' he said.

Nico carried Tante-Mar into Saint Ninian's, and placed her comfortably in a chair with half a dozen cushions. Jennet scornfully refused any such coddling. Bessie More, Annis Cairnie, Una MacAlpin and the girl Libbet stood with them on the women's side of the church. Norman More, old Robinet Loury, and the boys Davy and Gill stood on the other side. Gill had Seilie in his arms.

We left the doors open. The afternoon sun was bright as polished gold on the sea. I would not let myself think about the other time, or what followed. The one thing that was the same was that I had my mother's turquoises around my neck. Other than that I might have been a woman from the village, in a linen dress and a plain gauze veil.

Père Guillaume kissed his stole and put it around his neck, then opened his missal.

'Before these witnesses,' he said, 'I would hear your promises that you intend to wed.'

He nodded to Nico.

'I,' Nico said in a clear, grave voice, 'Nicolas de Clerac, promise to take thee, Marina Leslie, to be my espoused wife as the law of the Holy Church prescribes, and thereto I plight thee my troth.'

Père Guillaume then nodded to me.

I said, 'I, Marina Leslie, promise to take thee, Nicolas de Clerac, to be my espoused husband as the law of the Holy Church prescribes, and thereto I plight thee my troth.'

We joined our hands.

'I betroth you,' said Père Guillaume, 'and bear witness to your promises to take each other as espoused husband and wife, upon such day as you are dispensed by the Holy Church from the affinity between you.'

Jennet made a snorting sound. She thought little of affinities and dispensations.

'Now, *mes enfants*,' Père Guillaume said, with every appearance of sternness. 'You are espoused *de futuro*. Take care you do not come together as husband and wife, because if you do, you will no longer be handfasted, but married, legally, bindingly and for life.'

'We will take care, *mon Père*,' Nico said. He did not specify what we intended to take care to do.

'Great care,' I added.

And with that it was done. We went back into the Great Hall and ate a betrothal supper: pies of lampreys with pepper-spiced winesops, a roasted lamb and a soup of venison with wine, cloves and mace. Afterwards we ate cakes Bessie More had baked with fine white flour, butter and sugar, and custards with violet petals. The table was heaped with windflowers, wild roses and maiden pinks, and wreaths of purple-flowered trailing nightshade.

We left everyone else eating and drinking wine and singing, and slipped away up the ancient stone stairs to the Mermaid Tower.

'Are you certain?' Nico said. He ran his hand over my forehead and gently pushed back my veil. 'If we come together tonight we will no longer be handfasted, but married.'

'I am certain.' I pulled the veil free and let it fall to the floor. 'My hair has grown out a little.'

He smiled. 'So it has. Do you know what it feels like?'

'What?'

He closed his eyes and stroked my hair again. 'A sleeping fawn's fur. Silky and tranquil and yet awake in an instant if it is stroked the wrong way.'

'You have never stroked a sleeping fawn.'

He laughed. 'True,' he said. 'But I can imagine it.'

He began to unbutton his doublet. I took off my belt and untied the drawstring in the neck of my dress. Such was the advantage of country clothes – they were easy to put on and take off without assistance. I pulled the dress over my head and stood there in my thin shift, my arms and shoulders and most of my bosom bare. I closed my eyes and breathed the scent of the sea.

After a moment I felt the backs of his fingers, moving very lightly along the line of my jaw. He turned his hand and drew one fingertip from the squared corner of it to my chin, to my throat, to the hollow between my collarbones. He paused, then very slowly moved his finger lower, to the point where the loose round neck of my shift began. There he stopped.

'Your skin,' he said, 'is like the inner surface of a seashell. Transparent and white and luminous, all at once.'

'You are very gallant tonight, Monsieur. Do you think you are back at court?'

He touched his lips to my temple, just at the corner of my eye. I could feel the warmth of his breath. 'Do you not like compliments?' he said.

'It has been so long since I have had any.'

'From now on, you will have a hundred, every day.'

He took my face between his hands and kissed me very gently on the mouth. Involuntarily I lifted my own hands, caught at his arms, his shoulders, the hair at the back of his neck. Sensation contracted and then expanded, strong and warm and undeniable, in the very heart of my flesh and soul.

'I love you, Nico,' I said.

'I love you too, *ma mie*.'

'You need not take such care with me as you did the last time.'

'Indeed?' He smiled. 'It will not distress you, then, if I do this?'

I cried out. It was not from pain or fear. It was pure piercing sensation, and in the sweet silver moonlight it delighted my heart.

'Oh, no,' I said. 'It does not distress me in the least. And I am sure it will not distress you if I do *this*.'

He gasped with pleasure.

'*Sainte-grâce, ma mie*,' he said. His voice was breathless. 'Is this shameless sea-witch the same Rinette Leslie I have loved all this time?'

'The same,' I said, 'and not the same.'

By morning we were no longer handfasted. We were married, legally, bindingly and for life.

'Maman,' Màiri said. 'Why does Lilidh have a horn on her forehead?'

I laughed and hugged her tightly. 'That is not Lilidh, Màiri-Rose,' I said. 'Although I agree it does look like her, the way Monsieur Nico drew it. It is a unicorn. Can you say that? U-ni-corn.'

We were reading one of the tales in Nico's copy of my mother's book. Both Màiri and Kitte loved it, and Màiri already knew most of the stories by heart. She liked to repeat them and claim she was reading them. Seilie was curled at our feet.

'U-ni-corn,' Màiri said. 'Is it called that because it eats corn?'

'It eats stars,' I said.

'And it drinks angelica wine.' Nico came into the garden with a packet of papers in his hand. 'May I steal your maman away from you for a little while, *ma belle*?'

'I will read to Kitte,' Màiri said. She took the book and ran out of the garden. 'Kitte!' she cried. I could hear her voice growing fainter as she ran towards the castle keep. 'Tante-Mar, where is Kitte?'

I smiled up at Nico. I had no sense of foreboding at all until I saw his face. 'You have letters,' I said. 'Has Bessie given the messenger something to eat and drink?'

'Yes and yes.' He sat down on the ancient wall beside me. 'Rinette, she has married him.'

'The queen.'

'Yes. She has made him king by proclamation. Look.'

He handed me a silver coin. I turned it to catch the sun. It was a ryal, worth about thirty shillings, and it showed the heads of

Mary Stuart and Henry Stewart, Lord Darnley – King Henry now – facing each other with Darnley on the left, and around them engraved the letters HENRICUS & MARIA D: GRA R & R SCOTORUM.

'Henry and Mary,' I said. 'King and Queen of Scotland. His name first. She is mad.'

'Moray and Rothes have been outlawed, with all their adherents. She is seizing their properties.'

I jumped up. 'But Rothes is chief of the Leslies,' I said. 'I hold Kinmeall as his vassal.' Rannoch Hamilton's plot to take Granmuir in baby Kitte's name had been turned on its head by his death, and now it was I who managed Kinmeall as Kitte's mother and guardian. 'Oh, Nico, I do not want it all to start again. I thought we would be safe here.'

He laid the packet of letters down on the wall and put his arms around me. 'We are safe,' he said. 'I will go down to Edinburgh and see the queen. The king and queen. She is anxious for support – she has released young George Gordon from Dunbar, pardoned him and restored him to the Earldom of Huntly. She has welcomed Bothwell back into her favour. She will welcome me, too, and my assurance of our allegiance.'

'If you go, you will come back? You are certain you will come back?'

He laughed. 'Of course I am certain,' he said. 'Proserpine.'

I could not help but smile a little. 'Hades,' I said. 'What other letters are there? Who sent the messenger?'

He was silent for a moment, holding me, his chin resting on top of my head. At last he said, 'The new French ambassador, Monsieur du Croc.'

'Why would he send you messages, Nico? Oh, no, please do not tell me there is also a letter from Duchess Antoinette.'

'I will not lie to you.'

I turned away from him and looked out over the sea. I breathed the scent of the salt, and the garden. Nico's scent, bitter orange and myrrh. I closed my eyes and prayed, to God and Saint Ninian and the Green Lady of Granmuir.

'What does she want?'

'She is afraid for the young queen, which is not surprising.'

I said nothing. What could I say?

'Do you remember what I told you at Inveraray? That there were whispers of three *Escadron Volant* assassins in Scotland?'

I hated those words. *Escadron Volant*. I swallowed hard and nodded.

'Duchess Antoinette has heard rumours that there is indeed a third assassin, and that he – or she – is in Edinburgh. That Queen Mary herself may be the quarry, or perhaps the new king she has made.'

'Do you think it is true?'

Just as I spoke, a breeze off the sea caught the packet of letters and sent them swirling. They fluttered like guillemots, catching the sunlight, then swept over the edge of the cliff and out over the grey-green water.

'Whether it is true or not, she wants me to return to the court at Edinburgh, to watch over the queen,' Nico said. 'But her letter is gone now, *ma mie*. I cannot write an answer to it.'

I turned to him and we looked at one another. There were so many things we could have said, but we did not have to say any of them.

At last I held out my hand with the silver ryal on my palm. 'I do not want this here,' I said. 'The peony and the yellow cock's-comb cannot grow together – they will be the death of each other.'

'While the windflower and the nightshade,' Nico said, 'strange as it might sound, grow together and thrive.'

So they did, in Granmuir's own garden by the sea, masses of pink and white windflowers with golden threads at their hearts; climbing on the stone wall, appearing to embrace them, grew the trailing nightshade vine with its purple-and-gold flowers. Everything was flourishing. The wild roses and maiden pinks were thriving as well, and a new patch of borage, with its blue flowers hinting at a boy child, which had come up out of nowhere since we had been home.

I do not know if I can feel everything you want me to feel. My own voice, that afternoon in the Mermaid Tower, when we had first come together. *What I felt when I was young.*

And yet I felt it. I felt it now, filling me up, flourishing like the garden.

'I love you, Nico,' I said. I had said it before but this was different. It sounded simple but oh, it was not. 'I thought I would never be able to love you with all my heart, after – after everything. But I do. Somehow I do.'

He did not smile. He said just as simply, 'And I love you, *ma mie.*'

'Go in and make the arrangements,' I said. 'Remember that all our visits are to be short ones, and the sooner you leave, the sooner you will return. Take Lilidh, she is the fastest.'

He kissed me and went out of the garden. I remained among the flowers with Seilie, just long enough to throw the silver coin after the letters. It arched, glittering, and fell like a stone into the sea.

Acknowledgements

I would like to begin by thanking my husband Jim, the Broadcasting Legend™, who has been unfailingly supportive through the many ups and downs of writing this story I love so much.

Thanks are also due to my many writer friends, who laughed and cried with me and who understand in a unique way what it's like to tell a story.

In particular, I would like to thank Leslie Thomson of Edinburgh, who read the manuscript and made wonderful, meticulous comments on the places, times, language and personages of Scotland's rich history.

Special thanks also to Lisa Brackman, for her insights on pacing and continuity.

My agent, Diana Fox of Fox Literary, guided me well at every step in the process. Betty Anne Crawford and the team at Books Crossing Borders have taken me on a whirlwind trip around the world – my head is still spinning. Thank you all so much.

Finally, I owe the most heartfelt thanks to everyone at Preface – my brilliant editor Rosie de Courcy, managing editor Nicola Taplin, and the whole team of copyeditors, designers, publicists, and everyone else who has worked to make this book a success.

Author's Note

Rinette Leslie, the Leslies of Granmuir, and Granmuir itself are all fictional creations. Rinette's mother, Blanche of Orleans, is fictional as well. Granmuir borrows its general location and situation on a great rock beside the sea from Dunnottar Castle in Aberdeenshire. The ancient chapel supposedly built by Saint Ninian and the pagan spirit of the Green Lady are also associated with Dunnottar.

Nicolas de Clerac is another fictional character. Duke François de Guise is not known to have had any illegitimate children, which is why I shrouded Nico's birth with such secrecy. Given the time and place, however, it was not in any way considered a dishonour for a great nobleman, courtier and soldier like Duke François to have an illegitimate child or two.

Alexander Gordon of Glenlithie and Rannoch Hamilton of Kinmeall are also fictional characters. I felt quite comfortable in making Rannoch Hamilton an illegitimate brother of Grizel Hamilton, the wife of Andrew Leslie, the 5th Earl of Rothes, because Grizel Hamilton's father James Hamilton of Finnart is known to have had a staggering ten illegitimate children, by at least three different mistresses. In a case like that, what's one more?

Mary Stuart is one of the most enduringly fascinating

personages of history. She's been painted as a heroine and a villain, a misunderstood queen and a murderer. I have tried to portray her as the eighteen-year-old girl she was when she returned to Scotland, charming, mercurial and impulsive. Everything she does in the story is either taken from contemporary records or extrapolated from known actions and attitudes. The years of her early personal reign – from 1561 to 1566 – are often glossed over in fiction in order to get to the more dramatic years, of Riccio's and Darnley's murders, the Bothwell marriage, Queen Mary's forced abdication, imprisonment on Lochleven, and escape to England. Drama, yes – but by then the queen was at the mercy of the drama. I wanted to spend time with Mary in the years when she actually ruled, and had not yet made the choices that ultimately destroyed her.

The silver casket really existed – exists still, if the sixteenth-century silver casket at Lennoxlove House in East Lothian is truly Queen Mary's. Historically it entered the queen's story after she was imprisoned by the Lords of the Congregation, turned over to the Lords by one George Dalgleish, a henchman of Bothwell's. No one knows for certain what documents were in it at the time or how it came to be in Bothwell's possession, but it certainly played a stellar part in Queen Mary's trial – carefully called a 'conference' – at Westminster in England. By then it contained the infamous Casket Letters, the supposed proof that Mary was complicit in the murder of Darnley. Whether the letters were forgeries or not, their contents were damning enough to keep poor Mary in English imprisonment for the rest of her life – so perhaps there was indeed a curse on the beautiful little casket.

Edinburgh Castle is built on a crag of volcanic rock. There are persistent legends of secret tunnels and passageways under the castle, and although to the best of my knowledge no lava caves or lava tubes have ever been specifically discovered and explored in the heart of Castle Rock, it's perfectly possible they could exist in the volcanic basalt. The area now known as Crown Square within the castle was laid out over man-made vaults in the 1430s under James I and James II, and my maze of lava-tube passageways and the bubble-like lava cave under Saint Margaret's are a fictional extension of these existing vaults.

Lady Margaret Erskine, the mother of James Stewart, Earl of Moray, is generally considered to have been James V's favourite mistress. At the time of her liaison with the king she was married to Sir Robert Douglas of Lochleven; there were rumours the king had petitioned the Pope to arrange a divorce for her, and even rumours that her marriage to the king had actually taken place. This all came to nothing and instead James V married first Madeleine of Valois, and after her untimely death Mary of Guise. Sir Robert Douglas was killed at Pinkie Cleugh in 1547 and Lady Margaret did not remarry. She was obviously a beautiful woman in her day – she was a king's mistress and the character of 'Fair Ladie Sensualitie' in Sir David Lyndsay's *Ane Pleasant Satyre of the Three Estaitis* was said to have been modelled upon her.

How did she feel, having come so close to being queen herself, and ending as only the lady of Lochleven? I have given her ambition, both for her half-royal son and for herself, and I believe it would not only be a natural reaction, but fits with what little is known of her. Although she lived primarily at Lochleven, with Moray's prominence at court she would certainly have been welcome there whenever she wished, once her rival Mary of Guise was dead.

The *Escadron Volant*, the Flying Squadron of Queen Catherine de' Medici, really existed; it would have been in its early days at the time of this story. The secret sub-group of *Escadron Volant* assassins is a fictional creation, although in the time and place it seems perfectly possible. Blaise Laurentin is a fictional character.

Nostradamus, of course, is historical. He did write private prophecies and quatrains to individuals who had the position and wealth to pay for them. The *quatre-maris* prophecies written for Mary of Guise about her daughter Mary Stuart, however, are fictional.

Floromancy as a form of folk magic is as old as time. If you've ever pulled the petals off a daisy and said, 'He loves me, he loves me not,' you've practiced floromancy. In the sixteenth century it probably would have existed mostly in the countryside, among herbalists and 'white' witches. That said, astrology and alchemy, which were considered actual sciences at the time, incorporated flower symbolism. Flowers were associated with planetary influences and with the prevailing medical theory of the four humours.

Some of the flower lore I used in the book is based on ancient mythologies, some of it on astrology and alchemy, some of it on the planets, the zodiac, and the four humours. Most of it has some basis in folklore somewhere, although as an organised system, it's something I created.

I consulted many books, papers, articles and documents in the course of writing *The Flower Reader*; I was also kindly aided by wonderful historians, authors, and librarians. Whatever sins of commission or omission have crept into the story are entirely upon my own head.

Now read a chapter from Elizabeth Loupas'
thrilling second novel

The
Second
Duchess

Coming soon

FERRARA

5 December 1565

'He murdered his first duchess with his own hands, they say,' the Ferrarese hairdressing-woman whispered as she braided a string of pearls into my hair. 'She was so young, so beautiful.' And I, Barbara of Austria, neither young nor beautiful, would be the duke's second duchess before the pale December sun set.

What did the woman expect me to do, shriek and fall down in a faint? Jump up and swear I would not marry the Duke of Ferrara after all, but return straightaway to Innsbruck with my household and dowry and bridegoods down to the last box of silver pins? For all practical purposes I was married already, the contracts signed, the marriage-by-proxy performed. And truth be told, half-a-hundred people had already told me Alfonso d'Este had murdered his first wife.

I looked at my reflection in a hand glass. One loop of the pearls remained unfastened. 'You forget yourself, *parruchiera*,' I said.

The woman stepped back, a pointed braiding-bodkin gleaming in her hand, and for one incredulous moment I thought she meant to stab me with it. 'Do you think you will be safe here, Principessa, when she was not? The court of Ferrara is like a love-apple, beautiful and rosy-red and alluring to the senses, but poisonous, so poisonous—'

I put the glass down hard. 'Enough. You are dismissed.'

'The very pearls in your hair might be poisoned,' she whispered, sibilant as a serpent. 'That posset you have been drinking. Any piece of fruit, any flower you are offered. Your gloves. A flask of perfume. There are a thousand ways to envenom—'

'*Enough.* Madonna Lucrezia, ask the gentlemen-ushers to step onto the barge for a moment, if you please, and take this woman away.' The duke's elder sister raised her hand to the men waiting on the quay; her face was turned away from me and I could not see her expression. The men obeyed her gesture smartly and a scuffle ensued; there were a few cries of surprise and excitement from the ladies crowding the barge, and then the *parruchiera* was gone. My Austrian ladies, my lifelong friends, closed in around me. Lucrezia and Leonora d'Este whispered to each other behind their hands, their eyes glinting with things they knew and I did not. They had assembled my Ferrarese household, or so they told me, at the duke's command. Holy Virgin – had they deliberately chosen a madwoman to arrange my hair, so as to spoil my pleasure in my entrance into their city?

I picked up the glass. Fortunately, it was not broken. I could see them behind me, watching me, waiting to see what I would do.

'Sybille.' I spoke to one of my own women with deliberate steadiness. 'These pearls are too tightly braided. Would you loosen them, please?'

Sybille von Wittelsbach stepped forward at once. I watched in the glass and felt some of my distress evaporate as the arrangement of the pearls became less severe. Sybille often brushed and dressed my hair at home; her light, familiar touch calmed me further.

'I warned you, Bärbel,' she said under her breath. 'No foreigner can arrange your hair better than I. Did they think I meant to steal the pearls?'

'Of course not. It was the duke's wish for me to be dressed entirely by Ferrarese women before I entered the city. A symbol, nothing more.'

'A fine symbol. I thought she meant to stab you with that bodkin.'

As had I, although of course I did not say so. I closed my eyes, breathed deeply, and willed myself to be still. The magnificent ducal barge shifted and creaked beneath me, rocking gently on the waters of the Po di Volano. I could hear the rustle of a cold morning breeze in the imperial standard flying over me, and the faraway cries of cormorants and herons. I could smell the ancient river-scent, weeds and marshes and fish, and the milky sharp-sweet tang of the hot wine posset on the table in front of me.

The posset you have been drinking . . .

'Katharina,' I said to another of my Austrian ladies without opening my eyes, 'take the posset away, please.'

I heard her skirt rustle. The scent of the posset disappeared.

It was my wedding day, and posset or no posset, bodkin or no bodkin, whispers or no whispers, I would marry the Duke of Ferrara. It was my chance to grasp the thing I wanted more than anything else in the world: an establishment of my own away from the Austrian imperial court of my brother Maximilian and my Spanish sister-in-law. It was also my chance to escape the convent at Hall where three of my sisters were already preparing to immure themselves. Of course I did not delude myself that the Duke of Ferrara wanted me for my personal charms. His great rival, Duke Cosimo de' Medici, had betrothed his eldest son to my youngest sister, and if the Medici were to acquire an imperial bride, well, then, the Este must snap one up as well. That Duke Alfonso's ill-fated first wife had been Duke Cosimo's daughter simply added to the enmity between the two men and the titillation of the gossip. I did not care.

With Alfonso d'Este came the magnificent court at Ferrara, the sun, the stars, the court of my own I had coveted for so long.

The court of Ferrara is like a love-apple, beautiful and rosy-red and alluring to the senses, but poisonous, so poisonous—

The ravings of a madwoman, nothing more. I opened my eyes. My hair was finished. Ferrara lay before me, wreathed in icy river mists, my demesne, my dream, my golden city of courtesies and delights. I would embrace it and marry its duke and become its duchess and reign over its court. And I would never look back.

All Ferrara made merry that day for my entry into the city, with my train of ambassadors and bishops, courtiers and cross-bowmen, musicians and ladies and gentlemen from Austria, from Ferrara, and from all over Europe. My first impression, despite the pomp and clarions, was of narrow, twisting streets with buildings of stone and rose-coloured brick close enough to touch on either side. The air was dusty and ripe with the smells of ordure and rotting fruit despite the cold. The bells for sext pealed from half-a-dozen directions at once, and the horses' hooves struck hollowly on the ancient, uneven paving stones.

Then, all of a sudden, we crossed into a different quarter, and it was as if we had entered another city entirely. Sunshine. Fresh, crisp air. Broad, straight avenues. Trees, gardens, canals, beautiful open squares in the classical mode – this, then, must be the famous new section of the city. No wonder the duke had wished me to pass through the old city first, so I might properly appreciate the new city's wonders. Crowds of townspeople surged around my litter, cheering and waving. I gestured to my gentlemen to scatter coins and favours. What did I feel? Excitement? Delight? Apprehension? I was not sure – first one, then another, then some unnameable confusion of them all.

I wanted to remember every detail. I imagined myself as if in a great painting: the old city and the new city of Ferrara, the people of Ferrara, and at the center of it all a woman, white-skinned, unveiled in an open litter, wrapped in an ermine mantle and with ripples of reddish-blond hair streaming down her back. It was the fashionable colour, and I am sure many of the dark-haired Ferrarese ladies employed cosmetic means to achieve it, but mine was natural, the pure rosy-gold colour of fresh apricots in sunlight.

Every eye would be taken by that shining spill of hair, by the pearls gleaming at my forehead and temples, by my scarlet satin gown embroidered and re-embroidered with gold and pearls and rubies. Few would notice my long narrow face like a highbred filly's, or the unfortunately prominent lower lip that was the mark of my family. Few would realise I was twenty-six years old.

I could have made myself young and beautiful in my mind's-eye painting. I did not.

A girl-child stepped into the street before us, singing in a high, sweet voice, comparing me to some remarkable amalgam of Saint Barbara, Lavinia the wife of Aeneas, and Vesta the Roman goddess of the hearth. When she finished her song, she came forward, curtsied, and offered me a sheaf of magnificent out-of-season flowers, clearly from the duke's forcing-houses – roses and lilies and lavender and thyme.

Their scents were dizzyingly sweet in the clear December air.

Any piece of fruit, any flower you are offered . . .

I took the flowers from the child, gave her back one perfect pink rose, and kissed her on either cheek, much to the delight of the crowd. Neither she nor I fell over dead, thanks be to God. The procession passed on to the heart of the city – the four looming red-brick towers of the Castello di San Michele, the centuries-old fortress of the Este.

Two men awaited me on the far side of the Castello's famous moat, each with his own household and retinue. Although they were somewhat alike in looks, it was easy for me to tell them apart, even at a distance. One of them, of course, was the Duke of Ferrara himself, in purple velvet so dark it looked almost black, while the other, shorter man wore the scarlet of a prince of the church. This cardinal had to be Luigi d'Este, the duke's younger brother. With the duke's two unmarried sisters immediately behind me in the procession, I was surrounded by the Este, and the family in Ferrara was complete.

The duke I had met before, in the summer, in Innsbruck. He had courted me — what a mockery! Courted! — in a series of stiff, meaningless meetings, because the contracts were already signed, the dowry agreed upon, the bridal gifts proposed and accepted. The peculiar thing about the whole business was that had I not heard the blood-chilling whispers about the Duke of Ferrara murdering his first wife, I would not have disliked him. He was proud and vainglorious, true, and immoderately attentive to detail; all in all he gave me an uneasy impression of a glittering surface, like a calm sea, with ferocious serpents and dragons swimming in ritualised patterns beneath. But at the same time he was intelligent and cultured, a genuine lover of music and art, athletic, well-dressed, and cleanly in his personal habits. I would have to live with him, and for that matter bed with him; from what I could guess it would not be too unpleasant. He appeared to have much the same reaction to me. If anything, he seemed pleased I was not a lovely, alluring girl of fourteen — but then his first wife, of whom no one spoke, had been a lovely, alluring girl of fourteen. So perhaps I provided a refreshing contrast.

The procession came to a halt at the great gate of the Castello. I felt cold . . . hot . . . light-headed . . . resolute. I put my ermine mantle aside, and my master of horse assisted me to alight from the litter; the duke's sisters and my Austrian ladies formed themselves into ranks of precedence behind me. I stood very straight. The duke stepped forward and bowed with precise formality.

'Welcome to Ferrara, Principessa,' he said in his deep, rather cold voice. He had dark eyes, swarthy skin, black hair cut short in the current Italianate fashion, a close-cropped dark beard along the line of his jaw. His height was slightly more than my own; the true shapes of his shoulders and upper body were lost in the padding and slashing and pleating of his skirted coat and furred over-gown, but his legs in their tight hose were the fine, sinewy legs of an athlete.

He looked the same, yet he was not the same. Here in his own city, backed by the great fortress of his ancestors, his blood gave him power I had not fathomed in the salons of the Hofburg: the ancient princely blood of the Este, the royal Valois blood of his mother, the ruthless Borgia blood of his grand-mother. My own blood responded. I sank into a curtsy, my gemmed scarlet skirts rustling and flowering out over the dust of the paving stones. I made it a point to be careless with them, as if to say, *What is silk, what are jewels, to ones such as you and I?* Then I straightened and placed my gloved hand upon his.

'Thank you, my lord. I bring you my brother the em-peror's greetings and goodwill, as well as my own person and the first portion of my dowry, in token of his lasting friendship.'

'Let us not speak of dowries or policy today.' His face was an unbroken surface that gave no hint of what was con-cealed beneath. 'May I present my own brother, Luigi, the cardinal-deacon of Saint Lucia Septizonio, archbishop of Auch, and bishop emeritus of Ferrara? He will bless our union and offer the Mass.'

Undaunted by the weight of his ecclesiastical offices, Luigi d'Este bowed and held out his hand, his ring of office heavy and glowing upon his index finger. His resemblance to his brother was in his bearing more than in his features; he was clean-shaven and his colouring was somewhat fairer, his eyes more hazel, his hair more brown than black.

I withdrew my hand from the duke's and made another curtsy, a fraction less deep but with my head bowed. It caught to a nicety, I thought, the lesser respect due my husband's younger brother, and at the same time the greater respect due a prince of the church.

'My Lord Cardinal.' I touched my lips to his ring.

'My daughter.' He seemed to think something was an excellent joke – probably the fact that he was all of one year older than I. 'Welcome to Ferrara.'

'Thank you, Your Eminence.'

He lifted his hand and sketched the sign of the cross over me, then over his brother. The duke bowed his head briefly, then returned his attention to me; his hand was now resting on the hilt of a very fine dagger at his belt. Its design was unusual, but I would not have noticed it in particular if it had not been for the way he stroked his thumb over the damascened pattern, as if it were speaking to him in some way no one but he could discern.

'Your dress and jewels please me,' he said. 'Crezia and Nora chose your tiring-women well.'

Particularly the madwoman they selected to braid pearls into my hair, I thought. Aloud I said, 'I am pleased also. Although perhaps I will make one or two changes once I am settled.'

'Make what changes you wish. Have a complete inventory made of your costume, if you please, before the end of the day. I desire to have you painted as a bride.'

'Yes, my lord.'

With great formality he handed me back into my litter for the procession to the cathedral. The duke's sisters took their places again; the cardinal's servants led forward a white mule saddled in scarlet and gold and shod in silver, and placed a gilded stool for the cardinal to mount. The duke needed no such assistance to mount a white Andalusian stallion, trapped in blue and white and embroidered with the eagles and fleurs-de-lis of the Este, and the stylised flame that was his own personal device. He took control of the animal with one hand on the reins; with the other he acknowledged the cheers of his people. We moved forward; behind us a swarm of lackeys in ducal livery began throwing gold and silver coins to all parts of the crowd.

At the cathedral door we were married again, this time without proxies. Afterward we passed under a magnificent bas-relief of the Universal Judgment and into the nave for the nuptial Mass. *Jacta alea est*, Caesar said when he crossed the

Rubicon – the die is cast. I also had cast my die, and for good fortune or ill, I was now the second Duchess of Ferrara.

As I stepped into my litter for the procession back to the Castello, Sybille murmured into my ear that the Ferrarese *parruchiera*, with her mad whispers of love-apples and poisons, had escaped from the duke's guards and disappeared into the alleyways of the old city.

I see them, kneeling at the altar rail, looking chaste as two angels. How dare he? I hate her. I never loved Alfonso, but I hate the emperor's long-faced sister anyway, for taking my place.

My name is Lucrezia de' Medici. I suppose I should say Lucrezia, Duchess of Ferrara, but I'm not the duchess anymore. I'm dead. Mostly. Actually, not all the way dead, but in between – I'm an immobila, a still one, a watcher. I'm not sure why. Maybe it's because I didn't want to die.

When I was alive, I was the daughter of Cosimo de' Medici, Duke of Florence. He called me Sodona, 'Hard One,' because I hated my lessons and ran away from my tutors. He'd laugh and cuff me and swear that in my hardness and stubbornness I took after him. Maybe I did. He had a will of iron, my father, and a ruthless temper when he was crossed.

My mother, on the other hand, was melancholic and full of herself. I learned from her that acting frail was a good way to avoid doing anything I didn't want to do. The more my nurses and tutors scolded, the sicker and weaker I became. How I laughed when I was alone, or with my sister Isabella! I wanted no lessons, no books, no embroidery or dancing. I wanted to run free in the gardens and ride the horses in the stables. I wanted to sleep late every morning and wake up to cream custard with honey and little almond cakes with crisp, shiny sugar on top. Sometimes I managed to slip away and do as I pleased. Other times I was watched too closely.

Alfonso gave out I'd retired to the Monastero del Corpus Domini by my own will, but nothing could be farther from the truth. He had me taken there. Imagine — only two rooms and not even a window, for me, a princess of Florence, the Duchess of Ferrara! And the door was locked. Alfonso knew I couldn't stand being locked in. He did it deliberately, because he knew eventually I'd confess anything just to be free again.

That last night, I never expected to fall asleep, but I drowsed. I didn't hear the door open. All out of nowhere something was pressed down over my face, so hard its softness molded around my eyes and nose and mouth. It terrified me beyond anything I'd ever known. I felt as if my chest was going to collapse in on itself as I scratched and thrashed and struggled for air.

Then in one awful moment I burst free of my flesh. I didn't really, of course, but that's the only way I can describe it. The pain and fear stopped. Life stopped. I felt nothing. I was still there, in the monastery cell; I could see and hear and understand, but I couldn't make any of the living see or hear or understand me. I had become immobila.

I was seventeen, and it was April, and I was only just beginning to live! I can look at my favourite cherry tree now, but I can't